BEAUTY
IN THE
ASHES

MICALEA SMELTZER

Beauty in the Ashes
Copyright © 2014 Micalea Smeltzer

All rights reserved. This book or any portion thereof may not be reproduced or used in any manner whatsoever without the express written permission of the publisher.

This is a work of fiction. Names, characters, businesses, places, events and incidents are either the products of the author's imagination or used in a fictitious manner. Any resemblance to actual persons, living or dead, or actual events is purely coincidental.

Cover design and photography by Regina Wamba at Mae I Design
http://www.maeidesign.com/

Cover models Jeffery Hiedeman and Jenessa Andrea

Interior design by Angela McLaurin, Fictional Formats
https://www.facebook.com/FictionalFormats

BEAUTY
IN THE
ASHES

Caelan

Life is like a flame.
It burns bright for a while,
then it flickers and fades,
until finally one small breath extinguishes it
and we're left with the ashes.

THE HOUSE WAS quiet, but I still waited ten more minutes to leave, making sure I heard the sounds of my dad snoring.

I'd been grounded for a month the last time I got caught sneaking out.

I wasn't going to make the same mistake again.

I crept over to my bedroom window, sliding it up as quietly as I could. It squeaked and I halted my movements, holding my breath to make sure no one in the house stirred.

I all but jumped out of my skin when the door to the bathroom that connected my room to my sister's opened.

"Cael, what are you doing?" She asked, standing there in pajama shorts and a tank top. Her eyes were wide, reminding me of a doll.

"Isn't it obvious?" I whispered, nodding at my half open window.

"Mom and dad are going to kill you if you get caught," she hissed, padding into my room like she owned the place. Nosy little sisters were good for nothing. I missed the days when I could bribe her to keep quiet with candy.

"I can't miss this party, Cayla," I groaned. "I'm the

quarterback. I have to be there," I reasoned.

"I want to go," she squared her shoulders defiantly.

"No," I hissed through my teeth. No fucking way was I bringing my sixteen-year-old sister to a senior party. It wasn't because of her age that I wanted her to stay behind, but the way I saw my friends looking at her. Cayla was too sweet and innocent to get wrapped up in one of those fuckers. I'd kill them if they touched my sister.

"Fine, then I'm going to wake up mom," she turned on her heel to stalk out of my room.

I reached out and grabbed her arm, my fingers digging into her skin. "No," I said sternly. "Don't be a little tattle tale bitch."

Her eyes widened at my harsh words. Yeah, Cayla and I bickered like most siblings, but we also got along better than most too. She wasn't used to me being so rude.

"Let go of me," she yanked her arm from my grasp. "You can be such a dick, Caelan." She headed back towards the bathroom and stopped in the doorway. "I won't say anything to mom and dad about this, but you owe me."

"Deal," I smiled.

She started to leave, but something in me made me say her name. "Cayla?"

"Yeah?" She stopped, her blonde hair swishing around her shoulders.

I swallowed thickly. "I love you, you know that, right?"

She rolled her clear blue eyes at me. Cayla and I looked a lot alike—so much alike that many people believed we were twins.

"I see what you're doing here, you still owe me dickwad."

I chuckled. "Believe me, I know."

I was surprised she hadn't put up much fight. I think she knew the real reason I didn't want her to go, and probably wanted to avoid me getting in a fight—which would result in our parent's finding out that we had both snuck out.

"Have fun," she smiled, closing the bathroom door.

"Night, Cayla-belle," I said softly, so low that she couldn't hear me.

I eased the window up completely and eased outside, crouching on the roof. I waited a minute to make sure Cayla wasn't going to reappear—or one of my parents—then closed it.

I tiptoed down the eave of the roof, spotting the taillights of Kyle's car waiting down the street for me.

I lowered to my stomach, sliding over the edge and grabbing on. I dropped down to the ground, careful to tuck my body so I didn't injure myself.

Getting down was the easy part of sneaking out. Getting back up... now that was a different story.

I jogged down the street to Kyle's white car.

"Dude, what the fuck took so long?" He asked when I finally slid into the passenger seat.

"My sister caught me," I muttered.

Kyle grinned and I didn't like his smile one bit. "Why didn't you bring her? She's hot, I'm sure someone could've had some fun with her."

I glared at him, my fists clenched. "Don't talk about my sister like that."

Kyle raised his hands in mock surrender, a smirk playing on his thin lips. "It's the truth. A lot of the guys would love to have a piece of—"

I punched the side of his face.

I didn't care if he was my friend or not.

No one talked about my baby sister like that. Hopefully he'd learn from this and so would the other guys.

"Fuck, Caelan, did you really need to punch me?"

"Yeah, I really did. Maybe that will teach you that running your mouth about my sister is a bad idea," I retorted. "Would you want me to make comments about your sister?"

"My sister is fourteen," he countered.

"Mine's only sixteen," I continued to pin him with a glare.

"Fine, whatever dude. She isn't worth getting punched over for *no-fucking-reason*," he hissed.

He finally pulled away from the curb.

"Where's this party at?" I asked.

After we'd won the football game I had to head home for dinner—my parents were really big on family time. Sometimes 'family time' could be a major pain in the ass since it kept me from doing stuff with friends, but when I heard some of them talk about how messed up their families were I was silently thankful for my overbearing parents.

"The Cove," he answered, winding around a turn too fast. I knew better than to complain. He'd only speed up.

The Cove wasn't really a cove at all. It was a rock formation near the lake that provided great shelter from the surrounding neighborhoods. As long as we kept the noise level reasonable, most people didn't know we were out there.

"Leah is going to be there," Kyle said casually, watching me out of the corner of his eye for a reaction.

I'd been going after Leah for a few weeks now. She always tried to blow me off, but I could tell I was breaking down her walls. It wouldn't be long until I had her right where I wanted her. She was enjoying playing hard to get, and I was enjoying the chase, but it ended tonight. I'd have her.

Kyle parked a block over from The Cove and we walked from that point. People would get suspicious if a bunch of cars were parked too close.

"Cael?"

I turned at the sound of my name, my lips curling up as I spotted Leah.

Her shiny red hair was curling down her back, and her lips were coated in some kind of shiny gloss that I was desperate to taste.

"I'll see you later... I guess," Kyle winked, heading on without us.

"You know," I told Leah, "you shouldn't be standing out here all by yourself where anyone could get you."

"Oh," she purred, striding forward, "is the big bad wolf going to eat me?" She asked, purposely letting her breasts brush against my shoulder.

"Maybe," I smirked, staring down at her.

"And maybe," she stared brazenly up at me, "I want him too."

Aw, hell.

I'd been waiting weeks for this moment, and I wasn't going to let it pass me by.

I reached out for her, my hands finding the curve of her butt, and pressed my lips to hers.

She let out a soft little moan that stirred something inside me. I pressed more firmly against her as her fingers pulled at my hair. I knew she was a feisty little thing. I nipped at her bottom lip, and then plunged my tongue inside her mouth. I wanted her and I wanted her bad, but we were standing on the street, and I did value my life. If I got caught my dad would be pissed enough to string me up by my balls and leave me to die, so I broke away.

"That's hardly over," I warned her.

She giggled, reaching for my hand. "I hope not... and it certainly doesn't feel like it's over," she bit her lip, running her fingers over the hard-on pressing against my jeans.

My breath hissed through my teeth as she felt me up.

I led her through the tall grass and around the large rocks where the party was roaring. A small fire provided warmth—but wasn't large enough to attract unwanted attention. Someone played music from their iPod dock and bodies swayed.

"Dance with me," Leah pleaded, pulling me towards everyone else.

I wasn't a dancer, but I agreed just for the pleasure of watching her sexy little body move.

She grinded against me and I closed my eyes, tilting my head back.

"If you keep doing that," I warned her, grabbing her stomach and rubbing my thumb against the underside of her breast, "I'm going to haul you out of here and make you scream my name."

She looked up at me, her green eyes sparkling in the

moonlight. My throat tightened as her tongue flicked out to moisten her pouty lips. "I wouldn't complain."

"Fuck," I growled, my hands tightening against her.

I wanted her and I wanted her bad.

"Come on," I pulled her away from everyone else and into the tall grasses. I kept dragging her until we were far enough away that we wouldn't be found easily.

I sunk down on the ground, pulling her with me onto my lap.

"You've been teasing me for weeks," I lifted her shirt off her head. "This ends tonight."

"Just make it good," she challenged.

"Oh, trust me, baby, you don't need to worry."

WHEN WE RETURNED—clothes and hair mused, but completely satisfied—the party had grown even larger. It seemed like everyone in our senior class was in attendance.

People wanted to talk and congratulate me on the game. I smiled and nodded—but honestly, I didn't really care. Football was fun, but it wasn't my whole life.

I sat down on the ground, beer in hand, with Leah between my legs. Her head rested against my chest.

When the sun started to peek above the edge of the lake, we all knew it was time to leave.

I said goodbye to Leah, giving her a long lingering kiss. Tonight had been good and I wasn't ready to let her walk away just yet.

"Come on, Lover Boy," Kyle pried me away from her lips.

I laughed, calling to Leah, "See you later?"

She nodded, her cheeks flushed with happiness.

Kyle dropped me off at the same spot he'd been waiting for me earlier.

I walked slowly towards my house, my head bowed.

When I finally looked up, ready to cut across the side yard to the back, so I could get back to my room, I noticed that the front door was slightly ajar.

The hairs on the back of my neck stood on end.

Oh, shit.

My parents had woken up and found me gone. I was in so much trouble it wasn't even funny.

I swallowed thickly, my heart pumping in my chest as I made my way up the front steps into the house. There would be no point trying to sneak in. I had been caught and I had to face this.

When I pushed open the front door I was surprised to find the house in disarray. Drawers were open, lights smashed, and our belongings strewn about everywhere.

"What. The. Hell," I gasped.

My heart raced even faster.

Something bad had happened. It looked like someone had broken in and tried to rob us.

I walked to the back of the house, to the kitchen, expecting to find my mom and dad there calling the police, but it was empty.

"Mom!" I called. "Dad!"

Silence greeted me.

Maybe they had run to the neighbors' house? Or were at the police station? Or—?

Something told me that neither of those things had happened.

Dread settled over me, sliding through my body like toxic sludge.

I swallowed thickly, heading for the main staircase.

I took the steps slowly and came to a standstill when I reached the top.

Blood.

Blood everywhere.

My shoes were growing damp with it.

"Dad!" I dropped to my knees, not caring that his blood now soaked my jeans. "Dad!" I screamed again and again—willing him to answer. I rolled him over, choking on a sob as his lifeless eyes met me. There was so much blood. God, it was fucking everywhere, seeping out of a series of knife wounds on his chest.

I released him, running for my parent's room.

"No!" I yelled, when my eyes took in the sight of my mom lying on a blood soaked mattress, her eyes focused on the ceiling. There were cuts and slashes all over her. I couldn't mistake the sound of her blood dripping from the bed onto the hardwood floors.

Drip.

Drip.

Drip.

I ran to Cayla's room next, praying that she had hidden and was okay—or better yet, hoping I'd wake up and find this to all be a nightmare.

"Cayla!" I shouted, clutching my stomach as it heaved violently.

Like my mom, she was lying in her bed. Her eyes stared straight at me—the color so light it was almost white. Her normally rosy complexion was now a grayish blue color. Her throat had been slit open, the blood coating her, the bed, and the floor. Her mouth was open in a never-ending silent scream.

I fell to the ground, sobbing hysterically.

"Cayla," I cried, crawling on my hands and knees over to her bed. "Cayla, please! You can't die! Cayla!" I smacked her cheeks, shook her, yelled at her, and none of it did any good.

She was gone.

They were all gone.

I pulled my phone out, fumbling to press the right buttons.

"911 what's your emergency?"

"Help! You have to help me! They're dead! They're all dead!"

"Who's dead, sir?" The calm voice asked me.

"My family! They're dead! God, they're all dead!"

"Sir, what's your address?"

I couldn't answer the woman. I had lost all capability of

speaking. A strange noise was escaping me—half crying, half screaming.

I shook Cayla some more, hoping in vain what I saw would disappear and she'd wake up and tell me I was crazy.

I'd rather be losing my mind than face this reality.

When I knew that Cayla wasn't going to wake up I sat on the floor beside her.

I rocked back and forth, sobbing, my blood-covered hands running through my hair. I kept muttering under my breath, "This isn't real, this isn't real, this isn't real."

That's how the police found me.

Even five years later, I still felt like I was stuck in that room rocking back and forth beside Cayla.

Only now, I said, "This is real."

CHAPTER 1

Sutton

five years later

I STRODE INTO my apartment, clutching the last cardboard box tightly in my hands, and kicked the door shut behind me.

Sitting the box down, I placed my hands on my hips as I tried to regain my breath from carrying so many heavy boxes up the steps.

I looked around, a small proud smile on my lips.

This was it.

This place was mine.

I had never had my own place, having only lived with my parents and scumbag ex-boyfriend whose name I refused to even *think*.

After a crappy time back home, I'd been desperate to get away—as far away as possible.

So, now I was on this crazy journey to find my identity.

I strode over to the large windows, looking outside. My apartment was in an old part of town and I was in love with the charm. It was what drew me here in the first place. The town boasted unique shops and the building had exposed brick walls, old wood floors, and a magnetism that I couldn't help but be drawn to.

I found my smile widening as I watched the traffic below.

Moving twelve hundred miles away from home would probably scare most twenty-two year old women. Not me though. After finishing college, I'd needed to get away from my life and have a fresh start. I couldn't take the negativity and disgusted stares for a moment longer. I was tired of feeling like a piece of shit.

I'd known my whole life I was adopted, and I wasn't sure if that was the reason I always felt like I didn't belong... or something else.

I reached up, running my fingers along the long slender raised scar on my arm. Some people were frightened of my scar, it was big and red, and ugly, but it was a part of me. It reminded me that once I'd had a different family—a family I'd never know, because while I'd escaped the fire with nothing but this scar as a baby, my whole family had lost their lives. A mom, dad, and brother that I'd never know. All I had left of them was a lone photograph salvaged from the rubble. I missed them—which seemed impossible when I didn't even know them. There was an emptiness in my heart where they should have been.

I pulled away from the window, facing the mess of boxes. I didn't even know where to begin.

Eyeing the open windows, and realizing that it would be dark soon, I decided to leave the boxes where they were and run to the store. No way was I sleeping in here with windows wide open like that.

I grabbed my car keys off the tile kitchen counter and headed outside.

It had taken a few days to make the drive from Texas to Virginia. Forgoing the expense of a hotel, I'd slept in my car.

Before I left for the store I stopped someone on the street and asked for directions. I hadn't had time to explore and I didn't want to waste my time driving around like an idiot.

In no time I was at Target. I meandered through the store, grabbing necessities I'd soon need. Like, towels. I'd definitely need towels. And food. Yeah, that was a must.

When I finally checked out it looked like I was stocking up for the zombie apocalypse.

I hoped I could find my way back to the apartment without getting lost.

I got distracted when I spotted a sign that boasted: **KITTENS FOR SALE!**

I wanted a kitten.

I was alone.

I had no friends here.

A kitten would be nice.

I really hoped they were selling kittens and it wasn't a code word for cocaine or something.

I pulled up to the house and strode up to the front door.

It opened almost immediately and a harried young mother greeted me with an infant on her hip.

"Hi," I ventured, "I saw the sign about the kittens and I was interested."

"Oh, right. Come in," she nodded me inside her messy house.

Kids screeched, running around like they owned the place.

"Back here," she led me to a closed-in porch. "My cat got pregnant again and I can't keep them. I want them gone, so you can have one for twenty bucks," she explained, disappearing as she chased down a child.

I stepped into the room, looking around for the kittens.

It didn't take me long to find them cuddled against their mother.

I smiled, crouching down.

One of the kittens pulled away from its mom, bouncing up to me and playfully trying to nip my fingers.

It was cute and unusually colored. Half of its face was orange with a black ear, while the opposite was true of the other side. Most of its body was a dark gray with black stripes. Hints of orange dotted the mostly dark color—one of its paws was completely orange and there was a white patch under its mouth and front paw.

"Hi cutie," I reached out, letting it sniff me. "You wanna come home with me?" I asked, scratching behind its ear.

It rubbed its head against my hand, letting out a content purr.

I grabbed it up, cradling it against my neck. I didn't need to play with any of the others. This one had chosen me.

I stood up, carrying the kitten and cooing at it like one would a baby, and went in search of the woman.

I found her in the kitchen, consoling the screaming infant that had been on her hip.

She looked up at me, completely frazzled.

"You find one?"

"Mhmm," I nodded, pointing to the cutie in my hand.

She smiled. "Brutus is feisty. He'll keep you on your toes."

"I can handle him," I assured her, kissing his head. I handed her the twenty dollars and drove back into town to get supplies for my new friend. I knew my apartment had a one pet limit, so I was safe with Brutus.

Once I was home, I sat Brutus down in the apartment, as well as my bags.

It was getting late, the sun setting. I needed to get those curtains up.

Luckily, I'd had the forethought to buy a screwdriver while I was at the store. This would be a piece of cake, right?

Wrong.

Caelan

I STARED AT the canvas in front of me, willing my hand to move and make the strokes necessary to bring the image in my head to life. But I couldn't. Why? Because someone was making too much damn noise!

I threw the paint brush to the ground, not caring that

watercolor paint went flying everywhere—all over me, my clothes, and my hair, as well as the walls and floors.

Nobody in this whole fucking building had any respect for the fact that I needed *silence* to work. Noise was far too distracting when I was trying to paint. I needed to focus, and I couldn't do that when other people were—I had no idea what this person was doing, it sounded like they were trying to kill something. Well, *I* wanted to kill them. If it wasn't Frankie and his annoying girlfriend banging down walls with their raging sex life, it was Cyrus with one of his parties. *This* was neither of those things, and the commotion was coming from the apartment across from me. Somebody new had moved in. Whoever it was needed to learn real fast that I wouldn't stand for interruptions while I was working.

I shoved my fingers through my hair, no doubt spreading paint into the strands.

My temper flared as I paced. I reached for the bottle of Jack Daniels I'd been drinking from earlier and took a large swig, wiping my mouth with the back of my hand. My body vibrated from the leftover aftershocks of the hit I'd had earlier. Drugs and alcohol were my only true friends. Neither let me down.

I knew it wouldn't be long until I couldn't help but barge over to the new neighbor's place.

When I heard a crash, I couldn't wait any longer to say something.

I stormed out of my apartment and straight into the one across from me, since the idiot had left the door unlocked.

"What the fuck is all this noise?" I seethed, my fists clenched at my sides.

A raven-haired beauty stared up at me from the floor with wide puzzled eyes. She looked from me, to the open door in shock. I wanted to laugh as she realized her own stupidity about leaving the door unlocked. She might have been gorgeous, but clearly she was also lacking in the brains department.

I tapped my foot and crossed my arms over my chest as I

waited for her to answer.

She seemed to be battling some internal debate about whether to tell me to get the fuck out or actually answer my question.

"I'm trying to hang curtains!" She glared at me, her light blue eyes full of annoyance at me.

I sneered down at her, trying to appear angry and menacing, when really I was quite fascinated by her. I noticed she cradled her knee like she'd injured herself. That's when I noticed the chair fallen to the side. "It doesn't look like you're doing a very good job," I remarked, rocking back on my heels.

"Obviously," she snorted, rolling those pretty blue eyes at me.

Something about her attitude amused me. She was a spunky little thing.

I figured I wouldn't get any work done until those damn curtains were hung, so I turned sharply, heading back to my apartment for my drill.

It wasn't long until I was breezing back inside. The woman had picked the chair up and was attempting to climb back on to resume her poor job of hanging curtains. Who knew curtains could be so complicated? Why did she even need curtains? If someone looked inside and got an eyeful it was their problem and they shouldn't have been looking.

"Jesus Christ! Not you again!" She yelled and the chair teetered, causing me to edge closer in case she fell and I needed to catch her. Whoa... since when did I think about *helping* someone? I looked down at the drill in my hand. I was going to blame my worry about the threat of her falling and wanting to hang her curtains on the fact that I wanted her to be quiet. It had absolutely nothing to do with her being gorgeous. None at all. Nope.

I really wanted to know what she'd look like naked and what kind of sounds she'd make as I pleasured her.

I shook my head forcefully and scolded myself for undressing her with my eyes.

Ignoring her comment, I stepped around her, pretending that the coconut scent of her body lotion didn't have all the blood in my body running south.

I took the chair from her clenched hands and stood atop it to drill the brackets for the curtains into place.

She watched me with her mouth hanging open. I wasn't sure if she was impressed with my handy work, or still shocked that I had busted into her apartment like a crazy person. Probably both. Hopefully I could get some work done now. She might be hot, but my work was more important. So was drinking and getting high—as long as I numbed myself I didn't have to remember what happened to my family or how fucked up my life had become because of it.

Shaking my head free of my thoughts, I stepped down to make sure I had everything in place. No way was I going home only to have her start banging around some more because I hadn't done something right.

Sutton

HE APPRAISED HIS handy work before his light blue eyes landed on me. Slightly wavy blonde hair fell over his forehead, his nose was sharp and defined, and his lips were set in a thin grim line like I was an unruly teenager he wanted to reprimand. "Maybe I'll get some work done now," he snapped, striding towards the door. Something stopped him, and he turned back to me, a mocking smile on his lips. "Nice pussy."

"What?" I gasped, shaking my head. Surely I hadn't heard him right.

"Nice. Pussy." He said each word slowly like I was an idiot, and then nodded his head at Brutus.

Before I could retort, he was gone, slamming the door shut behind him.

I was stunned.

Had that really just happened?

I glared at the closed door, my anger getting the best of me.

I swung it open, striding to the door across from mine, assuming that was his since it sounded like it had just closed.

I slammed my fist against the door, refusing to let up until he opened.

When it did open, I nearly fell, but quickly straightened myself.

The man stood in front of me, with his hands braced above his head. He was watching me with an angry look, his lips curled into a snarl. He was a few inches taller than me, and slim like he didn't have much to eat, but still muscular. His clothes were splattered with different colors of paint and there was even some in his hair.

I shook my head, forcing myself to stop checking him out— even if he was insanely hot.

"I don't know who the hell you think you are," I pointed a finger at him, "but I don't appreciate you marching into my apartment like that. I don't even know your name!" I threw my hands in the air, letting them settle on my waist.

A single brow arched on his elegant face. "My name's Caelan, and—?" He paused, waiting for my name.

"Sutton," I responded, tapping my foot and giving off the air of being completely pissed off.

"Well, *Sutton*," he said my name slowly, rolling it around on his tongue, "it sounded like you were really struggling over there. I thought I'd be neighborly and help," he smirked. "You're welcome."

"You—" And that's the only word I got out of my mouth before he promptly slammed the door closed in my face.

I had my fist raised, ready to pound on his door again when another door down the hall opened.

A guy not much older than me stuck his head out, looking around, clearly disturbed by the slamming of the door.

When he spotted me, a slow grin lifted his lips and he looked me up and down.

"Did you piss off Gregory?" He chuckled. "Don't you girls know by now that he fucks you once, then he's done?"

"What?" I looked around, confusion muffling my brain. "Who's Gregory? Him?" I pointed to the door I still stood in front of.

The guy leaned against the doorway of his apartment and nodded. "Yeah."

"He said his name was Caelan!" I fumed.

"Oh," the guy frowned, "he gave you his first name?"

"Why wouldn't he tell me his first name? So Caelan is his name? You're confusing me," I admitted, venturing closer to the guy.

"His name is Caelan Gregory. He always tells his fuck buddies that his name is Gregory, so... if you're not another notch on his bed pole, who are you?" He studied me carefully like he was trying to get a handle on me.

"I'm Sutton," I answered. "I moved in there," I pointed back at my apartment. "And Mr. Rude over there busted into my apartment like a madman."

The guy winced. "Yeah, Cael, is kind of... well, you'll learn soon enough," he shrugged. "He's an artist, and he doesn't like to be... disturbed. Don't worry though," he added, "I'm more accommodating than Gregory."

I shook my head in annoyance. "I'm not interested."

He chuckled. "I have a girlfriend, so I'm not interested either. I *am* a nice guy, though. So if you need anything, don't hesitate to ask. I'm Frankie," he held out a hand for me to shake and I took it hesitantly. "My sister, Daphne, lives with me. I'd introduce you, but I'm pretty sure she's *still* sleeping off a major hangover."

"That's alright," I told him, backing away, "I really need to finish unpacking."

Before I disappeared inside my apartment, his voice stopped

me.

"Yeah?" I turned back around, my dark hair swishing around my shoulders.

"Try not to piss off Cael *too* much. He's already a pain in the ass to deal with on a daily basis. No one living here needs you to make it worse," he frowned, tapping his fingers on the wood of the door. It was obvious he hated sounding like a jerk, but he was more scared of Caelan than me.

"Trust me," I glanced at the door across from mine, "you have nothing to worry about."

CHAPTER 2
Sutton

When I awoke I was momentarily disoriented since I didn't recognize my surroundings.

I shook my head, clearing my mind of cobwebs.

"Meow."

I smiled, looking over at Brutus. "Hey," I greeted him, scratching him behind his ear. He twisted his head further into the palm of my hand and began to purr.

I pushed the covers off my body, heading into the bathroom.

The bathroom was the only room in the apartment that was closed off from the rest. My bedroom was open to the living room and kitchen. I didn't mind like most would. I didn't plan on having any sleepovers, so...

When I was finished in the bathroom I sat a bowl of food on the ground for Brutus. He happily chowed down, purring as he did. I couldn't help but crack a smile at him.

I'd picked up a coffee maker while I was shopping yesterday. Luckily, I'd taken the time to set it up last night, knowing I wouldn't have the patience to do it now. I pushed the button to brew it and hopped up on the counter to wait for it. I needed to do more shopping today and I also needed to find a job. Yeah, a job was a must.

My parent's were pissed that I'd spent four years in college getting a business degree, only to take off after graduation with 'no aspirations'. They were pissed at me for a lot of reasons, actually. Reasons that were far too painful to even think of.

I was only twenty-two. I wanted to have fun and live a little before I settled down. I had never had the true teenage experience. I guessed I was rebelling now. I wanted to go to parties and make friends with the wrong people. I wanted to work at some neat little shop and stay up all night. I wanted to get a tattoo and shout from rooftops.

Silly, I know, but it's what I wanted.

When the coffee was ready I poured the steaming liquid into one of the mugs I'd bought yesterday. I didn't need to add sugar or creamer. I took a sip of the bitter liquid and winced. It was perfect.

I drank all the coffee—my breakfast of choice—and showered. I pulled my wet hair up into a knot on my head and dressed in comfy clothes. I wasn't planning to head out yet. Right now I wanted to unpack and get settled.

I had only brought what I could fit in my car from Texas, which meant I was really lacking in anything except clothes and bedding. Luckily, I had enough money in my savings to get a couch and other things.

I sat on the floor, unpacking boxes and organizing my clothes in the closet. Brutus watched me with quiet curiosity.

Having Brutus around made me feel not so alone.

Not that I minded being alone.

When all the boxes were unpacked I flattened them down and tucked them under my arm so I could head outside to dispose of them.

"I'll be right back." I told the kitten that was currently scampering after me.

I bound down the steps and around to the side of the building. I dropped them in the dumpster, satisfied that I wasn't being a complete procrastinator and had managed to get all my unpacking done.

I rounded the building again, to go back inside, when I noticed a lean figure walking down the street—away from the apartments.

His head was bowed, as if deep in thought, and he walked quickly.

I knew who it was.

Caelan.

If I hadn't recognized the posture and overall attitude of the person walking away from me, the paint stained clothes would have given him away.

I didn't even know him, but I knew enough to see that he was a strange guy.

I couldn't figure out what his issue was. It was something more complex than him being an *artist*. There was more to him, I could see that, but I had no intentions of finding out what. Guys like Caelan were bad fucking news. I had come here to find myself, not to get wrapped up in some mystery.

Caelan

I FELT MY new neighbors eyes on me. I never knew that someone watching you could somehow feel like a caress.

I itched to turn around and look at her, but I kept my head bowed and continued walking.

I hadn't been able to get her off my mind last night, and for once I'd gone to sleep thinking about a woman, and not my family. Something about her was captivating. Yeah, she was fucking gorgeous, but it was more than that. I'd come across many beautiful women in the last five years and none of them did more for me than provide a quick escape. Sutton… I knew she'd be different.

I turned the corner and no longer felt her penetrating stare.

Rolling my shoulders, I burrowed into a protective stance as I continued my walk—heading for the place I came to at least once a week.

I was always sober when I came to the cemetery.

It was necessary in order to let the feelings of loss and abandonment seep into my pores.

This was the only time I couldn't allow myself to be numb.

I needed to *hurt*.

It was the least I deserved for letting them die.

I'd never forgive myself for not being there—for not saving them. I knew if I was there I could have done *something*.

Instead, I was out partying, and fucking a girl who in the end I couldn't even remember her face.

That night—finding them—destroyed some fundamental piece of my soul. It took away any feelings of joy and left in its wake a rotting black hole. I ruined everything I came into contact with. I was a shitty person. I did bad things and didn't feel a smidgen of grief for it. I liked to play with things, twisting and bending them to my will. I *really* wanted to play with Sutton. Her fiery personality ignited something in me that I couldn't quite pinpoint yet. She was dangerous for me and I'd do well to stay away. I feared that'd be impossible though. People like Sutton, they suck you into their orbit, centering you and becoming your gravity—even if only for a moment.

I didn't know the woman, and these were silly thoughts to have.

Maybe I was still high from the hit I'd had hours ago.

I knew that was impossible, but I would've liked to believe it, because it scared me to think that one person might have such a profound affect on me after only one encounter.

I tried to convince myself that it was her beauty that had me thinking such pining and poetic thoughts.

But it wasn't that.

It was... *her*.

She hadn't looked at me with disgust or pity. She'd certainly been irritated with me barging into her apartment, but I didn't see any of the usual looks on her face that I got from other people. In the last five years I had grown used to people looking down upon me. I didn't blame them for it. Fuck, I looked down on myself. I knew my parents would be ashamed if they knew how I turned out after their deaths. They'd probably string me up and flog me. The knowledge didn't serve to make me want to change though. I didn't think anything ever would. I had become far to use to letting drugs and alcohol take over every facet of my life so that I didn't have to deal with shit. Some called it self-medicating. I called it the-only-thing-that-didn't-disappoint-me. My family may have been the ones that died that night, but I might as well have too, because I sure as hell stopped living.

Kyle was the only person that stuck by my side, and even we weren't usually on good terms. For some reason, he refused to ditch my sorry ass. I think he'd never forgive himself if something happened to me. He felt responsible for my downward spiral since he thought if he'd come home with me that night he could have somehow kept me from breaking apart. Nothing could have prevented my reaction, but he didn't understand that. He hadn't had his only family ripped from him. Like everyone else, he couldn't relate no matter how hard he tried.

When I stepped into the cemetery a feeling of peace swirled through my body.

They were close.

I made the familiar steps to my family's graves.

"Hi guys," I said, taking my position between my sister and mother's graves. I lay down on my back, stretching my arms behind my head. "I've missed you."

I closed my eyes, pretending they answered and asked me how my day was.

"I painted a new picture of you, Cayla. I think you'd like it.

You were in the park, chasing butterflies like you used to do. Do you remember that?"

The wind tickled my cheeks and I smiled, imagining it was Cayla's laughter.

"Somebody moved into the apartment across from mine. Her name's Sutton. And..." I trailed off. "I don't know what to think about her—whether I like her or hate her. I think I like her. Hating her would be easier though." I whispered, my eyes still closed as I pictured my mom, dad, and sister all seated around the kitchen table as we talked like we used to. "I've hated everyone since you guys left me."

"Why, Caelan?" Cayla asked—or at least I wished she did.

"Because," I spoke, finally allowing my eyes to drift open to view the white puffy clouds above, "Loving you guys caused me unbearable pain and I refuse to ever go through that again. I can't lose someone else, so it's better if I don't care."

"Good luck with that," Cayla sassed. "You can't hate everyone forever."

"I can try," I growled, anger simmering in my veins at the imaginary voice.

"Love always finds a way in. Even if it's not the kind of love you're searching for."

I pushed myself to my feet, shaking off the grass that clung to my jeans. Talking to my dead sister was taking things too far—even for me.

I headed home, determined to drink myself into oblivion so that the words I'd pretended my sister was whispering no longer existed.

Sutton

"Again with the fucking noise!"

I wasn't surprised when Caelan came storming out of his apartment, angrier than he had been yesterday.

"They're bringing a couch in," I pointed to the furniture delivery guys, giving Caelan a bored look. "I'm sorry if their grunts disturbed you," I said, my tone dripping with sarcasm.

His blue eyes sparkled with fire and I was surprised steam wasn't coming out of his nose and ears. His hands fisted at his sides and his shoulders were tight with tension.

"Keep. The. Noise. Down. I'm working!" He shouted, his face red. A vein in his forehead threatened to explode.

My lips quirked into a crooked, challenging smile. Did this guy really think he could intimidate me? He was in for a rude awakening. I didn't cower under pressure. I thrived on it.

"Buddy," I started, eyeing him and completely unfazed, "you don't scare me. That might work with other people, but it won't work on me. Have you ever heard of these things called earplugs?" I pointed to my ears. "Or maybe headphones—then you could listen to music and forget the whole world still existed."

"You think you're real clever?" He seethed, but I swore there was amusement in his eyes, like he was enjoying the game we were playing.

"The cleverest," I retorted, moving out of the way so the men could maneuver the large couch through the narrow doorway.

"I guess no one told you the rules when you moved in," he gritted his teeth, "so I'm going to be nice and cut you some slack. Everyone knows, if you live here, you keep quiet. I need to work and I need silence."

"You don't own the place," I countered haughtily, crossing my arms over my chest. I didn't miss the way his eyes couldn't help but caress the skin peeking out from the tank top I was wearing.

"That may be true," he pointed a finger in my face, "but you don't want to get on my bad side, *Sutton*," he hissed my name like it was poisonous. I had to admit, I was surprised he remembered it.

"Trust me," I smiled slowly, "I don't want to be on any side of yours."

His eyes narrowed, but he knew he'd lost this round. He turned to go back in his apartment and stopped short of closing the door. "Quiet." Pleased that he had the final word, he closed the door.

I laughed, shaking my head.

This was going to be fun.

If he thought he could control me with a few bossy words, then he was in for a rude awakening.

Sutton Hale didn't bow down to anyone. Least of all some conceited dickwad that thought the world owed him a favor.

AFTER THE GUYS delivering the couch left I decided to dress up a bit and walk around town to see if anyone was hiring.

I went into a few places, but none of them felt right.

I wasn't even sure what I was searching for, but I'd know when I found it.

The stars were twinkling in the night sky when I entered a shop for a much needed coffee break.

I waited in line, watching the people seated around the shop.

When it was my turn to order I chose the house blend—sans sugar or anything else, of course.

"You look tired," the older man working there said, pouring my coffee into a cup and sticking a lid on.

I nodded. "Job hunting will do that to you."

"Job hunting?" he propped an elbow on the counter, ignoring the others waiting to place their order. "I'm looking for some help."

"You are?" I brightened. I had already decided I liked the atmosphere in the neat little shop.

"Yeah," he smiled kindly, "we're far too busy and understaffed. When can you start?"

My eyes threatened to bug out of my head. "That's it? I'm hired? You didn't even interview me!"

He chuckled. "Have you killed anyone?"

"No!" I scoffed in disbelief.

"See?" He shrugged. "You're safe enough. When can you start?" He asked again.

"T-tomorrow?" I hesitated, wondering if someone was about to jump from behind the counter and tell me I'd been Punk'd.

"Excellent," he clapped his hands together and smiled broadly. "Welcome to Griffin's," he held out a hand, "I'm Griffin, the owner and boss extraordinaire around these parts."

"Sutton." I couldn't help but smile at his exuberance and overall gruff charm.

Clearing his throat, he said, "Alright, now get out of here before people start thinking I have a heart."

I laughed, amused by my new boss.

I was headed out the door when I heard my name called. Startled, I stopped in my tracks. No one knew me here, so I couldn't see how they'd be speaking to me, but Sutton wasn't exactly a common name.

I turned around, scanning the interior of the shop when my eyes landed on arms flailing wildly.

I laughed, recognizing Frankie. He waved me over and I knew it would be rude not to join.

"Hi," I said hesitantly, standing beside the table he occupied.

His red hair stuck up wildly around his head and his arm was slung over the shoulder of a pretty blonde girl. Another girl sat beside him, and her hair color matched his, so I knew this must be the sister he had spoken of yesterday.

"Sutton, this is my girlfriend, Jen," he leaned over and kissed the cheek of the blonde girl, "and my sister, Daphne," he nodded to the other girl.

Both of them said hi, as I stood there awkwardly.

"Nice to meet you," I finally spoke.

"Sit down." Frankie pointed to the empty chair. "We're nice people. Stop looking at us like we kicked a puppy."

"Sorry," I laughed, my nervousness slipping away.

I pulled out a chair and took a seat, at a loss as to what to say. I wasn't a shy person, but I wasn't a great conversationalist either.

"So you moved in across from Caelan?" Daphne asked me, pulling her pretty red hair over her shoulder so it draped down her chest.

She was petite with alabaster skin and eyes that could only be describe as gold. Her nose was slim while her lips had that perfect pout most girls would kill for.

I nodded. "Nice fellow."

She rolled her eyes as the other two laughed. "Yeah, about as nice as a starving lion when it sees a gazelle." Tapping her bright purple nails against the lacquered tabletop, she asked, "Are you from here?"

I shook my head.

"Where are you from then?" She questioned, a curious brow arching.

"Ignore her," Frankie interrupted, "she's really nosy and will ask you a million and one questions."

"Whatever," Daphne grumbled.

"I lived in Dallas, Texas," I answered.

"And you came here?" She gasped. "To the middle of fucking nowhere? *Why*?"

I shrugged, may gaze sliding away from her face to look at my reflection in the shiny top. "I guess I needed a change of scenery," I whispered.

"It's so boring here," Daphne sneered, "seriously, nothing exciting ever happens."

"Except when Caelan has one of his episodes," Frankie inserted with a shake of his head. "Or when Cyrus has one of his parties."

"Huh?" I spoke up.

"You'll know soon enough," Frankie chuckled, leaning into his girlfriend and playfully nibbling on her ear. She appeared embarrassed at first, and then sank into his touch.

"Ignore them," Daphne slid closer to me. "They're sickeningly in love and it's disgusting."

I couldn't help laughing. "You sound jealous."

"Not at all," she muttered, and I noticed that her eyes zeroed in on a guy cleaning off a table. He was tall with tanned skin and dark slightly curled hair that fell in his eyes. Stubble dotted his defined cheeks and chin. He looked like he belonged on a magazine, not cleaning tables.

I looked back at her, noting her lust-filled eyes, and connected the dots. Since I didn't know her well, I didn't say anything, but filed this bit of information in the back of my mind.

"Anyway," she propped her head on her hand, smiling at me. "You're the one that pissed Caelan off so badly yesterday?"

I rolled my eyes. "I get the impression that everyone and everything pisses him off."

"This is true," she laughed, the sound light and musical sounding. "You have to learn how to deal with him."

"Yeah, well," I mumbled, my lips quirking, "I don't plan on bowing down to him."

"He doesn't frighten you?" She questioned with wide eyes.

I was a bit taken aback by her question, but I could see how Caelan could be an intimidating guy. He gave off a vibe of stay-away-from-me. "Not at all."

It was obvious that Caelan had demons. It was plain to see in his eyes to a keen observer. I didn't see anything there to fear though. He was broken. Life will do that to you—it toys with you, pushing you to your limits, waiting to see what it takes to make you snap.

She sat back, eyeing me.

"What?" I asked when she didn't say anything.

"I'm trying to figure you out," her eyes pierced me.

"There's nothing to figure out," I assured her.
"Everyone has a story."

With that, she came to her feet and left without a backwards glance.

CHAPTER 3
Sutton

AFTER DAPHNE'S DEPARTURE I didn't feel like staying and watching Frankie make-out with Jen, so I gathered my stuff to head back to the apartment.

I loved that there were so many shops in the vicinity of where I lived. I could walk around and find anything I wanted.

I stopped at a cupcake shop, the smell luring me inside, and picked out two to take home with me. Red velvet and double chocolate. I wasn't sure which one I'd eat first.

As I entered the hallway leading to my apartment, I struggled to maintain my hold on my coffee, the cupcakes, and my purse. *Something* had to go tumbling to the ground.

Of course it was the coffee and the cupcakes.

"Shit!" I yelled, stomping my foot in frustration and beginning to mourn the loss of the cupcakes and coffee. Well, I'd still eat the cupcakes. They might be smashed from the fall, but the box had kept them from touching the floor. So in my book, still edible.

"What's going on *now*?"

The door to Caelan's apartment came flying open at the commotion.

I was now convinced the guy freaked out over any sound—

even a mouse farting. *Do* mice fart? I'd have to Google it later.

"I dropped my stuff," I pointed to the mess, giving him a 'duh' look.

"Do you *enjoy* pissing me off? You've only been here two days and it seems to be a hobby of yours!"

His nostrils flared with anger and his blonde hair stuck up wildly around his head—like he'd been running his fingers through it repeatedly.

"Oh yes," I smiled slowly, "it fills my heart to be yelled at by men I don't know. Thanks for fulfilling my fetish."

He narrowed his eyes—eyes that I couldn't help but notice held an underlying sadness.

"You're a smart mouth, you know that, right?"

"I've heard that before," I told him, bending to pick up the box that contained my cupcakes and the now empty cup of coffee.

"One of these days, I'm going to shut you up." Smirking, he tilted his head and added, "I promise you'll enjoy my methods."

I wasn't surprised when the door closed and he was gone.

It didn't take long to learn that Caelan always got the last word.

I WOKE UP the next morning with nervous butterflies assaulting my stomach.

Day Three of my new life meant Day One of my new job.

Griffin had grabbed my arm before I left the shop yesterday, telling me to be in by ten in the morning.

That was completely doable.

He hadn't told me about a dress code though. Based on his casual attire, I assumed there wasn't one. None of the other people working there had been dressed a certain way.

After my shower I dressed in a pair of jeans and a white tank top with a worn blue plaid shirt thrown over top—it was my go to comfort outfit.

If Griffin wanted me to change, I was within walking distance of the apartment and could run home.

After my necessary cup of black coffee I cuddled Brutus for a few minutes before heading to work. I slung my cross-body leather and tie-dye fringe purse over my shoulder, and blew a kiss to Brutus who was rolling around on the floor pawing a dust bunny.

I stopped, eyeing Caelan's door. A sly grin spread over my face. Feeling like a mischievous child, I took two steps and leaned forward, rapping my fist sharply against the door.

I heard him cussing, and then something went crashing to the ground.

I ran down the hall and descended into the stairwell. I peeked around the corner to see him come busting into the hallway. He looked left, then right, and upon seeing no one slammed the door closed.

I couldn't help the giggle that bubbled out of my throat.

I didn't know why I enjoyed tormenting Caelan so much. There was something about him that I just couldn't help but *push*. I liked to make him tick. I was sure that meant I was a bad person, but I didn't really care.

With a smile on my lips, and a bounce in my step, I made my way to Griffin's.

Upon entering, a bell above the door dinged cheerily.

"Sutton!" Griffin waved from behind the counter he was currently wiping down with a damp rag. He tossed the rag over his shoulder and waved me behind the counter.

"I hope what I'm wearing is okay," I was quick to tell him, "you didn't mention a dress code, so..." I trailed off, shrugging my shoulders.

"You're fine like that," he said gruffly. Clearing his throat, he said, "You know I'm Griffin, but you can call me Griff. My wife,

Laura, and I own this place... obviously. The place has really expanded in the last few years," he shrugged his wide shoulders. "Started out as a coffee shop, now we serve food, and even alcohol," he winked. "The stage is back there," he pointed to a slightly hidden part of the restaurant from my vantage point. "It draws quite a crow. Plus, we're open twenty-four hours a day to cater to the college kids. So, I've had to suck it up and hire more people. That's where you come in," he winked. "The hours I'll need you will be kind of random. Are you okay working late?"

"Yes, sir," I answered immediately.

He eyed me with a stern look. "Don't call me sir... ever. Makes me feel old." With a shake of his head, swinging his gray ponytail, he scratched his bearded chin. "I'm going to start you off today training with my grandson, Emery. Emery!" He called, pushing open the door that led to the back.

The guy I had noticed Daphne checking out yesterday appeared in the doorway. He smiled easily, crossing muscular arms over his chest—stretching the thin cotton of the black t-shirt he wore. His jeans hung low on his hips, held up by a leather belt. His dark hair fell messily over his forehead, concealing a unique shade of blue-green eyes. They reminded me of the water you saw on tropical islands.

"Emery." His smile was lopsided as he held out his hand for me.

"I gathered that." Shit. My sarcastic side refused to stay reigned in lately. If my mom was here she'd try to wash my mouth out with soap. "I'm Sutton."

"I gathered that," he repeated my words back to me with a laugh.

"Now that we're all... acquainted," Griffin clapped his hands together, "let's get to work."

AFTER MY SHIFT ended, there was a slight pep in my step as I walked home. Working at Griffin's would be fun. The atmosphere was great and everyone was great to work with. Emery was sweet with a fun personality. I could see myself being friends with him.

When I stepped inside my apartment Brutus came up to me meowing and rubbing his small body against my legs. Clearly, he was happy to see me.

I picked him up, nuzzling him against my neck. Kissing his nose, I placed him on the floor and slung my bag on the counter.

I was tired, but happy.

A part of me was still in shock that here I was, over a thousand miles from home, and I was *fine*.

Well, except for my shitty neighbor across the hall.

A slow smile spread across my face as I pulled my iPod from my purse and placed it on the docking system.

I knew it was horrible of me to be looking for ways to torment my neighbor, but I couldn't resist the free entertainment.

I should've probably invested in a TV. Instead, I flicked through my songs settling on one by Evanescence. I turned the volume up as loud as it would go, and started dancing around wildly, shaking my ass as I sang along at the top of my lungs.

He liked silence.

I liked noise.

Messing with Caelan was wrong, but I couldn't resist. He'd get angry, and I... well, I liked to push people.

I knew there was probably a lot more to Caelan's behavior than I or anyone else knew.

I was sure he had a really interesting story—everybody does, just like Daphne said.

For now, I wanted to mess with him.

I wanted to make him angry.

I wanted to see that fire in his eyes.

Something about him called to me, drawing me in.

I didn't understand what it was about him.

Maybe his brokenness.

I stopped dancing and stood still in my kitchen.

What the hell was I doing?

Was I flirting with my neighbor?

Was this some kind of sick foreplay?

I scrambled to turn down the music—analyzing my own behavior—but I didn't get it silenced in time.

He pounded on my door, and from the sounds of those knocks he was *livid*.

Shit.

What had I done?

I forced myself to open the door and pretend that I wasn't internally freaking out over my thoughts.

"I thought we had discussed this," his voice was icy as his eyes glared directly at me, "you need to keep the noise down. Since you didn't heed my warning, it looks like I get to shut you up."

I found my back pushed roughly against the brick wall. One of his hands entwined with mine, pinning it beside my head, while he braced the other on the wall above my head. I was affectively caged in with nowhere to go.

My eyes closed as I found myself unconsciously cowering to his domineering ways. My hair fell over my left shoulder and a few strands tumbled forward in an effort to hide my face.

My heart beat wildly in my chest, threatening to break free, but my ribs kept it caged.

His sudden movements and overall officious way had surprised me.

"Are you scared, Sutton?"

My eyes popped open, my mouth falling a bit with shock.

"No," I answered with a challenging smirk.

Caelan Gregory didn't *scare* me. Not the way he thought at least.

He scared me in the sense that I couldn't figure out why I was so drawn to him. I'd only been here three days and I didn't even *know* him.

We had chemistry, and I knew he had to feel it too.

I didn't even know what I wanted from him.

Certainly not a relationship—after the disasters of my love life back in Texas, I wasn't ready for *that*.

I had a desire to get to know this man though.

He had demons.

And dammit if I wasn't insanely curious as to what they were.

My mom always told me I was attracted to '*broken things*' that I could never fix.

"Oh, Sutton. You can't save every broken thing you come across, dear. Some things... they're better off being left the way they are. They aren't worth saving."

That's what she told me when I tried in vain to save the dog dying on the road outside our house.

Her words weren't harsh. She was just being realistic.

Unfortunately, I could never grow out of my need to save things.

I should've been a doctor, not a business major.

Too late now.

"Wrong answer," he growled, the scent of alcohol hitting me in the face.

Before I could respond his mouth was on mine. His lips were harsh and demanding and the heavy stubble on his cheeks chafed mine.

I was so overcome by shock that I couldn't even push him away.

Was this really happening?

Oh, it totally was.

His lips were on mine.

And my traitorous lips were actually moving *with* his.

What the fuck?

Get it together lips! You're not supposed to like this doucheknozzle!

My lips *so* weren't listening to me.

Oh no, they were still toying with his and—
Oh, shit.
I moaned.
Like a low *oh-my-god-that-feels-so-amazing* moan.

Apparently I'd lost all control of my body with one touch of his lips.

That wasn't okay with me.

Trying to get myself under control, I wiggled my fingers free from his and braced them against his shoulders. He leaned in closer, as if my touch was drawing him in.

I let his lips linger against mine for only a second more before I pushed him away roughly.

His lips fell from mine as he stumbled back.

He looked at me with shocked, hooded, blue eyes.

He seemed stunned and confused, then arrogance stole across his face.

"After that," he closed the distance between us once more, leaning down so that his lips brushed against my ear, "I'm hoping you didn't learn your lesson."

He turned and left—humming pleasantly under his breath like he hadn't just attacked me with his lips and hands.

I moved to watch him enter his apartment. He turned back to me before closing the door and just stood there with that *smirk*. I wanted to wipe it off his face and force any other expression on his face except for complete and utter arrogant confidence.

He leaned against the doorway watching me. That signature cocky grin of his widened further. For someone as grumpy as Caelan, it was as close as he got to a smile. Stupidly, I was wondered what his real smile looked like.

"Oh, look. My kiss has left you speechless," his voice was bland, but there was a slightly pleased sparkle in his eyes that livened up their normally dull quality. "Don't worry. That happens to everyone. I've been told the affects eventually wear off… well, actually they don't," he shrugged. "Guess I've ruined you for all other men."

I opened my mouth to retort but it was too late. He had already closed the door, because of course he was going to get the last word. He always did.

I had news for him.

This. Meant. WAR.

Caelan

As soon as the door closed, I leaned my weight against it and let out a breath I hadn't known I'd been holding.

I'd intended to shut up Sutton with a kiss the next time she disturbed me, but I hadn't expected to enjoy it. I should have known, the way she called to me like a siren of the sea, but damn.

I shook my head, my hair brushing against the knotted wood of the door.

That kiss had been unlike anything else I had ever experienced in my life. It had seared me to my very core.

If Sutton hadn't pushed me to break apart the kiss, I'm not sure how far it might've gone. Probably too far. Out of this galaxy *too far*.

What the fuck was it with this one woman?

What was so damn special about *her*?

I wanted to believe it was the fact that she treated me like a human being—albeit one she messed with, but others were too afraid of me to try.

Not her.

"*Are you scared, Sutton?*"

"*No.*"

She should've been. She should have been terrified of me and what I was capable of. She had no idea what kind of monster lurked inside me. If she got too close, I'd explode, taking out the both of us—leaving nothing but debris behind, without a hint of who we once were.

CHAPTER 4
Sutton

I STARTLED AWAKE, the sound of music blaring roused me from my unconscious state.

I blinked my eyes into focus, turning to stare at the flashing green numbers on the clock beside my bed.

Three in the morning? Who the fuck would be throwing a party at this time?

I had *finally* fallen asleep, only to be roused by *this?* Great.

With a high-pitched groan I thrust the bed covers off of me. I slipped my feet into my bunny slippers—complete with ears, of course—and stormed towards the door.

I yanked it open so harshly that it banged against the wall.

The music and other noise was coming from the apartment to the left of me. With a fire simmering beneath the surface of my skin, I stomped down the hall, raising my fist and pounding on the door.

The sounds of people laughing, talking, and having a jolly good time met my ears.

The door finally swung open and I looked up into the dark eyes of a very good looking Asian guy. His dark hair was longer in the front and shorter on the sides. The wisps that hung in his eyes were dyed a neon green color. A lip ring adorned his plump bottom lip—and those lips were currently turned into a smirk as he watched me, leaning casually against the door with arms crossed over a chest that I was sure was well sculpted. I wanted to laugh at the fact that he was dressed in black slacks and a white button shirt with the sleeves rolled up. It seemed too fancy for a party being thrown at three in the morning—and for a guy with green accents in his hair.

"Can I help you?" He asked, boredom lacing his tone.

My sass instantly returned as I pushed all thoughts of his attractiveness out of my head. "Yeah, you can, actually. Turn the music down."

A single brow rose on his forehead. "No."

I wanted to roll my eyes.

The irony in this conversation didn't escape me, and I now understood how Caelan felt anytime he asked me to turn down my music—which he had done several times in the past week. I always refused.

What made the situations different however, was the fact that I was playing my music at a reasonable hour when people were still awake.

"It's three in the morning!" I cried, the sounds of an upbeat party song drowning out my words. The poor music choice was enough to make me gag.

"So?" He looked down and studied his nails like they were way more interesting than anything I had to say.

I bit down sharply on my tongue, but was saved from answering by Caelan storming out of his apartment.

His eyes were wide with anger and his jaw was tight.

Without saying a word, he surged forward, cocking his arm back and ramming it into the man's face. I saw blood spurt out before the man covered it with his hands.

"I fucking told you, Cyrus," Caelan seethed, spit flying past his lips with his words, "if you ever disturbed me while I was working again, I'd break your fucking nose! I always keep my promises!" His face was red and he breathed heavily as if he'd just run several miles.

Cyrus, I assumed, slid his back down the door, glaring up at Caelan.

"You're a fucking prick, Gregory." His voice was thick.

Caelan spread his arms wide. I noticed for the first time that he was unsteady on his feet and his eyes were slightly glassy. I assumed the way he'd come flying out of his apartment had distracted me from the obvious fact that he was raging drunk. "At least I own what I am," he slurred and then curtsied, I kid you not.

He stumbled back to his apartment and I looked from his door to Cyrus.

"I'll turn the music down." The lump on the floor finally spoke. "You know... from down here, your ass looks real nice."

My mouth popped open and my cheeks colored as horror filled me. I was in my underwear and a tank. That was it. In my haste to scold the party thrower, I'd forgotten clothes.

"Oh, and nice slippers."

I closed my eyes.

Those damn slippers!

"I'm Cyrus, by the way," he continued to speak from the floor, acting like his nosebleed was perfectly normal, "and yoooou must be Sutton, my new neighbor. Welcome, love," he waggled his eyebrows while mimicking a fake British accent.

"Oh, so you're British now?" I crossed my arms over my chest—trying to act like the fact that I was standing in front of him practically naked didn't bother me.

"I'm whatever you want me to be," he licked his lips suggestively.

I snorted, rolling my eyes. "Just turn the music down."

I turned sharply on my heel and went back to my apartment. I stopped short of closing the door when I noticed that Caelan's door wasn't quite latched.

I bit my lip, wondering if I should close it or leave it open.

I warred with myself for a moment, but finally curiosity won out. I couldn't help but wonder what his apartment looked like.

I tiptoed across the hall, noticing that Cyrus had picked himself up and his door was now closed—the music was still blasting, but it wasn't as loud as before. Still, I doubted I'd get any more sleep. That was normal for me though.

I placed my fingertips lightly against the door and gently pushed it open.

"Hello?" I called out softly. Normally I didn't care about making Caelan angry, but Cyrus had clearly pushed him past his limit and I didn't want to be next. I kinda liked my face and wanted to keep it bruise free.

"Caelan?" I ventured further into the apartment.

I silently cursed myself for still being mostly naked. Why hadn't I had the brains to put clothes on before I came over here? Oh, right, because I was a nosy bitch and wanted to know what kept him busy.

The place was surprisingly stark. No pictures, no mementos—making it appear as if *he* was the one that had just moved in, not me.

There was a couch with a coffee table in front of it, but nothing else, not even a TV.

Most of the space was occupied by an easel and canvases—some with paintings, others waiting to be used. There had to be hundreds of them occupying the space. I was surprised by how good he was. Crazy good, actually. I didn't even know Caelan, but he pushed my buttons, so it pained me to admit he was actually talented.

Every painting was done in watercolors, the colors of the portraits dripping down the canvases... almost like each person he painted was crying.

There was one that caught my eye... one person, actually, since there was more several paintings of her. My curiosity had definitely been piqued.

She was beautiful with light blonde hair and blue eyes. In every picture her eyes seemed... dead... haunted. I wondered who she was and what she meant to him. I mean, obviously she meant a lot to him if he kept painting her. I'd never carried on an actual civil conversation with Caelan, but I got the impression that he didn't let people *in*.

Unfortunately, being closed off was something I understood all too well. I didn't like talking about my feelings and I wasn't the lovey-dovey type. Apparently, those were the two very reasons why my ex-boyfriend cheated on me with my ex best friend. I hoped they were happy. Okay, that was a lie. I wanted both of them to fall off a cliff.

The fiasco with my ex-boyfriend was another reason I'd needed to get away from Texas. I was angry about what he'd done, that was for sure, but I wasn't *hurt* like I should've been. I guess that showed that I really hadn't cared all that much for him. I think there was something wrong with me. It was like I unconsciously held myself back from people—never letting them get too close.

So, why was I currently sneaking around Caelan Gregory's apartment in search of some clue to who he really was?

I was seriously screwed up in the head.

After studying the paintings—their swirls and colors almost hypnotizing—I couldn't help but notice white flecks dusting the coffee table.

I wasn't dumb.

I knew what that was.

Empty bottles of liquor were scattered along the floor. Some still had small amounts of liquid inside, but most were empty shells.

A syringe lay abandoned under the coffee table.

He clearly didn't care about cleaning up.

When I looked up I saw Caelan passed out in his bed.

His shirt had been ripped off, exposing his thin but muscular chest. The jeans he wore hung low, exposing the top band of his boxer briefs. I found myself inexplicably drawn closer to him like a moth to a flame.

My heart hammered in my throat, threatening to claw its way out.

I found myself standing beside him, my fingers grazing the side of the bed—the soft fibers of his sheets igniting a tingling sensation that spread from the tips of my fingers up my arm. Even in sleep his face was pinched into a scowl. His eyes moved restlessly behind closed lids and his breath gusted between slightly parted lips.

Lips that had been on mine.

God, I'd enjoyed that kiss when it should have disgusted me. I had thought about it more times than I'd care to admit in the last week—especially as we played our games with each other. Daphne and Frankie were highly amused by Caelan's behavior towards me. They told me he normally got violent when people pissed him off—like when he punched Cyrus tonight—but he didn't get that way with me. He enjoyed our games too. I knew it.

My eyes lowered from his face to crawl over his chest. I itched to reach out and run my fingers over the dips and curves of his abdominals. I was curious to see if his skin was as soft as it looked. My perusal stopped when I noticed a tattoo wrapping around his ribs. I tilted my head, squinting so I could make out the small swirling letters.

*** Life is like a flame.
It burns bright for a while,
then it flickers and fades, until finally one small breath
extinguishes it and we're left with the ashes.***

My breath faltered, catching in my throat. The words were beautiful, but so haunting, and I found myself saying aloud, "What happened to *you?*"

Of course he didn't answer, he was passed out drunk and who knew what drugs were currently snaking their way through his veins.

Surprisingly, I wasn't disgusted by him or what I knew

he was doing to himself.

I didn't even pity him.

I *understood*.

I knew how bad things could push you over the edge and make you do things you never thought yourself capable of. I'd been there. I'd experienced it. I'd lived it. Not to this extent, but enough that I could sympathize with the need to *escape*.

And wasn't that what I was doing anyway by moving to Virginia? Escaping?

I hadn't wanted to face my problems, so I chose to ignore them in the hopes that they'd evaporate.

I knew it didn't work like that.

That didn't keep me from hoping, though.

"Cayla!"

I jumped, my heart momentarily ceasing to beat in my chest at Caelan's sudden outburst.

His eyes were still closed but his body thrashed with the force of his nightmare. "Cayla! No!"

I looked around wildly, wondering if I should run out the door or do something to comfort the obviously distressed Caelan.

Decisions, decisions.

I ended up leaving, running away and across the hall to the comfort of my apartment. I couldn't risk him waking up and going crazy on me.

I did have some new information about him, though... well, my *only* information really, since I knew nothing about him except for his name, that he painted, and he hated noise.

Cayla.

It was only a name, but through it maybe I could peel back the layers of Caelan and expose the demons that lay behind his blue eyes.

CHAPTER 5
Sutton

A FEW DAYS later, I was showered and dressed, sitting on the couch playing with an excited Brutus when there was a knock on my door.

I stilled, my heart stopping briefly and then restarting with a vengeance.

Things between Caelan and I had been oddly quiet the past few days.

I had no doubts our games would resume though.

When I opened the door I was shocked to find Daphne standing there looking at me.

"Expecting someone else?" She smiled knowingly at my crestfallen face.

"Not at all." I stepped to the side waving her in.

"I won't be long," she kindly declined my offer to come in. "I wanted to stop by and ask if you'd want to go to dinner tonight. Frankie, Jen, and Cyrus are going so I was hoping..." She trailed off, biting on her bottom lip nervously and staring down at her toes—which I noticed were painted hot pink.

"You want me to save you," I interjected.

She nodded. "Cyrus is annoying, and if it's only the four of us it will feel like a date."

"What time?" I asked, caving easily to the pleading look in her eyes.

"Eeeeek!" She let out a high-pitched shrill squeal and started clapping her hands. "Thank you for this!" She attacked me, wrapping her skinny arms around my neck and squeezing me with more force than I thought it was possible for her to possess.

"What time?" I repeated, a bit put off by her excitement. I wasn't a naturally bubbly person and didn't do well around those that were.

"Six," she answered, releasing me from her stranglehold.

"I'll see you then," I told her, Brutus rubbing himself against my legs. "I can't be out late though, my shift at Griffin's starts at nine tonight."

"Oh, you're working late?" She frowned.

I nodded, reaching up to push strands of black hair from my eyes. "Night shift."

"How—uh—" She looked around uneasily, as if she wasn't quite sure she wanted to ask this question or not. "How's Emery? Do you talk to him a lot?"

I couldn't help smiling. Someone *definitely* had a crush on Griffin's hottie grandson. I couldn't blame her. Not only was Emery gorgeous, but he was a really nice and down to earth guy.

"He's good, I guess," I shrugged, purposely being evasive. "Why do you ask?"

"No reason," she shook her red hair around her shoulders and plastered on a fake smile.

"Uh huh," I muttered doubtfully, narrowing my eyes.

Backing away, Daphne said, "I'll see you at six. Oh," she stopped, "do you have a dress?"

"Why?"

"Weeeeeell," she drew out the word, looking anywhere but at me, "I've only seen you in jeans and this place is a little nicer," she bit her lip. If her goal was to make me question my decision to agree to attend the shin-dig, then she had succeeded with flying colors.

I stared at her, purposely scrunching up my face so that I appeared to be mad.

"I mean, if you don't have a dress it's—"

I decided to put the poor girl out of her misery. "I have a dress. I just wanted to mess with you," I laughed.

"Oh." She paused, appearing unsure of how to proceed. "Okay then."

I couldn't help but snort.

"I'll pick you up at six," she smiled.

Suppressing a laugh, I winked and blew her a kiss. "It's a date."

I closed the door before she could reply, snickering to myself. Poor Daphne didn't know what to do with my personality. I'd have to enlighten her of the mythical and powerful ways of sarcasm.

HOURS LATER, I stood in my tiny bathroom in a skintight black dress and wearing more make-up than I knew I owned. I felt like a stranger was staring back at me. My eyes looked wide—lined in black with gray shadows—and my plump lips were accentuated with a bright cherry red. I'd definitely have to come back home and clean my face off before I went to Griffin's. I wouldn't be recognized if I showed up like this.

I grabbed my perfume and sprayed a bit on my wrists. As I was placing it back on the counter there was a knock at the door.

I took a deep breath and muttered, "Showtime," at my reflection.

'Going out' wasn't something I enjoyed anymore. At one time, I had, but that felt like a lifetime ago. I was content to stay home and watch sitcoms or read a book. I would've felt bad turning Daphne down though. I felt like we could be friends, given the chance. Also, I wanted to save her from Cyrus. He seemed pretentious. Besides, I was already rooting for Daphmery. Yes, I already gave them a nickname, but it wasn't like I had named their children... yet.

I swung the door open—expecting to only find Daphne—but was greeted by the whole entourage.

"You look nice," Cyrus grinned, his eyes starting at my feet, which were clad in dangerously high strappy heels, and perusing their way up my body. "Although, I think I prefer you in your underwear."

My mouth fell open. Was this guy for real? "Did those words really just come out of your mouth?" I cocked my hip to the side and placed my hand on it, staring him down.

"They really did," his dark eyes held me hostage. I noticed a bruise had formed around his eye from the punch he sustained.

"You're an asshole."

"Thank you," he grinned, rocking back on his heels.

"That wasn't a compliment," I glared, tempted to slam the door in all of their faces and spend the evening with Brutus.

"I know," he chuckled.

"Ooookay," Frankie clapped his hands together, "now that Cyrus has thoroughly eye-fucked the new neighbor, I think it's time to leave. Memphis is holding a table for us."

"I'd rather be really fucking than just eye-fucking," Cyrus grinned at having silenced everyone with his douchebaggery.

"Keep dreaming," I muttered, pushing past him and heading for the stairwell, knowing they'd follow me.

Once outside I stopped, waiting for them to catch up. When they did I asked, "Are we walking, or driving?"

"Walking," Frankie spoke up, his arm wrapped around Jen's waist, "it's not far."

"Lead the way," I told him, swiping my hand dramatically through the air.

A few blocks later I found myself standing inside a nice restaurant and bar. It was definitely more upscale, but not overly so. The floors shined and the bar was chaotic. The noise level was through the roof and I wished I had some earplugs—ooh, maybe I should buy some on the way home and give some to Caelan while I'm at it. That would certainly be interesting.

Shit.

I was inventing reasons to see him now.

I needed to cut it out.

He was toxic, and I'd had enough experience with people that possessed baggage to know I needed to stay far away.

It didn't mean it would be easy.

"There's Memphis," Frankie pointed to someone I couldn't see.

I followed the group of misfits to the back of the restaurant where a large sectional type booth waited for us.

"You have no idea how difficult it was to hold this for you," a new voice spoke up.

Something about the sound of the man's voice made a shiver—a good one—run down my spine.

I looked up and my eyes connected with gray ones.

Lust filled my tummy and I found my body leaning across the table towards him without my permission.

I had moved here after a failed relationship and here I was finding myself attracted to pretty much every man I came into contact with.

Clearly, it had been way too long since I'd been laid.

You know, that should've been my first clue that my boyfriend—I refused to speak or even *think* his name— was cheating. It got to the point that he never wanted to have sex with me. At least I gave him a right good black eye when I found him in bed with my best friend. That thought left a satisfied smirk on my face.

"Hello? Do you have a name?"

I was jolted out of my thoughts and back into the present with the sound of the handsome man's voice.

"Oh, uh, my name is Sutton," I supplied, hoping he didn't

think I was weird for blanking out for a moment.

"My name's Memphis," he introduced himself and I finally let my eyes peruse over his features.

Messy bronze colored hair fell over his forehead in an effortlessly sexy way. His jaw was defined with a narrow nose and his lips... I was really wondering what they'd feel like on my body. There was a mischievous glint in his unique gray eyes as he checked me out too. He was tall and lean—not overly muscular, but enough that I was really curious to see what his chest looked like behind the sleek black button down shirt he was wearing.

Clearing his throat, Memphis smiled knowingly. He could tell I wanted to jump his bones, but he didn't act cocky about it. There was a sweetness to him, and I knew that like Caelan I should stay far away from this guy, but for completely different reasons.

"I better get back to work," he tossed his thumb over his shoulder towards the fancy bar, "anyone want drinks?"

Everyone around me rattled off their order.

"You?" He prompted, tilting his head to look at me.

"Surprise me."

His eyes widened a fraction. "I can do that."

"Well, new girl," Frankie chuckled, as he leaned back in the booth and draped his arm behind Jen, "you really get around."

"Excuse me?" I scoffed, my eyes threatening to bug out of my head.

He chuckled. "You and Gregory have some weird relationship that I can't even begin to understand," he eyed me, watching my facial expressions. "Do you know that the other day I saw him crack a smile at you when you had your back turned in the hallway? In the three years that he's lived there he's *never* smiled."

He smiled at me?

Why did that fact fill my body with warmth?

"Then Cyrus here can't stop picturing you beneath him." Frankie pointed to where Cyrus sat beside me, watching me out of the corner of his eye. "Now you've got Memphis watching you." The same finger he had used to point at Cyrus slid to point at the man behind the bar.

"It's the shoes," I said in a dead-pan tone.

Frankie snorted. "No, it's not the shoes. You've got that whole exotic look going on. The black hair, olive skin, and those blue eyes... not to mention your body... you're every guys *dream*."

Jen scoffed, throwing off his arm. She slid out of the booth, her face red with anger as she stomped towards the bathrooms.

"Shit," Frankie cursed under his breath, sliding out after her. "Baby!" He called. "I wasn't included in that statement! I like blondes!"

Cyrus laughed hysterically, clutching his stomach. "Oh, that was entertaining. He's going to have *a lot* of groveling to do to make up for that one, and Jen's going to hate your guts now," his gaze slid to my face.

Daphne rolled her eyes. "And I'll have to listen to the make-up sex," she gagged. "I really need to get my own place."

Cyrus looked across the table at her with a smile playing on his lips. "Trust me, the whole hall can hear them when they start going at it."

"Bleh." Daphne made a face of disgust.

Since it didn't look like Frankie and Jen would be returning anytime soon, I scooted away from Cyrus to place some distance between us, but the idiot only closed it. His thigh was pressed right up against mine and a cocky smile played on his lips. He knew what he was doing, only he didn't think I'd call him on his bullshit. He should've known better.

"Can you move?" I waved my hand, hoping if my words didn't give him a hint then my hand gestures would.

"No," he said simply, looking around the restaurant.

My mouth fell open. God, this guy couldn't catch a hint. He was hot, but he was also a major pain in the ass.

"Here's your drinks," Memphis grinned, carrying a tray towards us. Lowering it, he frowned, "We already lost those two?

I swear, if they're having sex in the bathroom again—"

"Frankie was being an ass," Daphne interrupted. "Jen's probably crying while he mutters I'm sorry over and over again." She reached up, taking her drink off the tray. She took a large gulp. "Oh, that's good," she said despite her wince from the bitter taste.

Memphis laughed, handing Cyrus his drink and one to me. He went ahead and placed Jen and Frankie's down too, optimistic that they'd return.

"Go on, try it," he nodded at me.

"Oh," I jumped slightly, startled by his command.

I eyed the concoction, hoping he hadn't slipped poison in it or something. I mean, if he had, that would make him a pretty shitty bartender.

I lifted the glass to my lips and took a sip.

"Hmm, not bad," I smiled up at him. It was surprisingly sweet tasting with just a hint of alcohol—I wasn't sure what kind though. "What is this?"

"It's a secret," he winked. "If I told you, I'd have to kill you, and wouldn't that be a shame?"

Without pausing for an answer he strode away and back to the bar.

I continued to sip on Memphis' magical mixture of goodness, completely ignoring Cyrus, and doing a poor job of conversing with Daphne.

If I was going to be her friend, I needed to do a better job.

"Are you in college?" I asked her, stealthily sliding the tiniest bit away from Cyrus in the hopes that he wouldn't notice.

He didn't.

He was staring at some chick's legs, where she was pressed up against the bar-top flirting with Memphis. I wrinkled my nose in disgust. Her dress did a poor job of covering her ass. It was more like a towel. She had the attention of most guys in the bar—except the one she was talking to. His eyes were locked on mine. He grinned slowly at me and my lower half squirmed.

"No."

"Huh?" I turned at the sound of Daphne's voice.

"I'm not in college."

"Oh," I tucked a piece of hair behind my ear. "Do you have a job?"

She shook her head, her lips turning down in a frown. "I'm trying to break into modeling."

"That's awesome!" I exclaimed loudly. Okay, maybe my drink had more alcohol in it than I realized. In a softer tone, I added, "I wouldn't imagine there are very many modeling opportunities in this area, though."

"More than you think," she replied, propping her elbow on the table and her head in her hand, "but not enough."

"Why don't you move?" I questioned.

"Finances." Her slender shoulders rose dramatically with a sigh. "Maybe I'll move to Manhattan one day."

"You totally should!"

Why was I yelling?

I glared at the drink that was mostly gone now. "You're dangerous," I muttered to it.

Daphne let out a small twinkling laugh. "Did you just talk to your drink?"

"I did." I pushed it away. "No more of that. I have to go to work."

"What's up with you and Caelan?" She asked and interest sparkled in her eyes.

Why did everyone have to keep bringing up Caelan? Didn't they know there was nothing to tell?

"Nothing," I answered honestly.

"Oh, please," she rolled her eyes. "You're the only person he ever seems to speak to."

"He yells actually. Yelling doesn't qualify as speaking," I reasoned. "And he also yells at Cyrus," I nudged the guy beside me.

"Hell yeah he does," Cyrus finally tore his eyes away from the woman's legs and ass to join the conversation. "He's always so grumpy for someone that's constantly got a different girl leaving his apartment every morning."

"You're one to talk," Daphne snorted. "I've lost count of how many girls I've seen leaving your apartment, and sometimes two at once." She shivered in disgust, her lips pursed.

My eyes threatened to pop out of my head as I turned to look at Cyrus. "What?" I gasped. What female in their right mind would want to fuck Cyrus? And a *threesome?*

He smiled innocently. "Variety is the spice of life."

"You're disgusting." The words tumbled out of my mouth before I could stop them.

Cyrus chuckled. "I've heard that before. It doesn't offend me, darlin'," he said in a southern drawl, his eyes twinkling. He was clearly amused by me.

Frankie and Jen chose that moment to return. I was forced to scoot closer against Cyrus once more. Jen's eyes were red and puffy and I wanted to kick Frankie in the shin for being so dumb with his words. Some girls—most, actually—were sensitive and took everything personally. Guys were too dumb to see that.

AFTER GETTING THE stink eye from Jen I decided it was time to part ways and head back home to get ready for work.

I felt Memphis' eyes on me as I shimmied my way past tables and bodies to get to the exit. I was suddenly glad I'd chosen the dress I wore. I knew it hugged my curves in all the right places.

He'd have to keep dreaming though.

The streetlights were just coming on as I made my way back to the apartment. The air was still warm with the heat of the late summer day. I looked up, watching as the last orange glow of the sunset disappeared behind a building and darkness set in.

"Nice dress."

I jumped about ten feet in the air at the sound of the voice.

Placing a hand over my racing heart, I turned to face Caelan sulking in shadows beside the building.

"W-what are you doing here?" I asked, my voice sounded breathless with fright.

"I was watching the sunset." His eyes lingered on my bare legs before they eventually rose to meet mine.

I was surprised he gave me an answer.

With his hands stuffed in his paint stained jeans, he pulled away from the wall. The movement brought him closer to me so that our breaths mingled together. I couldn't miss the tang of alcohol on his breath. I'm sure he could smell it on mine too, but while I only drank occasionally—rarely at that—I got the impression that Caelan was almost always in a state of drunkenness.

"I find some of my best inspiration while watching the sunset," he murmured, his eyes flicking down to my lips and I couldn't help but remember our kiss, "but *you*, you're an even better muse."

My eyes closed as I sucked in a surprised breath.

When I opened them, he was gone.

I turned, looking around me and towards the building. I knew I hadn't heard the door open and close, so he couldn't have gone inside. He had to be out here somewhere, but he wasn't.

He had vanished like the seeds of a dandelion blown into the air. Floating, wandering, lost... never knowing where they might land.

Caelan

I COULDN'T BELIEVE I'd just said that to Sutton.

You're an even better muse.

What. The. Fuck?

Clearly I was drunker than I thought and it had given me loose lips, which was unusual since alcohol seemed to spike my anger instead of turning me into a chatterbox.

As soon as her eyes closed, I'd slipped away like a coward, too afraid to face what was right in front of me—that there might be someone worth living for if I let her in.

I shook my head roughly back and forth, wishing I could dislodge my thoughts.

Shoving my hands in my pockets I walked as fast as my feet could carry me. Away from Sutton, away from my problems, away from everything that made my thoughts venture down a different path than I'd been on for the last five years.

I was beyond being saved, and being around Sutton gave me a false feeling of hope because she made me *tick*. The anger I felt towards her when she pissed me off wasn't comparable to the anger I felt towards others.

Rounding the corner, Kyle's white car came into view. It was the same car he'd had since we were in high school. I didn't know why the idiot was still friends with me. I certainly didn't make it easy for him. I had pushed everyone away after my family's murders, but Kyle wouldn't go down without a fight. So the stubborn ass and I were stuck with each other. In a way, I was glad I still had him. He was the only person in my life now that knew what had happened, what I'd been through, and remembered the guy I had been before.

I wasn't a good person then though.

I hadn't loved my parent's the way I should have. Always grumbling about them wanting me home and how they kept me from my real life.

Cayla and I had been close, but we'd still argued a lot, and I'd thought of her as my annoying little sister.

I'd been a cocky jock and expected everyone to bend to my will.

I'd give anything to go back and redo those moments.

But life doesn't have a rewind button. We're stuck with our decisions, our regrets, our fears—they're *always* there. They shape and define us into the people we become.

Unfortunately, mine had sent me down a destructive path.

And now, I was worse than I ever was.

Sutton

I PULLED MY hair back into a messy bun, securing it with a hair tie.

I had on comfy jeans and a tank top with a flimsy sweater thrown over top. Working at Griffin's had its perks—like not dressing up. In fact, when working the night shift, I got the impression Griff wouldn't have cared if we showed up in our pajamas.

I said goodbye to Brutus, making sure he had enough food in his bowl, and headed out the door. I hadn't heard Caelan return home, but with all the bumps and creaks in this old building, it wouldn't have surprised me if he was back, slaving away over a canvas and I just hadn't noticed.

His beautiful paintings had stayed with me. I couldn't believe that someone so angry and volatile could create something so beautiful. I was still curious about who Cayla was. I wanted to ask Daphne, but I didn't feel like I knew her enough yet to trust her to keep quiet about my question. Google didn't procure any viable responses—which I figured it wouldn't—and I wouldn't dare ask Caelan about the name he uttered. He'd probably kill me and chop my body into tiny pieces in his bathtub.

Slinging my purse over my shoulder, I left a meowing Brutus, and headed to work.

Griffin was already gone, and I was working with

Emery tonight. Griff partnered me up with Emery a lot. I wasn't sure if it was because he didn't quite trust me yet and thought Emery would keep tabs on me, or— I wasn't going there.

"Hey, sunshine," Emery greeted me with a wink. He thought his nickname for me was brilliant since I was anything but a ray of sunshine. I tried to act like the name didn't bother me, in the hopes that he'd get tired and drop it. Something told me he wouldn't though.

I rolled my eyes, letting the door bang closed behind me.

He chuckled at my non-reply as I headed past the swinging doors into the back. I put my purse in a locker—Griff had a locker for every employee—and grabbed the apron that tied around my waist.

"Hurry up, sunshine!" Emery sing-songed, poking his head through the doorway. "We have customers waiting to see your beautiful face!"

I flashed him my middle finger, which he found hilarious.

Once my apron was tied, I headed to the register, which was my station for the evening. There really weren't that many tables to wait on. Most people who came in the evenings were college kids. Despite the fact that classes must have only recently started, most looked exhausted and ready to fall over asleep— hence the need for caffeine. Some chose to stay in the restaurant to do homework, but I'd learned quickly that they didn't like to be bothered.

Emery returned from wiping down a table, his usual megawatt smile perfectly in place.

"How was your day?" He asked, leaning a hip against the counter and crossing his arms over his chest.

"Uneventful." It was the same answer I always gave him, but between Memphis and what Caelan said to me this evening, *uneventful* was actually the last word that came to mind.

"Liar," he smirked.

"I never lie."

"Mhmm," he remained unconvinced. "I have dishes to clean. Try not to drive away customers with your sparkly personality."

As he breezed by me, he used the rag in his hand to swat at my butt.

"Emery!" I shrieked.

As the door swung closed behind him I could still hear his chuckles.

Emery and I had formed an unusual friendship. We didn't talk much about our personal lives, but we were friends none-the-less. I'm sure the more time we spent together, the more we'd learn to trust the other and open up.

My eyes began to feel droopy as I stood there waiting for a customer to walk in. Griffin didn't mind when we worked the night shift if we helped ourselves to coffee, so I grabbed the largest size cup and poured myself some. That finished off the house brew, so I set about making some more.

The chime above the door dinged, sounding the approach of a customer.

I plastered on a fake smile and turned around, "Welcome to Griffin's, what can I get you?" My fake smile quickly turned into a real one, when my eyes met with now familiar gray ones. Butterflies took up residence in my stomach, fluttering around as they sought a way to escape.

"This is an interesting development," Memphis smiled crookedly.

"It is indeed."

I stared at him, completely forgetting what I was supposed to be doing. Shaking myself back to reality, I repeated, "What can I get you?"

Memphis looked up at the menu, biting on his lower lip as if in deep thought. When his eyes connected with mine once more, he said, "You."

"What?" I choked, shocked at his brazenness.

"Oh, I'm sorry," he shook his head, his smile widening, "that's not on the menu. I'll just have the house brew. No cream or sugar."

Oh, God. I was pretty sure he was perfect.

I gave him his total and he paid.

I poured the steaming coffee into a cup once it was ready and fixed a lid in place. Sliding it across the counter, I was careful to release my hold on the cup before our fingers could touch.

"So, what's your story?" He asked, bringing the lid up to his lips, his brows raised as he waited for my answer.

"My story?" It seemed like such an odd question to ask someone you had just met.

"Yeah," he shrugged. "You must have one. I've never seen you before and then we meet twice in one night. Coincidence? I don't think so."

"Not much to tell," I answered evasively.

"Ah," he breathed, his eyes twinkling, "so you're one of *those* girls."

I shook my head roughly. "What the hell does that mean?" I was offended that I could possibly be lumped into a statement such as that.

"You know, one of those girls that acts all mysterious to hook a guy."

"Trust me," I gave him a deadly glare, "I'm not acting. If you're sensing something mysterious," I shrugged lightly, "then I guess you are."

"Where are you from, Sutton?"

I stilled, enjoying the sound of him saying my name *way* too much. "I don't understand why you're so curious about me," I retorted.

He chuckled, still smiling. "Well, when a man likes a woman, he typically wants to get to know her. That means talking and asking questions. Does it scare you that you fascinate me?" He eyed me, making me squirm uncomfortably.

"No," I said too quickly. Swallowing, I added, "You don't scare me."

He shook his head. "That's not what I said and you know it."

Straightening, he shoved one hand into the pocket of his black slacks and kept the other hand wrapped firmly around his cup of coffee. "I can see you're not interested in answering a questionnaire tonight, so until the next time," he tipped his head in my direction, and pushed the doors open.

The chime clinked again and I was tempted to rip the annoying thing off the door handle.

Emery appeared from the back. "Well, that was fun."

I whipped around to glare at him. "You mean you were listening and you didn't help me! The guy could've been an ax murderer or something!"

He laughed heartily and I worried he might not be able to breathe. "Oh, Sutton, I hardly needed to save you. Rest assured, if you needed actual saving, I would've hopped aboard my mighty steed and come to your rescue."

I couldn't resist punching him in the arm for that ridiculous line.

"What was that for?" He still laughed, completely unfazed by the punch.

"For not saving me when I needed rescuing!" I retorted, throwing his words in his face.

"Trust me, Memphis is a good guy. You would never need anyone to protect you from him," Emery's voice softened.

"You know him?"

Emery nodded. "He comes in here a lot, and we went to school together. It's a small town," he shrugged like that explained everything.

I glanced at the door Memphis had departed through only moments before and then back at Emery. "Why do I feel like you're trying to play matchmaker?"

Emery smiled innocently. "I don't need to play matchmaker when fate will do the work for me."

CHAPTER 6
Sutton

IT HAD BEEN four days since I'd last seen Caelan. I didn't know why that fact bugged me so much.

No amount of noise I made sent him running out of his apartment.

I hated to admit it, but I missed our games... and maybe I missed him.

Nah. It wasn't possible to miss someone you didn't know.

I wondered where he was.

I hoped he was gone, but coming back.

A part of me worried that maybe he'd overdosed and was lying dead in his apartment and no one knew about it. I knew he was an alcoholic and drug addict. Seeing his apartment had confirmed that. But there were other signs too. Like the way he was always so jittery, and how sometimes his eyes would shift irregularly.

If he was dead, which I hated to even consider, I knew I should find a way to check on him. I couldn't exactly break into his apartment though. That would be embarrassing to explain if he turned up alive.

"Meow."

I looked down at the quickly growing Brutus. He tilted his

head, his strange greenish eyes watching me closely. I lowered, lifting him into my arms and tucking him under my neck. His warmth comforted me and something about rubbing his soft body instantly filled me with a feeling of calm.

With Brutus in my arms I stared out the window.

I had always liked to watch people—I found human behavior so interesting. I liked to imagine what the people below me were doing or saying.

I jolted in surprise when I saw a white car pull up the curb a little ways down the street and Caelan got out of the passenger side. He leaned back in, saying something to the driver. They seemed to be having some kind of argument. Caelan slammed the car door closed, shaking the whole vehicle with the force. I couldn't see the driver's face, but it was obviously a guy about my age, maybe a little older, and he shook his head in disgust. He pulled away quickly, the exhaust from his car filling the air with a hazy fog.

I jumped in surprise when I heard the door to Caelan's apartment slam closed.

I looked at Brutus in my arms and muttered, "Someone's grumpy."

"Meow."

Kissing Brutus' head, I set him gently on the floor.

I itched to provoke Caelan, but something told me not to. Now wasn't the time to push his buttons.

Tapping my fingers along the countertop, I tried to act like I wasn't listening to what was going on across the hall.

Things were definitely being thrown and it sounded like a piece of furniture crashed against the wall. I ducked, even though nothing was flying at me.

I wanted to check on Caelan, and based on what I heard I had the perfect excuse to investigate.

I bit down on my lip, pacing the length of my apartment.

Should I?

Or shouldn't I?

My mind warred with itself. I wasn't sure what would be the best move. He was clearly angry and I didn't want to be on the receiving end of that, but if I could calm him—

"Oh, screw it!" I exclaimed to no one.

I marched out of my apartment and across the hall. I was determined not to appear frightened.

Banging on the door, he didn't answer and the destructive noises didn't lessen.

I took the doorknob in my hand and I was surprised when it turned easily.

"Caelan!" I called out.

Crash.

"Caelan! Are you okay?" I tiptoed inside, afraid to anger the beast further.

He stormed past me from his bedroom area, his eyes flicked quickly over me, and then back to the task at hand—which turned out to be smashing his heavy boot into the glass tabletop of his coffee table. The sound of glass shattering made me wince, but I refused to back down.

"What's wrong?" I asked in a soft voice, like one might use with a wild animal.

Caelan stopped with his back to me, he looked out the window and his narrow shoulders rose and fell heavily. Now that the crashing and banging had stopped his heavy breaths were all that I heard.

"What happened? You can tell me," I pleaded, desperate to get him to say something to me other than to turn down my music or keep quiet.

He turned angrily at my words. His nostrils flared and his eyes were filled with fury. Something about him reminded me of a fallen angel. He was harsh and dangerous, but I knew something had to have pushed him over the edge. I wanted to find out what it was, but trust took time, and I hadn't earned his yet.

"I can tell *you? You?*" He laughed under his breath but there was no humor in the sound. "You don't fucking know me, so don't pretend you do!"

I would not cower down to him. Taking two measured steps forward, I stopped. "No, I don't know you, and you don't know me. If you gave me a chance, you might see that you could trust me."

"Trust is non-existent. It's a lie. The people I thought I could trust," he pounded on his chest with a fist, "where are they? They're gone, unable to handle my 'destructive' path. They wanted to *fix* me, but I don't need fixing, Sutton. Is that what you want to do? Do you want to fix me?"

Somehow, he'd ended up right in front of me. He was so close that our chests touched and you couldn't have fit a piece of paper between us.

"No."

"What?" He shook his head, seemingly taken aback by the word I'd dared to utter.

"No," I repeated. "I don't want to fix you," I swallowed thickly, grasping his forearms in my hands because I suddenly felt dizzy, "I want to know you."

He chuckled with a small smile. "Know me? I'm not the kind of guy any nice girl should want to get to know." His eyes narrowed and his lips thinned. "I'm angry, I'm bitter, I'm broken, I'm *lost*. I don't know who I am anymore. I don't recognize the man I see in the mirror." He clenched his teeth and looked away momentarily. I was shocked at his words, that he'd managed to open up that little bit. "I drink until I can't remember, I get high to dull the pain, I hit things to *feel* something. *That*, Sutton, is *not* a good person. I know it, but I can't stop. I don't want to."

"I'm not asking you to," I breathed, my words barely above a whisper. "I want to be your friend. I want you to trust me. I'm not some fragile little butterfly that you need to worry about breaking the wings off of. Talk to me, please."

He looked up at the ceiling, closing his eyes. There was so much pain etched into the lines of his face. I had never in all my twenty-two years of life seen someone so tormented. Something *broke* him. Something big. I knew it was none of my business, but I wanted to know. I wanted to gain his trust. I wanted *him*. I didn't know why. It made no sense to me, but something drew me to him. Maybe this was some latent teenage desire to bag a bad boy—but it didn't feel that way.

I believed that sometimes people were brought together for a reason, because they both needed something the other could offer.

"I need you to leave," Caelan finally said, his eyes were distant and his voice was resolved. I could tell that he was angry at himself for what he'd said to me. I may have been living across the hall from him for over a month now, but we were still strangers, and Caelan struck me as the kind of guy that didn't even open up to those closest to him—if there *was* anyone close to him, I thought back to the guy I saw in the car.

Finally, I nodded, knowing better than to say anything else.

I was almost out the door when he spoke up once more. "Keep the music down."

"In your dreams," I muttered, smiling at the fact that for once I'd gotten the last word.

Caelan

As soon as the door had clicked shut I went back to destroying things. Nothing was left untouched—not even my paintings that I cherished above all else.

I wanted to kill Kyle for what he had done—trying to shove me into rehab. I didn't need to go to rehab. Rehab was for addicts, and I was *not* an addict. I could stop whenever I wanted, but that was the thing, I didn't want to stop. The moment that I stopped would be the moment that I felt and I wasn't going to let that happen.

He'd picked me up days ago and I'd been staying at his house.

Then this morning, instead of bringing me home, the fucker tried to get me 'help'.

My reaction had been less than pretty. He'd ended up with a bloody lip and black eye, and the man who'd tried in vain to pry me from the vehicle possibly had a concussion from where I kicked his skull.

When Kyle saw that leaving me there would only end up with my arrest, he let it drop... as in, he didn't dump my sorry as there. Instead he lectured me like I was a child the whole time he drove me home.

The fact that Kyle was lecturing me was laughable. In high school, I had often been the one keeping *him* in line. Now that he was finished with college, had a job, and was building his life, he expected the same from me.

It wasn't happening.

I was destined to spend my life suffering in solitude. No sane human being could or *would* put up with my baggage and bullshit.

With my chest heaving I looked around at the destruction.

It was normal for my apartment to always be in some state of chaos. Be it because I was creating what I believed to be a masterpiece or I was just on a drunken binge. *Clean* was not the word anyone would ever use to describe this place.

I knew I should do the 'responsible' thing and restore it to order, but frankly, I didn't give a fuck.

Grabbing a bottle of liquor—I wasn't sure what kind since the label was gone—I screwed off the lid and brought my lips to the neck.

The burn and fog brought upon by the strong mixture was what temporarily cleansed me of my sins. That haziness cocooned me in a protective shield that I reveled in. I sat on the couch, swallowing down the rest of the liquid. I fell to the side, closing my eyes so that I was unaware of the destruction. I began to hum, letting the sound and alcohol now permeating my bloodstream block out everything around me.

Nothing else existed.

Not even me.

Sutton

I DECIDED I liked working the night-owl shift. I'd suffered with insomnia since I was a child, and that shift gave me something to do during the endless nights. Plus, Emery always seemed to work with me, and he was fun to have around.

Tonight, unfortunately, was one of the nights he wasn't working. I was stuck with Angela. The girl was nice enough, but she didn't really like to talk, so it made the long shift boring. While Emery and I joked around and had fun, Angela was all business.

"Customer!" Angela called to me, from where I'd snuck off in the back to check my phone. She acted as if I couldn't hear that annoying bell hanging on the door and I didn't understand why she couldn't tend to the customer. She knew how to work the register. Bitch.

I made my way to the front and stopped in my tracks, the door smacking me in the butt as it swung on its hinges, and I found myself face to face with Caelan.

I was shocked to see him there. I'd worked at Griffin's for a few weeks now and not once seen him set foot inside.

He smirked, chuckling under his breath. "I d-didn't know you worked here." His words were slurred and he swayed slightly to the side.

"I didn't know you came here," I countered, squaring my shoulders, and blatantly ignoring the fact that he was drunk.

His smile widened and there was nothing nice about it. "Are

you going to quit now?"

"What?" I was taken aback. "No. Why would I do that?"

His smile faded and his hazy eyes narrowed on me like a laser beam zoning in on its target. "Because I frighten you."

I let out a laugh that I couldn't contain. "I hate to break it to you, but I'm not afraid of you."

"You should be." He stated, bracing his hands on the counter to keep from falling over.

"But I'm not." I placed a hand on my hip, tilting my head to the side. "Now," I said slowly, "is there anything I can get you?"

He ordered an iced coffee and a blueberry muffin. I couldn't help laughing under my breath at Caelan ordering such a girly drink.

I didn't comment on his order as I made it and brought both items to his table. He sat in a chair with his head propped against the wall.

I knew better than to ask if he was okay. He wasn't.

"Here's your order," I said softly, lest he have a raging headache from his drinking binge.

He nodded in acknowledgement and I backed away.

I wanted to ask him about what I saw this afternoon, with the man in the car and why it had made him so angry, but I knew he wouldn't take kindly to my *spying*. I couldn't help it though. Caelan fascinated me. He wasn't the type of guy to spill his secrets. I would have to unravel his many layers of protective armor to figure out what kind of life altering experience could shatter a person so completely. I knew the bit I'd managed to get out of him this afternoon when I basically broke into his apartment—much like he had done to me the day I moved in—was only one layer of many.

Hours later, it was time for me to head home. Caelan had passed out with his head on the table and his mouth hung open. There was even a little bit of drool dangling from the corner of his mouth. It would have been funny if it wasn't so heartbreaking.

No amount of nudging or pushing or speaking of his name would get him to move.

I refused to go home and leave him there. I'd never get any rest if I was worrying about him.

"Fuck it," I muttered under my breath.

I breezed into the back, picking up a cup and filling it with water.

"What are you doing?"

I rolled my eyes at the sound of Angela's voice. God, she was annoying.

I looked over to where she had grabbed her purse from the locker.

"Nothing," I answered.

"It doesn't look like nothing," she closed the metal door with a bang, cocking her head to the right as she waited for further explanation.

"You know what it looks like to me?" I spoke with false sweetness. "None of your business," my tone turned icy.

Traipsing back out to the restaurant area, I lifted the red plastic cup high above Caelan's head. I tipped it slowly, then said, what the hell, and dumped the entire contents of cold water on his head.

He came awake with a wild flail of his arms and legs. He fell out of his chair, which came crashing down to the ground beside him.

I couldn't stop laughing.

He looked so funny sprawled on the floor covered in water. He kind of resembled a very wet and confused puppy.

"What the fuck was that for?" He peered up at me and droplets of water clung to his insanely long lashes.

I shrugged innocently, letting the plastic cup fall from my hand. It clanged to the ground, bouncing a few times before rolling under another table. "Oops. My hand must have slipped.

"Bullshit," he muttered, sluggishly coming to his feet. His sneakers squeaked against the now wet floor. He was angry, but at least he was awake.

"It's time to go home," I knocked my hand against his shoulder.

"Don't touch me," he growled, his face reddening as he roughly shrugged off my touch.

I rolled my eyes at him and stayed where I was. "This whole anti-social tough guy act is ridiculous. Anyone with eyes can see that you're hurting. You can try all you want to push me away, but it won't work. It just makes this game all the more fun."

He smiled and there was nothing nice about it. Pushing wet strands of blond hair out of his eyes, he said, "Act? I assure you," his voice lowered to a throaty growl, "it's no act."

"Believe me," I stood tall, which was really hard since I was about as short as they came, "I've known guys like you. You put out this fake persona to scare people away, when inside you're just a lost and scared little boy."

His smile disappeared at that. "Mind your own damn business, Sutton."

He pushed passed me and out the door.

I followed quickly behind him. I didn't bother to catch up to him, but I wanted to be sure he went home—which he did.

The whole walk—and even when we entered the building and made our way upstairs to our apartments across from each other—he never, not once, looked back at me.

CHAPTER 7
Sutton

"It's such a nice day," Daphne exclaimed, spreading her arms wide and leaning back in her chair. I was a bit afraid she might topple out of it.

She'd shown up outside my door thirty minutes ago, inviting me to lunch and a day of shopping. I wasn't much for shopping, but I was going a bit stir crazy, and talking to Brutus like he was a person probably made me even more of a nutcase.

"I love it here," she adjusted her sunglasses, and draped her hair over one shoulder.

"It's a restaurant," I stated. "How could you love it here?"

She shrugged. "I don't know... just the vibe," she did a little shimmy in her chair, "it's very relaxed."

Well, okay then.

Taking a sip of water, I ventured to ask, "Do you know who Cayla is?"

"Who?" Daphne sat up straight, a single brow rose with interest.

"Cayla," I repeated the name.

"Hmm," she thought, tapping a peach colored nail against her lips, "I don't believe I do. Why do you ask?" She leaned forward, expecting a juicy secret to spill from my lips.

"It's not important." I grabbed a napkin, wiping the condensation from my glass of water.

"It must be important for you to ask me," she sat back, tapping her heeled shoe against the floorboards of the outdoor patio we were seated at.

"It's really not," I muttered, looking out towards the street.

"You're a really bad liar, Sutton," she pushed.

"If I knew who this person was, why would I ask you?" I countered, getting huffy. "All I have is a name. I was curious to see if you had heard it before."

"And who did *you* hear it from? Hmm?" She studied my face, waiting for any sort of tick or flick of my eyes.

I let out an exasperated sigh. "I think you know."

"I think I know too," she drummed her fingers on the tabletop. Sobering, she added, "I know you don't know me that well yet, but I believe we could be friends," she momentarily placed her hand over mine where it rested on the table and then removed it.

I wanted to believe her, but I wasn't sure I could. After being screwed over by my best friend in Texas, I was leery to trust people. Her eyes were so sincere though, even if they were concealed behind dark sunglasses.

"Caelan," I whispered.

"I knew it!" She threw an arm in the air, doing a small fist pump.

"Seriously," I pleaded, "have you heard him mention that name before?"

"Not at all," she answered readily, taking a sip of sweet tea. "Granted, I don't really talk to Caelan. I think I've only ever said five words to the guy. He scares me," she shivered. Looking across at me, she asked, "Why doesn't he scare you?"

"I don't know," I answered honestly. "He just doesn't."

"So..." She paused, toying with whether or not she should continue. "When did he mention this Cayla person?"

"It was a while ago now," I shrugged, propping my head

on my hand. "He—uh—was passed out, muttering in his sleep. He didn't know I was there."

"Oh," she gasped in surprise.

"I tried to Google it, but with a single name I didn't find out anything useful," I muttered, irritation lacing the tone of my words.

"Ooh! Ooh!" She hopped in her seat and I wondered again how she didn't go falling to the ground. "Why don't you try searching *his* name?"

My mouth fell open in surprise. "Daphne, you're a genius!" I exclaimed and if I had been a lesbian I would've kissed her in that moment. "Why didn't I think of that?"

"It's worth a shot, right?" She smiled, clearly pleased with her brilliant idea.

"It's definitely worth a shot," I grinned, excitement filling me.

I knew it might be impossible to ever get Caelan to open up to me. If this worked, I may finally know what had destroyed him.

SHOPPING WITH DAPHNE proved to be one of the most exhausting experiences of my life.

I did have fun though.

She was always so bubbly, but she could have her serious moments too. After today, I counted her as a friend.

Sitting down my bags, I gave Brutus a small kiss on his head, and then dove for the laptop I had left on the kitchen counter. Some serious investigation was about to happen.

No amount of excitement over my new clothes and lingerie—lingerie I had no idea who I thought I was going to wear it for—could keep me from my desire to search Caelan's name in the hopes of information.

I typed his name into the search engine, hoping I spelled it right, and waited for it to load.

Almost immediately a news article popped up.

I didn't bother reading the tagline. I just clicked on it. It was an article about some high school, local to where we were now, and the football team. Skimming the article, I came across Caelan's name highlighted. Apparently he was the quarterback. I didn't know what the heck a quarterback did. I was *not* a sports person. Scrolling further down, I found a picture of the team. In the front, kneeling on the ground with his helmet in his hand was Caelan. His hair was even lighter than it was now. He was smiled widely in the image. There was a cockiness in the way he held himself. He was more muscular in the photo and a little heavier that he was now. Even in the picture, his eyes were piercing.

I pressed the back button, searching for anything else.

I stopped, an icy shiver making the hairs on my back stand on end when I read the headline.

Gregory Family Murders—One Survivor.

Swallowing down the sudden lump in my throat, I clicked on it.

I was immediately assaulted with a picture of a family—Caelan's family.

They looked so *happy*. The guy in the picture, a teenage Caelan, looked nothing like the man I knew. His smile was genuine and he had his arm wrapped around a girl that had to be his sister they looked so much alike. With a gasp, I realized she was the girl in many of his paintings.

I forced my eyes away from him and his sister to look at his parents. They looked kind and so in love. His mother looked like she could have been a movie star with blonde hair that matched her children's. Caelan had the exact shade of blue eyes that she had. His father had light brown hair and a proud narrow nose that he'd given his son, along with the same jaw and small dimple in their chin.

I couldn't help but look back at his sister. Her golden hair was long, falling over her shoulders. Her smile was big and her blue eyes sparkled with happiness and excitement.

It killed me looking at Caelan's image and noting the differences in the man I knew now.

His eyes were cloudy and he certainly didn't smile like *that*— so carefree and content. His hair hung limply in his eyes now, not styled back like in the picture. Even his skin tone was different now. While in the picture he glowed with a tan like he'd recently been to the beach, he was now so pale that he resembled a vampire... he kind of acted like one too.

The guy I saw staring back at me from the computer screen didn't seem anything like the one I knew.

While old Caelan glowed with warmth and light, new Caelan was dull and gloomy.

Scrolling past the picture, I began to read the article, and was quickly overcome with horror.

Eighteen-year-old Caelan Gregory walked in on what first appeared to be a home invasion only to discover his family murdered. Despite the fact that he was found covered in blood, he was unharmed and has been removed from the suspect list. Marcia, Paul, and Cayla Gregory all sustained multiple stab wounds.

I paused in my reading, stunned to have stumbled across the name I had been searching for.

Cayla Gregory.

His sister.

The vibrant, joyful, smiling girl in the photograph had had her life cut tragically short in such a gruesome way. No wonder he cried her name in his sleep and painted her picture repeatedly.

Taking a deep breath, I forced myself to continue.

Police are not releasing further details at this time while the perpetrator is still at large. If you have any information concerning the Gregory murders, please contact the police immediately.

At the bottom of the page there was an asterisk and I squinted to read the small font.

*At this time the Gregory murders still remain unsolved

It was dated only six months ago.

I pushed away from my computer and went running for the bathroom. I collapsed on my knees, heaving over the toilet bowl. But nothing came up.

No wonder Caelan acted the way he did. I knew there had to be a reason, but this was beyond anything I had imagined. This was... there were no words.

I couldn't imagine losing your family in such a grisly way.

I mean, I had lost my real family in a fire, but I'd been a baby. I hadn't *known* them. To come home and find your family like *that*... it had to haunt him. How could it not?

I suddenly, desperately, needed air.

I headed for the door that led to the roof, not wanting to stand on the street and have to face anyone. I couldn't handle it right now. I needed to be alone to breathe in fresh air and gather my thoughts.

When I stepped onto the roof I stopped in my tracks.

"Not now," I muttered, recognizing Caelan's familiar shape.

The door slammed closed behind me signaling that it was too late to turn tail and run.

His head turned in my direction as I took a few more steps closer.

A gasp escaped me as my eyes zoned in on him.

"What are you doing?" I asked him fearfully as I watched him walk the side of the roof like a balance beam.

"Testing death," he answered simply, "daring it to take me... to sweep me away." He purposely leaned further over the side where he could fall to the street below.

"Don't do that!" I cried, running towards him. I reached out to stop him, to do *something*.

He looked down at me and stopped moving, but still stood on

the ledge.

"Don't worry, I won't jump. I never do," he laughed humorlessly. His eyes were vibrant and there was no slur to his words. For once, he wasn't drunk or high on Lord knows what. "Staying alive is the punishment. Death is the reward."

"What do you mean?"

"When you're alive," he spread his arms wide, and where he stood with the sunset behind him it made it look like he had wings, "you *feel*. Feelings are a painful son of a bitch. But death, that's easy. It's peaceful. It takes away your pain and reunites you with the ones you love." He looked up towards the sky, his lips lifting in a small smile. Knowing about his family, I couldn't help but wonder if he was imagining their faces.

"But isn't life worth fighting for?" I responded, squinting from the brilliance of the sunset.

"Life is about surviving," he crouched down, still on that damn ledge. I was so afraid that at any moment he would lose his balance and fall three stories below.

"You call what you're doing surviving? I call it being a coward!" I stomped my foot, my fists clenching in frustration.

"You have no fucking idea what I've been through," he growled and spittle flew from between his lips. "What I saw..." His voice dropped below a whisper. "I have to numb myself so that I don't remember."

"What happened to your family, it was awful Caelan, but they wouldn't want you to have turned into this," I waved my hand at him.

His eyes threatened to pop out of his head and his face turned so red I thought a blood vessel had ruptured.

"Oh shit," I mumbled, realizing my mistake.

I wasn't supposed to know about this.

"How do you know about my family?" He roared, jumping off the ledge and stalking towards me. I found myself backing up. "Tell me!"

I flinched from his tone.

I swallowed thickly, moisture clinging to my eyes. "I-I was curious. So, I—uh—Googled you."

"Haven't you ever heard the saying, 'Curiosity killed the cat?'" he pushed me roughly so that my back was against the wall beside the doorway leading to the roof. The brick stung my hands where they'd scraped against the rough surface but I refused to show any sign of pain or emotion. "You had no right to *research* me like I'm some fucking science experiment. I know what I am, and I know why I'm this way, I don't need you to save me. I'm beyond saving, Sutton," he pointed a finger as he pulled himself away from me. Shaking all over, his jaw clenched tightly as he growled, "Stay away from me."

I turned my head, watching as he roughly swung the door open, and descended down the stairwell.

I knew after that experience I should have finally felt afraid of him, but I didn't.

If anything, I was only more determined to know him.

I wanted to see him smile again like he had in those photos— and I wanted those smiles to be directed at me.

Caelan

THE DOOR SLAMMED closed behind me and I paced the short length of the apartment. My fingers pulled harshly at the strands of my hair, yanking to the point that I winced in pain.

I had seriously lost my cool and hadn't been in control of myself.

If I hadn't left... I feared what I may have done to Sutton.

I hadn't been prepared for her to know about my family.

Nobody else here seemed to know—or if they did, they didn't talk about it. My family's murders had been a big thing in this area, but it didn't take long for people to move on, absolving themselves of their fascination, and eventually forgetting all together about the murders.

The fact that she knew scared and exhilarated me all at the same time. It was a strange feeling—like the jitters you get with fear and a dash of adrenaline.

Her knowing what happened meant I didn't have to hide—I didn't have to push her away.

I had feared getting too close to someone for so long, because I wasn't prepared to have to tell them about my family. Besides, my obvious addictions kept women from wanting anything more than a one-night stand.

Sutton had been able to overlook that from the start, I knew it.

Without either obstacle standing in the way of claiming her, what was I waiting for?

I guess I was waiting for fate to step in, tell me I was a fuck up, and I'd never deserve even a moment of happiness that the girl across the hall may bring me.

CHAPTER 8
Sutton

Rubbing my eyes, I padded across the room, making a beeline for the coffee maker. As soon as the heavenly aroma of coffee filled the air, I felt my body relax. I grabbed a coffee mug I'd recently bought at one of the stores in town that I found oddly fitting, since it declared in big bold letters that **GOOGLE IS MY BEST FRIEND**.

It was so true.

I hopped up on the counter as I took a careful sip of the hot liquid. I burned my tongue in the process, but I was so desperate for the caffeine rush that I barely noticed.

As I came awake completely, I noticed a piece of paper had been shoved under my door. I tilted my head, the slip instantly piquing my interest—but not enough that I was ready to abandon my spot and the coffee in my hand.

Once all the coffee was gone, I jumped down and grabbed up the paper.

Before I turned it over, I questioned whether or not it was from Caelan.

It wasn't.

It was an invitation to Cyrus' party Friday night. I had to laugh at the poor attempt he'd done of calligraphy on the piece of notebook paper. It looked more like chicken scratch with swirls tossed in for good measure.

> ***You are cordially invited to
> a party thrown by the out-of-this-world amazing
> Cyrus Mellark.
> This Friday (tomorrow, in case you didn't know)
> Be there.
> Because I said so.***

I shook my head, laughing under my breath.

The fact that he'd invited me to one of his parties after I'd requested him to turn down the music at the last one was laughable.

What was even more hysterical was the fact that I was actually considering going just to know what the fuss was about.

Daphne said they got pretty wild, and wild was just what I needed right now. I needed to spend at least one night without thinking about the C word.

I wouldn't let anything stupid happen at this party. I'd relax and hang out with Daphne—because I was so dragging her ass there, no way was I going by myself—dance a little or a lot, and drink as much as I wanted. It had been a long time since I'd been to a party like this one promised to be. Yeah, I was still young, but my ex-boyfriend was a stick in the mud who never wanted to go out. I wondered if he went out with my former best friend.

Ugh.

Thinking about him was not good. It only served to make me angry.

And the person I should be angry with was Caelan, but I didn't feel that way. I had bruises on my arms where his fingers had pressed into the skin and there were scrapes along my elbows from the brick. He'd been rough and borderline violent, and yet I wasn't cowering. In the moment I had felt a brief flicker of fear but it hadn't lasted long. I knew Caelan could be dangerous if provoked, but I didn't plan on stopping.

This was only just beginning.

I FOUND MYSELF knocking on the door to Frankie and Daphne's apartment.

This was a fashion emergency and I needed Daphne's help... like now.

A beaming Frankie opened the door. Based on his smile, I assumed Jen wasn't around and he didn't need to pretend to hate my guts.

"To what do I owe this pleasure?" He chuckled, sweeping his red hair out of his eyes with long fingers.

"I need your sister's help," I stated, trying to peer around him in the hopes of spotting Daphne.

"Why would anyone ever need Daphne's help?" He scoffed. "I'm sure I can help you with whatever it is."

I rolled my eyes. Guys could be so dumb sometimes... okay, all the time. "I don't suppose you own a size four dress that would make me so hot that every male in a five mile radius couldn't keep his hands off me?" I raised a brow, waiting.

His mouth gaped open and then he turned. "Daphne! Sutton needs your help!" Moving out of the way, he motioned me inside.

I'd never been invited inside Frankie's apartment before. It was bigger than Caelan's and mine with two bedrooms that actually had walls, a larger kitchen, and an expansive living space that boasted enough room for a dining table. Clearly I'd gotten the short end of the straw with my apartment, but I did like it.

Daphne stuck her head out of a bedroom. Spotting me, she grinned happily. She was such a carefree person. I wished I were that happy. I preferred to wallow in self-pity and coffee—not ice cream.

"Hey!"

"Hi," I waved awkwardly. Yes, I was twenty-two years old and still, quite possibly, the most awkward human being on the planet. "I came by, because I need a dress for the party. All I have is the one I wore when we went out before."

"I have *plenty* of dresses. I'm sure you'll like something," she stepped forward and grabbed my hand so she could drag me into her bedroom, since I wasn't moving on my own.

"Do you have anything that says, I'm-not-really-a-slut-but-you-can-treat-me-like-one-tonight?"

Her eyes widened as she paused with the door halfway closed. "Uh... and who are you wanting to wear this dress for?"

"No one in particular," I shrugged, looking around her room.

Her bed was against the exposed brick wall and the rest of the walls were painted hot pink. Her furniture was all various flee market pieces that had been painted bright colors. A neon green dresser caught my eye, as well as the gaudy gold mirror above it.

"Yeah right," she snorted, finally succeeding in closing the door to block her nosy brother.

"Seriously, I just want to look hot for the night," I mumbled, my eyes still perusing her bedroom. A crazy looking chandelier hung above the space. It looked like it had vines or something.

"And this has nothing to do with Caelan?" She gave me a look that said she was not about to be played a fool.

"Why would it?" I countered. "Caelan doesn't even come to Cyrus' parties."

She continued to stare at me, like she was searching for some hidden meaning behind my eyes and facial expression. I had news for her, I had no ulterior motive. I just wanted to look hot and have some fun. It was the only reason I had agreed to go to this stupid party to begin with. I was sick of being stuck in my apartment with Brutus. I did *not* want to be the crazy cat lady at my age. Maybe when I was seventy. Or eighty. Or never.

Finally, I sighed, exasperated with her stare down. "Come on, Daphne, you're a girl! Haven't you ever had one of those days where you just need to feel feminine and *wanted?* I need to feel sexy," I pleaded with her to understand. "Look at me," I pointed to my leggings and loose tank top. "I'm a mess."

Her face softened and her eyes held a twinkle of understanding. "You're not a mess."

"Trust me, I am," I muttered, crinkling my nose in displeasure. She hadn't caught the hidden meaning in my words. People only saw what was on the surface. As long as you looked normal, they didn't assume you had any problems. I'd become a master at blending in. "I'm quite a failure actually. Who just abandons their whole *life?*" My voice cracked and moisture filled my eyes.

Daphne tilted her head, studying me critically. "Are you okay, Sutton? Do you need to talk about it?"

I was so far past okay that I wasn't sure I could ever find my way back. I wasn't ready to open up completely about my life before here. I had done everything I could to bury those memories. This was my fresh start and I wasn't going to ruin that.

"No," I shook my head, forcing a pleasant looking smile.

"Okay," Daphne shrugged, skipping towards her closet.

I let out a relieved breath that she wasn't going to press me. If she had, I'd probably have run out of here like a crazy person and refused to ever speak to her again. I was nice like that.

Daphne pushed aside the shimmery purple beads that served as the barrier between her bedroom and closet, and started skimming the rack for an appropriate dress.

"What about this one?" She held out a glittery hot pink dress.

I tried to tamp down my gag reflex. "No way. I want sexy-sophisticated-slut, not I'm-pretending-to-be-a-hooker-bend-me-over-this-table-and-take-me-now."

She rolled her eyes and replaced the dress back in its proper space. "You're so weird. This?" She held a dress in front of her body for my inspection.

It was black on top with triangle cutouts that would show a bit of skin, but not too much, and the collar was low enough to show some cleavage without me having to worry about the lady berries springing forth into the world. The skirt part was attached to the top and it was white, black, and gold in an Aztec design.

Grinning slowly, I nodded, and reached out with grabby hands. "Gimme!"

With a shake of her head, she tossed it at me.

I caught it easily, surprised by the softness of the fabric.

"By the way," she turned around with a mischievous smile, "you borrow my dress, then I get to do your hair and makeup. No way are you leaving here looking half-done." She motioned to my face, which was currently makeup free, and the knot of hair on my head.

"Fine," I agreed. I wasn't going to complain about getting pampered.

"Yay!" She clapped her hands together, doing a strange little happy dance, where she basically stood on her tiptoes and jogged in place. "Girls day!" Looking me over, she said, "You need a shower."

"I showered last night!"

Eyeing the ball of hair on my head, she chuckled, "I'm not working with that."

"Fine, but I'm going home to shower," I raised my chin defiantly.

She agreed, and I headed home to get clean and, in her words, "do something with that monstrosity."

My hair wasn't even a mess—she should have seen me when I woke up. Then she'd having something to complain about.

Once I was showered, shaved, and buffed until I shined, I figured it was safe to return to Daphne's apartment.

"Took you long enough," she muttered when I knocked on the door.

She dragged me into the bathroom, where she blew my hair dry so that it hung straight with a slight curl on the end. "Simple, but sexy," she told my reflection.

When my hair was done, I was escorted to her room once more where I became her canvas.

"What are you doing to me?" I growled after ten minutes of her rubbing stuff on my face. I was terrified I'd end up looking like a clown, and clowns were not hot.

She stopped what she was doing, leveling me with a glare. "Patience."

With that, she went back to work.

"I have on so much makeup it feels like my face weighs ten pounds," I complained as she added *another* layer of foundation.

"Shush," she scolded. "It's not as much as you think. It's *buildable*, so I keep going over your face in *light* layers," she spoke slowly like I was too dumb to understand her words.

She finally laid the bottle aside and assessed me. Nodding, she went back to work, adding bronzer and blush to my face. Because of the dress, she added a shimmery gold color to the tops of my eyelids and heavy black eyeliner. After about fifty strokes of mascara over my lashes, she decided they were perfect. Last were my lips. She grabbed several tubes, twisting them out to assess the color. "No, not that one," she muttered to herself. "Where is it? Ah! There it is!" She picked a magenta color. Holding my chin, she swiped the lipstick over my plump lips and then motioned for me to rub them together.

I mimicked her motion. "Now can I please see myself?" I begged.

"No," she shook her head. "Dress first. You have to see the completed look."

"I wonder why I'm friends with you," I grumbled good-naturedly as I stood and swiped the dress off her bed.

I locked myself in the single bathroom and changed into the clingy dress. Thank God it fit, despite the fact that I was good six or more inches shorter than Daphne. The girl was a giant, and I was a shrimp.

I turned, assessing the dress and myself from all angles.

"Dang, I clean up good," I chuckled.

I spent so much of my time in jeans and a t-shirt that I didn't quite know what to make of the vixen reflected back at me. I was glad I had wanted to dress up this evening. It was nice to see yourself in different ways. The real me might have been a couch potato that lived in leggings and old shirts, but this me... she was capable of anything. And tonight was going to be all about having fun and being wild.

"THIS IS THE best night of my *life!*" Okay, it was safe to say that this was *not,* indeed, the best night of my life and it was just the alcohol talking, but I was willing to roll with it.

I stood on Cyrus' coffee table that was pushed against one of the far walls to clear the area in the middle, shaking my ass to the beat of the song, and screaming the lyrics at the top of my lungs whenever there was actually a line that I knew.

The party had been raging for a good hour now, and more people were arriving all the time.

When the door opened and in walked a familiar figure, I let out a cry of joy. "Memphis! I love you!"

Memphis turned at the sound of my voice, sweeping his copper colored hair from his eyes. He smiled widely, and I crooked my finger in a come-hither gesture. Yes, I had basically lost all rational thought.

"Come dance with me!"

He stopped in front of me, our eyes level from where I stood on the coffee table.

"I will if you get down from there," he chuckled like I was the funniest thing he had ever seen.

"I don't wanna," I pouted, still swaying to the beat of the song, my arms flailing above my head in what I hoped came across as an enticing gesture. I probably just looked like I was having an out of body experience, but it's the thought that counts, right?

"How about I go get a drink, and when I come back *then* you get down?" He suggested, amusement sparkling in his eyes.

I pointed a finger at him, nails painted gold to match the dress per Daphne's orders, and exclaimed, "Deal!"

With a shake of his head, he went in search of a drink.

I continued to move and shake my body. I felt the eyes of more than one man on me and God it felt good to be looked at. To be *wanted*. It had been far too long. And if I had my way, one lucky man would be accompanying me to my bed, because I seriously needed to get laid. It had been... I tried to count it up in my head, but it was futile. I was far too drunk and numbers were running together. Suffice to say, it had been a long time. Stupid, cheating, no good ex-boyfriend. After that experience, I was done with relationships. They only ended in disaster. No-Strings-Attached-Sex was *exactly* what I needed.

Somehow I found myself climbing off the coffee table and going in search of Memphis.

When I found him, he was surrounded by a group of guys, sipping on a beer.

"Hey!" I shouted when I found him.

He turned towards me, as did the rest of the guys.

"Let's have sex!"

Memphis spit out his beer, spraying it all across the floor. Thankfully it missed me, but hit a few of the guys, who were currently laughing hysterically at my declaration. I didn't see what was so funny. I was serious.

"Sutton," he wiped his mouth, trying to catch his breath from nearly choking, "I think you're drunk."

"No, I'm not!" I declared with a pout. "I'm perfectly in control of all my faculties."

"Uh-huh," he muttered, looking at me in disbelief.

"I am!"

It looked like I was going to have to take matters into my own hands if this was to progress to more fun activities other than standing here discussing my current state of drunkenness—which I wasn't, drunk that is.

I took his hand in mine, noting how his nearly swallowed mine whole and was rough with callouses.

Cyrus had all the furniture pushed against the walls, so the entire center of the apartment was cleared as a dance floor. I was surprised by how many people were packed into the small space. Well, it was larger than my apartment, a twin of Daphne and Frankie's, but still not the biggest space in the world and there were between thirty and fifty people.

"What are you doing?" Memphis asked, a slight chuckle to his tone.

"*We* are going to dance. Did you know that dancing can be great foreplay?"

"Sutton," he warned.

"I'm not drunk!" I hiccupped. "Okay, maybe a little. But let's just dance."

"Sure thing," he smiled with amusement.

I listened to the song for a few seconds before I started to move my body.

My hips rolled against his and his body instantly responded by coming closer to mine. His large hands grasped me just below my breasts, pushing me into him. Our bodies moved in sync, even our breaths taking on the same rhythm.

"Think of grandma. Grandma. Grandma. Grandma."

"Why the fuck are you muttering about your grandma for?" I questioned, my back to his front as I reached behind me to twine my hands around his neck. He felt so good, nice and muscular and warm. He smelled good too. Yummy.

His lips brushed against my ear, and he said, "I try to picture my grandma when I don't want to get a boner and think with the wrong head, and end up taking advantage of drunk girls that have *no* idea what they're doing."

Smiling coyly, I licked my lips. His eyes zeroed in on my tongue. "Oh, I want you to take complete and utter advantage."

"Grandma, grandma, grandma," he went back to muttering.

I turned quickly in his arms so that we were face to face. I grasped the silky strands of his hair in my fingers, and bit my lip in what I hoped was a seductive manner. I probably looked like I was hungry and my lip was there for the taking. "Would you shut up?"

And then, I stood on my tiptoes and kissed him. His body was stiff beneath mine, but then relaxed. I was in control of this kiss, and it felt nice to be in charge and take what I wanted. The kiss was hot and demanding, a tornado of desire. His tongue lightly flicked against mine, his fingers digging into my waist. A soft purr sounded in the back of my throat. This kiss was nothing like the one I'd shared with Caelan, where he'd been trying to make a point. This kiss was thick with *want*. But it was probably a bad sign that my brain, even while drunk, had thought of Caelan while I was kissing another man. I was a serious head case. Pissed at myself for thinking of Caelan, I threw myself even more into the kiss, taking it to scorching levels. I think someone told us to get a room. Didn't they know that was my plan? Duh.

When our lips broke apart, Memphis looked down at me with a small smile. "Well, that was something."

"Yeah, it was," I muttered, angry that when he looked at me I'd been hoping to see blond hair and blue eyes. "I need another drink."

Several drinks later, I thought it would be a good idea to give Memphis a lap dance. Alcohol was a wicked witch and it did dangerous things to my thought process. I was going to end up regretting this later... if I remembered it, that is. Right now, I thought it was the greatest thing ever.

I pushed Memphis down on a chair, praying that I didn't fall over my wobbly legs and that I could pull this off by looking sexy and alluring.

The crowd cheered me on, enjoying the show. Cyrus watched from the sidelines with a funny little smirk on his lips.

Swaying my hips to the latest Jason Derulo song, something

about talking dirty, I lowered my hips so my ass grazed Memphis' crotch. Air hissed out between his teeth. His hands reached up to cup my hips, but I slapped his arm.

"You can look, but you can't touch," I warned with a coy smile.

"Yes ma'am," he grinned, letting his hands fall to his sides. His eyes were now glassy with intoxication.

I dipped low, and then back up. I ran my fingers through my hair, lifting it up and then letting it fall as I turned my head slightly to watch his reaction out of the corner of my eyes. His mouth was slightly open and he swallowed thickly as his eyes grazed my body. At least he was no longer muttering about his grandma. This might be easier than I thought.

I turned around so I faced him, doing a little shimmy before grasping the back of the chair he was sitting in. The position all but shoved my boobs in his face. Poor Memphis was a saint for obeying my command of no touching, because I was right there in front of him, his for the taking.

I trailed my finger down his shirtfront, basking in the hard ridges of his pecs and abdominals. Mmm, I wanted to rip that shirt off so damn bad. *I* deserved to be inducted into sainthood for resisting the urge to straddle him right here.

"I thought you said no touching," he murmured, trying and failing, to keep his eyes away from the swell of my breasts.

"I said *you* couldn't touch. I was not included in that statement," I murmured, itching to kiss him again.

"Ah, I see."

I turned around so that my back was to him once more.

I moved my hips in a tantalizing rhythm, lowering so that with each sway of my hips my ass brushed against the growing bulge in his pants. I smiled in satisfaction.

And *that* was when Caelan came storming in and disrupted everything.

Caelan

THE PAINTING IN front of me was only half complete. The brush hovered an inch away from the surface, shaking with my anger. The music thumping out of Cyrus apartment had the whole fucking building vibrating.

I was working on a commission piece for some old lady and her five dogs. If I didn't get this right, I didn't get paid, and I needed the money. Cyrus was about to get a tooth knocked out for this. I hadn't sobered up for the night to listen to this shit.

Dropping the brush in the cup of water, I stormed out and down the hall. I banged my fist against the door, hard enough that some of the detailing on the door cut the side of my hand.

No one answered.

Bastard.

He couldn't fucking hear me knocking over the music.

Kicking the door roughly in my state of fury, I was shocked when it opened. Well, that was convenient. The idiot had left it unlocked. I guess that made sense, since he was throwing a party, but it did allow anyone, me included, to wander inside.

I was scanning the crowd—seriously, how did this many people fit in here?—for Cyrus, when I found Sutton instead.

I stopped in my tracks, stunned by what I saw.

I thought I needed to find a bottle of bleach for my eyes, stat.

She moved her body in a way that made it seem like she was dry-humping the guy she was giving a lap dance. Her eyes were glassed over with lust and drunkenness. He tried to touch her, but she slapped his hand away. Lifting her hair, she exposed her slender neck and gave the man a demure look. I was riveted—disgusted but unable to look away from the show playing out before me.

God, I wished I wasn't sober. Every sway of her hips had my mind reeling.

When she lowered and grinded herself against his dick, I lost my mind.

I stomped forward—a man on a mission.

I shoved people out of my way as I desperately tried to reach Sutton. I wasn't sure what had come over me. A latent hero complex? Maybe, but doubtful.

When I reached her, her eyes were closed so she didn't see me.

She was a tiny little thing—short but with hips my hands desperately wanted to rest on and her breasts weren't bad either, where I could see them swelling at the top of the dress.

Not giving myself another moment of thought, I wrapped my arm around her middle, and hauled her over my shoulder. She let out a high-pitched shriek that had people wincing.

"What the fuck?" The man in the chair looked at me.

He didn't deserve a response, and before he could react, I shifted my weight so that I didn't drop Sutton, and kicked that fucker right out of the chair.

I turned sharply, head held high. "Cyrus, turn the music down, or it won't be your nose I break." I said the words calmly, my show having caused all the eyes in the room to turn to me, so there was no need for shouting... unless I felt like it.

"Put me down!" Sutton shrieked, beating my back with her mighty little fists.

I admired her spunk. Normally, it would irritate me, but not with this woman. No, it made me tick in an entirely different way.

"Not happening sweetheart," I grinned, my step bouncing so that her stomach smacked against my shoulder.

"Ow," she moaned. "Don't do that."

Opening the door to my apartment, I carried her inside, flopping her like a rag doll on the couch.

She instantly rolled off, the whole front of her body pressed to the ground.

"Hello floor," she mumbled, waving her arms and legs like one would when making a snow angel. "I love you floor. You're cold."

I couldn't contain my snicker.

"You brought me home, you can leave now fucktard," she lifted one hand in the air, waving around her pointed middle finger.

I squatted beside her, my chuckle permeating the air. I hadn't been this amused in a long time. "Well, I would, but you're in my apartment. So that would make my leaving silly, wouldn't it?"

"Fuuuuck," she tried to push herself up on shaky arms but collapsed on the floor once more. "Take me home."

"Not happening," I shook my head. "If I did that, then that asshole you were grinding your ass against like you're a fucking pornstar would try to fuck you and that's not happening on my watch."

"Jealous?" She tilted her head to the side so she could look up at me through long thick lashes. I swallowed thickly. She was beautiful—in a natural way, where she didn't need makeup and fancy clothes, both of which she was wearing in abundance at the moment.

"No. I may be a bad man, Sutton, but I still don't condone rape."

"I can assure you, it would've been consensual. I didn't need you to be my black knight," she groaned. "I really love this floor."

My lips quirked up in a small smile. "Black knight?"

"You're sure as hell not a white knight. I don't see you helping any old ladies across the street," she mumbled and—what the hell? She was kissing the floor.

It was official. Sutton was the most entertaining drunk I had ever met.

"I'm sorry I haven't helped any old ladies recently."

I took a seat on the couch, wondering if I should leave her there, or what.

"You're mean. Always so grumpy. 'Turn your music down,'" she mimed my voice poorly. "And always so cryptic. You—" Her words stuttered to a stop as she jolted into a sitting position. "I'm going to be sick," she clapped a hand over her mouth. Coming to her feet, she ran around like a chicken with its head cut off as she searched for the bathroom.

I grabbed her by the wrist and led her there.

As soon as she saw the porcelain throne, she collapsed to her knees, emptying the contents of her stomach. Her small body heaved, and I reached down to pull her hair back. I was surprised by its silky texture. It was smooth between my fingertips and smelled of coconuts. In fact, she always smelled like coconut. It must have been her favorite scent.

"Whoa," I cried when she fell to the side.

Her eyes were closed, and she'd clearly lost the battle of staying awake. Most people didn't have a tolerance for alcohol like I did.

"All right, Sleeping Beauty," I groaned, lifting her into my arms once more. I cradled her against me like you would a child. She buried her face into my shirt, inhaling the scent.

I knew I should do the normal Caelan thing and take her to her apartment, dump her on the floor, and not care what happened to her.

But I couldn't.

No.

Old Caelan was resurfacing from a long slumber—resurrected from the dead—and Old Caelan didn't leave drunk girls to fend for themselves. Fuck, I was starting to *care* and that was such a bad thing.

Caring isn't bad, Cael. Cayla's ghost voice echoed through my head. *What you've been doing is bad.*

"Shut up!" I screamed at the voice.

Reigning in my quickly accelerating temper, I looked down at Sutton. She was beautiful. She was warm. She was vibrant. She was a *fighter*. She was everything I was not.

I needed to distance myself, before we were both destroyed.
My gut told me that would be easier said than done.

CHAPTER 9
Sutton

MY ARMS WERE wrapped around the softest, nicest smelling pillow I'd ever come into contact with. I squeezed it closer to my chest, inhaling the scent. There was something woodsy and masculine about the scent with bitter undertones of paint.

Paint.

Oh, shit.

I jerked awake, my eyes opening to take in the unfamiliar apartment.

With a scream, I fell out of the bed onto the floor.

I rubbed the sore spot on the back of my head where it had connected with the floor.

I heard rustling, then, peering over the edge of the bed was a boyish looking Caelan. His eyes were hooded with sleep and his blond hair stuck up wildly around his head. "Mornin'," he yawned. "You know, you talk in your sleep, and you like to snuggle. I don't like snuggling," he glared.

"Why the fuck am I in your bed?" I cried, clutching my head, which throbbed painfully from a killer hangover as well as from getting bonked on the floor. I tried in vain to remember what happened last night, but all I could recall was alcohol and dancing. Lots of dancing.

"You didn't know that rescuing idiot damsels is my second career? You really need to brush up on your Google searching skills. You're lacking," he tilted his head to the side. "Now that I know you aren't going to die, or be raped, you can leave," he waved his hand dismissively towards the door.

"You disgust me," I spat, trying to get my wobbly feet to hold my weight so I could stand.

He lay in the bed, his arms crossed behind his neck, smirking at me.

And *I* was staring at his chest.

I really needed to stop that.

"Like what you see?"

His words snapped me back to reality. "No."

Lie.

All I did was lie, or so it seemed.

When I moved my head to avoid staring at Caelan my eyes landed on a canvas lying against the wall beside his bed.

My mouth fell open slightly, studying the colors and the woman's face.

"That's me!" I finally cried.

He turned his head slightly to look at the painting I currently pointed an accusing finger at.

"Yeah," he said in a lazy drawl, like the fact that he had painted my image was the most normal thing he could do. "So what?"

"It's creepy!" I squirmed, realizing that upon further inspection I was sleeping in the picture, my features relaxed, and he must have done it last night. Which meant he'd watched me sleep. Weirdo.

"I paint lots of people's pictures," he waved his hand lazily to encompass the apartment. "Don't flatter yourself."

If I had been holding something I would have thrown it at his face to have something to do.

"You are—"

Before I finished speaking, he was out of the bed and had me pinned against the wall. He really had an annoying knack for slamming me against things.

"Don't finish that thought," he whispered, his eyes flicking down to my lips and then back up. My heart thundered in my chest, threatening to break free.

"What are you going to do, Caelan? Kiss me?" I challenged.

"No," he shook his head, so that the slightly wavy strands of blond hair tickled my forehead. "You can beg and plead, but I won't be kissing you again. Now, get out of my apartment," he released me, turning for the bathroom. Before he could close the door, I was assaulted with a memory of last night.

With a gasp, I asked, "Did you hold my hair back last night while I was puking my guts up?"

He stopped, his back rigid. "Absolutely not," he said without turning around. "That's something a nice guy would do and *I* am not nice." The bathroom door slammed shut and a moment later, I heard the shower turn on.

I *knew* he had held my hair back, the little liar. I couldn't remember much from last night, but bits and pieces were now starting to trickle in.

If he thought I was just going to let myself out, he was sorely mistaken.

Like the nosy bitch I was, I scanned all his drawers, and opened all the cabinets in the kitchen.

Basically, the only thing in the kitchen was varying bottles of alcohol. Not much food—unless a half-eaten box of Frosted Flakes counted as sustenance for a twenty-something male.

I never did find any stash of drugs. I knew he had them somewhere. I'd seen the evidence on the table and he'd admitted such. I got the impression Caelan didn't see the point in hiding his addictions. When you don't care, you have nothing to lose. I wasn't sure what I'd do if I found them—throw them away maybe? Move them to a different spot to mess with him?

I heard the shower cut off and figured I better get my ass out of there before he found me. I wasn't in the mood to argue with him thanks to this terrific headache.

Spotting the canvas beside his bed, I snatched it up. After all, it was me that he had painted, so I should get to keep it.

I scurried towards the door, and opened it as quietly as possible.

I scanned the hall and ran into my apartment, breathing a sigh of relief that no one had seen me. It would've been embarrassing if someone had spotted me leaving Caelan's apartment. They, no doubt, would have believed I was doing the walk of shame. Which I wasn't. So, why did I feel like I was?

Brutus brushed against my legs and I bent to scratch him behind the ears. "Sorry I didn't come home," I told the kitten—who had grown immeasurably since I'd moved here.

Placing the canvas on the counter, I set the coffee to brew.

While the scent of much needed caffeine filled the air, I jumped in the shower to rinse off, pulling my hair back in a sloppy bun on top of my head. I dressed in a pair of leggings and a loose flannel button down shirt. I wanted a comfy day, and luckily I didn't have to go into work until nine tonight.

Pouring a cup of coffee, I stood by the window, staring out at the street below. It had always amazed me how life went on around you. All these other souls, completely unaware of the turmoil churning around them, the secrets kept hidden. Ignorance really was bliss.

I was jolted from my thoughts by someone banging on my door.

Honestly, no one in this building had any respect. It was early, and I could have still been sleeping.

"What?" I bit out, opening the door with more force than necessary.

The person pushed past me and inside.

Caelan.

I didn't even have to look.

I knew.

I turned sharply. "What are you doing? You can't just barge in here!"

He spun around, his eyes wild and his nostrils flared with barely contained anger. "I can when you steal my fucking property!" He reached for the canvas, then clutched it against his chest like a small child would hold a stuffed animal. "You had no right to take this."

"I had every right! You painted a picture of *me!*"

"It doesn't belong to you," he muttered, "it's mine. I'm keeping it. You can't have it."

I rolled my eyes, exasperated with his strange behavior. He was acting like a petulant child.

"Fine, whatever. I don't care," I tucked falling strands of hair behind my ears. "Take it and get the fuck out."

"You don't like me," he stated.

No, I didn't like him. Not really, at least. He fascinated me, and that was an entirely separate thing from *liking* someone.

"You've given me no reason to like you," I crossed my arms over my chest and raised my chin defiantly.

"That's because I don't want you to like me, Sutton." He closed the few feet separating us. He was really good at that— getting in my personal space. His lips grazing my ear, he continued in a silky voice, "I *want* you to fear me. I *want* to watch your body shake with anticipation of what I might do." And then my traitorous body shivered a moment before he brushed his fingers lightly over my cheek. "We're not good for each other. I need you to stay away from me." The next word he said shocked me, gluing me to the spot where I stood. "Please."

"You look like hell," Emery said the moment I stepped inside the coffee shop.

"Thank you Mr. Observant. Would you like a sticker for pointing out the obvious?" My tone was snarky.

He raised his hands in defense. "Crabby too, I see. Is it that time of the month? Are you going to go all she-beast and try to eat me? I promise I taste *awful*, like rotting corpses and Sour Patch kids, 'cause those things are *nasty*."

His words had the desired effect and I couldn't help laughing. Emery always managed to make me feel better, even when I wanted to sucker punch him.

Heading behind the counter, I said, "Yeah, last night was pretty wicked. I don't remember much."

"Too bad," he shrugged, smiling. "I was looking forward to hearing all the details."

"You'll have to come some time," I pushed the swinging door open with my hip. Daphne would shit bricks if Emery showed up. I didn't know why she didn't make a move. She was gorgeous and nice—a winning combination. But she always turned insanely shy around Emery. I might have to resort to the very high school ploy of knocking one into the other so that they 'happened' to accidently bump into each other.

"Maybe," he shrugged, wiping off the already spotless counter. "Parties aren't really my thing."

Ignoring him for the moment, I headed to the back and dropped off my stuff and tied the apron around my waist.

When I returned to the front, I asked, "What is your thing then?"

Tucking the rag into the back pocket of his jeans, he pondered. "I don't know. I'm a simple guy. I like to sing... thought about making a career out of it, but..." He trailed off, his thought left unfinished.

"I've never heard you sing."

Grinning, he chuckled. "You're really missing out, Sunshine." Again with that damn nickname. "You should come by tomorrow at five. I sing then."

"I think I will," I smiled. It would be nice to have an excuse to get out, and not feel like a pathetic human being for only having myself for company. And Brutus. But I couldn't really take him shopping.

"We could get dinner afterwards," he suggested. At my bug eyed appearance, he added with a laugh, "As *friends*. Nothing more."

"Sounds good." I let out a breath I hadn't realized I was holding.

The next few hours were highly uneventful until around one in the morning. That damn bell on the door chimed, jolting me awake where I had nodded off. Standing up straight and smoothing my hands down my shirt, I looked up to find myself face to face with Memphis.

My mouth fell open as all the memories of last night finally resurfaced with startling clarity.

A blush stained my cheeks and I didn't know what to say or how to act. I'd basically mauled the poor guy last night.

"Can we talk?" He asked, clearing his throat and looking around awkwardly.

"Uh—"

"She can talk," Emery said from behind me.

I turned sharply and gave Emery a scathing look for throwing me under the bus. I think he wanted Memphis and me together as much as I refused to let go of my hopes for Daphmery.

His shoulders raised in a small shrug as a shameless smile twisted his lips. "We're not busy."

He was right. The place was empty besides us, and one lone college student reading a book in the corner.

"I hate you," I mouthed.

"No, you don't," he laughed, clearly enjoying my complete and utter mortification. Emery had no idea what I had done to Memphis last night. "Here, take these," he quickly poured two black cups of coffee into mugs.

Grasping the mugs, I forced a smile and turned around once more to face Memphis. "Where do you want to sit?" I asked.

He nodded his head towards a table and I came around the counter to join him.

I sat down, feeling out of place and uncomfortable. Staring into the dark depths of the liquid, I avoided his scrutiny, but it didn't stop me from feeling it.

"I wanted to apologize for last night—" He started, but was abruptly cut off when my head went flying up, a started sound escaping me.

"You want to apologize? *You*? If I recall, I was the one making a fool of myself, throwing myself at you like... like..." I was at a loss for words.

"But I wasn't stopping you," he cleared his throat, scooting the chair forward so that we were even closer.

"You tried to!"

"Initially, sure," he shrugged. "You were obviously drunk and I wouldn't take advantage of you, I'm not that kind of guy. I'm also not the kind of guy to have one-night stands. Just because I have a dick, doesn't mean I think I need to insert it into every pretty girl that walks by." That got me to smile. "But later, when you were dancing," he swallowed thickly, his gray eyes flashing a darker color for a moment before returning to normal, "I wouldn't have been able to stop myself from taking things further. You made it obvious that you wanted me, which made it impossible for me to reign in my desires." He took a sip of coffee, an obvious stall tactic. "I need you to know that I'm sorry. If I had known you had a boyfriend I would've never let you flirt with me like that. I know he was pissed and—"

I kept replaying that single word over and over in my mind. "Boyfriend? I don't have a boyfriend."

"Uh..." He leaned forward, looking perplexed. "Wasn't that guy that came in and hauled you out your boyfriend?"

"No!" I scoffed. "That's just..." I had no description worthy enough other than, "Caelan. He's just Caelan."

"And do you have a thing with him?" He probed.

"Absolutely not. He's just my nosy neighbor that can't mind his own damn business," I glowered at Memphis, and I wasn't even mad at *him*. Oh no, my anger was directed at an entirely different person.

"Are you sure?" He continued with his line of questioning. "The way that guy looked at me when he grabbed you up... I think he wanted to kill me."

"Don't you worry about him," I seethed. "He's just a very angry, confused person."

"Does this very angry, confused person think you're his girlfriend?" He continued, this time mischief sparkled in his eyes, but I was still livid.

"No! He is *not* my boyfriend! Not now, not ever!" My hand smacked sharply against the top of the table and a bit of coffee sloshed out of the mugs. "Now," I slid the chair back forcefully so it knocked into the one behind it, "I have to get back to work. As you can see, we're very busy," I said sarcastically, spreading my arms wide to encompass the nearly empty shop. I was irritated with Memphis for assuming that Caelan was my boyfriend—but frankly, I was more mad at myself for wishing there was something between Caelan and I.

I walked slowly into the back of the store where only employees were allowed. I refused to stomp my way there and act like a child, even though I felt like it.

"How'd it go?" Emery asked as he reclined on the couch and stared at the small TV that occupied the employee break room.

"I hate you so much right now," I unleashed my glare on him.

"What did I do?" He blinked innocently.

"You know exactly what you did," I groaned, burying my face in my hands. I was angrier with myself, than Emery, but it was so much easier to take that aggression out on him.

"Actually, I don't," he sat up straight, looking at me with concern. "What happened?"

"Nothing," I shook my head back and forth rapidly as I let my hands fall away from my face.

"Did something happen between you guys?" He questioned.

The way he stared at me made me feel as if I was a specimen being peered at through the lens of a microscope. I got the impression Emery didn't miss much.

I didn't want to talk about this with him, but I knew I didn't have any choice. He'd only keep pestering me.

"I guess you could say that," I muttered, looking at the ceiling.

"Did you guys...?" He let the thought trail off, but it was easy for me to fill in the blanks.

"No!" My tone softening, I added, "Almost. I wanted to."

"And he stopped it?" Emery tilted his head to the side, no doubt assuming that's what had happened and the reason for my current pissed off state.

"No."

"Elaborate, Sunshine. Don't make me imagine the details for myself," he waved a hand in a gesture for me to carry on.

"Someone stopped us," I admitted, my words were bit out painfully, the shaky sound barely above a whisper.

"Someone?" Emery raised a brow. "And who would this someone be?"

"Just my asshole of a neighbor. He doesn't know how to mind his own business," I grumbled.

"Well, you sure know how to get around," he grinned easily, laughing under his breath.

"It's not funny," I frowned. Forcing my fingers through the strands of black hair framing my face, I huffed, "Just don't bring this up again and stop pushing me towards Memphis. I don't need your help. Besides, you're a guy, so why should you care about my love life?"

The question was rhetorical but he answered anyway.

"I'm not. I'm just bored," he moved to lay back down on the couch, "and boredom makes me do dumb things."

I shook my head, not in the mood to talk to Emery anymore.

I returned to the front of the store and found Memphis gone.

I breathed a sigh of relief, but why did I still feel so stressed?

By the time my shift ended and I started home, daylight was reluctantly beginning to break through the clouds. I was exhausted and all I wanted to do was drop my bag by the door, flop face first on my bed, and cuddle Brutus.

And that was my plan until I opened the door and he didn't great me.

"Brutus?" I called. "Come here kitty."

No cat emerged from anywhere in the apartment.

I squatted on the floor, crawling on my hands and knees to peer under the couch and then the bed for the kitten.

Nope. Not there. Or there.

"Brutus?" My voice became high with panic.

I checked to make sure none of the windows were open and that he hadn't used one of his nine lives by dropping to the street below.

They were all shut and secured tightly.

How on Earth does someone lose a cat in an apartment this size? Seriously?

Despite the early morning hour, I headed down to the Daphne and Frankie's. I knocked on the door loud enough to wake the dead.

"What the—?" Frankie muttered, opening the door. He promptly slapped a hand over his mouth to stifle a yawn.

"Have you seen Brutus?" I pleaded.

"Who the hell is Brutus and why the fuck are you asking me about him this early?"

Before I could respond, someone from inside the apartment said, "Baby?"

A moment later Jen appeared. When she spotted me, she sent me a look that said she wished me a very painful death.

Instead of acting like a bitch, which is what I'd normally do, I appealed to her. She was a female, surely she would understand the importance of locating my cat.

I pushed past Frankie so I could see Jen fully, but didn't venture into the apartment. I was rude, but not that rude. "Hi Jen," I waved awkwardly. "I just got home and it seems that my cat is missing. You haven't by any chance seen him, have you?"

"Oh," her face softened, the anger draining away. "What does he look like?"

"He's about this big," I held my hands out. "He's kinda black with orange and some white." I clasped my hands together hoping she had seen him. I'd grown fond of the little fur ball.

"Uh..." Her brows furrowed together. "That sorta sounds like the cat I saw with Gregory earlier."

"Gregory—? Oh!" I jumped up in place. "You mean Caelan?" When she nodded, I added, "Thank you so much!"

The door closed as I raced back down the hall and pounded on his door.

No one came.

I smacked the palm of my hands against it harder in a slapping motion. "Open the damn door!"

Nothing.

"Fuck," I kicked the door.

If he had my cat, so help me God I was going to rip him to sheds. What kind of psycho steals a cat?

I reached out, my hand wrapping around the knob. I twisted it and relief flooded me when it turned. I pushed it open and stepped inside.

"Caelan!" I screamed.

I stormed inside, turning my head left then right, in search of the resident asshole.

I found him lying in bed, and there was Brutus snuggled up beside him.

Anger simmered inside me, churning and heating, ready to burst from me like a volcanic explosion.

I stomped over to where he was spread out across the bed fast asleep. He wasn't under the covers, and all his shirtless glory would normally have been a feast for my eyes but I was too angry.

My hand smacked sharply against the bare skin of his chest, the sound echoing through the room. Air gusted out of his lungs as he came awake and sat fully upright.

"What the fuck?" He looked at me with wide blue eyes. "Did you just *hit* me?"

"You stole my cat!" I screamed. "Hitting seemed reasonable. So does murder. You better hope I don't find a shovel because I'm not against smacking you over the head with it and burying you in the courtyard."

"We don't have a courtyard," he muttered, rubbing at the red imprint of my hand on his body.

"Then I'll toss your body off the roof and make it look like an accident," I glared.

Laughter burst forth from his lungs. I didn't think I had ever heard him laugh before. It was a shock to hear—oddly warm and masculine, I wanted to wrap myself up in it like a warm sweater.

Wait, I should so not be thinking such pleasant thoughts about the cat kidnapper.

"You've really thought my murder through," he tilted his head, still massaging the sore area. I was starting to feel bad that I hit him so hard but he *had* stolen my cat. "I'm glad you're so thorough. I believe I have some of those nasty smelling medical gloves around here somewhere if you'd like to use them so you don't leave behind any fingerprints."

"I hate you," I said through gritted teeth.

"I assure you, the feeling is mutual." He reached for Brutus and shoved the cat into my arms, his claws scratching my skin, clearly not pleased at having his slumber so rudely disturbed. "And just so you know, *Sutton*," he said my name slowly and with irritation, "I didn't steal your cat. When you left, the door didn't latch, and he got out. I found him outside my door."

"And if my door didn't close, you didn't think about maybe, I don't know, putting him back inside and closing the fucking door?!"

"You're a very ungrateful person," he remarked. "It didn't seem fair to leave him by himself when he so clearly wanted my company."

"Do ridiculous things just fall out of your mouth? Or do you think you're cute?"

He shook his head, a small smile playing on his lips. "Don't act like you're not attracted to me." He slowly raised his head, his eyes connecting with mine. My pulse jumped in my throat. The look he gave me... it was indescribable. I was once again reminded of this insane *thing* between us. "I'm glad you don't deny it."

He stood from the bed, getting into my personal space once more. Brutus, clutched tightly in my arms, was the only thing keeping our chests from touching.

My breath quaked and then stopped all together as his thumb brushed against my bottom lip.

I desperately wanted to close my eyes to avoid his stare, but I couldn't. I was riveted, wondering what he was going to do next.

He was so hot and cold that it made him completely unpredictable.

One minute I could see a glimmer of the guy he'd once been and the next a monster was in his place.

A smart girl would have turned tail and run far away. A smart girl would never speak to Caelan Gregory. A smart girl wouldn't keep coming back for... nothing. He offered me nothing. We were *nothing*.

But I wasn't smart.

I followed my heart.

And my stupid heart liked this crazy, moody, egotistical artist for some insane reason.

We were both lost in a sea of self-torment and anger,

searching frantically for a buoy to hold ourselves up.

In that moment, I decided that's what we were to each other.

A buoy.

God, I hoped neither of us let go, because I just might drown.

"What are you going to do?" I whispered, my breath caressing his lips.

"I don't know," he murmured, his thumb still making lazy strokes against my lips.

He may not know what he wanted, but I knew what I wanted.

I dropped Brutus and he went scampering away.

Before Caelan could react, one of my hands grasped his shirt in a tight fist and the other wrapped around his neck, pulling him close.

Our lips connected and it was like fireworks went off in my body.

This kiss was nothing like our first. With that kiss, Caelan had been trying to make a point.

There was no point to this—nothing but pure unadulterated lust and passion colliding into a fiery explosion.

My whole being yearned for him in an uncontrollable act of defiance.

His mouth moved effortlessly against mine as if our lips were only ever supposed to touch each other's.

His fingers dug painfully into my waist and I knew his mind was warring with whether or not he should push me away or pull me closer.

Closer, ultimately, won out.

He twisted his body so that my legs were against the bed, then he lowered me onto the bed as he hovered above—never, not once, breaking the kiss.

I clenched the short hairs at the back of his head, my fingers curling around them. Somewhere, in the back of my mind, a voice scolded me, telling me that this was wrong and I needed to stop. After all, I was making out with the cat stealer. But I told that voice to shut up. The moment I decided to pick up my life and move here was the moment I decided to throw reason and logic out the window. I wasn't going to start thinking like a sane person now.

"You infuriate me," he breathed, pulling his lips from mine and then raining kisses down my neck.

My body arched, aching for his touch and the pleasure it could bring. No man had ever made every cell in my body feel so alive.

His hand ventured lower, lifting the edge of my top. My breath stuttered as the button on my jeans popped and then his hand eased inside.

His fingers caressed the soft skin there before delving inside.

My gasp echoed around the apartment and my hands grasped onto anything to hold, settling on the curve of his upper arm.

His darkened eyes met mine momentarily. Before he looked away I saw confusion, lust, passion, and anger swirling in their depths.

As his fingers stroked me roughly, his lips sought mine. We were hungry for each other and I knew that every moment we'd shared, no matter how brief, had been leading to this. I wasn't sure if this would be a one-time thing or what. Right now, as pleasure vibrated through my body and I shook with want, I didn't care. All I wanted was for him to make me feel good.

The games we'd been playing for weeks now had been building a frustration inside both of us—a frustration that only we could relieve by giving into the unavoidable.

My hands slid from his arms to clutch at the bed sheets. My hips grinded against his fingers, aching for more and the release that was so close.

I tore my mouth away from his and my teeth dug into his shoulder as the most powerful orgasm I'd ever had ripped through my body—and he wasn't even inside me yet. Oh God. Could it get better?

Panting, I collapsed beneath him, my limbs lying languid at my sides. He pressed his forehead against the curve where my neck met my shoulders. We both breathed heavily and were unable to move.

Finally, he lifted his head. I thought for sure he was ready to continue to the grand finale, but that wasn't the case.

His face was full of hatred—whether aimed at himself, or me, I wasn't sure.

"Get out," he hissed venomously, pushing himself off the bed and away from me.

I couldn't move.

I was shell-shocked.

My mouth opened and closed.

Tears of anger pricked my eyes as I slowly sat up, snapping the button on my jeans back in place. I hated him in that instant, because he'd made me feel such insane pleasure and then yanked it away so quickly. He was impossible. I couldn't figure him out at all. What kept holding him back? I wasn't asking for a relationship and flowers and sweet words.

God, why did I always have to do this? Get involved in broken things that weren't mine to fix?

I was beginning to see that there was no fixing Caelan. He had been far too damaged and his scars ran too deep. Mine did too. Only I didn't show mine like he did. I didn't lash out. Or drink. Or do drugs.

But I hurt too.

Couldn't he see that I was as broken as he was and we needed each other? Why was he able to so easily ignore the powerful force twining us together?

"Get out!" He yelled, his hand whipping into the lamp on his bedside table.

My eyes closed and I flinched as the plug was wrenched the outlet and the lamp went flying across the room, smashing on the floor with a crash.

"Get the fuck out, Sutton!"

My eyes flew open as he grasped my arms, his fingers digging in to the point that I felt bruises forming. He shook me forcefully, so that my teeth clanked together.

He kept shaking me and I felt like a rag doll clasped between his hands.

"You're hurting me!" I screamed. "Let me go!" I wiggled. "Caelan! Stop!"

As quickly as he had grabbed me, his hands were gone.

His mouth parted with shock. His fingers thrust through his hair as he stared at me.

"I-I—" Words failed him.

His Adam's apple bobbed with a hard swallow as he backed away from me. "No, I couldn't," he whispered to himself and I had no clue what he meant. His eyes were haunted and he looked *scared*. I didn't understand what he had to be afraid of. Shouldn't I have been the one running and screaming? He'd assaulted me.

He kept walking away from me until his feet touched the tiled floor of the bathroom. He slammed the door shut and I heard a crash. I could only assume he'd broken the mirror.

I stood slowly, gathering my cat, my dignity, and my pride.

I would not let Caelan Gregory break me down. I was a fighter and I stood strong. Nothing scared me. Not screams. Not pain. And certainly not his temper. I stopped being scared a long time ago.

CHAPTER 10
Caelan

MY FIST STUNG where the tiny shards of glass penetrated the skin. I couldn't believe what I had done. I'd lost complete control of my mind and body. I'd been in plenty of fights, especially over the last five years, but I had never laid a hand on a woman like I did with Sutton. She hadn't shown it, but I knew I'd hurt her. What the fuck was wrong with me?

Trickles of blood dripped from my hand, down to the floor.

I stared at the shiny red rivulets, instantly transported back to that god awful day I couldn't fucking forget.

The blood had been *everywhere*.

Even now, I felt like I couldn't scrub it from my skin. It had seeped inside of me, poisoning my very being, and turning me into a monster. I wasn't sure if the transition had been immediate after their murders or if it had been gradual. I just knew that I wasn't the same person anymore. I'd been okay with that. But maybe, not anymore. Going after Sutton like that was a wake up call. Losing my shit wasn't cool. I couldn't rationalize it to myself. Things had gone too far, but I didn't see how I could stop.

I banged both of my fists, one injured and one not, against the porcelain sink. The harder I hit it, the worse the pain was. It filled me up, blocking out all thoughts. As long as the pain remained, I didn't have to remember what I had done to her.

Sutton was destroying the very foundation I had built my life upon after the murders. She was an earthquake, shaking down my walls and exposing the Caelan that had long ago been buried. I didn't want that Caelan to come back. He was better left dead. That Cael felt too deeply. He was weak.

Anger bubbled inside me, coming to a boil.

I lost all control.

I ripped the bathroom door open. It smacked against the wall hard enough to crack the tile.

Between Kyle and Sutton I was in a constant state of pissed off, it seemed.

I wanted to tear my apartment apart, rip it to sheds, so that it would resemble the state of my insides—a chaotic, uncontrollable mess.

I was spiraling out of control. I had been for a while.

But Sutton was my undoing.

I had known from the moment I stormed into her apartment, irritated about the noise she was making trying to hang those damn curtains, that there was something different about her.

I had tried to fight it.

God, I was still fucking fighting it.

I had pushed her away.

I had told myself to stay away.

None of it was doing any good.

She was a drug to me—one far more powerful than what currently ran through my veins. Those drugs shut me down. Sutton woke me up. The high was that much more intoxicating because of it.

I stared around me, breathing slowly. I needed to calm the fuck down.

I headed up to the roof. It was a safe place for me. I hadn't been up there since the night Sutton appeared and revealed that she knew about my family.

It was weird having her know.

Even more odd was the fact that she didn't look at me or treat me any differently than she had before.

To her, I wasn't broken glass that she had to tiptoe around lest she be cut.

Everyone else avoided me when I let my true nature show, but not her. She was a mysterious creature that I couldn't begin to fathom. Her reactions to dangerous situations were... non-existent. She didn't flinch or show any signs of fear.

Sitting on the edge of the roof, staring up at the night sky so full of beautiful clear stars, I decided that Sutton had been hurt too. There was more to her than I had even begun to know.

I sat on the ledge for hours.

For the first time in years, I wasn't thinking about my next hit or how much I could drink before I passed out. It was a peaceful feeling, but one I knew wouldn't last. I had to bask in it while I could.

Sutton

I SHOULD'VE BEEN sleeping.

I couldn't.

That wasn't anything new, but there was something different about it this time. It wasn't the typical feelings of insomnia—so tired but unable to fall asleep.

No, my current lack of restlessness could be described in three words.

Caelan Fucking Gregory.

I kept replaying what had transpired between us.

His hands had felt good on me—too good, actually.

Our chemistry was explosive and undeniable. A dangerous and toxic combination. His reaction had proven that I needed to stay away.

I never did what was good for me, though. The things I'd been through in my life had turned me into a masochist and I always came back for more. Hurting, whether the pain was physical or emotional, I thrived on it. I was as sick as Caelan, but in a different way.

We were two broken souls, desperately trying to put ourselves back together.

But not everything could be fixed.

"Are you okay?" Daphne's voice broke through my thoughts.

I shook my head, jolting myself back to reality. We were at the same restaurant we'd had lunch at before. I swirled a fry in ketchup before forcing myself to nibble on it.

I wore a floppy black hat on my head to block the sun. It also provided excellent coverage from Daphne's curious gaze.

"Yeah, I'm fine. I didn't get a lot of sleep." More like none at all. After lying in bed for hours, unable to fall asleep, I'd gotten out of bed and showered. Then I asked Daphne to lunch, which turned out to be a very bad idea.

"Is this about Callie?"

"Who?" I finally looked up at her.

"I thought that would get your attention," she smirked. "Callie, Cael, Caelan, Gregory, whatever you want to call him," she winked, taking a sip of wine, despite the fact that it was the afternoon and hardly an appropriate beverage to have at this time. She propped her elbow on the table and her head on her hand. "I assume something happened with him to make you so mopey. You're not normally like this."

I narrowed my eyes. I was *never* rainbows and sunshine, so what the fuck did she mean I wasn't normally like this?

As I stared her down she started to squirm. "Okay!" She surrendered, throwing her hands in the air. "It sounded like he was throwing stuff in his apartment, which is normal, but then we heard his door open and close while the banging was still happening. That's *not* normal." Chewing on her lip, and looking around, she added, "So I kind of opened the door and caught you going home."

Shit.

I was caught now. I couldn't lie.

"Caelan doesn't sleep with anyone that lives here," she eyed me with a deadly gaze, but I refused to wither, "Lord knows I've tried to get that man to do me. He might be fucking crazy, but he's hot as hell, and I'd *love* to know what he's hiding under all those dirty paint stained jeans. So spill, girl," she leaned forward, trying to create a bubble around us.

"There's nothing to tell," I insisted, lowering my sunglasses to hide my eyes.

"You slut!" She cried, causing heads to turn our way and more than one man to take notice. Look the other way fellas, these goods were not for sale. "You can't fuck the resident bad boy and not give your best friend the details! I *need* to know!"

I sent withering glares at the people staring. God, couldn't people mind their own damn business? My sex life, non-existent at that, was not news worthy information.

"Nothing happened!" I insisted. Glaring at a man that had started over to our table, I held up a hand and said, "Look elsewhere bud, no free blowjobs here." His steps halted and he returned to his table of buddies, all of who laughed hysterically at how I shut him down. Seriously, I didn't know why if a dude heard a girl say the word sex, they suddenly thought she was down to do it with anybody. Honestly, men could be the stupidest creatures on the planet.

"You're such a liar," Daphne whispered. "You can tell me! Please?" She pouted, clasping her hands together. "Who am I going to tell? Until you came along I didn't have any friends."

That caused me to pause. "What?"

She frowned, looking down at the table and tracing a grain in the wood. "Well, yeah, you're like my only friend. Besides Frankie, but he's my brother so he has to like me, therefore he doesn't count."

"You have friends."

"No, I don't," she shook her head sadly. "I have acquaintances but not friends," she shrugged, like as if the topic didn't bother her, but I could tell it did.

I instantly felt bad for being such a lousy person and not spending more time with her. She was clearly lonely.

I reached over and placed my hand over hers in a comforting gesture. "Well, it's a good thing you have me then. I'm so fucking awesome that you don't need anyone else."

She grinned at that and I felt a little lighter.

Eating another fry, I said, "We didn't have sex—" She opened her mouth to cut me off but I shushed her. "*But*," I added, giving her a warning look, lest she interrupt me again, "there was some touching involved."

She almost fell out of her seat at that. "You or him?

"He touched me," I whispered, and found myself squirming—not typical behavior for me.

"Oh. My. God." She fanned herself dramatically, licking her lips. "What I wouldn't give for that man to touch me."

I eyed her.

"What?" She laughed. "Every girl has to have at least one bad boy in her life, and that man has *dangerous* written all over him. Was it good?" She asked, bouncing in her seat a bit. Clearly she wasn't lying about not having friends, because I didn't see how this was the least bit interesting.

"Mind-blowing," I replied, taking a sip of water to cool down my racy thoughts.

"So," she frowned, "what happened to set him off? Giving a girl a so-called mind-blowing orgasm doesn't seem like a reason to start breaking stuff."

I stiffened in my seat. I couldn't tell her that he hurt me. I'd been lucky that today was slightly windy and I was able to wear a light sweater to hide the bruises without anyone being suspicious. I shrugged. "You know him better than I do. He gets mad for no reason a lot."

"That's true," her lips puckered in a frown, "but it sounds like things were getting pretty steamy, so what's there to get pissed about? Oh! Could he not get it up?!" Her eyes lit thinking she'd guessed right.

I was too busy snickering over her high schoolish term. Finally I regained control of myself and said, "Trust me, he was primed and ready." I wiped away a tear of laughter.

"Oh," her face fell. Eventually she shrugged. "You're right. He is weird."

Luckily she dropped the conversation after that. Unfortunately for her, I was no longer quite there with her. My thoughts were circling around Caelan. I couldn't understand why he had stopped and lost his cool like that. Sex was sex, right? I knew from the other people living there that he was hardly a monk and since I'd moved in, I'd heard at least two women sneak out of his apartment. I didn't like to think about that though. I knew that whatever this sick, twisted relationship of ours was, that it wasn't exclusive. Or even really a relationship at all, so he was free to sleep with whomever he wanted. It sure didn't keep him from messing with my sex life though. He'd had no problem hauling me over his shoulder cave man style and taking me away from Memphis. Cock blocker.

"I have to go," I stood suddenly, grabbing my purse and slinging it across my body.

"O-okay?" Daphne said, her brows furrowing together.

Slapping some cash on the table to cover my meal, I said, "This was great. We should make this a weekly thing or something."

Before she could reply, I jogged down the deck steps and onto the street.

I knew exactly where I was headed.

The bar was only a few blocks from the restaurant, so it took me no time to get there. I busted inside, striding forward purposefully. I was a woman on a mission and no one better dare try to detain me.

"Ma'am we're not open yet, you can't be here," a waiter warned, trying to grab my arm to steer me away.

I skidded around him, ignoring his calls to stop.

The guy I searched for looked up at my approach.

"Sutton, what are—"

I climbed on a barstool, leaned forward, and grabbed him by the collar of his shirt.

I had to know.

It was wrong to use Memphis like this, but I could barely remember our kiss the other night, and I needed to see if kissing him was as good as kissing Caelan.

His eyes widened as my body splayed over the counter and my lips connected with his.

The other workers in the bar, preparing for opening hours, cheered at the display. I wondered if they'd be cheering if they knew the real reason I was kissing Memphis so passionately.

My tongue grazed his lips and his mouth parted, his teeth tugging lightly on my bottom lip. The kiss was certainly hot enough, and I did feel *something*, but nothing like the storm that raged through my body with a single look from Caelan.

I pulled away, ending the kiss. My forehead was pressed against his as we both panted. Finally, my head rose and I pressed a tender kiss to his forehead. "I'm sorry," I whispered.

His eyes closed and a shadow of pain flickered over his face.

He knew.

"I'm sorry," I repeated once more before I pushed myself off the chair and ran out of the bar, impervious to the looks of bewilderment from the staff.

I had used Memphis to make a point to myself. It had been

wrong to drag him into the middle of this, but I had to be sure.

I was upset at myself for my silly, spur of the moment, decision, but I'd had to know if I was imagining things with Caelan.

With my head ducked, I walked at a brisk pace back to the apartment building. I was a woman on a mission.

I jogged up the steps of the building, my purse thumping steadily against my thigh—thumping just as hard and fast as my racing heart.

I was taking the bull by the horns here.

I stopped outside Caelan's door. My pulse jumped in my throat, a nervous and irritating flutter.

He'd stopped things this morning, but that wasn't happening anymore.

We were destined. Yeah, I knew that totally sounded ridiculous, like I was under some kind of love spell or some other shit. But it was true.

I believed that in our lifetime, there were certain people we were meant to meet and that they could have a profound effect on our lives if we let them.

Okay, that sounded even sillier than the fact that I believed we were destined.

Clearly, I'd been watching too many fucking Hallmark movies.

Taking a deep breath, I poised my hand above the wooden door, preparing to knock. Only this time, unlike that moment several weeks ago, I wouldn't be running away.

I was seizing the moment... well, more like *making* the moment.

I squared my shoulders, and knocked.

CHAPTER 11
Caelan

I RAISED THE bottle to my lips, taking a drink of the bourbon. I tilted my head to the side, studying the painting in front of me. I frowned, anger simmering inside me. I couldn't seem to get her lips right. They weren't as plump looking on canvas as they were in person. I also struggled to get the right shade of blue for her eyes.

For so long, unless it was a commission piece, all I had painted was Cayla. Her image haunted my nightmares—a beautiful life cut so short. I carried an immense amount of guilt for her death. If one of us was going to die, it should have been me. Not her. She was so bright and happy, the kind of person who lit up a room. Compared to her, I was nothing but a poser. Looking back on that night, I'd wished a million times that I had let her come to The Cove with me. I could have spared her a tragic fate with one decision. I knew deep down, in what was left of my twisted and tortured soul, that if Cayla had lived, I wouldn't have descended into this never-ending spinning hole of madness. She wouldn't have let me.

But the image in front of me wasn't of Cayla.

It was Sutton.

Now, she was the one overtaking my nightmares. She was

always there, hovering in my mind. Day or night. I had become addicted to her, and I'd barely had one hit. She was a dangerous and powerful toxin for my bloodstream, because she didn't dull me. She made me feel alive.

I wiped the paint that had gotten on my fingers onto my jeans.

I swirled the brush in the cup of water, contemplating what I needed to do to fix the lips and get them right.

A little voice in my head told me I could always "study" them up close and personal.

I wanted to agree with the voice in my head, but after how I'd hurt her this morning I doubted she'd ever come near me again. My true colors had *really* shown through then. I hated to admit it, even to myself, but it had scared the crap out of me. I hadn't been myself, not at all.

A knock on the door sounded, jostling me from my thoughts. I took another swig of the bourbon and set it down along with the paintbrush.

Sighing, I raked a hand through my hair.

Unlike normal, I wasn't angry at being disturbed. I was too tired.

I opened the door and my mouth fell open as I looked down at the petite, raven-haired, woman standing in the hall.

My heart picked up speed in my chest.

The last time I'd felt this... overwhelming need and desire for someone was the night I lost my family.

Somehow, Sutton was resurfacing the Caelan I'd believed to be long gone.

I stood there, looking at her, unsure of what to do or what to say.

She made the decision for me.

She pushed past me, into the apartment and stood there. "Close the door," she said calmly. "I have some things I want to say to you and you're going to listen."

I nodded, surprising her and myself, by listening to her

instructions. I closed the door and stood in front of her. A few feet separated us. It was like she needed space to speak.

Taking a deep breath, she dropped her purse on the ground, as if it was weighing her down and she needed to rid herself of it before she sank.

"I'm not scared of you," she said slowly. "I know you think I am after what happened, and if I was a sane person I would be, but I'm not sane Caelan. I've been through things too," tears pricked her eyes but she dammed them back. "You and I, we *need* each other. I know you feel it too, so don't you dare try to fucking contradict me. I know we're fucked up and neither of us is whole," she bit her lip, "we're a *mess,* Caelan. Together we're like a damn war. I know in a war there are casualties, but fuck it if I don't want to try." She took a deep breath. "I *know* I should stay far away from you, but I can't. I know you think you're nothing but a druggie and a bad person, but you're not Caelan! There are a lot worse people out there than you!" She spoke with such passion that my heart clenched in—what was that? Pity? Remorse? I couldn't understand it. But I realized that Sutton had been through a lot. Maybe, just as much as me. Spreading her arms out, she continued, "Anyone can be a villain, but not everyone can be a hero. I'm not asking you to change for me, or to even date me," she laughed humorlessly. "I just want you to stop denying this undeniable cosmic connection we have. It's real!" She stomped her foot. "It's fucking real." Her voice softened and her breath gusted between her parted lips.

I didn't know what to say.

But I knew what to do.

I'd been alone for so damn long, and God if it didn't feel right with her. She *got* me. No one else did.

I closed the gap between us, claiming her lips with mine.

She was stunned at first, but slowly her body responded to mine. A small moan escaped her and it sent all the blood in my body rushing south. I cupped the back of her neck in one hand, and the other pressed against her slender waist, causing her body to melt into mine.

Her fingers curled in my hair, wrapping around the small strands, as she surrendered herself to me.

I knew then, that she was mine for the taking.

To cherish.

To worship.

To bend.

To break.

I would take whatever she gave me, for as long as she'd give it, until I fucked it up.

Her arms draped around my neck and she jumped slightly, her legs wrapping around my waist.

I grasped her slender hips and carried her to my bed, lowering her down with my body over hers.

I kissed her deeply, with all the heart I had left inside me, which granted, wasn't much. I only hoped it was enough to be worthy of this beautiful, stubborn, woman.

My fingers skimmed under the edge of her sweater, tickling her sensitive skin. She let out a small giggle.

"Ticklish?" I whispered, my lips brushing against her neck. It was the first time I'd spoken since she'd shown up.

"Shut up," she growled, low and throaty and sultry and delicious and everything I didn't fucking deserve.

Her lips claimed mine once more. Yes, claimed.

She fucking owned me from that moment on.

Sutton

I COULDN'T BELIEVE this was actually happening.

I must have walked into a strange, alternate universe.

Either that, or he was really drunk and high and wasn't aware of his actions.

There was no way he was entirely sane right now.

Caelan could not possibly be about to do this.

But he was.

We were.

The faint taste of alcohol clung to his lips, but it wasn't overpowering, so I knew he wasn't really drunk. It just seemed like the most reasonable explanation. He always put up such a fight that I wasn't expecting him to give in so easily.

I guess he knew just as well as I did.

We were fucking inevitable.

A train wreck that you couldn't avoid.

"I know you deserve someone who will make love to you," he whispered, then bit into my neck, "but sweetheart, I fuck."

My neck arched in pleasure at the sharp sting of pain.

Gathering my senses, I mustered up my strength and used it to rise up and push him down, so that I was now straddling him. Rolling my center against his, I smiled down at him, my hands splayed against the soft material of his shirt.

"Good, because that's the only way I like it."

His eyes rolled back into his skull and he let out a pleased groan. "We're a match made in heaven."

Pushing his shirt up his chest and pressing kisses to his stomach, I said no more.

Now was the time to let carnal pleasure overtake everything else.

He sat up, removing his shirt and tossing it somewhere behind me. I did the same with mine.

I lowered, my hair swishing around us.

His hands skimmed up my back, hovering over the clasp of my bra, but he didn't undo it. They continued a lazy journey to my front and I couldn't help but moan against his mouth when his hands tested the fullness of my breasts.

I had never wanted anything more than I wanted to be owned by Caelan Fucking Gregory.

His lips devoured mine, eating me alive in a deliciously slow torture.

Something told me I'd just sold my soul to the devil.

Certainly no one of this realm could produce such an otherworldly response from me.

Pulling roughly on the strands of his hair, I whispered in his ear, "Don't hold back." Then I bit the lobe, the pressure, no doubt border-lining on painful. I wanted him to know that I wasn't some dainty flower that he needed to be careful with. I was like him. A fucking beast, I just kept my inner monster on a tighter leash.

"I never do," he growled.

In a lightning fast motion, he had my bra removed and my breasts were bared to him. Staring down at him, I waited with baited breath to see what he'd do next.

He sat up, holding me in his lap.

His stare was intense and unwavering.

I knew that he wouldn't stop this time.

Whatever had made him halt this morning, that cloud of doom was gone. Right now, it was just he and I, and what our bodies could give each other. Our demons still hovered there, but for now, they didn't weigh us down. We were escaping.

His mouth closed around my breast, taking the nipple between his teeth. My eyes shut and my neck bowed back. My breath was embarrassingly loud, but I didn't care.

His tongue swirled around the tip and I moaned, biting down on my lip. When he looked up at me through hooded lashes, I knew he saw the lust in my eyes.

Kissing and nibbling his way down my chest to my stomach, his fingers found the button on my jeans. He slid them down my thighs, but since I was straddling him they didn't get very far. He was content with that though. His fingers found the edge of my panties. Pulling the fabric to the side, he slipped a finger inside. First one, and then two. I swallowed thickly. My heart beat rapidly and I lowered my head to the crook of his neck. I closed my mouth around the area where his shoulder connected with his neck, and bit down. Hard. A hiss escaped between his teeth.

I was branding him with my mark the only way I knew how.

Before I knew what was happening, I was beneath him and he had my arms pinned to the bed. A vein throbbed in his forehead, and he growled, "Be a good girl, Sutton, and *later* I'll let you be as bad as you want."

I stroked a finger over his heavily stubbled cheek, and then moved that same finger over his parted lips. "Promise?"

He didn't answer me.

With a jerk, my jeans and panties were gone, lost somewhere in his apartment. His clothes followed quickly. It was obvious that Caelan wasn't the kind of guy for much foreplay. Lucky for him, I believed it was overrated.

He grabbed a condom from the night table and slid it on.

He held my hips in a vice like grip, but didn't move. I tried to roll my hips forward, but his hold tightened painfully until I whimpered.

I was scared he'd changed his mind, and like earlier he was about to lose his shit.

I braced myself, my body tightening as I waited for him to slap me or do something. He had that dangerous look men got in their eyes just before they hit you.

But then, he surprised me, and his blue eyes softened.

Staring in to my eyes, he said, "Before we do this, I need you to promise me something." He shuddered, like it killed him to hold himself back from taking what he wanted and thrusting inside me.

"Anything," I breathed. At that point I would've cut myself and signed my name in blood. I wanted him inside me *now*.

"Whatever you do, don't fall in love with me."

That was an easy enough promise for me to make. I lost the capability to love a long time ago. I focused on the beautifully broken man in front of me.

"Promise."

Without another word, he slammed inside me.

My nails dug into his back, my mouth falling open as I cried, "Oh my God." It had been way too long since I'd had sex and my body was unaccustomed to the feeling.

Caelan didn't wait for me to adjust, which I didn't expect him to.

The pain gave me as much of a high as the sex did.

His forehead pressed against mine and he stared into my eyes in a surprisingly intimate gesture that I hadn't expected from him. I let my walls fall away so he saw what I kept hidden. He'd know that I was like him. The same, but different. I might not have had a substance abuse problem like he did, but my addictions were just as dangerous.

I was addicted to bad men, and Caelan was the worst of them all.

He was a drought, sucking the life from everything around him, and I was willing to let him take my very essence.

I never claimed to be very smart, but smarts ultimately had nothing to do with it. Life had fucked me over real good and turned me into the kind of woman who thrived off being hurt. I was the person others looked down upon and hated, because I wasn't normal.

I craved things that hurt me.

It was sick and twisted, but for me, it was an undeniable desire that had to be sated.

I scratched my nails into his back, my pleasure doubling as he hissed from the sting. There was surprise in his eyes when he looked at me.

He kissed the skin below my ear, then bit it, and finally his tongue flicked out to soothe the wound.

He repeated the motion over different parts of my body.

I loved every second of it.

His thrusts quickened and my fingers dug into his arms, urging him on.

Oh God, I needed this.

We'd been dancing around this for weeks and now that we

had finally connected, it was so worth the wait.

"Harder," I pleaded. "I'm not going to break."

He was more than happy to oblige.

He fed the monster inside me, the one that wanted to be punished.

I wasn't into anything hardcore, but I *needed* sex to be rough. Any other way and I was lost, not knowing how to function.

An orgasm tore through me and I shook all over from the force of it. I had never experienced anything as powerful as that in all my life. From the look Caelan gave me, he was well aware.

My hands braced against his shoulders, and sensing what I was about to do, he grabbed them and pinned them above my head.

"No," he growled, his hold tight and his glare withering.

I let him take control, but my stare was defiant. I wanted him to know that I wouldn't always let him have his way. I wiggled my fingers and smirked as his hold tightened.

He lowered, his lips brushing tantalizingly against the skin of my jaw. "Don't fucking move."

He covered my lips with his, quieting anything I might have said in protest. He hadn't needed to say anything. I just wanted to see that anger flare in his eyes. Yeah, I was sick, and I knew it. But like Caelan, I had no wish to change. I was happy being fucked up. It gave me something to live for when there was nothing else.

I bit down on his bottom lip and a low growl clawed out of his throat.

We were a sick pair, destined to meet and destroy each other.

His hold on my wrists continued to tighten as his thrusts increased.

I knew he was close to falling apart.

Since he had my arms pinned, I raised and lowered my hips to match his.

The moan that escaped me was loud and unrestricted. I wasn't holding myself back from him like I did with other people.

I was laid bare to him. Every flaw, physical and emotional, on full display. I let him have it all, because it wasn't a gift. It was a fucking curse.

He kissed me then, and I was surprised by the gentleness of it. The heavy stubble on his cheeks scratched me and I reveled in the burn—anything to hurt me, so that I didn't have to relive my past.

When it was over he pulled out and his weight disappeared.

My eyes had closed and I was unable to move.

A part of me, a big part actually, was embarrassed that I'd let him see that side of me. The less people knew about me, the better. But I knew Caelan wasn't the type to talk about other people's business. Besides, did he even have any friends? I thought back to the guy I'd seen him arguing with.

I was startled when my clothes were dropped on top of me.

I slowly blinked open my eyes to look at him.

He wasn't angry, but he wasn't happy either. His face was unreadable. He stood there with his hands on his hips, low hanging sweatpants barely clinging to his narrow frame.

"I won't tell anyone," he finally said.

"Wh-what?" I stuttered, thinking he was talking about what had transpired between us. If anyone was home, they had to have heard. We weren't exactly quiet. Okay, he was, but I definitely wasn't.

He swirled a finger at me, watching me with a calculated gaze. "Whatever it is that haunts you. I won't tell anyone. Your problems are your own. And I promise I won't Google you," his voice dropped low and anger flared. "Your business is your business. Whatever happens between us," he pointed at himself and then me, "I don't need to know what your problems are. *This*," he hissed, "isn't a fucking relationship. It's just sex. Okay?"

I couldn't help laughing hysterically at that. Did he really think I wanted more than that? The two of us could *never* work. People like us, we didn't fall in love, and we certainly didn't get a fairytale ending. Life wasn't perfect. I wasn't going to heal him and he wasn't going to heal me. Our problems were far bigger than something we could solve so easily.

"Okay."

And so it began.

CHAPTER 12
Sutton

WHEN I OPENED the door to leave Caelan's apartment, luck was not on my side.

Cyrus was also leaving his.

He saw me and stopped in his tracks, a slow smile spreading over his lips as he fought laughter.

"'Bout time," he finally said.

"Shut it, Cyrus," Caelan growled from behind me, his body suddenly pressed against mine as he glared daggers at our neighbor.

"What?" He shrugged innocently. "Everyone's known since she moved here that it was only a matter of time."

"Don't make me break your nose again!" Caelan seethed, trying to get around me so that he was the one facing Cyrus. I stayed put though, wanting to avoid a fight.

Cyrus merely chuckled. "Go for it. It makes me even more ruggedly handsome and the ladies love it. It makes them think I'm a badass," he winked at me.

"Or," Caelan said between clinched teeth, "it makes them think you're a pussy who can't throw a punch."

Cyrus shook his head, his dark hair blocking his eyes for a moment. "Wow, Cael. Never knew you could get so worked up over a female leaving your apartment. Guess she really is special. Wish I could get a taste," he cackled as Caelan tried to lunge for him once more.

Whistling, Cyrus left, tossing us a wave over his shoulder before he descended the steps.

"I hate that guy," Caelan glared, his knuckles turning a ghostly white where he grasped the doorframe.

"Doesn't everybody?"

He grumbled something under his breath.

Now that the coast was clear, I headed across to my apartment.

I felt Caelan's gaze on me and I held my breath as I waited for him to say that this could never happen again.

When I swung the door open, he said, "See you later."

I turned around to look at him, but he was already gone and I was met with a closed door.

"You're in a good mood," Emery remarked when I breezed into Griffin's a quarter till five, so that I could hear him sing and we could get dinner. Despite the fact that I'd only gotten an hour of sleep once I returned home from Caelan's I had more energy than I'd had in a long time.

"Sex will do that to a person," I joked, dancing past him and onto a stool. It felt weird to be here and not working.

He followed and took the seat beside me. "Whoa, missy, you can't say something like that and leave me hanging." He kept his voice low so no one else heard, but with the crowd gathered we could shout and they still wouldn't hear us.

I turned to face him. "What? I'm not giving you the details if that's what you think."

He rolled his eyes. "Trust me, I don't want them. Memphis?"

I shook my head.

His eyes widened in surprise. "Who then?"

"I'm not telling."

Emery pondered for a moment. "It was your neighbor, wasn't it?" I turned away guiltily and he clapped his hands together. "I knew it!"

"You know nothing," I grumbled, resting my head on my hand.

He laughed heartily. "Whatever makes you feel better, Sunshine."

I groaned at the ridiculous nickname, but said nothing about it. I was still hoping it would wear off.

"You're up," Griffin said, patting Emery on the shoulder as he passed us.

Emery wiggled his eyebrows and I couldn't help but laugh. "Are you ready to be amazed?"

"More like bored out of my mind," I laughed.

He rolled his eyes and stood. "Whatever. Come on," he nodded his head towards the back where the stage was. "You can't see the show if you stay out here."

I followed Emery and since there wasn't an empty table, he grabbed an unoccupied chair and moved it to the corner. "Sit," he commanded.

I did as he said, mostly because people were staring and I was too damn happy to make a scene anyway.

The couple on stage finished their duet and Emery took his place, an acoustic guitar slung over his shoulder.

He introduced himself and the crowd clapped.

He started to sing and I was surprised by his voice. It was husky and warm and gravelly in places. I didn't recognize the song he sang and I realized it was an original piece. I hated to admit it, but I was wowed. He had talent—too much talent to be stuck here serving people coffee and making food. He needed to be out there in the world trying to make his dreams come true. I resolved to tell him as much when we had dinner.

As he sang, his eyes closed, and I knew he *felt* the music. There was so much passion and feeling in his words and the way he sang them.

I felt a single tear tickle my cheek and I reached up to wipe it away, hoping no one had seen.

The last note hung in the air and Emery's eyes opened.

Clapping ensued and I sat there, mesmerized. There was so much about him I didn't know. It felt wrong to call him my friend. I knew I needed to get better about letting people in. I had closed myself off so long ago that I didn't know how to open up. The people I had trusted, despite being good people, had abandoned me when the truth was revealed. I rubbed the scar on my arm, a nervous habit I had never been able to break.

"You okay?" Emery asked, hopping from the stage.

"Yeah, I'm fine," I forced a smile.

He looked at me skeptically but didn't press the issue, for which I was thankful.

With a hand barely touching the small of my back, he led me away. "I'll be right back," he nodded towards the Employee Only door and lifted his guitar slightly so I'd know he intended to put it away.

I waited by the door for him. Griffin kept a careful eye on me and I wondered what he was seeing. Did I look as broken as I felt? My good mood had gone south in no time.

Emery appeared, smiling crookedly. "Dinner, m'lady?"

I rolled my eyes. "As long as you're paying."

He bellowed a laugh at that. "They have a name for people like you," he whispered in my ear as he held the door open for me to walk out.

"And what would that be?" I forced a smile. I was determined to have a fun dinner with my friend and regain my good mood. Maybe I'd even get to see Caelan again later. Although, I really did need to get some sleep.

Chuckling, we walked side by side, as he answered, "You're an opportunist."

A genuine laugh bubbled out of my throat and it felt good. "Hey, someone's gotta be," I countered.

His smile was easy as we walked through town. I didn't realize where we were going until it was too late.

I wanted to speak up and tell Emery that this was the last place I wanted to be, but I knew he'd tell me I was silly and parade into the bar anyway.

My heart raced in fear at possibly seeing Memphis.

After our last kiss and my muttered apologies, I knew things would be beyond awkward between us. I'd been hoping to avoid this.

Emery led me to a high top table in the corner. Like a gentlemen, he pulled the stool out for me to sit.

"Thanks," I told him.

Sitting down across from me, he said, "This is dinner as *friends*, just in case you think I'm trying to woo you." He winked and I couldn't help but smile.

"If you were trying to woo me, it wouldn't work," I assured him.

"And why is that?" He picked up a menu, scanned it for a few seconds, and put it down. His hands clasped together and he leaned towards me.

"I'm immune to charm," I stated, pretending not to look for a certain copper haired man.

"Bullshit," he chuckled, smiling crookedly. "Between your neighbor and Memphis I'd say you're definitely not immune."

A single brow crawled up my forehead as I eyed him. "And how do you know that it isn't *my* charm that's working?"

"Touché," his laugh vibrated around us.

A waitress appeared to take our drink order and I decided I better figure out what I wanted to eat.

The fact that we were where Memphis worked had caused my appetite to disappear, but I knew I better order something.

I decided to get the grilled chicken sandwich and hoped the

waitress hurried back. The sooner she took our order, the sooner our food came, and that meant the sooner I could haul ass out of here.

However, there was no avoiding Memphis.

"Emery. Sutton," he turned to me, setting my glass of water down, and his smile wasn't nearly as friendly as usual but it certainly wasn't hostile.

I squirmed in my seat. I knew I needed to talk to him, but now wasn't the right time. Well, there would *never* be a right time. I knew I was going to have to apologize for the kiss and its purpose. Memphis wasn't dumb. He'd figured it out. But he deserved to have me say it.

He walked away and didn't look back.

"That was interesting," Emery remarked.

"Don't start hypothesizing," I warned him.

His hands rose in the air in mock surrender. "I'll keep my thoughts to myself," he mimed zipping his lips.

Our waitress finally returned to our table, looking frazzled. "Sorry about that. Can I get you something to eat?"

We each placed our order and she ran off once more.

I figured since Emery liked to meddle in my love life that it was time I returned the favor. "So," I used my straw to swirl around the ice, letting it clink against the sides of the glass, "do you know Daphne?"

"Daphne Hart?" He questioned, and I noticed a slight tick in his jaw.

"Yeah," I narrowed my eyes, watching him carefully.

"We grew up next to each other," he shrugged.

"Mhmm," I nodded. There was more there than either of them said. I wanted to press him for more information, like he always did with me, but his eyes were far away and something told me to back off. That didn't mean I was done talking about her though.

"She's nice," I continued, crossing my legs, and sipping my water like this was a simple and easy conversation. I didn't want him to get scared and change the subject. "Did you two ever date?"

"Not really," he shrugged, tapping his fingers on the tabletop in a random beat.

"Care to elaborate?"

He was quiet for a moment, contemplating what he ought to say. "I don't think sneaking around when you're sixteen counts as dating."

I nodded, trying to figure out what to do with this information. He'd said more than I expected him too. "Do you think you'd ever date her now?"

He groaned, scrubbing a hand over his face. "I don't know. I'm not sure if there's really a spark there."

"Don't you think it's worth finding out?"

He looked away from me, a muscle in his jaw jumping. Finally, he huffed out, "Why is this so important to you?"

"It's not." I sat back, the picture of ease. "I thought I sensed something between you guys."

"Well, you're mistaken."

His face was twisted with anger and irritation. I knew I'd pushed too far and I needed to let the poor guy off the hook.

"Excuse me, I need to use the restroom."

I slid from the stool and headed back towards the restroom area, but I didn't enter.

My real purpose for escaping was so I could locate Memphis.

He wasn't manning the bar and I didn't see him dropping stuff off at any of the tables.

I was about to give up hope when I spotted our waitress. I grabbed on to her arm before she could enter the kitchen doors.

"Do you need something?" She asked, pushing strands of hair out of her eyes.

"Uh... I'm looking for Memphis."

"Oh," she frowned, "are you a friend?"

"Something like that," I muttered.

She pondered for a moment, nibbling on her lip. Looking

around, she said, "I'm not supposed to do this, but come on."

She led me through the kitchen and out a back door. "He's on break. You can usually find him down there somewhere." She started to close the door and leave me outside, but stopped. "Please, don't tell anyone I did this."

"Of course not," I assured her.

"Thanks," she flashed a relieved smile.

I walked past the dumpsters and trash bags. I finally found Memphis sitting on the concrete with his arms dangling over his knees.

He took a deep breath as my shadow caressed his body.

Slowly, he looked up. I wasn't prepared to see the hurt in his eyes. I was so shocked by it that I couldn't even speak. He saved me the trouble. "Hi."

"Hello," I squeaked. Why did I have to go and make things so awkward between us? Memphis was a good guy. He was the guy every girl dreamed of ending up with. He was kind and sweet. He had a steady job. He was funny. He was everything I wasn't ready for.

From his point on the ground, he tilted his head and looked up at me. "I assume you didn't just come out here to say hello. If that *is* the case, you've done that, and you can leave now." His words may have sounded harsh, but they really weren't, and they were less than what I deserved. He spoke them softly, with no hate, just a resigned bitterness.

"No," I finally spoke, "that's not why I came out here."

"I didn't think so," he looked back down at the ground.

"I want you to know that I'm really sorry for what I did."

"For using me?" He flicked his copper colored hair from his eyes. "Because that's what you did."

"I didn't use you, not the way you think," my tone of voice took on a pleading quality. I wanted him to understand that I wasn't as callous as he believed. "I do like you, Memphis."

"But there's someone else," he stated. "I wish you would've told me, instead of lying and telling me that you didn't have a boyfriend and—"

"I didn't lie. I don't have a boyfriend. Things are complicated."

"So, yesterday... the kiss...?"

He was going to make me say it. "I... I... Oh God," I turned away from him, not sure if I was prepared to tell him my true fucked up thought process.

"Just tell me. I'm a big boy. Why. Did. You. Kiss. Me?"

I startled at the feel of his hand on my shoulder, forcing me to turn around. I hadn't heard him get up.

I swallowed thickly, staring at the buttons on his shirt.

With his thumb and forefinger he forced my chin up.

"Look at me, Sutton."

My eyes flicked from the ground to his. It was beyond painful to look at him. His gaze was unwavering as he waited for me to answer him.

My breath left my lips with a shakiness that I didn't like. I was used to being strong, but right now, I felt anything but that.

I gaped like a fish for a moment, unprepared to say the words aloud. "I-I needed to know."

"You needed to know what?" His voice was soft with no irritation.

Tears coursed down my cheeks and he reached up with his large hands to wipe them away.

"That what I feel for him is more than what I feel for you." My words were barely above a whisper, almost covered up by the wind, but he heard.

His eyes closed and he let out a deep breath. "I knew it. I knew it the moment he hauled you away."

"I'm sorry," I said for the thousandth time, and something told me it wouldn't be the last time I apologized to Memphis. I leaned my forehead against his solid chest and sobbed. My gut told me that Memphis was the kind of guy I needed in my life, to heal and to ultimately love. But I wasn't ready to accept that. Caelan was what I craved.

His long fingers smoothed through my hair. "I'm sorry too." I felt his lips brush against the top of my head.

I don't know how long we stood there—too long I'm sure.

"I'm a mess," I mumbled when I pulled away, wiping mascara off my cheeks.

"Wait here," he commanded and disappeared back inside the building.

He returned a moment later with a damp rag. I held my hand out to accept it from him, but he wouldn't let me take it. "Let me," he whispered.

Tenderly he wiped the black streaks from my face. I didn't understand his kindness. I'd just rejected him. He should hate me. But he didn't. Memphis wasn't that kind of a guy.

He was one of the few good guys left in the world.

And I'd turned him down.

What the hell was wrong with me?

When my face was clean, he tucked the rag into his back pocket. "I'll see you around."

Before I could think of a reply, he was gone.

I couldn't seem to move and I knew with as much time as had passed that Emery was probably worried about me.

When I could finally manage to put one foot in front of the other I walked around the building and entered from the front, for fear of getting the waitress in trouble.

Our food had already arrived and Emery was almost done.

"Did you fall in or something?" He raised a brow and then his mouth slowly fell open. Pointing in the direction I'd come from, he asked, "Did you just come from the front?"

I nodded.

"Why?"

"It's none of your business," I grumbled. I looked around for our waitress and when I caught her eye I waved her over.

"Yes?" She questioned.

"I'm not feeling so well. Would you mind bringing me a box?"

"Sure, no problem."

"Thanks," I said, but she was already gone and didn't hear the words.

"Are you really sick?" Emery asked skeptically.

"I think so. My stomach," I mumbled.

I really did feel nauseous, but I knew I wasn't really sick.

"I'm sorry I'm such a sucky friend," I told him. "My treat," I pulled out a credit card and handed it to the waitress when she breezed by with the box.

"What? No," he protested.

"It's the least I could do for ditching you." I put the uneaten food in the box and stood. "Next time," I pointed at him, "you're paying."

With a laugh, he said, "Deal."

The waitress handed me my credit card and I signed the slip of paper.

Surprising Emery, I wrapped my arms around him in an awkward hug. "Thank you."

"For what?" He asked skeptically. "I didn't do anything."

"You're my friend." I paused, then added, "I hope."

"Of course," he replied quickly without any hesitation.

"I know that being my friend is hard. So, thank you," I repeated.

I left before he could say anything else.

I went home to my empty apartment, which seemed even emptier thanks to my cold and shriveled heart, and cried.

CHAPTER 13
Sutton

I'D CALLED IN sick to work three days in a row.

I wasn't sick though.

Unless depression counted as an illness.

Well, I guess it did.

Telling Memphis the truth had cut me deeper than I expected it to. I guess I really did have feelings for him.

I knew it was nothing compared to the all-consuming inferno I felt for Caelan.

Speaking of Caelan, I'd seen a lot of him the past few days while I ditched my adult responsibilities. There hadn't been much talking involved, which I was perfectly okay with.

Now, though, I was alone once more. Had been for hours.

I didn't like being alone.

When I was alone, my thoughts wandered far too much. The bad things became real again. It hadn't been my brightest idea to move so far away from my home, from my *life*. But that life had been a lie. Nothing about it was *real*. While my family and the friends I'd grown up with lived in Dallas I was really more alone there than I was now.

Sitting on the counter sipping the scalding black coffee, I realized that while I wasn't happy, I was far better off now than I had been.

Healing was a slow process, and while I hadn't quite begun, I was almost there.

I sipped on my coffee, letting my thoughts carry me away. When the coffee was gone, I set the cup in the sink.

Like a small child, I kicked my legs against the cabinets.

I was bored and Caelan had been MIA for twelve hours now. I knew he was holed up in his apartment working, he'd told me such when he kicked me out. I didn't want him to think that now that we were sleeping together that he held some kind of power over me. So, I reached for my iPod, hooked it up to the speaker and scrolled through my songs. I finally settled on one, turned the volume all the way up, and pressed play.

I couldn't wipe the evil grin off my face when only seconds later there was a knock on the door.

As I hopped off the counter and strode across the room, I couldn't ignore the rush zinging through my veins.

When I opened the door, he stood there with his arms crossed over his chest in a sleeveless shirt and jeans. His lips were turned up in amusement. He didn't appear to be angry, almost like he'd been expecting me to do this.

"You know," he swirled a finger in the air, "if you wanted me to come over, all you had to do was ask." Crossing his arms over his chest, he added, "Although, you do seem to love making a lot of noise to get my attention."

With a laugh, I grabbed ahold of his shirt and yanked him inside. The door closed with a slam. "I want to make even more noise," I whispered, my lips brushing against his collarbone. Standing on my tiptoes so I could reach his ear, I continued, "And I need your help to make this noise."

"Is that so?" He chuckled, his fingers digging into my hips.

"Mhmm," I kissed his neck.

"I guess I could take a break."

"You can most definitely take a break," I assured him, unzipping his jeans.

"Eager, are we?" He grabbed ahold of my arms and pulled them away.

I pouted in frustration. "Always."

"You know," he eased my shirt up and my eyes fluttered closed as his fingers grazed my bare stomach, "I haven't ever had sex with the same woman as much as I have with you."

My eyes came open and I smirked. "Mr. Gregory, should I be honored?"

"Absolutely," he winked and I was surprised that he'd just cracked a joke. I didn't know he had it in him.

I lifted my arms and he completely removed the top, his eyes perusing my body.

I couldn't control the shiver that ran down my spine at the look he gave me—like I was the most delicious dessert he'd ever seen laid before him and he was starved.

His fingers brushed lightly down the curve of my jaw. My lips parted as a breathy sigh escaped me. I cherished every moment he touched me, because a part of me feared it might be the last. "You're different."

He was right. I was different, but he had no clue how true that statement was.

I'd already shown him too much—my inner pain and suffering—and I had no plan to open up anymore.

Secrets were kept quiet for a reason. They had the power to destroy worlds.

I wrapped my arms around his neck and kissed him. In part, to keep him quiet, and because the man was the best kisser I'd ever had the pleasure of locking lips with.

He backed towards the bed and I went with him.

He sank down on its surface with me straddling him. This was the first time I'd had him in my bed. It excited me, like having him here cemented whatever this fucked up arrangement of ours was.

"My bed. My rules," I whispered.

His soft laugh rumbled through my body. "Whatever you say, sweetheart."

Grinning like the cat that ate the canary, I splayed my hands over his chest and looked down at him. "Get ready for a wild ride. I promise it'll blow your mind."

Caelan

I WASN'T ONE to linger after sex. It wasn't in my nature. I didn't want to cuddle and do the whole, 'let's talk about our feelings' thing. Who the hell has time for that bullshit?

But what was I doing?

Lying in bed with my arms wrapped around Sutton and my face buried in her neck. I never wanted to leave and that fact scared me. I was a man of many addictions. Drugs. Alcohol. Art. And now I could add Sutton to that list.

"You're not leaving," she stated.

I knew she was surprised. It was evident in the tone of her voice.

The other times, I'd made it clear that when we were done she was to leave. She didn't seem to mind. Now, here I was in *her* bed and I was the fucker that didn't want to move. Go figure.

"Do you want me to?"

Please say no.

"No."

She traced a finger down my chest and my eyes closed from the pleasurable touch. Her nail dug in and I hissed.

"That hurt." I glared at her.

"It was meant to," she giggled, now lightly caressing the area she'd just scratched. Like I needed illegal substances to numb my memories, Sutton needed pain to drown out whatever haunted her.

Feeling bold, after all, she knew about my family—nosy bitch—I asked, "What happened to you?"

She stiffened in my arms and started to pull away but I held tight. She wasn't going anywhere.

"I know something, or someone, hurt you. You know about my past," I growled, getting angry at the distant look on her face, "isn't it fair that I know about yours?"

"There's nothing to tell," she muttered.

"You're a really bad liar, Sutton."

She sighed heavily, her whole body shaking with it. I knew she wasn't going to say anything. I might not have been a good guy, but I knew how self-destructive it was to keep painful memories bottled so tight. It slowly ate you alive until there was nothing left but a rotting black hole that destroyed everything you came into contact with.

In a gesture that wasn't like myself, I laced our fingers together and held them up, marveling at how amazing something so simple could feel. Her skin was soft and silky, her hand fitting perfectly into mine. "Why don't you tell me how you got this scar?" I probed, determined to get *something* out of her. This wasn't me trying to get to know her. Not at all. This was simply one broken person speaking to another.

She swallowed thickly and I could practically see heart racing in her chest.

"Why do you want to know?" She whispered, staring over my shoulder at something so she didn't have to look at me. "I thought this," anger laced her tone, "*thing* we're doing, was just physical. Don't act like you want to get to know me when you really don't."

"Who's to say I don't want to get to know you." The confession tumbled out of my mouth before I could stop it.

Gathering the sheet up, she rose and her glare was withering. Her dark hair tumbled around her shoulders. "I call bullshit. Pretty much everything that comes out of your mouth is rude, I doubt you want to know anything personal about me. Just because we had sex doesn't mean you need to know everything about me."

I snorted, rubbing my hands over my face. She was a fucking pistol. "This has nothing to do with the sex, Sutton. Don't be so dramatic, it's unbecoming of you. Let's face it, you know way more about me than I know about you," I reasoned and her face began to soften with realization. "I don't even know your last name."

She stared down at the white sheet, wringing it through her fingers. "Hale."

"What?"

"Hale. My last name is Hale."

"Oh..." I smiled slowly. "See, that wasn't so hard, was it?"

"No," she admitted, frowning.

"And the scar?"

Her head snapped towards me. She didn't appear to be angry anymore. Just tired.

"Do you really want to know?"

"Yes," I reached for her hand once more, guiding my hand over the ridge of the scar. I sat up, and bent forward, placing a soft kiss against it. "I really want to know."

Her body shuddered. "I got it when I was a baby. There... there was a fire. My family didn't make it. I escaped with only this," she nodded down at the scar. "They died," tears pooled in her eyes, "and I escaped with a minor burn."

I didn't know what to do with that information. The fact that we had such similar pasts scared me. Maybe Sutton really did understand more about me than anyone else ever had, or ever could.

"I don't even remember them," she whispered, lying down once more and clasping her hands under her head. "I was too little." Breathing deeply, as if to calm herself, she said, "I have a picture of them. That's it. If I didn't have that I wouldn't even know what they looked like."

"What happened to you after the fire?" I asked. For the first time in five years, I was more worried about someone else's pain than my own. I didn't know what to make of this development. It was strange, to say the least.

"I was adopted by friends of the family. My grandparent's were too old to take on a baby and I guess no one else wanted me."

Her voice and eyes were full of sadness and I knew there was more she wasn't telling me. But I knew how much I hated it when people pushed me and I refused to do the same to her. One day, we'd both have to come to terms with the fact that the horrors that haunted us were never going to go away, and therefore we had to find a way to live with them instead of only coping.

CHAPTER 14
Sutton

"Not so fast, Sunshine."

Emery cornered me in the backroom. I tried to get by him but he crossed his arms over his chest and refused to let me pass.

"Emery!" I stomped my foot like a child, the stress of everything catching up with me, and therefore making me lash out.

"You've called in sick for four days, and after the way you fled our dinner the other night, I know something is going on with you. Spit it out."

"There's nothing to tell," I said in a calm, reassuring tone. "I wasn't feeling well."

"Something tells me this has to do with Memphis and your mystery lover," he continued, still blocking my path.

"Why are you so obsessed with my love life?!" I shouted. "It's none of your business! Stay out of it!"

Hurt flashed on his face and I instantly felt bad.

"I'm sorry," my voice lowered, "I shouldn't have yelled at you like that."

"But you did," he glared, a muscle in his jaw jumping. "I'm just *trying* to be your friend, but you make it really damn hard." He turned sharply, then stopped abruptly and spun around to face me. "By the way, Memphis is a good guy. I've known him for a long time and he'd never hurt you. Whoever this guy you're currently wrapped up in is, I can tell he's bad news. You've been together barely anytime and he's already turned you into a different person."

"Maybe it's just my true colors showing!" I spread my arms wide.

He shook his head, a smile that was hardly pleasant graced his face. "If that's the case, then I'm glad you cut Memphis loose."

"Why do you want us together so bad? What does it matter to you?" I hated that Emery's words were cutting me so deeply, like he'd plunged a knife in my chest and wiggled it around.

"It doesn't *matter* to me," he thrust his fingers through his dark hair and it stuck up in every direction, "but I can see that you're perfect for each other and it's fucking ridiculous that you're blind to it."

Smirking, I tried and failed to insert some humor. "You sound like a girl."

"Whatever, Sutton," he laughed humorlessly. "I'm done here."

My mouth fell open in shock as he pushed open the swinging door and left.

I sat down for a moment, unable to move.

Normally Emery's words would have gone in one ear and out the other. I did what I wanted and I didn't need someone else's judgment. But this time, it hurt to know that Emery didn't think very highly of me.

I pushed myself up, rushing to the restaurant area to apologize, but he wasn't there.

I looked around and around, but he was gone.

Griffin spotted me and grabbed my arm. "Are you looking for Emery?"

I nodded.

"He left."

I'd deduced as much.

"He looked upset," Griffin continued, "and asked for the night off. I called Angela, she'll be here in an hour."

Great.

Emery was pissed at me and I was stuck with Angela—at least I was on the day shift today, which meant we were busier than at night, and I could avoid her.

Knowing that work was exactly the kind of distraction I needed—from Emery, from Memphis, and from Caelan who'd managed to pry some information out of me—I grabbed my pen and notepad and settled into the monotony of taking and filling orders.

Caelan

I OPENED THE door and let Monique inside.

"Hello Cael," she purred, gliding her finger down my chest.

I grabbed her hand and placed it back by her side.

She was undeterred though. She was a pushy lady and I'd grown used to her advances. She was my best client though. She always requested a new commission piece. Despite the fact that her husband was rich, and she had kids, she was always eager to let me know that she'd be more than happy to pay me for other services. I was an artist, not a fucking male prostitute. I guessed every woman wanted to bang a bad boy.

She adjusted her very large, very fake, breasts and smiled.

"You're looking better than usual," she remarked, standing a bit too close for comfort.

"I'm not drunk," I stated, "although now, I'm questioning whether or not sobriety was the best decision for this meeting."

She let out a high-pitched cackle that made me think of a witch. Swishing her overly dyed blonde hair over her shoulder, she followed me over to the easel.

"You know," I started, "you don't have to come over every week to check on the progress."

"I know," she swatted playfully at my arm. She was laying it on thick today. "But I like to."

"It's annoying." Yeah, I said it, but it was true.

She laughed again, tossing her head back. I hated looking at her face. It was all bloated with that shit women put in their faces. What happened to aging gracefully? Did women really think men cared if they had a wrinkle? No matter our riches and possessions, we all get old and we all die. It's the way the world works.

"Oh stop it," she smiled, running her fingers down my arm. "I know you like my visits."

Shrugging off her touch, I pointed to the easel. "As you can see, it's almost done. You could've saved yourself a trip if you waited till I called. It'll be ready in a few days."

"Oh, nonsense," she waved a hand, "it's no trouble at all. The drive isn't that long."

It was over an hour. I knew, because I'd had to deliver a piece to her home once. She opened the door wearing nothing. I knew I should have severed ties with her then and there, but I didn't sleep with her and I was never going to sleep with her. Our relationship was strictly professional and no flirting on her part could change that.

"It's beautiful, Cael!" She gasped cooing over the painting of her dog.

Yes, I had stooped so low as to paint a fucking pug.

Well, I guess I did a lot worse things than paint a pug.

"Nugget looks so cute! You captured the emotion in her eyes perfectly!"

Who the hell names their dog *Nugget?* And emotion in the dog's eyes? Was she batshit crazy? It was a fucking dog! What kind of emotion did it have?

I didn't say any of that, though. I did my job and played along.

"Yes, the emotion. The love shining in her eyes has touched

my heart," I patted my chest, trying not to laugh at my ridiculous words.

"You're an amazing artist." She surprised me by wrapping her arms around me in a hug. I didn't return the gesture.

"Uh..." I muttered when thirty seconds later she hadn't released me. "You can let go now."

"Oh, right." She released me. Turning back to the painting, she said, "Do you think you could deliver it when it's done?"

Since she couldn't see me, I wasted no time rolling my eyes. After the last time, I wasn't going there again.

"Sorry, no delivery service anymore. You'll have to either come pick it up or pay for it to be shipped."

"Not a problem," her voice was husky and seductive sounding, but even in my worst state it had never done anything for me. "I'll drop back by and pick it up when it's ready. I already have something else for you."

"Of course you do," I muttered, unable to keep the words bottled inside.

"It's my goal to have my entire house covered in your art."

God, she was ridiculous. I would've thought after a year of this that she'd know by now that I wasn't going to sleep with her. I wasn't that desperate. Besides, she was probably fucking her pool boy and gardener and... the list was endless. A woman like this didn't just want one man to have an affair with.

"I'm sure your husband would really enjoy having watercolors all over his house."

Laughing, she said, "Oh, he doesn't care. He doesn't care about a lot of things," her voice dropped low. She stalked towards me and I suddenly felt like I was prey she was about to devour. Her hands found my chest and she tried to yank my shirt off. God, couldn't the woman take a fucking hint that I wasn't interested. I really wished I was drunk, because then I could blame my reaction on that.

I grabbed her wrists in my hands and squeezed as I pried her hands from my clothes. "Don't fucking touch me, Monique."

"Oh, come on." She was relentless, trying to kiss my neck.

"Stop," I growled, shoving her away. Her mouth fell open in shock as she stumbled back. She strap of her dress fell off her shoulder and she hastily replaced it.

"You need to leave." My voice was deadly calm. I wanted her out of my apartment, and I didn't care if she ever came back. Her behavior was ridiculous. "I'm not going to fuck you, so just get over it."

She stuck her nose in the air haughtily and strode towards the door—her five-inch heels clacking on the floor. Seriously, how did women walk in those?

She threw the door open and turned back to me. "I won't be needing your services anymore, Cael."

Surprise, surprise.

"You still owe me for this time," I told her, throwing my thumb over my shoulder towards the easel.

"I'll put your check in the mail." She straightened the skirt of her dress and fluffed her hair, before leaving.

I watched her go, and as I did, my eyes latched onto very vibrant, very hurt blue eyes.

"Sutton," I breathed.

Shaking her head, she stomped forward. I expected her to say something. Instead, her hand reared back and smacked against my cheek hard enough that my teeth clanked together.

It dawned on me then why her eyes had looked so hurt.

She didn't go across to her apartment, instead trekking towards the door that led to the roof—to *my* sanctuary.

I forced my fingers through my hair, an irritated groan coming out of my mouth. I didn't need to deal with these fucking female hormones. It's why I'd avoided a relationship forever. I warred with whether or not to go after her. I finally decided that I had nothing to hide and I didn't deserve her anger—unfortunately now *I* was angry. Between her reaction to seeing me with Monique and the psycho cougar pawing all over me, I was done.

I stormed up the stairs after her. The door to the roof slammed closed behind me. Her back was to me as she sat on the ledge and she flinched at the sound.

"Sutton," I growled.

"I have *nothing* to say to you," she said, bending her head forward as she looked at the ground below her feet.

"Well I have a hell of a lot to say to you!" I shouted. I didn't care if anyone heard us. Let them watch us make a spectacle up on the roof.

"Like what?!" She finally turned, and swung her legs around so she could stand. "The fact that you let that woman *pay* you for sex?! God, Caelan! I feel so fucking dirty now!" She rubbed her hands over her body like the taint of my sins clung to her.

"You have it all wrong!"

"Do I?" She tilted her head, glaring at me. I had never seen her this mad. Was it wrong that it turned me on? "It looked pretty straightforward to me!"

"Listen to yourself!" I pointed at her. "You're so fucking judgmental and you have no idea what's going on!"

"Then explain." Her voice softened and she crossed her arms over her chest. She wasn't going to go easy on me. "You have five minutes to explain yourself."

I wanted to turn around and leave. Stuff like this wasn't worth the hassle, but from the moment I hung those damn curtains, Sutton had me. Something about her was different and she'd managed to weasel her way in to my rotting heart. What I felt for her wasn't love, but an overwhelming need. She didn't judge me. She *got* me. And that's why I didn't leave and stayed to explain myself.

"She's a client—"

"See!" She exclaimed, throwing her hands in the air. "A client! As in a sex client!"

"No," I pinched the bridge of my nose, rolling up the sleeves of my shirt. "You know, you're making this entirely unpleasant. I don't owe you an explanation for my actions. I didn't do anything wrong. But here I am, trying to get you to see the truth and you won't fucking listen!" I yelled. I wanted to take her in my hands and shake her for being so stubborn. She infuriated me like no other. She reminded me of my little sister who'd gotten under my skin in the same way. Cayla always believed she knew everything, when really she knew nothing, and Sutton was the same way.

"Fine," she inhaled deeply. "I'll be quiet." She then mimed zipping her lips and locking them with a key, which she then pretended to toss over her shoulder for good measure. A little smirk twisted her lips and it took everything in me not to march forward and claim those plump lips with my own.

"Like I was saying," I forced myself to say the words, instead of giving in to what I wanted, "she's a client. She's commissioned several pieces of art from me." Sutton's mouth fell open into a perfect O of shock. "She's never and will never pay me for sex. I'd be lying if I said she hadn't tried. I may be a bad man, Sutton," I stepped forward, three long strides closing the distance between us, "but even I wouldn't stoop that low for sex and money or even drugs. I may be desperate, but I'm not pathetic."

Unable to control myself any longer, I reached up and cupped the side of her face in my hand. Her skin was silky, like the softest blanket you could imagine, and unblemished.

I didn't deserve her, not for even a moment, but our pain brought us together. That pain would also be our downfall.

She placed her hand over mine and turned her head so that she could place a small kiss on the palm of mine.

"I'm sorry. I jumped to conclusions and it was wrong of me," she whispered, her eyes hooded.

"You're right, it was wrong of you," I breathed, my other hand finding the nape of her neck. "I think you need to make it up to me."

She chuckled, her breath tickling the skin peeking out of the collar of my shirt. "And how do you expect me to do that?"

"Weeeeell," I drew out the word, "I've never had sex on the roof."

"And I've never had sex in a public place," she nipped on my earlobe, "I'm liking what you're thinking."

"I'm glad we're on the same page," I murmured, pulling her shirt off. I wanted her naked, like now.

We wasted no time undressing each other and when I sank inside her it was like coming home.

We were opposites in every way.

She was the Beauty to my Beast.

But somehow, together, we completed each other—each filling that desperate, aching, hole of loneliness left behind from trauma.

I knew that someone like Sutton, with a genuine heart, wouldn't be with a guy like me if she didn't have her own demons. I knew they ran deeper than the burn on her arm. She might never tell me, and that was okay, because I'd gladly take the *now* that I had with her. It wouldn't last forever. People come and go from our lives all to often. I had nothing to offer her. She'd get sick of me and my addictions and leave eventually.

"Cael? Cael? Caelan?"

Her hand reached up to brush my cheek, forcing my gaze to hers. "Where'd you go?" She breathed.

Thrusting into her, I buried my head in her neck, and whispered, "I don't know."

"Harder," she pleaded, pulling on my hair.

I couldn't help smiling against her neck.

I grasped her hips in my hands and used it as leverage. Her mouth fell open and the moan that escaped her did crazy things to me. Sex had always just been sex to me. Nothing more. But with Sutton I found myself in tune to her likes and dislikes, noting the way her body responded to me. I wanted to please her and I'd never cared about a woman's pleasure before—only taking what I wanted and needed.

"Do you like it when I fuck you? Do you like having my cock inside you? Tell me you like it, Sutton. Tell me," I grasped her chin in my hand and forced her to look at me.

"I fucking *love* it," she breathed, raking her nails over my back.

Our mouths sealed together and she moaned against me. Her neck arched and my hand found the curve where her neck met her shoulder.

She grasped my biceps, her tongue twining with mine.

We were both mad with pleasure.

Her body pulsed around me and a groan tore from my throat. No one had ever felt as good as Sutton. It was like she was made for me. With most women, once was enough. Sometimes I did go back for seconds. But with Sutton, I knew I'd never get tired of feeling and hearing her.

Her nails scratched against my back once more and I knew they'd leave a mark. I wasn't blind to what she was doing. She wanted to make me hers, so that others, like Monique, would stay away. I wasn't sure how I felt about that, but I wasn't asking her to stop. I didn't want to be her boyfriend any more than I believed that she wanted to be my girlfriend, but I didn't want to see her with anyone else either. That probably made me a sick bastard, but I didn't care. For the last five years I'd taken what I wanted and not cared what kind of damage it caused, and now, I wanted Sutton more than anything else. I was more addicted to her than anything else. Dangerous? Yes. Unavoidable? Yes. Potentially explosive? Definitely.

Together we were a fire that couldn't be contained, but once we were extinguished we'd never be the same.

She pushed me onto my back, straddling me. Sutton liked to be in control even more than I did.

"Stop thinking," she lowered, her hair creating a shield around us, "just feel."

Feeling with Sutton was hard. I was scared of what she stirred in me.

She rolled her hips against me and finally all thoughts flew out the window.

She raked her hands down my chest, and then placed small

kisses to soothe the sting.

I took her breasts in my hands, kneading the fullness. God, she was perfect.

"Mhmm, that feels good," she moaned when my thumbs brushed against her nipples, so I did it again. Her back arched as her breaths quickened. Her core clenched around me and I knew she was coming. "Oh, fuck! Caelan!"

I loved it a bit too much when she said my name, but when she screamed it like it was a fucking prayer? I completely and utterly lost it.

"Caelan," she panted my name, coming down from her high. "Oh my God."

I couldn't hold back any longer. "Sutton," I growled her name.

She collapsed on top of me, our damp bodies clinging together. I wrapped my arms around her, burying my face into the curve of her neck.

I wanted to melt inside her and get lost, so that none of my past ever existed. I wanted to be able to start fresh and release the strings tying me down, but I wasn't there yet. Maybe one day, but it was still too hard and I needed to escape.

CHAPTER 15

Caelan

I LAY ON the ground, between the graves of my family. Lately, I'd been coming here more often. I found solace in the eerie quiet of the cemetery. It soothed my wounded soul being close to them. I couldn't bring them back, but I did have the power to never forget them, and that was something.

I reached out and plucked a withered piece of grass from the ground. Summer had left and fall was upon us.

I twirled the blade of grass between my fingers, staring up at the blue sky and the clouds floating by.

I wondered if that was what heaven looked like—bright, happy, warm, and full of promise.

I knew I'd fucked up royally and there would be no peaceful afterlife for myself. I'd never be reunited with my family. I was destined to burn for my sins. A part of me was angry about that, but I knew I deserved it for how I'd acted, how I still acted, after their passing. I'd destroyed my family's name instead of honoring it. What kind of person does that? Me. That's who.

Looking back, I knew I should've accepted help after they died. A counselor would've been able to help me move past their deaths and cleanse myself of those last memories of them. No one should ever have to see the people they love slashed open like a fucking sacrifice.

I had wished so many times that I died with them, so that I didn't have to deal with this pain.

I'd forgotten a long time ago what it felt like to be happy.

The emotion held no meaning for me anymore.

To be happy, you have to care, and I cared about nothing.

"That's not true." Cayla's voice floated through the air.

"What do you mean?"

"You care for Sutton," she whispered, like she was afraid I'd get mad. Which I did.

"No, I don't. You don't know anything!"

"I know more than you think, Cael." She said, and it was almost like she was alive again, looking at me like I was the silliest thing she'd ever seen. I missed her so much. I missed them all. I would give anything to have one more day with them. To tell them I loved them and I missed them and that they were the best family any one could ever ask for, and that I was sorry for not realizing it sooner.

"You have to let people in if you want to get better. Open up, Cael. Share your pain. It's okay. Let her see it all." I swore it felt like someone tapped my chest, right where my heart lay.

I placed my hand on the spot.

"And what if it scares her? What if my darkness swallows us whole?" I asked.

"Then it wasn't meant to be, but you accomplished something by trying," she mused. "If you do nothing but fear rejection, you'll never do or try anything."

"I hate that you're smarter than me," I smiled, crossing my arms behind my head.

"I'm dead, I see and know everything, so of course I'm smarter."

"How do I know I'm not just hallucinating your voice?" I questioned.

"Maybe you are, maybe you aren't. I guess it's up to you to

decide what you believe."

"I miss you." My voice was barely above a whisper, painfully choked out. "I miss all of you so much. It hurts so much having you all gone."

"I know, Cael." Her voice sounded sad. "We miss you too."

I closed my eyes swallowing thickly. Listening to her voice, I tried to envision what a twenty-one year old Cayla would have looked like. But I couldn't. I could barely remember what any of them looked like. Time had slowly erased my memories of them. The most vivid recollection I had of them was when I found them... like *that*. While I'd forgotten everything else, that was one thing that refused to leave. I wished it would. I'd often woken up from a nightmare feeling like their blood was caked into my skin, seeping into my pores. No matter how raw I scrubbed my skin, it was there. Some things never left.

I took a deep breath, trying to remember something from before, but all that existed was the after.

As I slowly drifted to sleep there in the cemetery, the memory of the day I had to bury them resurfaced.

Was it possible to have a heart attack at eighteen?

I was no doctor, but it sure felt like I was having one. The pain in my chest was unbearable, like a heavy weight sat atop it.

My breaths were loud and people kept staring.

I knew I looked like a zombie. My hair was limp, my skin was gray, and even in a weeks time I'd lost so much weight that if a heavy gust of wind surfaced it would blow me over.

I was a mess.

Staring at their coffins, all three lined up in a row, I felt the overwhelming need to join them.

I was alone.

I literally had no one.

I was drowning in my grief, trying to stay afloat, but I wanted nothing more than to sink beneath the surface into oblivion.

"Hey," Kyle said, walking up and standing beside me. "You okay?"

Why did everyone keep asking me that? How could I possibly be okay?

"No."

"I'm sorry."

They kept saying that too. 'I'm sorry'. What did they have to be sorry for? They hadn't killed my parents and my sister. They hadn't taken a knife to them and ripped them to shreds, gutting them like fucking animals. If I ever found out who had done this, they'd suffer ten-fold of what my family did. I'd make them pay.

"Just stop," I mumbled, staring ahead. The clouds above were dark gray, the threat of a storm looming. How appropriate.

"What do you mean?" He asked.

I turned to my best friend. My grief and anger evident in my posture and facial features. "Everyone else is asking the same fucking questions. I'm sick of it. I don't need you doing it too."

He raised his hands in surrender. "Okay, I won't."

I turned back to face the caskets.

People were crying and chatter abounded.

"Such a tragedy," someone said.

"Can't believe something like this would happen here." Another piped in.

"I heard the son was a suspect."

I felt eyes boring into the back of my skull.

I bet most of the people here didn't even know my family. They were just curious about the murders that had taken place in their own backyard.

"Shut up!" Kyle yelled. "What the hell is your problem?" He turned to face the group of gossiping women behind us. I didn't turn to see their reaction. I didn't care. I knew people thought I'd killed them. After all, there was more evidence pointing at *me having done it than a stranger. The police hadn't been able to find anything left behind by the killer—oddly enough, that was what kept them from pining the murder on me. Without a murder weapon, they could only speculate as to what happened. I knew some of the officers, as well as the community, believed something had made me snap and I'd done it. Innocent before proven guilty was a bunch of bullshit. Everyone always thought you were guilty before evidence showed otherwise.*

I grabbed Kyle's arm. "Leave it."

"No way," he shrugged off my hold. "Apologize," he glared at the woman.

"Sorry," I heard her squeak from behind me.

I didn't acknowledge her. People would believe what they wanted to believe, and I wasn't going to waste my breath trying to prove them other wise.

Slowly, people started to leave as the service ended.

I didn't speak at the funeral. I couldn't. Talking about them in the past tense didn't feel right.

The cemetery emptied and only Kyle was left by my side. He was a better friend than I deserved.

"You should go," I said.

"Cael—"

"Go!" I yelled. "I need to be alone right now."

Kyle heaved a sigh. "Fine."

His steps faded away and I was finally alone.

My knees gave out and I sunk to the ground. Tears drenched my cheeks. I had never cried so hard in my life. With each painful sob, my gut clenched. I clutched at the grass, dirt getting under my nails.

As I watched the caskets being lowered in the ground a scream tore out of my throat.

This was goodbye.

They were really and truly gone.

This wasn't a nightmare I was about to wake up from.

Real life fucking sucked.

"You should go." One of the workers told me as others spread tarps over the open graves. "It's going to storm soon. You shouldn't have watched this anyway."

I didn't say anything to him, but I refused to move.

Once the graves were covered the men disappeared.

I leaned my forehead against the ground, my sobs shaking my whole body. It was the first time I'd cried since they'd died. I'd been unable to until now—and now my emotions spilt forth like flood.

I felt raindrops hit my neck. They picked up speed and soon I was soaked and my clothes became muddy where I knelt against the ground. It was like the sky was crying with me, mourning the loss of three good people who died before they were meant to.

The trees in the cemetery shook from the force of the wind and my body quickly felt like it was turning into a popsicle. I was so cold, shivering uncontrollably, but I couldn't leave. Not yet.

The moment I left, it would be like I had finally acknowledged that they were really dead.

Like a small child I believed if I wished hard enough that this wasn't real someone would have to listen to my pleas and grant my desperate request.

Lightning lit up the sky and thunder cracked—the sound overpowering my choking sobs.

I tore at my hair.

I wanted to die.

I didn't want to have to live without them.

It wasn't fair.

"Caelan?"

"Go away!" I screamed at Kyle. I should've known he had waited for me.

"I'm not leaving. Not until you do."

He sat down beside me and I turned my head to see him

drawing his knees up and draping his arms across. His wet hair stuck to his forehead as he looked ahead. "I know you believe you're alone, but you're not."

He was wrong.

I was alone.

No one could understand what I was going through. They couldn't grasp the pain that ripped through my body with every second that I was alive and they were dead. Sure, people tried to get it, but they couldn't.

I didn't say any of that to him, though.

As days turned to weeks he, like everyone else, soon realized that I would never be the same.

I awoke with a start. I couldn't seem to catch my breath. I buried my head in my hands, trying to forget what I'd remembered. I knew it was stupid, but I couldn't help wishing that there was some magical device that would allow you to erase the things you didn't want to remember, and keep the things you did.

I stood slowly, looking around the empty cemetery.

No one else was here.

There hardly ever was anyone here.

The living feared the dead because they represented an all too present fate for themselves. Therefore, they avoided cemeteries, like the place alone was going to cause them to drop dead.

As if I wasn't already weird enough, I found peace here.

The dead weren't nearly as judgmental as the living.

"Ha! I'm totally judging you!"

"Cayla," I groaned.

"Seriously, get your shit together."

I frowned.

"I know you don't think you can," she continued, "but you're wrong."

"I've fucked up everything, Cayla," I said, staring at her grave. "How can I possibly fix this mess now?"

"By not talking about it and *doing* it," she spoke. "Take that first step, Cael. Do it. Not for me. Not for Sutton. But for *you*."

I took a deep breath. "I'll try."

I was already doing better than I had in a while. I was drinking less and I hadn't used any drugs in a few days—when in the past I couldn't go a few hours without a hit.

"That's all I ask."

CHAPTER 16
Sutton

THE SUMMER HEAT melted away, replaced by cool winds and the warm colors of fall. Looking out my window, I watched the red, yellow, and orange leaves swirl from the trees down to the street below where they were then scattered by passersby and traffic.

Autumn had always been my favorite season. The crisp cool air always made me want to bundle up in my most comfy clothes. The colors of this time of year were beautiful—so warm and inviting, a direct contrast to the cool greens and crisp blues of summer. Even the smells of fall were better, like pumpkin spice coffee.

The curtains began to shake, momentarily directing my attention away from the window.

"Brutus!" I yelled, grabbing up the cat and cradling him in my arms. "You can't climb the curtains! You'll hurt yourself!"

The cat just peered up at me like I was crazy, which was probably true since I was talking to an animal.

With Brutus still cradled in my arms, I continued to watch the leaves swirl around. Something about them practically hypnotized me.

Soon though, it wasn't the leaves that held my attention.

Light blond hair caught my eye and my eyes followed the

man's quick gait. His head was bowed as the wind tousled his hair. He bundled his coat tighter around himself and blew on his hands for warmth.

He'd been gone for a while. He disappeared a lot. I always wondered where he went, but despite my nosiness I didn't try to follow him. I figured he was off buying drugs or something and that was information I didn't want to be privy to. My gut told me that he went somewhere else, though. I knew I should ask—bridge that invisible gap that divided us and kept us from opening up about the ghosts that haunted us.

I watched him until he disappeared inside the building and then I finally pulled myself away from the window.

I set Brutus on the ground and he jumped on the couch, peering at me innocently like he hadn't just been about to use up one of his nine lives with his acrobatics.

I opened the door and leaned against the jamb.

Caelan's head snapped up, his eyes connecting with mine, as he topped the steps.

He smiled playfully and I was struck by just how amazing his smile was—even when I knew it was slightly forced.

"Spying on me?" A single brow rose on his forehead as he stopped a few feet away from me.

I shook my head. "You wish."

His eyes narrowed. "So you're what... getting some fresh air? I think you have to go outside for that."

A small laugh escaped me. "No, I was looking out my window at the leaves."

"At the leaves," he repeated. "That seems rather boring."

"Says the man who stares at a blank canvas for hours on end until inspiration strikes." The more time we spent together, the more I learned about Caelan's quirks. One of which being, he couldn't start painting until it 'felt right'. Sometimes he'd stare at a canvas for only a moment before his hand would start moving, making the necessary dips, curves, and swirls needed to bring about the vision in his head. Other times hours would pass and

I'd eventually leave, bored out of my mind. I could never knock his talent though. He was incredible—the kind of artist you read about in fancy magazines and saw their art exhibited in galleries. I knew if Cael ever got his act cleaned up, he could do great things.

He shrugged, my words having done nothing to faze him. "Why don't I give you an art lesson?"

I gaped. I hadn't been expecting that.

"Uh..."

"Oh, come on, Sutton," he chuckled, "it's just a little paint."

I finally shrugged. "Okay, why not." The worst that could happen was he'd be turned off by my lack of artistic ability. Over my shoulder, I called, "Brutus, behave."

Caelan's laughter filled the hallway. "Do you always talk to your cat?"

Tilting my head I gave him a significant look as I shut the door. "At least he doesn't sass me."

I was surprised when a snort escaped him at my words. Unlocking his apartment, he waved me inside. "So, basically, you're saying that your cat is better than me."

"Yep. Buuut," I sing-songed, "he also tries to climb curtains and kill himself, so..." I trailed off.

"Who's a bigger pain?" He asked.

"Huh?"

"Who's a bigger pain?" He repeated. "Me or the cat."

"You. Definitely you," I replied, spinning through his apartment.

It was a lot cleaner now than the first time I saw it. Either he was drinking less or he was picking up the bottles. I *wished* he was drinking less, but I knew in my heart that he wasn't. There was no changing someone like Caelan. They had to make the decision to save themselves.

It did appear that he wasn't relying on drugs as much. At least not the heavy stuff. The other day when I'd been in his apartment, I'd discovered a needle in the trashcan, but I didn't mention it. Some things were better left unsaid. And there were still small tiny pin sized pricks in his veins, but not as many. That was a start, right? Or was I trying to delude myself into believing something that wasn't true?

"So... what am I painting?" I asked as he set up a blank canvas on the easel.

He shrugged. "I don't know. That's up to you to figure out."

"What if I want to paint a giant blob?" I tilted my head as he grabbed a stool and pulled it up the easel, then another.

"Then you paint a giant blob," he smiled, waving me over. "Art is subjective. Eye of the beholder and all that jazz. Paint what's in here," he pointed to my heart.

"What if it's not pretty?"

"The painting?" His brows rose as he looked at me quizzically.

"No," I shook my head. "What's in my heart."

His face softened. "There's no one here to judge you. I have no right and I wouldn't anyway. *This*," he waved his hand to encompass the apartment, "is our safe place."

He held his hand out, waiting for me to place mine on top. When I did, he pulled me forward into his arms.

I was surprised when a giggle passed through my lips. The sound of it was so carefree and happy. Genuine.

He pressed a quick kiss to the corner of my lips and directed me to sit down.

He grabbed a wooden board and started squirting different colors of paint on it. When he was done he handed it to me, along with a brush.

"And now you paint."

I let out a laugh. "Really, Caelan, I'm no artist."

His eyes darkened and his voice grew husky. "Then let me show you."

Grasping one of my arms, he reached around with his free hand and wrapped it around my wrist. His breath tickled my ear as he slowly guided my hand to dip the brush into orange paint. He then brought my hand up so the brush touched the canvas.

He directed the brush down and then released my hand. "See, you're painting."

"It's just a line," I stated.

"Ah, but it's *your* line."

"Technically, I think it's your line, since you helped," I remarked.

He chuckled and sat back on the stool, his hands resting on his knees. "You're over thinking it."

"I thought you said you were going to give me an art *lesson* as in *teach* me. So far, I'm not getting a lot of teaching."

"That's because I know you're too stubborn to ever listen to a word I say," he countered, a small smile playing on his lips.

"Then why offer?"

He chuckled, scratching at his stubbled jaw. "You're like a little kid. You know that, right? You always answer everything with a question."

"It's a gift," I winked.

"Come on," he rested his chin on my shoulder. "Paint something."

"Did you know that you can be annoyingly persistent?" I asked, arching a brow.

He didn't say anything, instead staring me down. I found myself squirming. "Stop looking at me like that."

"Like what?" Now it was his turn to ask questions.

"Like you want to eat me."

"Well," he grinned crookedly. "I will bite. But only if you want me to." With that, he lightly nipped at my shoulder.

"Stop," I lightly pushed him away and he went with a smile—one that almost reached his eyes.

It was like in the weeks we'd been together, he was getting better, and I was getting worse. I found myself frowning. I'd thought by moving here I could leave my past behind me, but it always has a way of catching up to you.

"Hey, are you okay?" He asked, brushing strands of dark hair off my shoulder and kissing the skin it exposed.

"No," I answered honestly. Before he could question me further, I started painting. I didn't paint anything in particular. Just a bunch of lines and colors blending together. While I was no artist like Caelan, it felt good to focus simply on what was in front of me. I was beginning to understand now why he did this. It took your mind off of things.

While I painted, he did everything he could think of to distract me.

"Stop it," I laughed, pulling away so that his hand fell from my shoulder where he'd been playing with the strap of my tank top.

"I can't help it that you're irresistible."

"You're the one that wanted me to paint, so why don't you let me paint."

"Fine," he grumbled, sitting back and watching me. It wasn't long until he pulled lightly on my hair.

"Caelan!"

Finally he left, retreating into the kitchen where he poured a bowl of Fruity Pebbles, added milk, and proceeded to eat.

The drug addict eats kid's cereal. Go figure.

"Want some?" He asked when he noticed me watching.

"Sure."

I tried and failed to hold in my laughter at the sight of Caelan pouring me a bowl of cereal. We'd come a long way since he busted in my apartment. I never would've thought we'd end up here. Life works in mysterious ways like that. I couldn't help feeling like I'd been meant to be here, in this place, with him. Maybe not forever, but for now, and I'd take that over nothing.

"What are you laughing about?"

"You." I covered my mouth in the hopes of suppressing my laughter, but didn't succeed.

"Me? What did I do?" He asked, rifling through a drawer for a spoon.

I waved my hand to encompass him standing there in the kitchen with two bowls of cereals. "This," I laughed. "It may only be cereal, but I never thought we'd be where we are now."

"What can I say?" He shrugged, dropping the spoon in the bowl and picking up the box of cereal. "You're very persistent."

"Me?!" I gasped.

"Yes, you," he chuckled, dropping some dry cereal into his mouth and crunching. "If I recall correctly you showed up here and practically mauled me."

I rolled my eyes. "Whatever you need to tell yourself so you feel better."

I had turned back to face the painting when I got pelted in the back of the head with something. "What the hell?" I gasped, noticing whatever I'd been hit with was now also stuck in the paint, as well as my hair. Peering closer at the object congealed on the canvas, my mouth fell open.

I whipped around, pieces falling from my hair, to face Caelan with an open mouth. "Did you seriously throw Fruity Pebbles at me?"

He snickered, batting his eyes innocently. "Me? No way."

Shaking my hair around me, even more pieces of multi-colored cereal fell from it. "Did you throw the whole box at me?" I asked, noting the significant pile of cereal now on the floor, as well as the bits stuck in the paint.

"Of course not. A man's got to eat." He promptly shoved another handful of cereal into his mouth.

I narrowed my eyes and chose to ignore him as I turned back to the canvas. I was almost done and I wasn't going to let his childish games distract me.

He sat down beside me once more and held out the bowl for me. I set the paintbrush aside so I could take it from him.

We sat side-by-side, eating cereal as he appraised the now paint splattered canvas. We were an odd pair, that was for sure, but we were far more similar than someone on the outside would ever realize.

"How bad is it?" I asked, when he had been too silent for far too long.

"It's interesting."

"That's code for, 'It's horrible.'" I mumbled around a mouthful.

He chuckled. "No, it's not horrible. It's..." He tilted his head, searching for the right word, "Abstract."

"I guess that's better than horrible," I shrugged.

"I wasn't expecting you to paint a masterpiece."

"So, you knew I'd suck?"

"That's not what I meant," he rolled his eyes, standing to deposit his now empty bowl in the sink.

When I finished my cereal, he took that bowl as well.

I looked over my shoulder at him, and the words tumbled out of my mouth before I could stop them. "Where were you?"

He looked up, his brows furrowed in confusion.

"When I saw you coming home, where had you been?"

He shook his head and one of the bowls crashed in the sink. Looking down, he braced his hands on the counter, shoulders taut.

"Sutton," he growled my name, a muscle in his jaw jumping. "I thought we didn't talk about personal things."

"I was curious," I squeaked.

His knuckles turned white where he grasped the counter. "Fine," he finally spat. "I'll tell you where I go—" I brightened but the feeling was short lived, "*but* you have to tell me something personal about yourself first."

Fuck. I should've known better. Of course he'd want something from me.

Was my curiosity so great that I could give up a part of myself to know something about him?

Yes. Yes it was.

"Fine," I relented.

"You. First." He growled. I was trapped. I had to tell him something now.

I swallowed thickly, my pulse jumping. I'd learned a long time ago not to let people in. Once people knew the real me, they didn't like what they saw. I decided to settle on something safe. "I moved here because I caught my boyfriend sleeping with my best friend."

"You're lying."

My eyes widened at the words he spat out so quickly after I told him something about myself he didn't know. "No, I'm not."

"I'm not doubting the truth in the situation. What I'm doubting, is that you moved here because of it." Tapping his fingers on the tile countertop, he said, "You know, I don't understand why you want to know so much about me, but you refuse to let me know anything about you. You've let me see," he stared into my eyes, recalling our first time together, "that you have things that haunt you, but you won't *tell* me about them. How is that fair, Sutton?"

"It's not like you told me about your past!"

His eyes narrowed to such thin slits that I was surprised he still saw me. "Only because you Googled me. Something tells me Google wouldn't procure any results on you, though."

"You're right about that," I muttered under my breath.

"You can tell me anything, Sutton. I want you to know that," he said, his voice and posture softening. "I wouldn't tell anyone. Anything you tell me, I'd take it to my grave."

I closed my eyes, my breath faltering as tears pricked my eyes. "It hurts so much," I confessed.

"I know. Believe me, I know."

And I knew he did. If I hadn't found out about his past on my own, he probably would've never told me. But then again, watching the way he was looking at me right now, maybe he would have.

"If-if—" My voice shook. "If I tell you *everything*," I put emphasis on the word, "then you owe me the same."

All the muscles in his body tightened and his teeth clenched. I saw a million thoughts flicker through his mind. "Don't you know everything already?" He countered.

In a calm tone, I said, "Hardly." Grasping his shirt between my hands, I rested my forehead against his chest. "I've never opened myself up to anyone, not completely at least. If I do this, I need there not to be any secrets between us. I think we both need someone who knows the whole truth and won't judge us." Looking up at him a sigh escaped my lips. "I think you're that person for me, I only hope you believe that I'm that person for you."

A shaky breath gusted out of his lips. "I don't know if I can," he cupped my cheek, "but for you, I'll try."

"That's better than nothing," I breathed.

We were both two entirely fucked up people, who'd been dealt a bad hand, if we couldn't trust each other with our sins then they'd stay bottled inside us until one day we exploded.

The one time I had sought help for the damage that had been done to me, the results hadn't been pretty.

I was going out on a limb here, trusting Caelan with my secret after being burned, but he deserved to know what he was dealing with.

He brushed a piece of hair off my shoulder, his fingers lingering against the bare skin longer than necessary. My eyes closed and years of pain and self-loathing flooded my body.

"Hey," he brushed his thumb over my lips and I forced myself to look at him, "it's okay. Take your time. This is hard for me too you know?"

"It is?"

He nodded. "The intensity of my feelings for you scares me more than anything," he confessed, forcing the words past his lips. "Not caring has become a way of life to me. I keep everyone at a distance." He looked up briefly, taking a deep and steadying breath before letting it out. "You successfully knocked down every wall I've built around myself." His hand settled at the nape of my neck, his thumb roaming in small, slow circles. "You make me want things a guy like me has no right to have." He swallowed thickly and tears shimmered in his eyes. Seeing a guy like Caelan this close to breaking down made my insides twist together. I itched to hold and comfort him, but I knew it was best to stay quiet and let him say what he needed to. "I know there might not be a future for us, I mean," he chuckled weakly, "we're kind of a mess, but right now *this*," he leaned his forehead against mine and lightly pressed his lips to my nose, "is enough."

My hands shook as I grasped the collar of his shirt. "If there was ever anyone I could trust with this, it's you."

"You can," he assured me, his voice soft—a direct contrast the harshness I was used to from him. "We all need someone in this world that we can trust with our darkest secrets. I didn't actually believe that until I met you. I didn't even tell you about my parents, and, well," he shrugged lightly, "it's not like I hide my struggles with addiction. Still, though, you never judged me. Not at all. Everyone else looks at me like I'm... tainted somehow. I guess I am," he let out a soft chuckle. "The way people look at me... it makes me feel..." he paused, searching for the right word, "dirty and useless. Like I'm *less* because I turned to drugs to erase my problems. People only see addiction. They don't see behind that, to what drove that person to destroy their life. An addict doesn't become an addict for the hell of it," he whispered, his eyes full of pain, "we all have a story."

There that word was again. *Story*. First Daphne, then Memphis, and now Caelan had used it to describe life. I truly understood what it meant now. People tend to only look at the surface and see what's there. If they look at a cheerleader, that's all they see. Someone happy, peppy, and smiling. They don't look further to notice the bruises on her arm in the shape of fingertips. If they see a kid shoplifting, he's just a thug. But maybe he stole that thing to take care of someone. We're all too quick to think we know everything and pass judgment when we have no right. Humans are selfish like that. We naturally think we know everything, when we know nothing. It's our fatal flaw and our ultimate downfall.

I stood slowly, shaking all over.

I blocked out all thoughts of possible rejections. After all, if we spent too much time thinking of rejection, we'd never accomplish anything.

I knew that this moment, right here and right now, could be my turning point—if I allowed the dreaded words of my haunted past to leave my lips. The thing about healing is it's hard. Really fucking hard. Impossible sometimes. But it's up to us to let it happen. Some of the worst scars we carry are from ourselves and our own self-doubt—we're our own worst critic and biggest bully. We tear ourselves down over things that aren't even our doing. It's pretty damn sucky. I blamed myself for what happened to me—still do. It's a natural reaction. If I had done this or that, then this wouldn't have happened. But it's not true. No one asks to be hurt. And I was hurt in one of the most dehumanizing ways.

I went to the place I always felt the safest—the window. Looking out at the world below, it was easy to pretend that what happened to me was nothing but a distant nightmare.

I placed my palm against the glass.

In the minutes since I'd left my apartment a downpour had descended upon us.

The rain beat against the glass, the sky a stormy dark gray, and the leaves blew around dangerously from the wind.

Caelan didn't say anything, but I felt him behind me.

He might have hurt me in the past, but I felt safer with him than I ever had with anyone else.

His presence reassured me and gave me the confidence to speak.

"You know I was adopted," I whispered, my throat catching. "I always knew I was adopted. It was pretty obvious," I shrugged. "I look nothing like my adoptive parents. They're good people and they loved me like I really was their daughter. I always felt wanted and cared for. There were times where I missed my birth parents, where I wondered what my life had been like if they'd lived..." I wet my suddenly dry lips with a flick of my tongue. "I wondered that a lot as I got older," I huffed. I watched the rain beat against the glass for a moment, marveling in how cold my hand had become from the rain-slicked surface. "They have a son, Marcus. He... never liked me, to put it simply," I laughed. "He wished I never came along and disrupted his perfect life. Suddenly, he wasn't the center of his parent's universe and he didn't handle it well. He was four years older than me." I tapped my finger against the glass and closed my eyes. *Tap. Tap. Tap.* "It started out with typical childish pranks at first. It didn't take long till they escalated." I swallowed thickly. "When I was eight he pushed me out of our tree house. I wonder if he hoped it would kill me," I snorted, shaking my head as a disgruntled smile settled on my lips. "I ended up with a broken collar bone. He told his parent's it was an accident. They believed him, of course, and I was too scared to tell them the truth. I thought if I did, they'd toss me to the side. After all, I wasn't their biological child."

I took another deep breath and turned away from the window. I sank down on the floor, drawing my legs up to my chest and wrapping my arms around them protectively. I wanted nothing more than to curl into a ball and roll away. I was good at hiding. It's what I'd done my whole life until... well, *until.*

"I slowly pulled myself away from them, from my adoptive parents. I thought if I didn't care about them, if I stayed away from family activities, that Marcus would eventually grow bored with terrorizing me. I was wrong," I mumbled as Caelan sat down across from me. He listened carefully to every word I said like it was precious. I was surprised by how intent he was. He didn't appear to be bored just... concerned. Caelan Gregory concerned? It was a laughable concept. My oh my how things had changed since summer.

"Marcus was very popular in school, and he always made sure that everyone hated me. I had no parents and then I had no friends. I was alone, just the way he wanted. With no one to trust and no one to talk to about my problems." I picked at the hole in my jeans to have something to busy myself with. "He made me hate myself. I thought about killing myself at least once every single day. The only thing that stopped me," I finally looked up at

Caelan once more, "was that then, I'd be letting him win. I couldn't give him that satisfaction." My lower lip trembled and tears began to leak out of the corners of my eyes. I wiped them away, my breath coming out shaky. "He took *everything* from me. Happiness. Love. Friendship. Hope. Even my virginity," I said the words steadily, waiting for a reaction, but he didn't flinch at my words. "When I was twelve years old, just a little kid, he held me down and he raped me. I cried, I screamed, I bit him. He didn't stop. He didn't care. And you know what he did?" I sobbed, unable to keep my emotions in check any longer. "He fucking *laughed* at me. He laughed! When he was done, he told me it was my fault that he had to do it and not tell anyone, because they wouldn't believe me and they'd hate me even more. So, I didn't. Not then. Not the next time. Or the next. I eventually lost count. I eventually stopped fighting him too. I gave in to what was unavoidable, because he'd already accomplished it—he destroyed my soul."

Shaking all over, I wiped my tears away, my hand coming away wet.

"I *dreaded* going to my room at night, just *waiting* for the knob to twist. I never knew when he'd come, so I'd lie there, staring at the door, praying that it didn't open. And when it did, my heart would stop. In those moments, I'd wonder why I hadn't ended my life yet." I let out a soft laugh that held no humor. "You were right when you said that staying alive is the punishment. It really is. Every day of my life was a fucking nightmare. There were so many times where all I could think about was the different ways I could end my life. I could hang myself, maybe even drown in the swimming pool, or jump off the roof. The possibilities were endless. But I never did it." I leaned my head against the wall, trying to regroup. "The rape went on for years, even after he went to college, when he returned home he was back at it. Sometimes," I closed my eyes, "it still feels like his hands are on me. I guess I have him to blame for my need for rough sex. He always hurt me, so having someone be... gentle... it just seems wrong now. I feel like I need to be punished over and over again. Sick, I know." Caelan watched me closely, but didn't say a word. I appreciated that. He was going to let me get it all out. "He turned me into this person that..." I paused, frantically searching for the words to describe myself, and coming up empty.

"You don't even know?" Caelan supplied, his voice no more than a whisper.

"Yes, exactly," I nodded. "If he hadn't hurt me, over and over again, I wouldn't be so fucked up. But then again... if he hadn't done that to me... I wouldn't be here right now."

Caelan shook his head. "Here isn't a very good place."

"I think it is."

He shook his head once more, muttering unintelligibly under his breath. Finally, he looked me in the eye, and said, "There's more."

Of course he wouldn't pose it as a question. He could see straight through me. I was always able to keep my thoughts and emotions in check—no one being able to see what lurked behind the depths, but Caelan he saw it all, even more than what I meant to show him.

"I... I finally got the courage to tell them... my adoptive parents and my boyfriend." I frowned, looking down at my hands that were clenched tightly into fists. "No one took it well. My parent's called me a liar and told me to get out of the house. My boyfriend, Brandon," I forced his name past parched lips, "he never looked at me the same after that. It was like I was suddenly... tainted or something. He made me feel dirty and like I wasn't good enough. We grew apart, but didn't break up. I don't know why," I snorted, shaking my head. "I loved him, I did, but I was never *in* love with him. I was too foolish to see the difference. I craved the stability a relationship provided, but we weren't good for each other. I was too damaged and he was too concerned with upholding his public image—because Lord knows he was a fucking prick behind closed doors. I would've left him, eventually, but catching him with my best friend was the final straw. I couldn't keep torturing myself over something that was never real." Tracing my finger along a groove in the wood floors, I continued, "So, I packed up my stuff, sold what wouldn't fit in my car, and left. I didn't tell anyone where I went. I didn't want word to get back to *him*."

Caelan nodded in understanding.

"My parent's haven't tried to contact me once since I told them. I guess I should have expected it. He is their flesh and blood. But it hurts, you know? They raised me as their child and when I finally worked up the courage to tell them the truth, they called me a liar and an attention seeker." I rubbed my fingers over the raised scar on my arm. "I *wish* I was lying about it. No one should ever have to go through something like that." Leaning my head against the wall, I said, "Everyone in my life who I should've been able to trust and believe in, has let me down. It really fucking sucks. But you have to deal with it."

Caelan was quiet then, and so was I. The only sounds that filled the apartment was the quiet whir of a floor fan in the corner and the symphony of our breaths.

I kept waiting to see the pity in his eyes or—God forbid—loathing. I hated myself more than anything. I didn't need other people to too.

Without speaking, he slid across the floor to sit beside me. One arm wrapped around me and with his other hand he coaxed me to rest my head on his shoulder. I was surprised by the comfort he offered. Caelan wasn't the lovey dovey affectionate type and we weren't a couple. But he knew I needed this.

Silent tears streamed from my eyes.

I always tried to keep everything bottled inside, but it could be really hard. Sometimes you had to let it all out.

"Do you ever hear from him?" Caelan finally asked.

"From Brandon?" I sniffled, wiping away the moisture from my cheeks.

"No," I felt him shake his head, "from Marcus."

"Oh."

"So, you do?" He prompted, gliding his fingers down my cheek. The touch caused me to shiver.

"Yes," I admitted. "He texts me all the time. I never reply, but it doesn't deter him. He's extremely stubborn."

"Why don't you change your phone number?"

I let out a sigh, nibbling on my lip with nervousness. I slowly tilted my head up to look at him. "I know it probably sounds silly, childish even, but I keep hoping that my parent's will call me and it'll all be okay."

"No," he breathed, his eyes heated with affection, "it's not silly. It's normal to hope for things—even impossible things. Once you lose hope, you lose everything."

"You're being oddly insightful," I muttered.

He chuckled, his lips brushing against my hair. "When you're so filled with anger and resentment, you tend to shut yourself off from everyone and everything. It allows a lot of time for *thinking*, so yes, I can be insightful."

"You know what I hate the most?" I whispered.

"What?"

"Despite the fact that they didn't believe me, I still love them and miss them."

"Your parents?"

I nodded to answer his question. "Isn't that dumb?"

"Not at all," he spoke, his voice barely above a whisper. "They're your parents, by nature you're going to miss them and love them no matter what."

"I hate myself for it, though," I admitted. "After the things they said..." I trailed off, shaking my head. I sat up straight, no longer using Caelan's body for support. "I should never want to see or hear from them again. But I can't help feeling like if my mom called me right now, and said she was sorry, that she believed me, I'd end up on a plane back to Dallas tomorrow."

I hid my face behind my hands, ashamed of my admission. I wanted so desperately to hate them, but I couldn't. That fact made me angry. I mean, I was certainly *mad* at them, but there's a huge difference between being mad and hating someone.

"Hey," Caelan said. "Hey," his voice grew louder and he grabbed ahold of my wrists pulling my hands away from my face. He was now crouched in front of me. I turned my head away, unable to look at him. I could barely *breathe*. I felt like I was suffocating—like the truth was killing me. Why had I thought this was a good idea? Why had I shared this with him? It was far too painful having it out in the open. Having him *know* changed everything, and we'd both be lying if we said it didn't. "Come here," he finally murmured. I didn't move. I didn't have to. He wrapped his arms around me and pulled me against his chest. We lay down together on the floor, wrapped in one another's arms. The smell of his soap comforted me and helped to still my racing heart.

"Shh," he hushed, his fingers tangling in my hair. "Shh, I'm here, Sutton. I'm here and I'm not going anywhere."

Sobbing, I clung to him—my whole body twined around his.

How was it possible that it hurt to tell the truth, but felt so incredibly liberating at the same time?

"It's okay," he whispered, his lips lightly pressing against my forehead in a tender kiss. I found my eyes closing and a soft contented sigh passed between my parted lips. It felt so good to be held and comforted—by Caelan Gregory of all people. He'd frustrated me at first, pushing all my buttons, but I'd known there was more to the addict across the hall. I was right. And he had a heart of gold—even though he couldn't see it. One day he would, though. I'd make sure of it. He wasn't all bad like he believed. Yeah, drugs and alcohol are some bad shit, and he could be downright abusive, but there was so much more to him than that. He wasn't mean for no reason. He was haunted, and when you have monsters hiding in your closet, it makes you lash out. That's why I understood him when no one else could. We were far too much alike.

"What happened to you—all of it—was horrible, Sutton," he

spoke after several long minutes of silence. "But you're not tainted because of it."

I breathed deeply, savoring his words like they were a delicious wine and my taste buds couldn't get enough. I slowly sat up, my hair falling over my shoulder to brush against the fabric of his thin cotton shirt. "You're not either, you know."

He breathed out roughly, his whole body shaking with the effort. "It feels like it. I feel like everyone is judging me, watching me, waiting for me to fuck up even more and do something irreversible." A frown marred his beautiful face. "Everyone gave up on me after they died. Instead of pushing me to get help, they thought I was beyond it, and let me be. They didn't try hard enough. And I know I shouldn't hate them for it, because it's my fault too, but I was just a kid."

"We both were," I whispered, crossing my arms and laying them across his chest where I then rested my head. We stared at each other, cataloging our features, and soaking in one of the rare moments where you were connected to someone who understood you. "Tell me about after they died," I whispered. "Please," I added, when his face hardened.

His eyes closed and his whole body shuddered as the memories resurfaced. I knew what it was like to remember things better left buried. Each time you recalled them, another piece of you died. I hated myself for asking such a selfish question—I should've left it alone—but I needed him to share a part of himself with me. 'Always so curious, Sutton,' my mom used to say. She was right. I had innate need to figure out and understand everything that confounded me.

He wet his lips with a quick flick of his tongue and his eyes opened once more. The pain that shown there was excruciating and I wasn't even the one that felt it. My heart broke further for Caelan Gregory. My body, my heart, and my soul ached to comfort him, but I knew that's not what he needed. Right now, he needed me to listen, because he was finally going to open up. We would no longer be two people using each other to fulfill selfish desires. We were crossing a line in to dangerous territory—one where our hearts would entangle and be altered forevermore.

"It was November when I lost them, and myself," he said the words slowly, swirling them around in his mouth like they were a foreign language. "Two weeks before Thanksgiving," he snorted humorlessly. "Since you Googled me," he looked at me pointedly, "I'm sure you know all the gory details. How I found them, like *that*," he paused, swallowing thickly. I saw his pulse jump in his throat and his whole body shuddered painfully once more. "There was so much blood, Sutton. It was *everywhere*. Sometimes I still feel like it's on me and I can't get it off, no matter how hard I scrub my body it's *always* there clinging to me, reminding me of what happened." A look of revulsion tore over his facial features. His chest rose and fell with a shaky exhalation. "Sometimes, when it should be quiet, I hear screams... and I can't help but feel like I'm hearing their last moments even though I wasn't even there." My hands fisted, the nails digging into the palms as I fought against the need to provide him comfort and reassurance. I knew he needed to get this out and there would be time for the other later—if he allowed.

"After they died... nothing else mattered to me," he whispered, staring up at the ceiling away from me for a moment. "I moved in with my grandparents after." He chuckled to himself, and then explained the reason for his outburst, "*After*," he repeated. "My life exists in *before* and *after*. How pathetic is that?" He struggled for composure, but once he gained it, he continued. "I retreated in to myself. I didn't care about school. Or going to college. Or friends. At that time I didn't even care about girls." He gave me a wry smile. "I fell in with the wrong crowd." Laughing again, he asked, "How cliché of me." Shaking his head, he bit his lip and struggled for words. "My grandparents didn't know how to handle me. My grandpa took the tough love route and my grandma... well, I think she was afraid of me. Kyle, my friend since we were in diapers, he never gave up on me even though he should have. He's tried to get me to go to rehab several times. The last time was a few weeks ago when you found me destroying my apartment. I was so angry that he couldn't understand that I *need* the drugs and the alcohol. Without it, the pain is all too real. It consumes me." He rubbed one hand up and down my back and used the other to scrub his face. "I often wish I could forget everything, but then that means I wouldn't remember my family, and do I really want to forget them? No." He answered his own question. "So, I'm stuck in this endless vortex of pain and suffering and hatred and it's all that exits."

"That's not true," I whispered.

"Isn't it?" He countered. "I've let it rule every facet of my life—changing all the plans I had for my life because I couldn't *deal*. I'm a weak and useless excuse for a human being."

"You're wrong, Caelan. So, so wrong. You're none of the things you think you are. Is the stuff you do bad? Yeah, it is. But the damage is reversible if you choose to fix yourself."

His lashes lowered to flutter against the high planes of his cheekbones. "I'm scared to make the decision to get help. This is all I've known for so long. I don't think I can function as a normal person. I've forgotten what it's like not to have the need to get high, or drunk to dull the pain, or to not be angry." His hands fisted. "There's so much anger inside me, Sutton," he continued, "that I can't feel much else. It runs through my veins all the time. I'm angry with the person who killed them. I'm angry with my grandparent's for abandoning me when I needed them. I'm angry with Kyle for caring too much. I'm angry with myself for letting it go this far. I'm angry at you because you make me *care*," his voice cracked. "And worst of all," tears shimmered in his eyes, waiting to spill over, "I'm angry at *them* for leaving me. How wrong is that? They didn't ask to die, and I'm mad at them for it anyway."

"I think that's a perfectly normal reaction," I commented.

"Is it?" An elegant brow arched as he looked at me. "It seems pretty fucked up to me."

I shrugged. "Yeah, it's messed up to harbor anger like that towards them, but I don't think there's something wrong with you because of it. I'm angry at my parents for not believing me, and angry that they were too blind to see what was happening when I was a child. But really, is it their fault? No. They chose to see what they wanted and believe who they wanted, and I could have gone to them at any time... maybe if I'd still been a child they would've handled things differently. I'll never know now."

He let a pent up breath whizz past his lips. "I'd give anything to have *one* more day with them. Just one. To tell them I loved them and I'm sorry that I wasn't a better son and brother. I have so many regrets and there's no magical do over button for life so I'm stuck with them."

With a slight chuckle, he added, "You know, they say to appreciate the little things in life. That is so fucking true. I miss all the small things from my old life. The sound of my mom and dad laughing as they made breakfast. Cayla singing in the shower. Our 'forced' family dinners where we each had to say two truths and a lie about our day, then guess which was the lie. I hated it all at the time, and now it's what I hold closest to my heart." Looking at me, he breathed out deeply. "I don't drink or do drugs to *forget* them, I do it to numb the pain *remembering* causes, because I never want to pretend that they didn't exist. If I don't remember, who will?"

"Oh, Caelan," I sobbed and finally gave in to the temptation to wrap my arms around him. He held me close, his fingers entangling in the strands of my hair as my face found the crook of his neck. I scooted my body as close to him as possible, wishing I could burrow inside him and drive away the darkness that plagued him. I didn't want him to have to hurt and suffer any longer. I knew the pain he felt was far worse than mine, and that was saying something. I knew how easy it was to dwell on things you couldn't change, how it ate you alive. It was a horrible existence and he deserved better. So did I.

"You wanted to know where I went today," he whispered, his chest vibrating beneath my ear when he spoke.

I nodded when he didn't continue right away.

"I go to the cemetery. I like to visit them," he admitted. "I don't want them to be alone and I..." He stopped himself.

"And you what?" I prompted.

"It's not important," he sighed, his fingers tightening around my hair to the point that it was almost painful.

I didn't press the matter, not wanting to push too far. After all, he had given me more information than I expected. I knew when to back off and now was one of those moments.

We laid on the floor, wrapped in each other's arms, for a long while.

I think we both needed to bask in the peacefulness of having it all out in the open. No lies and no secrets separated us right now. We were just two people, clinging to the support the other provided. I'd never had anyone like Caelan—someone I cared about so completely and so selflessly. He was a beacon of light in my dreary life. I knew he didn't see himself that way, but he was to me at least.

I couldn't help but believe that some cosmic force had pushed us together, making sure our paths crossed. I'd thought I was coming here for no reason, but now I believed that I had come here for him.

We were destined to meet and destined to heal one another.

I was more sure of that than I was of anything else.

His fingers lazily brushed up and down my arm. A light hum buzzed in the back of his throat and the sound of it calmed my racing heart.

After a while, he brushed his lips against my cheeks, the scruff adorning his chin chafing my skin. "Be my canvas." His voice was a husky whisper against my ear.

His fingers found the strap of my bra and he grasped it in his fingers before pushing it off my shoulder and trailing his soft lips down the side of my neck.

I found my body arching off the floor and a soft moan escaped my throat.

"Wh-what?" My voice shook, distracted by the feel of his tongue on my skin.

"Let me paint you," he kissed his way over to the other side of my neck.

"You want t-to paint a picture of me?" I asked, my head rolling back to allow him better access. "Didn't you already do that?"

"No, not *of* you. I want to paint you... your body."

My heart sped up in my chest at his declaration.

He kissed the swells of my breasts and I lost all coherent thought. Caelan knew exactly what he was doing to me, smug bastard. I had to admit, though, there was something deliciously erotic about the thought of Cael painting on my naked body.

The feel of the brush.

His fingertips ghosting along.

Maybe even his mouth and tongue.

I shivered at the very thought of it.

"Yes," I gasped breathlessly, my fingers finding the hairs on the back of his head and pulling his mouth to mine. His lips branded me, burning me all the way down to my toes.

He nipped at my chin, and murmured, "Mmm, this is going to be fun."

He stood and held out a hand for me, pulling me up and into his arms. He held me for a moment, his hands warm on my arms, as his nose glided along the curve where my shoulders met my neck. His tongue glided out with a quick lick. "You always smell and taste so good."

His fingers found the bottom of my tank top and he eased it off.

All of his movements were calm and calculated. Nothing like the frenzy I was used to when we collided.

"You're so beautiful," he breathed, his breath tickling my skin. I shivered as Goosebumps broke out across my body. I swallowed thickly, my heart racing even faster than it had moments before. I felt something in our relationship irreversibly shift in that moment.

For once, we weren't trying to hurt or punish or use one another. The air in the room crackled with barely contained passion. We were combustible and it would only take one small spark to burn us completely.

His lips found mine and we sank into each other. One of his hands held the nape of my neck, pressing me close, while the other rested against my now bare waist. His tongue glided leisurely against my slightly parted lips. Slow. Slow. Slow. Everything he did to me was with unhurried movements.

After confessing everything to him, I didn't feel the need for rough, uncontained, sex. We'd both been using it to mask things we didn't want to acknowledge. Now that it was out in the open, we didn't need that anymore, and God did it feel amazing.

"I want you, Sutton," he growled against my skin, "I want you so fucking bad, but I'm not good enough for you."

I understood what he meant. I felt it too. With our problems, we might understand each other, but could we ever really *love* one another? Could we provide the stability we ultimately needed? I wasn't sure, but right now I didn't care.

"You have me," I breathed.

"For now," was his reply.

His lips covered mine, and then descended down my neck to the tops of my breasts. His fingers found the clasp of my bra and he unsnapped it easily. It slithered down my arms and dropped to the floor.

He got down on his knees, placing small light kisses on my stomach.

My head fell back and my eyes closed—overwhelmed by the sweetness. *Sweet* wasn't a word you'd typically use to describe Caelan or me, and definitely not together, but right now, that's what it was. I'd never been okay with sweet. Marcus had ruined that for me, just like the death of Caelan's family had ruined it for him. Right now, though, it was what we both needed. We had exposed ourselves in more ways than one—and neither of us ran.

My eyes popped open when I felt something cool touch my skin—a shiver shaking my whole body. I lowered my head to see his finger drawing an intricate lace-like design on my abdomen with purple paint.

At the feel of my stare, he stopped, his eyes flicking up to meet mine. My heart tightened in my chest at the look he gave me. No man had ever looked at me like that... like I was perfect and unflawed. I reveled in it.

He kissed the skin just above my naval and went back to painting. He continued the design around my back and then up my spine. I swept my long hair out of the way, so it now shielded my chest.

I felt his lips press against the back of my neck and a small sigh of pleasure escaped me.

I never knew it could feel so good to be *worshipped*.

He didn't say the words, but for the first time ever, I felt truly *loved*. He knew everything and he didn't look at me with disgust, or leave. He was here. He was with me. He didn't care. To him, I wasn't flawed. I was a normal girl and he was a normal guy—together at last and truly one.

He stood and I noticed at some point he had removed his shirt. I'd been so absorbed in the feel of his hands and the paint on my body to notice.

His hand curved behind my neck, drawing my lips to his. He didn't kiss me, though, just held me close enough that our lips brushed together when he spoke. "Your turn."

With a body-racking shudder, I reached for some paint. I didn't even notice the color I grabbed. I smeared it on my fingers and then glided my hands down his chest, swirling it around. I was no artist like him, so it looked more like a child's doing, but from the look on his face, it was the best thing ever. He was clearly enjoying this.

I swallowed thickly, moving my hand back up to cup

his cheek—green paint getting in the heavy stubble on his cheeks. I wanted to tell him I loved him, but the words were lodged in my throat, unable to come out. I couldn't do it. I was too scared.

With the paint still sticking to his fingers, a grin lit his face, and he smeared a large chunk over my cheek.

I paused as my mouth fell open and then I surprised us both by laughing. A real, genuine, carefree, *laugh*. I hadn't laughed like that in so long.

He smiled too, letting out a soft chuckle as his chest brushed against mine. His shoulders raised in a small shrug. "I couldn't resist."

I put some on his nose. "Me either."

"Oh, it's on now!"

I let out a shriek as he grabbed me, smearing the paint on my torso with his hands. He held me caged in his arms and smeared some on my nose so that I now matched him.

I tried in vain to reach for more paint, but he was stronger than me.

"Caelan," I panted around laughter, "let me go."

"Never," he whispered, turning me around so that we were chest to chest. His nose brushed against my cheek and then his fingers glided lightly over the same spot. One of my hands rested on his shoulder and my eyes closed. His other hand grasped my side to keep me from moving. Swirling his finger around my cheek, he said, "You're mine."

His lips claimed mine in a demanding, soul-stealing kiss, preventing me from saying anything. I didn't need to.

I had no idea where we were going and where we'd end up, but I knew, no matter what, a piece of me would always belong to Caelan Gregory.

Paint smeared all over our bodies as we kissed, but neither of us cared. It only added to the beauty of it.

He released my lips with an audible pop and I felt slightly dizzy. "I want to try something," he breathed.

"What?"

"You'll see."

He strode away and I was left swaying. He opened a closet door and returned with a large roll of canvas. He slowly unfurled it and laid it on the floor like a blanket.

He smirked as he grabbed several different colors of paint and squirted them all over the canvas. I think I had an idea where he was going with this, and my God it had my blood pumping even more than the idea and action of him painting *me*.

When he was satisfied with the colors on the canvas, he placed the bottles back, and stood in front of me once more.

He undid the button of my jeans and slid them down my legs, along with my panties. I trembled at the look in his eyes. They were passion filled and swirled with lust. I stepped out of my jeans and he tossed them to the other side of the apartment where there was no danger of them being ruined by the paint.

"Lay down, Sutton." His voice was husky and commanding.

I did as he said, not worried about the paint getting in my hair—not worried about anything, really. He stared down at me, his eyes skimming every curve of my body. His fingers twitched at his sides and I couldn't help wondering if he didn't wish he could sketch me. His Adam's apple bobbed as he swallowed. "You look like an angel."

My whole body flushed at his words and gaze.

This, right here, having someone look at you like you're everything, was what life was about—finding that one person that woke you up and made you feel alive.

"Are you going to join me?" I crooked a finger, beckoning him to me.

A wry smile tilted his lips. "In a minute. For now, I want to look."

I bit my lip, letting him look at me. I had never been shy, but the way he looked at me made it hard to resist the urge to cover myself.

The only thing that stopped me was his scrutiny didn't make

me feel dirty—quite the opposite actually.

"Please, Cael," I finally begged, when I couldn't stand it any longer.

I needed him on me.

Inside me.

Filling me completely.

"Please," I repeated when he didn't move.

He removed the last of his clothes and lowered.

Every nerve ending in my body hummed when his skin touched mine.

I needed him like I required oxygen to breathe. That kind of desire was dangerous, but I didn't care. He filled a void inside me that had existed for far too long. He thought he was bad, but he was wrong. He healed every broken piece of me with each tender kiss.

I thought I couldn't be saved.

But he proved me wrong.

In even the darkest moments of our lives, there's always a beacon of light if we look hard enough.

That light was shining blindingly bright right now.

He cupped my cheek, smearing more paint against my skin, but now it wasn't a game.

My fingers found the strands of his hair and I held on tight. "Kiss me."

And he did. Oh God, how he kissed me—devoured me, was a more accurate description. I felt like I gave him a piece of my soul.

I let him have it all.

The good and the bad—he took it away.

His hands rested beside my head, smearing the paint.

He nipped at my jaw and then took my earlobe between his teeth. "I'm not going to fuck you, Sutton."

"Y-you're not?" I was shocked. I thought—

"No," his breath ghosted along my hair, "I'm going to make love to you."

My eyes closed and my body clenched in the most delicious way at his words. I'd never been ready for that before, but I was now, with him. He was the person I could give everything to.

"Yes," my fingers curled into his hair further, "I want that. Please."

He kissed down my neck and over my breasts. "This won't be like the other times."

"Oh, I know." My back arched as his lips found my stomach.

"You're going to give me everything."

"Yes... everything," I gasped as his lips made contact with my heated flesh. "Oh, God."

I was coming undone and he'd barely done anything to me yet, but his words, knowing that this time would be unlike anything I'd ever experienced, had my body on the brink of explosion.

He paid careful attention to every surface of my body, making sure no spot was left bare from his touch and his kiss.

The paint swirled around us in a dizzying array of colors.

"Look at me."

When I did, he slowly eased inside me. My mouth fell open in a perfect O as my hips lifted to meet his. His head fell back and a smile broke out across his face. "You feel so amazing. You were fucking made for me."

He moved his hips in slow, deliberate circles. The sensations in my body were unlike anything I'd ever experienced. He hadn't been lying. He really was making love to me, and it was beautiful.

A tear slid down my cheek and he frowned. Wiping it away, he said, "Why are you crying? Should I stop?"

"No," I placed my hand against his cheek and swallowed thickly, "never stop. This is perfect."

He said no more. It wasn't necessary, because our bodies did all the talking.

He held himself above me, refusing to kiss me. I knew why. He wanted to see what he was doing to me, and I was more than willing to let him watch. I wanted him to know how affected I was—how only he could reduce me to this.

Our breaths mingled together in the space between us.

With each movement, our bodies stuck slightly together due to the paint and the misty sweat clinging to our skin.

He dipped his hands in some of the paint spread around us, then cupped my breasts, massaging the paint into my skin.

I could feel him everywhere—in every single pore and fiber of my being.

I wrapped my legs around his waist and held on to his arms. I needed something to anchor me, so that I didn't go flying away.

He flipped over, holding onto me and pulling me up with him so that I was now straddling him. My knees slipped in the paint and I let out a small giggle as I grasped his shoulders so I didn't fall. We stayed connected and once I was righted I tried to find my rhythm. I didn't go fast—even though a part of me still wanted to. Sensing my internal struggle, he grasped my hips, guiding me in a slow up and down motion. My hands splayed on his chest and I looked into his eyes. A fire surged inside me—a fire only he created. From the moment we met our attitudes had collided. We were like a thunderstorm—loud, violent, and out of control... but when the storm cleared, we were also that clear light peeking out of the shadows of the clouds.

In a tangle of limbs, we moved together, creating art and releasing our demons. It was the most amazing thing I'd ever done in my entire life.

As the hours passed, he showed me again and again just how beautiful making love could be. I was ruined now. I'd never be able to go back to my old ways. Caelan Gregory had forever changed me—and I was perfectly okay with that.

Spent, my body curled against his. He kissed me deeply, robbing me of breath.

He nuzzled my neck and the words he spoke stopped my heart and even my world.

"I love you is too simplistic of a description for what I feel for you." His breath tickled my skin. "I live for you." He kissed my neck, then my chin, and finally my lips. "Yes," he hummed, "that's much more accurate."

I tilted my head towards him, lifting my hand to cup his cheek as my hair tickled his skin. "I live for you," I repeated his words back to him.

He was right. What we had... it couldn't be defined as love. It was different... infinitely more.

CHAPTER 17
Caelan

WE'D FALLEN ASLEEP on the canvas. Waking up with Sutton in my arms filled me with a joy I'd never felt before.

As she slept, her face buried in the crook of my neck, I couldn't help but marvel at how she'd shared her past with me. I was honored that she trusted me enough to tell me the truth. It was a gift I'd cherish for the rest of my life.

She stirred in her sleep and made the cutest little moan.

God, I could watch her sleep forever.

Her nose crinkled and I itched to reach out and touch it.

Slowly, her eyes blinked open and she looked up at me. She turned her head away and yawned before looking back at me. With a bashful smile, she asked, "What time is it?"

I raised my body a bit to look out the window. "Well, it's dark now."

She laughed. "That doesn't answer my question, but okay." She suddenly frowned and started to pull away. "I should go."

I tightened my hold on her. She wasn't going anywhere, not yet.

"Stay," I breathed, rolling on top of her and pinning my hands beside her head.

"You... you don't want me to leave?" She questioned, a small crinkle in her brow.

I let out a small chuckle and rubbed my nose against hers. "No way, sweetheart."

"Oh." She let out a soft sigh and smiled.

I frowned, realizing that when she had awakened she'd believed things had gone back to the old way between us. She was crazy. That wasn't happening. The truths and passion we shared had forever altered us. There was no going back.

I kissed he, pulling her plump bottom lip between mine and releasing it. Her eyes dilated with lust and I loved that I made her come alive.

"You know," I grinned, tilting my head, "we should probably shower."

She laughed—her face transforming with the emotion—and reached up to run her fingers through my hair, which was caked together with paint. "That's probably not a bad idea," she wet her lips. "Are you going to make sure I get very, very clean?" Her arms wound around my neck.

"Mmm," I pretended to think. "I'll make sure there's not a speck left."

"Good," she giggled, wiggling her hips, "because I'm pretty sure I have paint in places I don't even want to *think* about."

That was probably true of the both of us.

I peeled my hands off the canvas and stood. I reached a hand out for her, and when she grasped it I tossed her over my shoulder.

"Caelan!" She shrieked as I carried her to the bathroom. Her laughs filled the air as I turned on the shower and waited for it to warm. Once the water was heated, I lowered her and pulled her inside under the spray.

The water caused the paint to blend together on our bodies in a kaleidoscope of color. I took a mental picture, never wanting to forget this.

I grabbed my soap and lathered it in my hands. "I have to

admit," I inhaled the scent of the soap, "I kind of like the fact that you're going to smell like me."

She laughed, rolling her eyes. "You're such a dude. You all want to mark your territory like a damn dog."

"Well," I reached out, rubbing the soap on her body, the white foam running in rivulets down her abdomen and legs, "when a guy has a beautiful woman like you, he can't help but want to make sure everyone knows she belongs to him."

"Trust me," she smiled coyly, "you have nothing to worry about."

"There's no one else?" I questioned, cupping her breasts and rolling my thumbs over her nipples. "What about the guy you gave a lap dance?"

Her body stiffened and she frowned. "He's no one."

Ice drenched my veins. She was lying. I could see it. She had feelings for him, feelings she didn't want to admit.

"Don't lie to me, Sutton," I growled.

"He's just a friend," she assured me, placing her hand on my chest where my heart beat proudly. "What I feel for him, in no way compares to what I feel for you."

I took a deep breath, marveling at her words and how *relieved* they made me feel.

I kissed her in a punishing manner. I wanted her to know that she belonged to me. Her body melded against mine and then her legs wrapped around my waist. Under the spray of the shower, I held her in my arms with her back against the tiled wall, and sank myself deep inside her. I wanted to stay buried there forever, so I didn't have to face reality. And the reality was if I ever wanted to have a healthy, lasting relationship, I had to clean up my act.

As she climaxed around me, and I reached my own peak, I said the same words to her that I had spoken after we made love. "I live for you."

It was true.

I lived and breathed for Sutton Hale.

And that was a dangerous fact.

WHEN WE FINALLY had all the paint scrubbed from our bodies, I grabbed towels from under the sink. I wrapped one around my waist and tossed the other one at her.

Fluffing her wet hair, she smiled. "I think you got all the paint. Thanks for being so thorough," she winked.

I swiped at her towel, trying to pull it away from her body. Laughing, I said, "Maybe I should check and make sure it's actually gone. I wouldn't want to any to have slipped through the cracks."

"No, no, no," she backed away, wagging a finger. "You've had your way with me too many times. My body needs a break."

I frowned. "Can you at least be naked then?"

She let out a bellowing laugh, and the sound of it filled me with joy.

"I don't think so, but nice try." She redressed in the clothes she'd had on earlier.

Pulling on a pair of sweatpants, I grabbed her and pinned her against the dresser. I lifted her up, so she sat atop. Her hands framed my face and she shook her head. "What are you doing, Caelan?"

"I don't want you to leave," I admitted. "Stay with me."

She frowned. "I should really go home, Brutus—"

"Bring Brutus over here," I replied, before she could continue. With a smile I added, "I've grown quite fond of your pussy."

She smacked my shoulder and scoffed. "You're disgusting."

"Pussy*cat*. Better?"

"No."

I laughed, and lowered her to the ground once more. "Please, come back," I rested my forehead against hers, my fingers tangling in the belt loops of her jeans. I hated to sound like I was begging, but after everything we'd just shared, the last thing I wanted to do was watch her walk out the door.

"Okay," she relented. "I'll get Brutus and be right back."

My relief was audible and embarrassing.

Her hand found mine and she gave it a reassuring squeeze.

She left the apartment, and in the moments I was alone, I assessed the canvas spread on the floor. It was kind of crazy to think we'd made this beautiful piece of art by making love. The colors swirled together in a hypnotic blend. If you studied it closely, you could make out the occasional hand and foot print and was that—? Yeah, that was the imprint of my ass. Or maybe it was hers. I tilted my head, trying to figure out. Realizing she would be back any second with the cat I picked the canvas up off the floor in a gentle manner, laying it delicately across the drying board. It was still damp in spots and the last thing I wanted was for Brutus to walk on it and ruin it. Although, I guess we could always make another one and wouldn't that be fun.

I heard the door close and turned to look behind me. Even though she'd only been gone no more than five minutes, I couldn't help feeling relieved that she was back.

Clearly, there was something wrong with me or maybe I was returning to normal. I'd spent so long in a drug induced haze that I'd forgotten what it was like to yearn for a human being—for the comfort only a relationship could provide, not just a one-night stand.

"Oooh, I want to see!" She clapped her hands together, dancing over to where I stood.

Even Sutton was different since this afternoon. She was lighter and happier. She smiled and laughed more. There wasn't a cloud of doom hanging over her head anymore. I hated that I hadn't seen at first how much she hurt. I was a selfish bastard like that, but hopefully I could make up for it now.

"Wow," she gasped when her eyes lit upon the canvas. "We did that?"

"We did," I chuckled. "What do you think?"

"I think it was so worth getting paint in my hair."

I grasped a dark wet lock of hair between my fingers. "Yes, definitely worth it."

"What are you going to do with it?" She asked.

I was lost for a moment, staring at her and remembering the things we'd done hours earlier.

With a shake of my head I jolted back to the present. "I'll wrap it around a frame," I pointed to some of the wooden boards I had lying in the corner, "and probably hang it up."

Eyeing the boards, a smirk lifted her lips. "Now I know why you had a drill."

I raised a brow in question.

"That first day when you hung my curtains. I wondered why you of all people had a drill. You seemed so..." She paused. "Unhandy," she finally supplied with a small shrug of her slender shoulders.

"Me? Unhandy? What are you talking about? I'm quite handy. I give Bob the Builder a run for his money."

She snorted at that. "The fact that you know who Bob the Builder is, is highly amusing."

I shrugged. "When I was little I used to want to build houses like..."

"Like?" She questioned.

I bowed my head, air whizzing past my lips. "Like my dad."

"Oh, Caelan," she placed a gentle hand on my arm.

"It's okay," I shrugged. "Our dreams and hopes for our future are always changing. This may not have been the life I imagined for myself, but it's not all bad," I took her hand in mine, squeezing gently.

She looked over at the canvas and back at me. "Why do you paint?"

I should've known that question was coming. "Artistic abilities run in the family. My mom was a very talented artist. She did paintings and pottery from the house—made a decent living off of it too. And Cayla, my sister, she was always insanely talented too. I was too invested in myself and football and hopes for a scholarship that I never bothered to see if I had any talent of my own." Shrugging, I continued, "Once they died, it seemed like a good way to connect and honor them. Turns out, I'm not that bad."

"You're *very* talented," she smiled. "Have you ever thought about opening a studio and showcasing it?"

I couldn't contain my laughter at that, it slipped past my lips and filled the air, echoing against the walls. "That's funny. An addict owning an art gallery—that sounds like a bad comedy in the making."

"You're too hard on yourself." Her lips turned down in a frown.

"No, I'm not," I shook my head. "Just realistic."

She rolled her eyes and I knew she thought I was crazy.

I didn't want to talk about it anymore so I asked, "Are you hungry?"

"Starving," she replied, sucking her plump bottom lip between her teeth and releasing it.

Fuck. Now I wanted to eat her. She was a temptress.

I strode away from her before I took action—like kissing her senseless and taking her to my bed. We really did need to eat if we were to keep up our strength for later, because I wasn't done with her.

I looked through the refrigerator and cabinets. Uh...

"I don't have any food."

She rolled her vibrant blue eyes and tapped her fingers on the tile countertop. "You boys are all the same. You never have any food except cereal and chips. How do you not fall over dead from starvation?" With a shake of her head, she started towards the door. "I'll be right back."

Brutus rubbed against my legs and I picked up the cat, cradling him in my arms. You know, he was kind of cute... in a weird way. I'd never seen a cat with as many colors as he had. It was like he didn't know if he wanted to be brown, black, orange, or white.

I scratched him under his chin and he immediately began to purr.

Sutton returned with a bag filled with items from her fridge. "Get," she waved me out of the small kitchen area, "you're in my way."

I chuckled, still clutching Brutus in my arms. "Has anyone ever told you that you're extremely bossy?"

An elegant brow arched and she cocked a hip to the side, placing her hand on it. "Yes, I'm well aware that I'm a bossy, nosy bitch. Happy?"

"Very," I smiled, rubbing the top of the cat's head. He curled his body into me, his purrs becoming louder. "Need any help?"

She whipped around to face me. Her still damp black hair slapped against her skin with the movement. "I'm guessing since you have no real food to speak of in this place, that you don't know how to cook. So why on Earth would I need your help?"

I suppressed my chuckle. "Point taken."

"Go paint a picture or something," she muttered, turning a knob on the stove so it would heat.

"Bossy, bossy, bossy," I muttered under my breath, letting Brutus down on the floor.

"I heard that!"

"I meant for you to," I smirked, backing towards my easel. "I think I better go paint that picture now, before you toss me off the roof."

Her lips lifted in a smile at the memory. "This won't take long."

While she cooked, I worked. I should've been working on a commission painting, but right now I needed to get this image out of my head.

My hand glided over the canvas, the pencil leaving behind a light gray outline. I didn't sketch much, preferring to do everything in paint, but when an image was this clear in my head I knew sketching it would provide a much needed depth.

Brutus tried to jump in my lap and I brushed him away, so that he didn't mess me up.

The image quickly came to life. To anyone else looking, they would've seen a bunch of gray lines that made no sense. But I saw the end result.

I blended a deep blue-violet for her hair and worked on that first. It filled most of the canvas with its long and flowing waves. Smearing it with my fingers and adding water, I let it drip. I always loved the more drippy watercolor paintings. I guess in some part of my brain, it made them seem more meaningful. Like each image was melting and would only last a little bit longer—making me want to memorize it before it disappeared forever. My paintings were always a chaotic mess of colors, spinning and merging together to form the image I desired. For me, it symbolized the chaos of life and the ever-changing colors that made up our environment and personalities. I didn't know what someone else saw when they looked, and I didn't care. Art was subjective. It meant anything to any number of people. The point of art was to find your own interpretation. No one was wrong and no one was right. The artist was the only one that held the true knowledge of what lay behind the eyes of the painting— but what it meant to us, wasn't important. It was what it made people *feel* that mattered.

I dipped a clean brush into the brightest blue I found and blended a bit of black and white into it until I had the exact right shade of her cerulean eyes. When I was confident that it was perfect, I pressed the brush lightly against the canvas.

Once her eyes were painted I focused on creating a magenta for her lips. I wanted them to pop and compete with the beauty of her eye color.

Next, I moved on to her eyelashes. Instead of going with the traditional black, I made them a rainbow, then the let the colors drip down the canvas.

I didn't pause when Sutton sat down on the floor beside me,

watching me work. I wasn't used to people being around while I painted, but I didn't care. With her, I was comfortable.

Soon, the image I'd seen in my head stared at me from the canvas.

I set the brushes aside and appraised it.

"Is that... me?" She asked, her voice soft and hesitant.

"Yeah," I nodded, "it's you."

"Wow, it's... just... wow. I have no words. It's beautiful, Caelan. Completely different from the other I saw, and that one was amazing, but I love this one more."

I knew which one she was talking about, the one I'd demanded she give back. That one had been a more realistic portrayal of her. While this one with it's rainbow of colors, could have easily been someone else.

"It's my favorite too," I concurred.

She didn't know that I had even more paintings of her lying around.

She'd invaded my every thought, and become the only thing I wanted to paint.

We sat looking at the canvas for a little while longer until her stomach rumbled.

She smiled bashfully and stood. "The food is getting cold."

I turned around to see that a meal was spread out on the tile bar top. I had the urge to spread her on top, but I knew we needed to eat. The other would come in time.

She'd prepared a salad, baked potatoes, and some kind of fish. It smelled heavenly and I couldn't remember the last time I'd had a meal like this.

She appeared apprehensive. "I hope this is okay."

I laughed, pulling her against me and placing a kiss on her lips. "Don't go getting shy on me now, Hale. Where's that know-it-all attitude I love."

She pulled out of my arms and gave me a light shove. Crossing her arms over her chest, she said, "Alright, I worked hard to make you a nice meal. Eat it and like it."

"Yes, ma'am," I mock saluted her.

I sat down at one of the barstools and noted the fact that she'd poured us each a glass of cold water. No alcohol was in sight.

Maybe I shouldn't have left her alone in the kitchen. I wouldn't put it past her to dump out all my drinks.

She picked up her fork and looked at me. "Eat!"

I laughed. I might give her grief for it, but I loved her bossy attitude.

I took a bite of the fish and flavors exploded across my tongue. "This is really good," I assured her as she stared me down, making sure I ate. "You might have to cook all my meals."

She rolled her eyes, and muttered, "Let's not get carried away."

We bantered back and forth easily through the meal. I hadn't laughed or smiled that much in... well... five years.

When we'd finished eating, we both cleaned up—goofing around and making a mess of the bubbles in the sink. It felt so good to have fun and act my age for a change.

Grasping her by the waist, I spun her around, dancing to the sound of our beating hearts.

I lifted her on to the counter, and pressed kisses against her neck where her pulse raced. "You have no idea how many times I've pictured you spread out here with me inside you."

She wiggled away, and slowly eased up her shirt until her full breasts were exposed, held by a lacy black bra. I'd been too occupied earlier to notice how good she looked in that bra.

"Why don't we make that fantasy a reality?"

At her grin, I knew my eyes had darkened with lust. I didn't see how I'd ever tire of this woman. I wanted her all day, every day. Maybe even for the rest of my life.

"Mmm," I hummed, capturing her lips with mine, "yes."

When she tried to pull my shirt off and was unsuccessful, she then moved to my jeans. I grabbed her hands in mine and pinned them beside her head. Laying across her torso, I swept my nose along the curve of her neck. "Slow, Sutton."

Her mouth parted slightly and with hooded eyes, she nodded.

Going slow was just as hard for me as it was for her, but I knew it was what we both needed.

I wanted to worship her, and show her that she didn't need to be punished for what happened to her. She had been a little girl, and she didn't deserve that. If I *ever* saw the fucker that did this to her I'd send him to an early grave.

Pushing all thoughts of that man out of my mind, my fingers curled into her soft hair. For once, she didn't smell like coconuts. She smelled like me.

"I want to hold you forever," I admitted, almost hoping I'd spoke the words too soft for her to even hear. But she did.

"Forever is a very long time," she murmured, gliding her finger over my lips.

"It is," I concurred, "but it's never enough."

When you think about it, we're each gifted with little bits of forever. The time I had with my family—while short—was our forever. It was the time we were given, because we didn't need anymore. I'd always be able to look back and remember them. That time didn't disappear. It was always there. Thus, existing forever. The short term could be as powerful as the long term. We were all a bunch of ticking time bombs, and it was up to us to utilize every second of our lives and make it count. I'd been throwing my seconds away for a long time, but not anymore.

I tenderly explored her body with my fingers and mouth. I wanted to make her feel safe. After the horrors she'd experienced, she deserved no less.

When I eased inside her, she gasped my name and satisfaction filled my body. Her lips were made to say my name and my ears were made to hear it.

I kissed her, pouring every ounce of passion in my body into it. I needed her to know that I cared—maybe even too much. I didn't know where this was headed, but life doesn't come with a map, and after all, isn't it the bumps along the way that make it all worthwhile?

As our bodies melded together, the love we were scared to share with anyone else created an impenetrable bond, blocking the world around us.

Sutton Hale had irrevocably changed me, and I wouldn't have it any other way. I hoped one day I could find the proper way to thank her. For now, this was enough.

CHAPTER 18
Sutton

"I WANT TO get a tattoo."

I don't know what made the words tumble from my mouth, but they felt right.

Caelan blinked his sleepy eyes open, yawned, and stretched his arms above his head.

"Are you dreaming? Or are you serious?"

I rolled my eyes and let out a laugh. Lightly punching his shoulder, I said, "I'm serious." I propped my head on my hand and faced him. "Where'd you get your ink?" I nodded towards the script adorning his ribs.

"A place in town."

"Annnnd," I scooted closer, "I was wondering..." I paused, hoping this wasn't forbidden territory I was about to enter.

"You were wondering?" He prompted, swishing his hand through the air.

"What's the poem from?"

He swallowed thickly, rolling on his back to stare at the wooden boards crisscrossing the ceiling. "My mom wrote it."

"She did?" I gasped.

He nodded, still refusing to look at me. He was lost in another place and time.

"She was a very creative person, as you know from what I said previously, but she wrote poems for fun. I never knew about it, not until... not until she was dead. My grandparents found the book when they packed up my stuff and gave it to me. When I read it, this one stuck out to me. I knew I wanted to make it a permanent part of me." He finally flicked his gaze to me and smiled sheepishly. "I got the tattoo the day after their funeral. I guess you could say it was the start of my rebel ways. My grandma just about had a heart attack the first time she saw it."

"Well, I think it's beautiful, and the meaning behind it makes it even more special." I reached my hand out, tracing a fingernail over the elegant script.

"Yeah," he sighed loudly, his chest rising with a shaky breath. "It's a good reminder," he rolled over onto his side to face me. "We're not guaranteed tomorrow, life can end at any moment and we need to cherish each moment we have." Rubbing his hand over the tattoo, he said, "Every time I look at this I can't help but wonder if she had some premonition that it was going to happen." He let out a nervous laugh and said, "This poem... it was dated the night they were murdered."

I reached for his hand, entwining our fingers together. Remembering that the information on the website had said that the murderer had never been found I ventured to ask him about it. I really hoped my question wouldn't upset him, though. The last thing I wanted to do was cause him pain. "I... uh... remember seeing that their murderer was never found."

His lips twitched in a smile that was anything but happy and shook his head. "Nope. Never found the guy. The police had a few suspects, myself included," he tapped his chest. "But there was never enough evidence to make a definitive case against anybody."

"Do you..." I paused, nervously biting my lip, not sure if I should go *there*. "Do you think you know who did it?"

"I have an idea," he admitted. "My dad had fired a guy for stealing from the job site at the construction company he owned.

The guy... he didn't take it well. I remember overhearing my parents talking about it. My dad told my mom that the man showed up and basically assaulted him." Tears pricked my eyes and my heart ached for Caelan and the amount of torment he had to live with. It was plain for me to see that his pain was even greater than mine. "And if it was that guy, he's out in the world with his freedom intact. Even if it wasn't him, there's someone out there that killed them and they don't have to deal with the fucking consequences. It tears me up inside. Someone should be punished for this. And now, this many years later... people don't care anymore. It's old news. It doesn't matter to them, because it isn't their family. They don't have to walk down the fucking street and wonder if each person they pass knows something or did it!" He jumped from the bed, tearing at his hair. "I-I need a minute." He padded into the bathroom and closed the door. A second later I heard him let out a heart-wrenching sob. My stomach clenched and I bit down on my fist to block my own cries. My heart constantly broke for Caelan. I didn't want him to live with this pain anymore, but I didn't know how to help him break free.

I chose to leave him alone, knowing the last thing he needed right now was for me to push him.

I grabbed up Brutus and headed back to my own apartment.

I showered and changed into clean clothes. I braided my hair to the side and set about making my necessary cup of black coffee.

I was about to take a sip of the steaming liquid when someone pounded on the door. I let out a sigh, having a pretty good idea who it was.

When I opened the door Caelan stood there with damp hair and a pair of jeans hanging low on his hips. His hands were braced above the doorframe and it did amazing things to the muscles in his chest.

"You left me," he whispered.

"I thought you needed to be alone," I shrugged.

"No," he reached out, gently cupping my cheek in his hand and looking at me seriously. "I need you, Sutton. You keep me grounded."

I swallowed thickly and stepped aside to let him in.

"Coffee?" I asked him.

He smiled wryly and sat down on the couch. "No. I don't really like the stuff."

"Ah," I nodded with a grin, "now I understand why you ordered that fancy iced coffee when you came in to Griffin's."

He let out a chuckle and bowed his head. Strands of blond hair fell forward to hide his face. "Yeah, those are actually good."

"They have hardly any coffee in them."

Pointing a finger at me, he grinned boyishly—I was surprised by how much it transformed his face. "And that's why I like them."

I finally made my way over to the couch and sat down beside him. He grabbed my legs and placed them in his lap. I smiled, letting myself relax. I couldn't believe how far we'd come since August.

"So," he started, "you want a tattoo?"

I nodded.

"Why?"

I rubbed a hand over my face, searching for the best words to explain myself. I finally settled on, "It's time."

He chuckled. "It's time? That's all you've got?"

"I've always wanted one, but I never thought of anything that I really wanted permanently on my body," I explained.

"And," he glided a finger over my foot where it rested on his lap—my foot twitched when he hit a ticklish spot, "what is it you've decided to get?"

"Freedom," I whispered, leaning my head against the couch cushions. I prayed he didn't think it was silly.

His smile was slow, almost forced, and I knew he was thinking about what happened to me. "It sounds perfect."

His fingers slowly crawled up my legs and I let out a giggle.

"Stop that! It tickles!"

"Oh, it does?" His touch was merciless as his fingers found my stomach and the spot on my side that was quite possibly the most ticklish spot on my body.

Our laughter filled the apartment as I tried to tickle him back. I failed—of course.

I sank down on his lap and wrapped my arms around his neck. His hands rested on the small of my back as we looked into each other's eyes. So many things passed between us in that moment. Both our feelings were on full display once again and neither of us was running. I could see the fear in his eyes, and I was sure it was reflected in my own, but what we had was worth pursuing. He closed his eyes and tilted his head forward to kiss me, but feeling devilish, I pulled away.

His eyes popped open and he let out a chuckle. "Playing hard to get, Ms. Hale?"

"No," I eased off his lap and pulled the band from my hair, releasing the braid. "But if I let you kiss me, things are likely to go too far, and then the whole day will have passed and nothing of importance will be accomplished."

He smirked, clasping his hands together and leaning forward. "Sex is important."

I rolled my eyes and crossed my arms over my chest. "I'm going to get a tattoo, maybe walk around town for a while, and *then* I'm going to work tonight."

"So, no sex?" He pouted.

I laughed, and as I walked by the couch I bent over him, wrapping my arms around his neck. I whispered seductively in his ear, "Maybe. If you behave."

He licked his lips suggestively. "I thought you liked it when I was bad?"

"Oh, shut up," I laughed, retrieving my jacket from the closet and shrugging it on. I slipped on a pair of shoes and looked over at him. "Are you coming?"

He pretended to think. "Um, I might need a shirt."

"Then get a shirt," I laughed. "And maybe a coat too, since it's kind of cold out."

"I don't own a coat," he said, standing and stretching his arms above his head. Staring at his body flex and ripple, I suddenly didn't want that tattoo as bad anymore. I shook my head, silently telling myself to get it together.

"You don't own a coat?"

"Nope," he shook his head. "Don't worry, I'll put on something with sleeves." With a wink, he was gone.

By the time I walked out of my apartment—careful to make sure the door latched and locked since I didn't want Brutus to escape again—Caelan had emerged from his.

We didn't say anything, just headed outside. I stopped by my car, but he shook his head. "It isn't far. We can walk. Besides, the air feels nice."

"Okay," I agreed, falling in to step beside him.

After walking a few blocks, he grabbed one of the shops doors and held it open. "After you milady," he said with a flourish of his hand.

I pretended to curtsy and entered the shop.

I didn't know quite what to make of this new playful aspect of our relationship. I'd never had someone who I could be that way with.

The woman behind the counter straightened at our arrival. She was about our age, with dyed black hair with vivid red streaks. She had a nose ring, and both arms were adorned with colorful tattoos. "Hi," her lips spread into a smile, "I'm Alba. What can I help you with? Well," she laughed, "I assume you're here for a tattoo. Do you know what you want?"

We both nodded and she tilted her head, studying Caelan. "Do I know you?"

He nodded. "Sort of. I've been here before." He lifted his shirt up and exposed his tattoo.

She squinted, leaning forward to read the tiny script. "I remember now," she smiled.

As she and Caelan spoke, I looked around the shop. The walls were painted black with silver glitter sparkling in it. The couches were shiny red leather. Mirrors and chrome accents were scattered about. It had a cool vibe, much like the woman herself. Judging from her appearance and store's color décor, I assumed she was the owner—not a diehard employee.

Eventually we were led back to a room. I volunteered to go first, lest I lose my nerve. Caelan leaned against the wall while I sat in the chair. Alba fluttered about the room, getting everything ready.

"What do you want done?" She asked.

"I want the word 'freedom' here," I pointed to my wrist.

"Easy enough," she smiled. "Do you mind if I try something with it? If you don't like it, we'll scrap the sketch. No worries."

"Yeah, sure," I shrugged.

"I'll be right back," she smiled at each of us.

When she returned a few minutes later, she held up a piece of transfer paper. "What do you think?" She asked, appearing nervous as to what my reaction would be.

"It's perfect," I breathed. The word 'freedom' was done in a simple font, but the top part of the 'm' was floating away, the ends turned up to look like a bird's wings. "It's beautiful," I continued.

"Great," she smiled, pulling up a chair and sitting down.

She got everything set up and pulled out the tattoo gun.

"Need to hold my hand?" Caelan joked from somewhere behind me.

I rolled my eyes. "Not likely."

The whir of the machine filled the room. I closed my eyes and laid back. It didn't hurt—not at all, at least to me. The slight sting of pain was actually pleasant.

"All done," she said, wiping excess ink off my wrist. She wrapped it up, going over care instructions. Then it was Caelan's turn. He handed her a slip of paper that I was sure contained what he wanted. After discussing placement and font, she left us alone again.

"What are you getting?" I asked.

"You'll see," was his smart-ass reply.

"Come on, tell me," I pleaded, but he wasn't having it. I didn't get to see the script until she placed the outline on the skin of his upper back. "Fate is always there to carry us home," I read. He glanced over at me with a sad look in his eyes. "Your mom wrote this, didn't she?"

He nodded simply and turned away, staring ahead.

I repeated the words in my mind, marveling at their meaning. It made sense, if you believed in fate—no matter what we did, or who we became, some things were meant to be. You couldn't fight it. You couldn't question it. You had to accept it.

Once his tattoo was done we paid Alba and said goodbye.

We walked around town—not holding hands, our relationship would never be lovey-dovey, no matter what—and went in and out of a few shops, eventually stopping to eat a late lunch.

Weird, could not even begin to describe what I felt sitting in a restaurant, in broad daylight no less, eating a meal with Caelan Gregory. We didn't talk very much. I think we both felt extremely awkward. So far, our entire relationship had pretty much taken place behind closed doors.

On our way back home, I spotted something in one of the many stores and forced him to wait outside while I went in. Once I had the item purchased, I walked back outside and handed him the bag. He raised it in question and shook it. "What is this for?"

"It's a gift," I smiled, swaying back and forth.

"A gift? For what? Are we celebrating something?"

"No," I laughed. "I saw it," I pointed to the store behind us, "and knew you had to have it."

"Oh," he murmured as we started walking once more. "Can I open it?"

"Yeah, of course."

"You know," he said, reaching into the bag, "I can't remember the last time someone gave me a gift."

I frowned. "Well, you're getting one now."

He pulled the item out of the bag and unwrapped the tissue paper.

He stared down at the doll in his hand, reading the inscription. Finished, he looked at me with a playful smile. "A Dammit Doll? Really, Sutton?"

I shrugged innocently. "It seemed fitting. When you get mad, just take it out on this and not..."

"You? Someone else?" He bowed his head in shame, and I was sure he remembered all the times he lost his cool with me.

"It's just a joke," I shrugged. "Please, don't take it to mean anything else. Honestly."

He forced a smile, swallowing thickly. "Thanks," he muttered, putting it back in the plastic bag.

I suddenly felt unsure of my gift and hoped I hadn't upset him. I'd meant it to be funny.

In the stairway of the apartment, I grabbed his hand and stopped him.

"What?" He snapped, his voice gruff.

Yeah, I soooo shouldn't have gotten that stupid doll.

"There's something I want to do."

A smirk slowly lifted his lips as he looked around. "You want to have sex here?"

"No," I laughed, shaking my head.

"Okay, what?"

"Well..." I paused, glancing down in embarrassment. "I've... uh... always wanted to... okay, this is going to sound really silly," I blushed.

He chuckled, leaning back against the wall. "Spit it out."

I suddenly couldn't get the words out of my mouth because it was so *stupid*. I guess since my childhood wasn't much of one, I felt the need to rebel now and do things unbefitting of my age, but I didn't care.

"I'll show you."

I jogged up the rest of the stairs and he followed. I headed for the door that marked the pathway to the roof.

With everything that had transpired in the last twenty-four hours, I needed the whole world to know that I was happy. I didn't know how long this joy would last, so I wanted to revel in it for as long as possible.

"Sutton, what—"

My scream cut off the rest of his words.

I twirled around, whooping with joy, because *I was finally free.*

Caelan laughed, shoving his hands in his jeans pockets, rocking back on his heels.

I screamed again and again and again. My hair swirled around me, with my movement, and with the wind. The cool air tickled my skin and the sun warmed my face—two contrasting things, working together as one.

For so long I'd been ashamed of what happened to me, somehow twisting it in my mind so that I believed it was my fault—that I had asked for it or something. Marcus was good at manipulating people. He'd convinced me to keep quiet, instilling fear into every fiber of my being. He had everyone else fooled too. Anyone that met him thought he was an upstanding citizen. In school he'd made the best grades, went to the best college, and now worked as a... wait for it... teacher. The man that had single-handedly destroyed my life, was now guiding our youth. Lovely. No one, except me, could see the darkness that lurked inside him. While everyone has a little bit of bad in them, Marcus was pure evil.

I let out a squeal when Caelan's hand snaked around my waist. Then he did something that completely surprised me.

He began to dance and scream with me.

I knew this moment would be stored in my mind forever as one of my favorite memories.

Eventually we stopped screaming like banshees and he held me. He wrapped both his arms around me and the comfort I was filled with was unparalleled. I hadn't felt safe in a long time, and Caelan gave that back to me.

CHAPTER 19
Sutton

HOURS LATER, AND before I had to go to work, we sat on the ledge of the roof. A wine bottle sat between us, one which we took turns drinking from, and a cigarette dangled from Caelan's fingers. I guessed he was trying to stay away from the harder stuff, and this was his compromise.

Taking a sip of the wine, I ventured to ask, "Have you been back?"

"Huh?" He questioned, flicking the ash from the tip of the cigarette over the side of the building.

"Back to your house where... where it happened?"

"No," he let out a laugh that was anything but pleasant. "Absolutely not. I don't think I can ever set foot in that house."

"Does someone else own it now?"

"It was left to me, but I haven't been able to part with it. Dumb, I know," he shrugged, taking a drag from the cigarette, causing his cheeks to hollow. "I should sell it, but I can't. Doing that feels wrong somehow."

"I think it makes complete sense," I said and meant it. "It's a part of your life. It's where you grew up. It's normal not to want to part with things that hold a special place in our hearts."

"You think so?"

"I know so," I nodded, taking another drink. I needed to pace myself before I ended up drunk and had to go to work. God, I hoped I was working with Emery tonight. I didn't think I could tolerate Angela. Gathering my thoughts back to the topic at hand, I said, "I do think it might be healing for you if you went back."

He swiveled to face me, his eyes full of anger. "Are you fucking crazy? I can't go back there!"

"Hey," I raised my hands in surrender, "don't get mad. It was merely a suggestion."

His face softened and he mumbled an apology under his breath.

I hoped he wasn't terribly mad at me for bringing it up, but I really did think it would help to move on if he went back. He needed to come to that realization on his own, though. I only hoped the seed had been planted and it grew.

I circled my legs back around, so that they weren't dangling off the side of the building anymore. I grabbed the bottle of wine and swung it between my fingers, a little bit spilling on the ground. "I have to get ready for work," I told him.

He flicked the cigarette over the side of the building, watching it fall. "Okay."

I thought maybe he'd tell me that he wanted me to come to his apartment when I got home, but he said nothing. That was Caelan though, and I didn't take it personally.

"I'll see you later, Gregory!" I called as I left.

He didn't say anything. He didn't even turn to watch me leave.

Caelan

I HEARD THE door leading back into the building click close behind her. I knew I should've said something more to her besides 'okay'. At least a goodbye. But I'd been unable to utter anything.

I kept replaying what she suggested—going back to my childhood home.

Would it be good for me? Could I do it? Or would it send me into an even bigger downward spiral?

I was really sick of questioning everything. What happened to living?

I reached over for the wine bottle and found it gone. Damn, Sutton.

Time for another cigarette then.

As the end of it glowed orange, I stared down at the street below. While it had been dark for hours, the street below was bright with the glow of the handy dandy old-fashioned looking street-lights.

You know, I think I'd been numb for so long—thanks to drugs and alcohol, and my own ability to block any feelings I didn't want to have—that I didn't know how to function like a normal human being anymore.

I rubbed at my chest, where my broken heart resided.

Looking below, I saw Sutton dart out of the building. Her dark hair was pulled back in a ponytail, and her bag thumped at her side.

I loved her, I did, but I also knew my love was flawed and it would never be enough. It wasn't the love she deserved either. She needed someone that would put her first, and I was smart enough to know that I wasn't that guy. I knew if I was a good person I'd cut her loose right now, instead of dragging this out further. But I wasn't a good person. I was selfish, and that was why I wanted her for as long as I could have her.

I took a deep breath and blew it out. It fogged in the air, and I watched the random shapes swirl around before eventually disappearing. I wished I could disappear like that—float away and cease to exist. Life fucking sucked, and more often than not, I didn't want to live. But my heart kept beating, because it was the exact kind of punishment I deserved. Those that die were the lucky ones, because Earth was a pretty shitty place.

I jumped when the ashes of the cigarette burned my fingers. I'd completely forgotten about it.

I let it fall, joining the countless others that littered the street.

I shivered from the cold air, but I didn't go inside. Not yet. The chilly night provided a much needed clarity.

Kicking my legs back and forth I forced myself to remember something besides the pain of *after*. It was hard, but the memories were there. I reached out, grasping on to the thin tendrils, and pulled.

"Mommy! Can I stir the batter?" I begged.

"No, it's Cayla's turn, you know that."

"But—"

"Stop frowning," she warned. "You did it last time."

I glared at my little sister, sitting atop the counter, clapping her chubby hands together. Her blonde curls bounced with the movement. "I hate having a little sister."

"Oh, don't say that, Cael. You know you love her, and one day you'll be so thankful that you have a sibling."

"Whatever," I grumbled, crossing my arms over my chest. My mommy glared at me, warning me to check my attitude. "Besides," I continued, "she's too little! She won't stir it right!"

"Caelan Reese Gregory!" She yelled. "You need to be nice. It'll be your turn next time."

I glared over at my little sister. I hated her. I didn't know why my mommy and daddy thought they needed another baby. Wasn't I good enough?

And then Cayla pushed the bowl closer to me. "Cael, stir!" She yelled in her garbled baby talk.

"No, sweetie, it's your turn," mommy told her, rubbing her fingers through Cayla's hair.

"Cael!" Cayla shouted again.

I smiled. "Can we do it together?"

Mommy nodded. "That would be okay."

I climbed up on the counter and Cayla and I stirred the batter together. Maybe she wasn't that bad. In fact, I kind of liked her.

The memory melted away and another quickly replaced it.

"Come on, Cael! You can do better than that!" My dad yelled when I dropped the football again. His smile cut out the bite his words could've had.

"I'm too short," I pouted.

"Aw, kid, you'll grow. Besides," he crouched in front of me, ruffling my hair, "Our size has no effect on the person we become. You can accomplish anything if you believe you can and you love what you do," he poked my heart.

"I really do love football," I said, my voice small.

"I know you do, Cael. Practice makes perfect. If we practice every night, you'll be surprised at how good you get."

"Really?" My eyes lit up. My dad never lied. If he said practice would make me better, then it would.

"Really."

A smile lifted my lips at the memories. God, I missed them. I yearned for them every day. I realized that grief never really went away. It may shift and recede, like the tides of the ocean, but it was always there. It became a part of you.

"So," Cayla bounced on my bed, smiling giddily, "I have a boyfriend."

I stopped in my tracks by my dresser where I'd been looking for a shirt.

I turned around, facing my fifteen-year-old sister. "No way! You're too young!"

"Jesus, Cael," she rolled her eyes, "You had a girlfriend when you were thirteen, chillax."

"You're my baby sister, I will not chillax," I mimed her tone.

"I thought you'd be happy for me," she stood from my bed, starting towards the Jack and Jill bathroom that connected our bedrooms. "Guess I was wrong."

"Yeah, you were wrong. You're a little kid!"

She stopped in the doorway and turned abruptly to glare at me. "I'm not a little kid. Stop treating me like one. If it was left up to you, I'd never date and die a virgin!"

My eyes threatened to bug out of my bed. "Cayla!"

She slammed the door closed between us, and a second later I heard the lock click into place.

I knew I needed to back off. She was getting older. But I was her big brother, and I felt like I needed to protect her.

When the memory faded into the recesses of my mind once more, dampness clung to my cheeks. For years I'd been protecting Cayla from everything. Back then I had a major case of hero-complex. But on the night she and my parent's needed me most, I was gone out having fun and partying the night away.

Sutton was right. I needed to go back. I wouldn't be able to move on until I did. I hoped she would go with me. I knew I couldn't do it by myself.

The thought of stepping foot into that house once more sent my mind into a frenzy.

I knew the only thing that could calm me.

I headed inside in search of my undoing.

When I found what I craved I sat down on the couch and went through the motions. I'd done it so often that it was now second nature. The needle slid into my vein and the numbness soon settled over me like a cloud. As everything faded around me I smiled to myself. This was the best feeling in the world. I didn't have to think. Or feel. Or hurt. I simply existed.

CHAPTER 20
Sutton

WORK WAS PRETTY uneventful.

Up until Memphis walked through the doors.

I would've thought after our last conversation he'd do everything he could to avoid this place. I was so very wrong.

I wanted to crouch down and hide behind the counter, but it was too late. The shop was lit up and he had to have seen me through the windows.

An endless chant of, *Fuck, this is not good,* circled through my mind.

I was trapped with nowhere to go, and of course Emery was in the back. The rascal always seemed to know when to hide.

Memphis stepped up to the counter and tilted his head to study me. "You look good."

"Ha!" I laughed. "Hardly." My hair was pulled back in a messy ponytail, I had on the bare minimum of makeup, and I certainly wasn't dressed up.

"I'm serious."

"And you're a liar," I countered.

"I'd never lie to you, Sutton," he winked. "Just a coffee," he finally ordered, pulling his wallet out of his back pocket.

As I rang it up, I forced myself to say something instead of standing there like an idiot. I wouldn't let Memphis rattle me. No one else could, so he shouldn't have that power over me either.

"Late night working?" I ventured to ask. That sounded casual, right? I didn't want to give him the wrong idea.

He nodded. "Yeah, and then after we closed I found myself wandering around. Somehow I ended up here," he shrugged.

"It's the coffee," I winked, fixing his cup. "Best in town. Your nose couldn't resist."

"It's not the coffee," he said, running his fingers through his copper colored hair so that it no longer hid his eyes.

"I assure you, it's the coffee." My tone wasn't very nice as I slid the coffee cup across the counter.

"Whatever makes you feel better," he muttered under his breath.

He took the coffee and left.

While he was there I hadn't noticed how my heart rate spiked and how sweat was sprinkled across my forehead. But I was aware of it now. I didn't understand my reaction. Not one to over analyze, I pushed it out of my mind.

For now.

THERE WAS A homeless person sleeping outside my door.

Okay, upon closer inspection it was Caelan, but still.

I crouched down to wake him and found him unresponsive.

"Caelan?" I shook his shoulder as roughly as I could. "Caelan? Wake up!" Desperation laced my voice. I grew frantic, shaking him and slapping his cheeks in the hopes of getting a reaction. "Caelan! Please wake up!"

Eventually he uttered a groan and relief filled me. I'd feared he was dead. Puke stained his clothes, clung to his lips, and his skin had taken on a sickly grayish pallor.

I knew I needed to get him into my apartment and cleaned up, but I couldn't move him on my own.

That left two options.

Cyrus and Frankie.

With Cyrus, I'd risk him hitting on me.

With Frankie, I'd risk the wrath of Jen.

I didn't wait long to make a decision.

"Really, love?" Cyrus asked, his hair sticking up wildly around his head—the pieces that were once an electric green were now blue. "It's..." He pretended to look at a watch, but his wrist was bare, "too fucking early in the morning for a wake up call... unless," he smiled cockily, "you'd like to join me in bed."

"Stop acting British," I hissed with irritation. "And I will never in a million years get in your bed. I need help getting him into my apartment."

Cyrus took one look at Caelan's form and said, "No."

He started to close the door, but I inserted my foot so that it wouldn't latch.

Cyrus glared. "Move. Your. Foot."

"Not until you help me."

He muttered unintelligibly under his breath. "If he tries to break my fucking nose again, I'm dropping him on his head."

"Thank you!" I cried in relief, slinging my arms around his neck in a hug. I then realized he was practically naked and pulled away awkwardly. "Oh... uh... sorry."

He shook his head. "Let me get some pants on."

"Yeah, that would probably be a good idea," I concurred.

I stood in the doorway, in case he tried to go back to bed without helping me. He finally returned. "You owe me for this," he muttered as he passed me. "I accept blowjobs as payment." Upon settling his eyes on Caelan, his nose wrinkled. "Oh, fuck, he's thrown up all over himself. Not cool. I didn't sign up for this!" He glared at me.

I shrugged innocently. "I need someone's help."

"Ugh," he groaned. "I need to fucking move so I don't have to deal with this shit."

He bent down and got one arm under Caelan's legs and the other behind his back. With a grunt, he lifted him up. "The scrawny thing is heavier than he looks. Get the door open."

I did as quickly as I could, and then had Cyrus put him in the bathtub. I figured that would be best since I had to get him cleaned up.

Once Caelan was in the tub, Cyrus stood with his hands on his hips and looked at me steadily. "This is really what you want?" He pointed to Caelan. "A *boy* who can't get his shit together?"

"You wouldn't understand," I muttered, maneuvering Caelan's arms around so I could rid him of his soiled shirt.

"You're right. I wouldn't. But I do know you deserve better." With those parting words, Cyrus left me alone.

I took a deep breath. Pushing his statement out of my mind I set about removing Caelan's clothes. I dumped them in a trash bag and tied the string, then set the bag outside my apartment door so that the smell didn't permeate the air.

Back in the bathroom, I turned the water on. I thought for sure it would wake him up, but it had no affect. He was out cold. Once he was cleaned up, I used a towel to dry his body. I frowned, rocking back on my heels. I was at a loss as to what to do. I couldn't ask Cyrus for help again and I didn't see how I could get him out of the bathtub on my own.

With a sigh, I realized it was going to be a long night—er, morning—because I was going to have to sit up and keep watch over him to make sure nothing bad happened.

I brewed a hot cup of coffee and created a makeshift bed on the bathroom floor.

Oh, the things we do for the ones we love. It's comical really, the lengths we'll go to.

Caelan

I HEARD SOMETHING crash in the house. It sounded like something big.

Then footsteps sounded on the stairs, but everyone was sleeping—which meant someone was in the house that wasn't supposed to be.

I heard my parent's bedroom door open, and then my dad spoke.

Screams, his screams, filled the air.

I was up and out of my bed before I knew what I was doing.

I had to get to Cayla, and then I had to get to mom. It sounded like it was too late for dad—his cries had ceased. Oh God, what was happening?

You heard about these kinds of things on the news all the time, but you never imagined it would happen to you.

Cayla was sitting up in her bed when I entered the room. She looked around wildly and gulped greedily at the air. She was beyond scared. I was too. But I had to stay calm. The minute I'd start to freak out would be the minute I'd forget how to think. We had to get out of the house, that was for sure.

I held a finger up to my lips, urging her to be quiet. She nodded, easing the covers off her body.

I nodded my head towards the window.

We could climb out on the ledge of the roof and jump down.

Silence had fallen in the hallway, but now mom's screams started up.

I bit down harshly on my tongue, to the point that blood was drawn, to resist the urge to yell out for her.

Her shrieks quieted almost instantly.

I knew Cayla and I had only seconds to get out of there.

"Go, Cayla!" I nodded towards the now open window. A

breeze swept into the room, causing her curtains to billow.

"Hurry, Cael," she hissed, starting out the window.

I reached out towards the door, to lock it, but it was already being opened.

The man wore a ski mask to hide his identity.

Before I could shout for Cayla, he slammed a fist into my face and a knife into my abdomen at the same time.

I fell to the ground, clutching at my side, willing the blood to stop flowing. I needed to help Cayla and I couldn't do that if I was bleeding out on the floor.

I twisted my body to see the man grab her by the hair and yank her back through the window. She yelped in pain and started to shout for help. Why couldn't the neighbors hear us? Couldn't they sense that we needed help?

He dragged her over to the bed. She kicked, and yelled, and bit at him, but it did no good.

I felt myself fading, my vision becoming blurry.

I saw the knife penetrate her skin over and over again. Her screams echoed through my skull, torturing me.

When the man was done, he turned to me once more. The knife pointed towards the floor, blood dripping off of it.

He surprised me when he spoke. "This is your fault."

And then, everything else faded away, and I died with them.

I woke with a start. My heart beat too fast and sweat drenched my skin. My cries echoed around me and I stared around at the unfamiliar place.

"Shh," someone crooned in the darkened room. "Shh, it's okay. You're safe."

"Sutton?"

"Yeah, it's me." I felt her hands on my face, but I couldn't see her. Why couldn't I see her? I blinked my eyes but everything remained black. Had I gone blind?"

Pushing her hands away, I reached and found that my eyes were actually still closed. I felt relieved. Forcing them open, I flinched the moment light hit my retinas. They closed automatically and I decided that darkness was better for now.

"Does the light bother you?" She asked, her voice soft and sweet—everything I didn't deserve.

I nodded.

"Let me fix that." She replied. Her warmth left my side and I heard the sound of a light switch being turned off. "You can open your eyes now."

I did, slowly. As promised, the room was now bathed in darkness except for the glow of a nightlight plugged into the outlet. I noticed the door was closed, but... Sutton's room didn't have a door... and neither did mine.

"Where are we?" I asked, confused.

"The bathroom," she laughed, reaching for my hand.

"The bathroom," I repeated, the words tasting funny in my mouth. "Why?"

"Because when I got home from work this morning, you were passed out in front of my door. I needed to clean you up."

"Ohhh," I drew out the word, realization dawning on me. If I had been in the kind of state I believed I'd been in I wondered why Sutton had bothered helping my sorry ass.

"Why were you screaming?" She asked.

"I-it was a nightmare," I muttered, suddenly realizing how out of breath I felt.

"It's over now," she whispered, crouching beside me. Her fingers gently glided through my damp hair. My eyes closed at the soothing touch.

"It'll never be over," I whispered. "When I wake up, the nightmare is real, except..."

"Except what?" She prodded.

"Except, when I'm sleeping... I die with them."

"Oh, Cael," she sobbed, grasping onto my shoulders and trying to pull me close. I didn't move. I couldn't. Fear paralyzed me to the spot. I didn't want her crying for me. I didn't deserve her tears, not at all.

In a sweet gesture, she kissed my forehead. "I love you," she whispered, "it'll be okay. You have to know that."

I swallowed thickly at her words. She shouldn't love me. Someone like me didn't deserve it.

I didn't say that to her though. Instead, I replied with the truth that I'd only uttered two times before. "I live for you."

She held me tight for a while longer. She didn't seem bothered by the fact that I didn't reciprocate the comfort.

"Do you want anything to eat?" She asked, and in the dim light I saw her swipe at her face, removing any traces of tears.

"I'm not hungry," I muttered.

"Okay," she whispered. "Well, I am. I'll make a little extra in case you change your mind." Standing, she wiped her palms on the legs of her pants—a nervous gesture. "You might want to shower. I only rinsed you off. I'll—uh—get you some clean clothes. I threw away what you had on. It was ruined."

"Thank you," I whispered before she exited the room.

She stopped, her hand wrapped tightly around the door. "You're welcome."

It then dawned on me that I didn't think I'd ever thanked her for anything. She deserved more than a thank you for everything she had done for me.

I slowly got myself to my feet.

Since I was already in the bathtub, I closed the curtain and turned the shower on. I didn't bother with a light. My eyes were still too sensitive.

I used Sutton's soap to clean my hair and body. Like I had suspected, it was coconut scented. I would never be able to look at anything coconut related the same way again.

Once I was clean, I wrapped a towel around my waist. It had been conveniently left on the counter. My clothes, however, were not there.

I figured Sutton was trying to force me out of the dark bathroom.

She was smarter than I gave her credit for.

Sure enough, I found my clothes lying across her bed. While it was brighter in her apartment, than the bathroom, she had been kind enough to close the blinds and curtains. I guess I couldn't grumble about her stupid curtains anymore, because right now they sure came in handy.

She was in the kitchen, finishing up whatever she was cooking, and paid me no attention as I dressed.

I knew I must have been in a bad state when she found me last night.

After the realization that returning to my childhood home might be a good thing, I resorted to the same thing I'd done the last five years to block out emotions better left buried. Drugs and alcohol were always there when I needed them. I didn't have the willpower to stay away. Was I doing better? I guess so. But I think last night proved that I needed more help than I was prepared to ask for.

Once I was dressed, I ventured over to the kitchen.

My stomach rumbled—an unusual occurrence after I went on a rampage like I had last night.

Sutton turned towards me with a little smirk on her plump lips. I wanted to grab her and kiss her, but I was afraid after last night she might be disgusted by me. I couldn't blame her if she was. *I* was disgusted by myself.

"Sounds to me like you're hungry," she noted.

"A little," I shrugged, shoving my hands in the pockets of my jeans for lack of knowing what to do with them. "Do you need some help?" I asked.

"No," she shook her head. "I'm almost done here."

"Oh," I mumbled, moving out of her way and taking a seat at one of the stools. "I'll stay out of your way then."

She rolled her eyes. "You weren't in my way, Caelan."

I shrugged like it was no big deal.

She set a plate in front of me, and another on the spot beside me.

I studied the scrambled eggs and toast, fighting a laugh. "A little late for breakfast, isn't it?" I pointed to the edges of the windows where enough sunlight streamed inside to tell me it was much later than morning.

She rolled her pretty eyes at me once more. I could tell I was getting on her nerves and needed to watch myself, especially after what I put her through last night.

With a sigh, I muttered, "Sorry."

"Yes, it is much later than breakfast time," she replied like she hadn't heard my mumbled apology. "In fact, it's nearly two in the afternoon. But considering I didn't get much, if any, sleep and you spent the night passed out in front of my door, and then in the bathtub, I thought breakfast might be beneficial." She let out a breath as her lengthy run-on sentence finally ended.

"It was a brilliant idea," I forced a smile.

She took several deep breaths to calm herself.

Palms on the counter, she leaned forward, leveling me with her gaze. "I didn't like finding you like that, Caelan. In fact, it scared the shit out of me." Her lower lip began to tremble. "I thought you were *dead*," her voice cracked. "You wouldn't wake up or make any response. Do you have any idea what that did to me?" She continued on, so I assumed the question was rhetorical. "It tore me up inside. I felt so helpless," her hands fell to her side as she held back tears. "Don't you *ever* do that to me again." She pointed a finger in my face like one would with an unruly child they were scolding. "I don't think I can handle it if you do," she sighed.

I frowned. "I'll try not to."

She flinched, and this time tears did stream down her pretty face. "But you're not promising." It was a statement, not a question.

"No." I said the word simply and honestly. There was no point in lying to her, and the fact of the matter was I didn't want to break a promise to her. If there wasn't one in the first place, then I couldn't really mess things up... could I?

She grabbed a paper towel and used it to dry her face.

Throwing it away, she finally sat down beside me and began shoveling food in her mouth.

When both our plates were clean, I said, "I thought about what you said, and you're right."

"About what?" She looked over at me, her head twisted to the side, studying me like I was a fascinating scientific specimen. "I'm right about a lot of things, so I need you to clarify." Her smile was sweet, and I hoped that meant that our early conversation was forgotten.

"About going back..." I paused, swallowing thickly. "T-to the house. To my house," I clarified.

"You want to go back?" An elegant brow arched on her forehead. "You're ready?"

I nodded. "I think so. I mean..." I chuckled humorlessly. "I might freeze the moment I see the place, but I think I'm ready to try, and that's worth something, right?" I suddenly felt unsure of my decision.

She smiled widely and my heart warmed.

"It's worth everything," she replied.

I grabbed our empty plates, stacking them on top of each other to go clean them. As I stood, I began to feel shaky. Sutton reached out, grabbing ahold of my arm. Realization dawned on her. She stood too, taking the plates from my hands. "I've got this. You should lay down," she pointed to her bed.

"Are you sure I won't be in the way?" I questioned, suddenly feeling like I was an unbearable burden in her life. "I can go back to my place."

Rinsing the dishes off, she said, "If I wanted you to go, I would've said so. I'm not one of those girls that has a double meaning with everything. If I say something, I mean it."

"Yes, ma'am," I chuckled, crossing the room to lie on her bed. It was soft and smelled like her. The bed covers were some lavender flowery design. It didn't quite seem like Sutton to me, but at the end of the day, what did I really know about her? Not much. I didn't even know what her favorite color was.

How pathetic was that?

Eyeing me, she warned, "I really need to get to sleep so, no—"

"Sex?" I supplied, cutting her off. Covering my face with the crook of my arm, I said, "You have nothing to worry about, sweetheart. I'm too exhausted."

"Oh... of course," she floundered. Peeking through my arm, I saw her cheeks flush with color. I loved when I made her embarrassed. It didn't happen often enough.

Once the dishes were clean, she climbed into the bed beside me. Yawning loudly, she pulled the covers over her body.

"Come here," I reached for her, pulling her against me.

She bit her lip, her palm flat against my chest where my heart beat. "Is this okay?" She asked.

"It's more than okay," I murmured as I coaxed her to lay her head in the crook of my neck, "it's pretty fucking perfect."

Well, as perfect as my life got.

CHAPTER 21
Sutton

WHEN I WOKE up Caelan was still asleep. He was too peaceful to disturb, so I let him be as I slipped from beneath the sheets.

I changed my clothes and since my hair was a hopeless mess it ended up in a messy bun on top of my head.

I left Caelan a note, letting him know I'd left for work. I didn't want him to wake up and worry. In the state he was in I feared he'd have forgotten me mentioning it earlier.

I kissed his forehead, my lips lingering longer than necessary, before slinging my purse across my body and heading to work.

Despite the hours of sleep I was still exhausted. I'd been so worried about Caelan, and warred with myself most of the morning about what to do. The responsible thing to do would have been to call for an ambulance, but I hadn't done that.

Why?

Well, because I feared if he woke up in a hospital, and knew that I'd called for help he'd hate me.

Silly, extremely so, in a life or death situation.

I hung my head in shame.

I should've called for help.

But he was okay.

What if he hadn't been? A little voice inside my head told me.

The messed-up-ness of the situation was through the roof. There was something majorly wrong with me. Well, maybe not just me. It was us. We were both poison, and together, we tainted each other even more. In helping each other we only made things worse. I saw that now, but I didn't see anyway to stop this train wreck. And I didn't want to. I may have confessed my horrid past to Caelan, and he may have accepted me, but history was repeating itself. I was attracted to broken things, and Caelan was the most broken of them all. He was like glass, cutting in to me repeatedly. Making my wounds deeper. But... wasn't I doing the same to him? I was. Somehow, despite our feelings for each other, we were making things *worse* instead of better. We were like an avalanche—bound together, rolling down a hill, gaining speed, until we obliterated everything around us.

My chest constricted.

I knew I should cut all ties with him and save us the heartbreak we'd no doubt face in the future.

But I knew I couldn't, because I was weak.

There was nothing I could do now, but let the pieces fall where they may.

Caelan

My heart raced as Sutton drove closer and closer to the place where it all began, and ultimately ended.

It had been a week since I made the decision to come here.

And in that week, I'd changed my mind about doing this more times than I could count.

I kept telling myself that Sutton was here and she'd make it okay. She would keep me together when it all fell apart. I'd become more dependent on her than was healthy.

"Are you okay?" She asked me for at least the hundredth time since we'd gotten in the car, and I knew it wouldn't be the last.

I nodded, looking out the window at the bare trees passing by. How quickly the colors of the leaves changed, and before you could enjoy their beauty they fell away, scattered by the wind.

"Don't lie to me, Caelan," she warned.

"I'm as okay as I can be," I grumbled.

It was the truth. There was no way I could be entirely all right with this. I'd avoided this place since the police carried me out. My grandparents had gone to pack up my stuff since I refused to set foot in the place. So, yes, the last time I'd been here was when... I swallowed thickly, not wanting to go there. I didn't want the memories to overwhelm me. I wanted them to stop. I didn't want to have to remember that day anymore.

"If you need to talk about it, I'm here for you."

"Shut up!" I screamed, my voice filling the small confines of the car with its ferocity. "You're not a fucking shrink, Sutton! Just stop!"

She frowned, but stared straight ahead, shoulders squared. My words didn't faze her. Sutton wasn't afraid of anything.

"You don't need to act like a jerk," she said calmly, turning the blinker on and making a right. "It was a simple statement."

Only Sutton could put me in place and make me feel an inch tall with her words.

I glared out the window, choosing not to make a comment. For once, I'd let her have the last word. I didn't want to fight. Not now. I just wanted to get this over with. My chest had already tightened with fear and we weren't even there yet.

"We're almost there," she said five minutes later, listening to the directions from her GPS system, since I refused to utter them.

"I know," I snapped, my tone harsh. "Don't you think I fucking know where the house is?"

She sighed dramatically, letting me know I was wearing thin on her nerves. That was fine. She was tap-dancing across my last nerve as well.

"I'm beginning to think this was a bad idea," she muttered under her breath, not caring whether or not I heard.

"You think?"

She smacked her palm against the steering wheel and glared at me briefly before her eyes returned to the road. "Should I turn around?" She asked, her tone biting. Yep, she was pissed. But I deserved her anger for my behavior.

"No," I muttered, bowing my head in shame like a small child. "You were right. I need to do this."

"Mhmm," she murmured, tapping her fingers to the song playing on the radio.

"You know," I started, "maybe, since I'm doing this, you should think about contacting your parents."

Her fingers immediately stopped tapping. "Absolutely not." The words tumbled out of her mouth without a breath in-between. "I took the leap by telling them in the first place, I don't need to put myself through even more heartbreak. I couldn't..."

"You couldn't what?" I prodded.

"I won't be able to handle them rejecting me a second time. It hurt enough the first time." Shrugging her shoulders lightly, she continued, "I believe we can only handle a certain amount of heartbreak." Frowning, she added, "I've met my quota. Anymore would just... crush me."

I hated hearing her speak so negatively, but I understood.

The closer we drew to the house, the more nervous I became.

Sweat broke out across my body. My palms grew damp and I rubbed them on my jeans.

I really needed *something* right now. *Anything.* All of it. I'd take any high to knock me out at this point. I wanted oblivion. I found my fingernails digging into the skin until it drew blood. Sometimes physical pain was as freeing as the mind-bending numbness brought on from drugs.

"Caelan," Sutton called my name, trying to pry my arm away. "Caelan! Stop it!"

It was like she spoke to me from a tunnel. I heard her, but she sounded far away. I didn't want to listen to her anyway. I needed to feel the pain. I needed to focus on it, let it seep inside me, so that the other stuff wouldn't matter as much.

"Caelan, you need to stop! You're hurting yourself!"

I continued to ignore her, focusing instead on the sharp sting on my arm and the rapid beating of my heart.

The last five years of my life had been leading to this.

Acceptance.

Yeah, I knew they were dead.

But it was a lot easier to ignore everything that had happened.

Not anymore, though.

"Caelan," she said my name again, trying to break through the walls I'd built around myself, "I'm right here. You're not alone in this."

I laughed under my breath at her words.

She might be here at my side supporting me, but I was still alone. She couldn't begin to understand what I felt right now.

I heard the blood rushing in my ears and it felt like everything was closing in around me.

I felt so hopeless, because going back home would only further remind me that there was nothing I could have done.

I'd replayed that night over so many times in my mind that it would forever be burned inside me.

And like my nightmares showed, even if I had been there, the outcome would've still been the same. Only, I would have died with them.

I pried my nails away from my skin and looked over at Sutton.

I was beginning to realize that living wasn't such a bad thing. If I had died that night, I would've never met Sutton, and I wouldn't have had a chance at a future. True, I'd thrown the last five years of my life away, but I could still find redemption, right?

I closed my eyes and rested my head against the seat. We should be there in...

Five...

Four...

Three...
Two...
"We're here."

Sutton's voice was soft and hesitant. I knew she was unsure how to handle this... how to handle *me*.

"Give me a minute," I told her, grasping the car's seats between my hands.

You can do this, Cael. I heard Cayla's voice inside my head. *Just get out of the car, and go inside, and...*

And what? I asked her silently.

And it's time for you to say goodbye. You need to let us go.

I began to hyperventilate. Say goodbye? Could I really do that? Could I just let them go like sand scattered in the wind?

Breathe in.

Breathe out.

I knew this was going to test me, but aren't the hard things in life supposed to be the most rewarding? I only hoped this could be a turning point for me—a good one.

"Caelan—"

"Not yet," I barked.

I needed to calm down and prepare for this, and that took time. If I got out of this car before I was ready... well, things wouldn't be good. It probably wouldn't go well anyway, but I could try.

"There's a car in the driveway," she whispered.

"I know," I responded.

"You know?"

"Yeah," I muttered, staring at the ceiling. "I called my friend Kyle to be here in case..."

"In case what?" She prodded.

I slowly turned my head towards her and blinked my eyes open. "In case I go in there... and lose it. I don't want to hurt you."

"So..." She paused, nibbling on her delectable bottom lip, "you called him to protect *me* from *you?*"

I couldn't tell whether she was touched by the gesture or angry. "Yes."

"You really think I need to be protected from you?" She snapped, pushing her black hair out of her eyes. "Jesus, Caelan. I can handle you."

"I'm trying to keep you safe!" I yelled. "I don't want to hurt you again, not like—"

"You didn't hurt me," she cut me off.

"Yes. I. Did." I bit out each word, wanting to beat them through her thick skull. This was Sutton's problem; she couldn't sense danger because she was attracted to it.

She let out a dramatic sigh. "If you hurt me, why am I still here?"

I narrowed my eyes. "Do you really want me to answer that question for you? Because I'm pretty sure you already know the answer."

Her teeth clamped shut and she stared ahead.

Mustering up all the courage I had left in my body, I opened the car door and stepped out.

Upon seeing me, Kyle got out of his car. Sutton trailed somewhere behind me as I walked slowly up the driveway. My head bowed and my eyes were trained on my feet, so I hadn't gotten my first look at the house yet.

"Hey, man," Kyle muttered, clapping a hand on my shoulder. "I hope you aren't still mad about the last time."

"It's okay," I shrugged. "I understand why you did it." Lifting my head, I looked him in the eye. "Just don't try it again."

He chuckled, but didn't reply. I knew that meant he wasn't going to make a promise he might not be able to keep.

Clearing my throat, I placed my hand on the small of Sutton's back, pulling her against my side. "This is Sutton."

"Nice to meet you." Kyle shook her hand. With a smirk, he looked at me and back at her. "I didn't know that Caelan had a lady friend."

Lady friend? What the hell?

Sutton laughed, the sound light and sweet. She acted as if our conversation in the car had never happened. "I'm not his friend. We just fuck around." She looked up at me, smiling evilly.

"Oh, is that what this is?" I snapped.

Her eyes widened in false surprise. If she was looking to piss me off, it was working, and I certainly didn't need to deal with this bullshit right now. Not today. Not when I was about to force myself to do something I absolutely didn't want to do.

"Isn't it? Am I wrong?"

"I don't have time for your bitchiness," I growled, my voice low. "Are you on your fucking period or something? There's a drugstore down the road. Get some tampons and a bar of chocolate."

Her face reddened and her glare was withering. "You know why I'm mad," she spat.

"Hey," I stepped away, towards Kyle, "I was only looking out for you."

"Uh..." Kyle squirmed, clearly uncomfortable. "Is this some kind of lover's quarrel? Should I leave?"

"No."

"Yes."

"Sutton," I scowled.

"Caelan." She crossed her arms and tapped her foot against the driveway.

"She's mad that you're here," I explained to Kyle, not caring if it pissed her off further. She was being dumb.

"No," she shook her head adamantly. "I'm mad that you don't think I can handle myself. I think I've proven that I'm stronger than I look."

I let out a sigh. I was about three seconds away from dragging her ass back to the car and making her wait there.

"*This*," I shoved a finger over my shoulder at the house I had yet to take one look at, "is going to be really hard for me. Impossibly so. Stop acting like a fucking child. This isn't about you, and you know it."

She smiled slowly and then flounced by me, heading for the house. "It got you to get out of the car, didn't it?"

That little faker! I was going to toss her over my shoulder and spank her ass for this.

"Come on," Kyle forced me to turn around. "It's time to get this over with. You've been putting this off for..." He counted on his fingers, and then said, "Too long."

I sighed. He was right. Sutton was right. Everyone had been right. I had to face this. Every day that I stayed away only made this harder.

Are you there? I asked Cayla.

I'm here. Her voice echoed through my skull. *Even when you can't hear me, I'm here for you. Always.*

I closed my eyes as I soaked in the warmth I always felt when Cayla was near. Before their murders, I'd never believed in ghosts or anything like that. But now? Yeah, there was definitely *something* to the afterlife.

Finding some inner strength I normally lacked, I opened my eyes, and looked at my house for the first time since I'd been taken away in a police car—handcuffed.

I couldn't breathe.

It was like all the oxygen in the world was suddenly gone and I was suffocating.

The house... it hadn't changed. It was still *exactly* the same.

It was a two-story brick front home. Steps led up the front door that was painted a cherry red color. A wreath still hung on the door—the same wreath that had been there that night.

I don't know what I had expected, but it wasn't this.

I guess I thought the yard would've become a jungle, overtaking the house and everything else. I believed the paint would be faded and chipped and it would have the overall appearance of being abandoned—because it was.

That's not what it looked like though.

It was exactly like my parent's had left it.

They'd both prided themselves on our house looking nice.

They'd been the people always working in the yard. My dad mowed the grass and my mom planted flowers that she spent the entire summer tending to.

I felt relieved that it hadn't changed.

"It's the same," I whispered.

"You didn't think I'd let the place rot, did you?" Kyle asked.

"You did this?" I asked.

He nodded. "I knew one day you'd come back, and I didn't want it to be any harder on you than it needed to be. I thought if I kept things up... maybe it wouldn't hurt as bad."

I sighed, squinting my eyes from the reflection of the sun. "You're a far better friend than I deserve."

He chuckled, scratching his jaw. "Let's just say, you owe me a lot."

"I know."

"I didn't have a key though, so..."

He didn't need to finish his sentence. I understood. I needed to be prepared for the worst.

I forced one foot in front of the other. Even though the front door couldn't be more than twenty feet from where I stood, it seemed like twenty miles. I thought I'd never make it there.

Sutton stood off to the side. Her being there meant a lot to me. I might not have shown it, because I was under so much stress, but I knew I couldn't have done this without her.

I stopped at the door.

I ran my fingers along the wood, my touch lingered over a small slip of tape still stuck there—the tape that had once labeled this a crime scene.

I leaned my head against the door.

A crime scene.

That's what this was.

I had to keep reminding myself of that.

"Caelan," Sutton whispered my name a moment before I felt her hand touch my back, "it's going to be okay. You can do this. I know you can."

I swallowed thickly. "I'm scared."

I was so overwhelmingly afraid of what my reaction might be the moment I opened the door. I had no idea what to expect. I feared that the house would still be in disarray and that their blood would still stain the upstairs. But I also feared that everything would be clean and perfectly in place. Which was worse? I wasn't sure, and I wouldn't know until I opened the door.

I dug in my pocket for the key. When I found it, I handed it to Sutton. She closed her hand around it so that it didn't drop.

"You do it," I breathed. "I can't."

She nodded, slipping in front of me. I stepped back to allow her room.

"We're here for you," Kyle said from beside me. "Remember to breathe."

That was easier said than done.

The lock clicked, but Sutton didn't open the door.

She looked over her shoulder at me, her eyes sad. "Are you ready?"

No. "Yes," I said instead.

Her hand wrapped around the knob, twisting it. The door swung open and I froze.

She turned around, and upon seeing me immobile she reached her hand out for mine. I reluctantly placed my hand in hers. "It's okay."

With her pulling me inside, and Kyle behind me, I took my first step into the house.

Memories rushed over me, threatening to drown me with their startling clarity.

The house was exactly the same—in the sense that nothing was out of place. Someone had taken the time to clean up the mess and restore order. It looked like your typical suburban family home, except for the fact that it carried an emptiness. The air was still and it felt unlived in. This wasn't a home, not anymore. It was an empty shell that stood in commemoration of what once was. There was no happiness here anymore. It was a reminder of the horrors that happened here. I wondered if the neighbors that lived here were the same ones I remembered or if they'd moved on, taking with them the memories of what happened. I guess what I really wanted to know was, did any of them still *care*?

I moved further into the house, gliding my fingers along the walls.

Dust clung to everything in a thick coat. Pictures of my sister and me still hung on the walls. Upon entering the kitchen, I found several dishes still lying in the sink.

The house was stuck in a time warp—forever frozen in place in testament to the last activities that had taken place here.

I felt Sutton's hand tighten around mine.

I hadn't even realized she was still holding my hand. I was thankful for her support, because inside I felt like I was crumbling.

Surprisingly, so far, this wasn't as difficult as I'd believed it would be.

Granted, we hadn't gone upstairs yet, and that's where the true test lay.

In the living room, I found a family photo of all of us at a neighborhood barbeque. I picked it up, running my fingers over the glass.

Cradling the picture close to my heart, I realized that missing them would never get easier. You don't suddenly stop remembering or missing someone. That ache is always there, but if you work hard enough it can become bearable. So, that's what I was striving for.

"I want to take this with me," I whispered, clutching the frame tight.

No one said anything as I finally started up the stairs—to the place where it all ended.

I stopped in my tracks, staring at the carpet. Someone had obviously tried to clean it, but there was still a faint pink ring where my dad had lain there.

"Oh God," Sutton gasped, smacking a hand over her mouth.

"I found my dad here," I said. My voice was oddly detached, like this had happened to another person, and not me. Maybe it had.

"I think we should go," Kyle grabbed for my arm, trying to get me to turn around. He sounded as horrified as Sutton.

"No!" I pulled from his hold. "I didn't come this far to leave without finishing this. I *need* this."

Closure was necessary. I saw that now.

Kyle sighed, muttering under his breath.

I stepped by the stain, heading for my parent's room. The bed was stripped, even the mattress gone, so there were no lingering traces of blood there.

I didn't linger long. There was no point.

Instead of going to Cayla's room, I went into mine first.

"This was my room," I told Sutton. My words were unnecessary, though. It was obvious who this room belonged to. I was sure it seemed strange to her, having been in my apartment multiple times. The two places were nothing alike. They marked the significant difference in Old Caelan and New Caelan. This Caelan had been a boy. Only concerned in pleasing himself and being a star. Getting the girl. Having the perfect life. The person I was now didn't care about any of those things. Except maybe getting the girl. The right girl.

I released Sutton's hand and picked up the football lying on top of my dresser. Funny, Old Caelan loved football, but New Caelan hated it. Watching it on TV bored me... or maybe watching it reminded me too much of the life I left behind.

Staring at the football, and the other memorabilia in my room, I wondered how my life would've turned out if they hadn't died. Would I have continued with football? Gone pro?

There are a series of decisions we make that ultimately decide our course in life. Saying yes instead of no to something can drastically alter the outcome and there's no do over button. You only get one chance to make it right.

I think most of us failed.

It was easier to mess up than it was to succeed.

My bad decisions had led me down a path I never imagined—a dark, twisting thing that never seemed to end. There was the occasional bright spot. Like my art. Or Sutton. I did feel joy, but not as often as I used to. So when the emotion did make its presence known, I grasped onto it, holding tight for fear that it would leave me at any second—because the fact of the matter was, I was afraid to let myself live and be happy. If I moved on, it would be like I was accepting that they were gone. It seemed wrong to allow myself to be happy, when they were dead.

Oh, Cael. You were always so stupid. Cayla's voice hissed. *Of course we want you to be happy. We want to see you move on and start a life. You can be happy and still miss us. It's not like you're choosing one over the other.*

That was Cayla. Always the wise one. Even at sixteen she was smarter than I gave her credit for her. I loved my sister, but I also picked on her endlessly. I wished now that I'd been a better brother. A better son too. Once people are gone, it's all too easy to let yourself look back and regret. But regrets are just that, and there's nothing you can do to change them. We're stuck with the decisions we made.

"I'm ready," I whispered, leaving my room.

Going into Cayla's was the true test.

I stood in the hallway, staring at her closed door.

Sutton's hand rubbed soothing circles on my back.

I opened the door and that's when it all fell apart.

I sunk to my knees, unable to bear the emotions rushing me. I was flooded with memories of that night—of sitting in this room and watching the blood drip onto the floor, helpless to do anything. Seeing someone you love gutted like a fucking animal was unbearable, and I had to witness it not once, but three times.

Of course it changed me. How could it not? If I carried on like everything was normal, wouldn't that have been worse than the way things turned out?

"It's not fair!" I cried. In my anger I threw the picture frame. It smacked against the wall. The glass shattered as it fell apart.

The broken picture only served to upset me more.

"No!" I rushed over to where the pieces lay, trying in vain to put it back together. Luckily, the picture was relatively unharmed. I picked it up, not caring if I cut myself on the glass. I stood up and held the picture carefully so that I didn't damage it.

I forced myself to look around the room. I took in everything, searing it into my memory like I had with the rest of the house. I knew this would be the last time I came here. It was too painful, and I knew in my heart that it was time to sell it. There was no point in keeping a house I had no intentions to live in. We'd had a good life here, except for that night, and it was time for a new family to live here and create their life story.

"Are you okay?" Kyle asked.

I nodded.

"You're crying," Sutton gasped.

I reached up, my fingers connecting with dampness. "I didn't know I was."

They grew quiet and gave me all the time I needed. I made one last lap through the whole house before I stopped at the front door.

Looking at Kyle, I said, "I'll be calling a relator on Monday."

He nodded. "Good."

Standing on the front porch I watched as he closed the door.

They always say when one door closes, another one opens. I really hoped that was true.

CHAPTER 22
Sutton

I WAS SURPRISED by how well Caelan handled returning home. He was obviously shaken up, but his reaction was relatively mild. I took that as a good sign. He needed to move on, and I think he saw that now too.

He'd reframed the picture of his family and it now resided on the table beside his bed.

Like he told Kyle, he'd contacted a relator and the house was going on the market in two weeks. In that time, everything was being cleared out of the house. Caelan refused to have any dealings with that part, and I didn't blame him. Kyle was taking care of it, along with the help of some of the other guys Caelan went to school with. Even though I didn't really talk much to Kyle I liked the guy. He wanted Caelan to get better too, and was willing to do whatever it took to make it happen. I'd only known Caelan a few months, but Kyle had known him his whole life. I imagined it had been hard for him to watch his best friend fade away and helpless to stop it.

"Are you going home for Christmas?"

"Huh?" I shook my head, bringing myself back to the present.

Daphne sighed, the steam coming off her cup of coffee creating a shield between us. "Are you going home for

Christmas?" She repeated her question. Before I could answer, she said, "Where have you been lately, Sutton? I barely see you anymore and when I do, you're here in person," she waved a hand at me, "but off in la la land."

"I'm sorry," I mumbled. "I have a lot on my mind."

"Caelan?"

I nodded. "And to answer your question about Christmas, no, I won't be going home." She didn't know, but it wasn't like I had a home to go back to. The townhouse I'd lived in had been owned by my boyfriend and I doubted my parent's ever wanted to see me again. I hoped one day that their rejection wouldn't sting as much.

"You look sad," she commented.

"I suppose I am."

"Why?" An elegant brow arched with the question. She lifted the cup of coffee to her lips and took a delicate sip. I wished I looked like that drinking coffee. I probably sounded like a dog sloshing around in its water bowl.

I shrugged. "This time of year should be about family, and for me it's not." *Anymore.*

"Oh, Sutton," she reached out, gently placing her hand overtop mine. "You can come to my parent's house with Frankie and me. My mom always bakes enough to feed the entire neighborhood and there's an extra bedroom. You wouldn't be intruding, promise."

Sadly I was tempted to take her up on the offer, but I didn't. "Thanks for the offer, but no. I'll hang out here. I might bribe Caelan with sexual favors in order to make him get a tree and put up decorations."

In a very un-Daphne-like gesture, she spit out her coffee. It splattered over the table and some landed on my shirt. Great.

"Sexual favors? Really, Sutton? Have you ever heard of TMI?"

I rolled my eyes and leaned forward to wipe up the mess with a napkin. "We're both adults, why can't we talk about sex?"

She squirmed in her seat. "We can, but not in public. Please?"

I looked around at the mostly empty coffee shop. "I'm sure the dude in the back listening to music is scandalized by my use of the word 'sexual.'"

Daphne's cheeks flushed.

Grinning, I said, "Sex, sex, sex, penis, sex, vagina, sex, sex, sex."

"Oh, God." She covered her face, completely mortified. "I hate you so much."

"What's going on here?" Emery asked, pulling out a rag to wipe up some of the mess I had missed.

"Nothing!" Daphne shrieked.

"Just talking about sex," I shrugged innocently.

Daphne's face grew so red that it matched her hair.

Emery let out a husky chuckle as he looked between us. He tucked the rag in his back pocket and crossed his arms over his chest, only accentuating how muscular he was. I figured Daphne was about two seconds away from melting into a pile of goo.

"Sex, huh?" He smirked. "Sex with who?"

"Just sex," I said, then to embarrass Daphne further I added, "although my friend here is really in need of being laid. Know anyone interested?"

"Oh. My. God." Daphne peeked through her fingers. "I'm mortified."

Emery chuckled, playing along. "I'll put a flier up and see if there are any interested suitors."

"I hate you. I hate you. I fucking hate you," Daphne shook her head, her hair swishing around her shoulders.

"Love you too, Daph," I smiled.

Emery left us then and her color slowly began to return to normal.

"I don't know why I'm friends with you."

"It's because of my bubbly personality, of course." I reached for the muffin I'd ordered when we arrived at Griffin's and tore off a piece, popping it into my mouth.

"'Bubbly' is not the word that comes to mind to describe you."

"What would you go with then?" I asked, taking another bite of muffin.

She tilted her head, studying me. "Secretive."

I nearly spit out my muffin at that. "Secretive? You really think that about me?"

"Well," she tapped a finger against her lips, "yeah. I don't know much about you."

"Trust me," I laughed humorlessly, "there's not much to tell."

"And that's the kind of answer someone who's secretive gives," she countered.

I pretended to be unaffected by this conversation. "What do you want to know?" I asked and my heart raced in fear that she'd ask something I really didn't want to answer. I'd hate to make a scene by running out of there like a crazy person.

"I don't know," she leaned back in her chair, holding her cup of coffee. Various gold rings glimmered on her fingers. "Did you go to college?"

"Yeah," I nodded, trying not to laugh. It seemed like such an odd question to ask someone when I knew she really wanted to know something more personal. Maybe she was building to that.

"What did you study?"

"Business..." Propping my head on my hand, I said in a hushed tone, "What do you really want to know? Something tells me it has nothing to do with what I studied in college. Come on. I don't bite."

She shrugged her thin shoulders. "I guess I wondered why out of all the people on the planet you seem to connect so much with Cael. For as long as I've lived there, he's never let someone in like he has with you. True," she raised her hands in front of herself like a shield, "I don't know what goes on behind closed doors. So, maybe it's only sex, but it seems like more than that."

"It is more," I whispered. "I don't know how to explain it to someone else, but what we have it... it's special."

She looked at me with pity.

"Why are you looking at me like that?"

She sighed. "I don't want to see you get hurt and the two of you together... that has *suffering* written all over it."

"What do you mean?" I asked.

The pity in her gaze increased. "Do you really think that a relationship with him will last?"

I began to squirm. "You don't know what you're talking about."

"Don't I?" She countered. "I've known him a lot longer than you have."

"You don't know him like I do."

She let out a sigh, looking at me like a parent dealing with an unruly child. "Sutton, you're a smart girl. He might be doing better now, at least it seems that way, but he's always going to choose the drugs over you. He will never be able to put you first in his life and you deserve so much better than that."

"I thought you were my friend," I snapped, my tone cutting.

"I am," she groaned, "that's why we're having this talk. I want you to see that this is going nowhere before you end up hurt."

I wrapped my hands around the coffee mug, letting the heat penetrate my chilled fingers. "I don't think you understand our relationship, therefore you can't know how things will end up."

"I may not understand, but I'm not stupid. These things always end badly, Sutton. Don't you think there's someone else out there that's a better fit for you?"

I hated that my mind automatically went to Memphis.

"No," I lied. "Caelan's it. I love him. Things might be hard for us, but it's worth it. *He's* worth it."

She shook her head, looking at me like she thought I was incredibly dumb. Maybe I was.

"Do you really believe that?" She asked. Then, not waiting for me to reply, she shook her head and said, "Never mind. Don't answer that. I don't want to make you mad at me. Let's talk about something else... hmmm... how's work?"

I laughed at her ridiculous change in subject. "It's work. What do you expect?"

Looking over her shoulder at Emery, where he lounged against the counter, she grinned. "At least you have nice things to look at."

I snorted. "Only I'm not looking."

"'Tis a shame." Biting her lip, she studied Emery. "He has such a nice ass."

Laughter bubbled out of my throat. "I can't believe you just said that."

"What? I might not say the things you do, but it doesn't mean I don't think them."

"I knew there was a reason I liked you so much," I smiled.

She suddenly frowned. "I am sorry for what I said about you and Caelan. I shouldn't—"

I raised a hand, silencing anything that might have further escaped her lips. "Don't apologize when you don't really mean it." My words weren't harsh, but it was the truth. I hated when people said they were sorry and they really weren't. Own what you say.

She sighed and picked up the coffee mug, emptying the last of the contents. "You're right."

"Aren't I always?" I smirked.

"Oh, Sutton," she rolled her eyes. "You know, I've never quite had a friend like you before."

"Is that a good thing or a bad thing?" I inquired.

"I think it's a good thing. You speak your mind and you don't care what other people think. It's refreshing. I wish more people were like that."

I frowned. She didn't know the half of it. I might act like I didn't care—keyword being, *act*—but inside I was as lost and scared as everyone else. Pretending I had some control over my life gave me peace of mind, but it wasn't the truth. I'd lost all control a long time ago.

"I really admire you," she continued.

She *admired* me? Me? I had done nothing worthy, but fake it till I made it. I'd rather plaster a smile on my face than wallow in the self-pity I felt on the inside. I didn't see how that made me admirable.

"Trust me," I glared down at the table, "I'm no one you should admire. I'm not perfect."

"No one's perfect," she laughed.

"That's true," I agreed. Finishing my muffin and coffee, I stood. "My break's over. I better get back."

"Oh," she shook her head, her red curls bouncing around her shoulders. "Of course. I forgot you were working," she giggled. "I'll see you later then."

I watched her gather up her stuff and leave, a frown turning down my lips. I liked Daphne, a lot, and I did consider her a friend but this conversation only served to remind me how much she didn't know about me. I knew I didn't need to share everything with her, but it seemed like if we were to be friends I should open up more. I didn't know if I could. Letting someone see your vulnerabilities was a difficult thing. I mean, I'd managed to do it with Caelan, but he was... Caelan. He was like me. He'd been hurt. He understood how the tortures of your past could change you. I wasn't sure Daphne would, and I couldn't handle it if I told her and like my parent's and Brandon, she acted as if I was disgusting and wrong and that... and that it was my fault.

No one asks to be hurt, so why does society always want to blame the victim?

"Earth to Sutton," Emery snapped his fingers in front of my face.

"Huh?"

"That's what I thought," he laughed. "You disappeared for a minute there."

"Sorry," I mumbled, heading to the back to throw my stuff away and wash my hands.

When my shift ended I was more tired than normal. I knew it wasn't because of work, or even the things Daphne said.

It was this time of year.

Everywhere I looked there was a reminder that it was

Christmastime, and this year I didn't have a family to celebrate it with. That hurt a lot. My mom had always made a big deal out of the holiday season. The house was always filled with the scent of something baking, while she'd stride through the house singing Christmas songs. I wouldn't experience any of that this year... or ever again.

I knew pouting about it was stupid. It wouldn't change anything. I needed to accept things and move on. I couldn't dwell on it forever. Eventually I had to find the strength to let go.

I went to my apartment, instead of Caelan's, when I got home. I was sure he was still up painting, so it wouldn't be like I might disturb him, but I needed to be alone for a while.

After showering, I climbed into bed, promising myself that when I woke up I'd put this behind me.

We had to create our own happiness, and that's what I was going to do.

***

"YOU WANT TO get a Christmas tree?" Caelan looked at me like I'd lost my mind, a paintbrush dangling from his fingertips.

"Yeah," I nodded.

"Okay, so get a Christmas tree. I don't see how I need to be involved in this."

"I want it to be *our* tree," I explained. "Don't you want to celebrate Christmas?"

"Not really," he grumbled. "Christmas is a reminder of what I don't have. I'm already having a hard enough time with selling the house. I'm not sure anymore if it was the right thing." He stared at the half-completed canvas in front of him.

"That's exactly why we should do this. We both need a distraction."

He sighed, pinching the bridge of his nose. "You're not going to leave this alone, are you?"

"Nope," I smiled.

"Fine," he agreed, "we'll get a tree and some decorations, whatever you want. But it's not going in here. You'll have to find room for it at your place."

"Thank you!" I cried, wrapping my arms around his neck and hugging him close.

His smile was genuine. "Only you could talk me into this."

I batted my eyes. "You can't resist this face."

He chuckled. "It's when you pout those pretty lips that it really gets to me."

He tugged on my hips, pulling me down on his lap. I straddled him, running my fingers through his silky hair. He laid his head against my chest and grew quiet. When he did speak, it was to say, "I'm trying. I am. But it's so, so hard."

"I know you are," I whispered. "Trying is better than not. Remember that."

He nodded and pulled back a bit to look at me. "I see that you're hurting a lot right now," his finger glided down my cheek, "and I don't know how to fix it."

"Some things are unfixable. You have to learn to deal."

"Story of my life," he grunted, resting his forehead against mine.

Rubbing his hands along my thighs, he sighed. "Let me clean up and we'll go get your silly tree."

"You won't be calling it silly when you see how pretty it looks," I countered.

I stood up and sat on his couch while he got everything in order and changed his clothes. Things were changing between us. It bothered me, but I was powerless to stop it. We both seemed to be drifting away from each other. I was beginning to think he shouldn't have gone back to his home. Then again, that might not have anything to do with it. It could just be... us.

"I'm ready," Caelan said, shrugging his shoulders into a black sweatshirt that was far too large for his thin frame.

He didn't have a car, so I ended up driving. I decided to head to Target first for decorations. I didn't want a naked tree.

Caelan reluctantly trailed through the store with me. He appeared irritated, like he'd rather be doing anything else.

"Which one?" I asked him, holding up two lollipop ornaments in different colors.

"Uh... both?"

I sighed. This was pointless. I ended up picking out all the decorations on my own. Hopefully he'd be more excited about getting a tree. Probably not, but I could hope.

He helped me load the shopping bags into the trunk of my car and then put the cart away.

I stopped at the local nursery that sold Christmas trees.

We walked down row upon row of evergreens. "What do you think of this one?"

"It's okay," he shrugged.

"This one?"

"Nah."

Pointing to another, I asked, "Do you like this one?"

"Sutton! They're all fucking trees! They're the same! Just pick one, so we can go!"

His words froze me. I looked around at the other people around us and they all gaped in surprise. One parent had slapped her hands over her kid's ears.

"Fine," I snapped, "I pick this one."

"Good. Now we can go." He grabbed the netting wrapped around it and dragged it behind him. I paid for the tree and the man working there helped us strap it to top of the car.

I wanted to be mad at Caelan, I really did, but I knew if the holiday time was hard for me, it had to be a thousand times harder for him. I was trying to understand, but it was difficult. I knew when I met Caelan that he was moody and at times impossible to get along with. In the past few weeks he'd been so much better that it was a bit of a shock to have to deal with this version once more.

Silence filled the car. Caelan rubbed his face and I knew he wanted to say something, but was struggling to find the right words. "I shouldn't have acted like that," he finally said after a few minutes had past.

"No, you shouldn't have," I agreed. "But you did."

He sighed, staring out the window.

"I understand that Christmas is probably a hard time for you and—"

"It's not just Christmas," he interrupted. "It's this whole time of the year. It's supposed to be about family, and I don't have one anymore. I lost them before Thanksgiving. I can't help but think of them all the time right now. I mean... I never really stop thinking about them, but it's harder right now. The wounds are deeper. Fresher."

With my eyes on the road, I reached over and put my hand on his knee. "I understand, but you can't keep carrying this baggage around with you. You have to let it go."

He laid his head back and pinched the bridge of his nose. "I know. I do. It's so hard though."

That's when I realized that I was in a better place than Caelan was. While what Marcus did to me would always leave lasting scars, I'd finally moved past it. Now, I was more hurt by my parent's reaction than anything else. Telling Caelan had helped me heal even more, because he didn't judge me. He'd listened to everything I had to say and comforted me. Since that day he'd never looked at me differently. He'd given me peace, but I saw now that I hadn't really been able to do the same for him. I wanted nothing more than for him to let all this go and live his life happily. I worried that it might never happen.

"You know what would make this hot chocolate better?" Caelan asked, lifting the mug in the air, his nose crinkling in irritation.

"What?" I asked, hanging a silver snowflake ornament onto one of the spiky sprigs.

"Whiskey."

I snorted, digging through the plastic bag for another decoration. "I doubt that would be as good of a combination as you think. Add some more marshmallows," I pointed at the bag sitting on the counter.

He frowned. "Um, no." He set the cup down on the table and watched me.

"You can help, you know."

"Ah, but why help when the view I get watching is so much better?" He smirked.

Picking out one of the lollipop ornaments I focused on the task at hand.

Music started up next-door and Caelan groaned. "Every fucking week. I seriously don't know how he manages it," he said, referring to Cyrus and his never-ending stream of parties and guests. "He's not even a likable guy. Who would want to go to one of his parties?"

"Hey, they're not all bad."

His eyes narrowed. "Thank you for the reminder of me having to watch you grind your ass against some other guy's dick. Bravo, Sutton. Would you like a round of applause?"

I laughed. "Are you seriously still mad about that? It was so long ago. Besides, we weren't even together."

"And are we together now?" He questioned with a playful smile. His tongue flicked out to moisten his lips.

I put the ornament down and strode over to him. I sat down and straddled his lap. "Hmm," I kissed my way up his neck before settling on his lips, "we better be. If we're not, then this," I made a face and indicated me pressed up against him, "is pretty awkward. I should probably move." I went to get off his lap but his hands found my hips and kept me there.

"You're not going anywhere," he chuckled. Kissing the

sensitive spot below my ear, he said, "I'm sorry about earlier today. I shouldn't have gotten snappy with you."

"Snappy? Did that word really just come out of your mouth?" I giggled when the scruff on his cheeks tickled my chin.

"It did." With his long fingers he pushed my hair out of my eyes, his hand settling at the nape of my neck. "Let me make it up to you."

"And how do you propose to do that?" My neck arched at the feel of his lips against my collarbone.

"I could kiss you here." His lips lingered against the spot where my pulse raced. "Or here." He hovered millimeters away from my lips, but didn't kiss me. Fucking torturer. "Maybe here," he moved his lips lower, to the spot between my breasts, which were exposed by my low hanging shirt. "And maybe, if you say the magic word, I'll take your clothes off and kiss you everywhere."

"What's the magic word?" I breathed, my eyes fluttering closed.

"Ah," his breath tickled my skin, "I can't tell you that. It would be cheating."

His lips continued to skim over the exposed parts of my body—which wasn't much, considering it was winter and I was clad in jeans a long-sleeved tee.

"Please," I begged, my voice breathless. "Please, Cael."

He pulled away slightly, one hand cupping the side of my face. "Did someone tell you the magic word?"

"Oh thank God," I cried, my arms winding around his neck as I tackled him down on the couch cushions. I silenced his chuckle with my lips as I kissed him deeply. No guy had ever been able to drive me as crazy as Caelan could. Their touch had never ignited fireworks in belly. With him, it was different. He was the first man I wanted to touch me because I *liked* it. With everyone else, I'd always felt dirty.

"Someone's eager," he growled, grasping my sides as he flipped me over so he was on top.

"I want you," I breathed, melding my lips with his.

His fingers skimmed under my shirt, and my insides felt like they might burst into flames from his touch.

My need for him was unlike anything else I'd ever experienced. In the short time I'd known him, he'd become my everything. That scared me. I wasn't one to be dependent on another person. But I honestly didn't know what I'd do without him—and that thought filled me with fear. When I'd come here I'd wanted to find my independence and stand on my own two feet. I needed to find myself. Instead, I found Caelan.

He removed my shirt and his lips seemed to be everywhere. His hands too. The man was talented.

I pushed all my thoughts and all my worries out of the way and let myself *feel*.

It was harder to do than you'd think.

Our thoughts were always there, flitting through our mind forever bugging us about something, and with thought came worry. It was a vicious cycle really. But in moments like this, where the man I loved held me, I wanted all my focus to be on him.

"Sutton," he breathed my name against my lips and it sent a shiver down my spine. I moaned in response.

He undressed me slowly, taking his time exploring my body.

I didn't miss rough sex, because this was so much better. Before, I'd thought I had to have it because it gave me control, but there was something more freeing about letting go and trusting him not to hurt me.

"Open for me," he growled low and husky, his hands on my thighs. He didn't have to ask. My legs fell open and he settled between them, easing inside me. I whimpered, fighting the effort to beg him to go faster. Oh so slowly he inched further in.

I was ready to burst, scream, cry, you name it, it was about to happen.

"Caelan," I panted. "Please."

He shook his head no. Fucker.

Brushing his nose against the hollow of my throat, he said, "You know I love you, right?"

"I know."

I did. I saw it in the way he looked at me. The way he touched me. I felt his love all around me in everything he did and said. Even when he was angry, like today, his love was still there. Love wasn't something that went away, it ebbed and flowed, but it was always there. It was ever changing, but once it was given it couldn't be taken away. It was forever.

As he made love to me I thought nothing could ever ruin this.

I. Was. Wrong.

CHAPTER 23
Caelan

I WAS SUFFOCATING on the inside.

All the cells in my body were slowly being depleted of oxygen.

I couldn't breathe, and yet, air still managed to reach my lungs.

I realized then it was the drugs my cells were yearning for, not air.

Lying in bed my whole body broke out in a sweat as I fought against the overwhelming *need* to take a hit. I'd been using every day for years now... in the past few months, I'd gotten better, only getting high a few times a week. But I'd made the decision to quit. I'd tossed out everything—all the drugs I had stashed around, particularly heroin, which was my go to, and even the alcohol. I had *nothing*. And I needed it. Bad.

A scream tore from my throat.

I need it.

I need it.

I need it.

This was fucking painful. It was like there were tiny pins piercing my body everywhere.

I pressed the heels of my hands against my eyes.

Sleep. I wanted to sleep.

But there would be no sleep as long as I felt this.

What was I thinking?

Throwing it away had been a bad idea.

Anger filled my body and I tore through my apartment. I went through every drawer and looked in every nook and cranny in the hopes that I had missed tossing something.

I hadn't.

I need it.

I need it.

I need it.

I got dressed as quickly as possible.

I was sure the people in this small town weren't aware of all the crime and drug dealing, but when you're a druggie like me, you know it all.

So I knew exactly where I could find what I needed on this chilly December night.

I had almost made it to the stairs when I heard her behind me.

The crashing and banging had no doubt awakened her.

"Caelan?" She asked, her voice small and groggy with sleep. "Where are you going?"

"Out," I snapped. I turned around and saw her standing there in only a t-shirt, her sexy legs crossed and that damn cat standing beside her. I swallowed thickly. I wished I was enough for her. I wished I could fight this and be the man she deserved. But I was weak and I couldn't. Besides, I'd learned a long time ago that wishing got you nowhere.

"You're stronger than this," she whispered, tears swimming in her eyes. She might have been half-asleep but she was alert enough to know what I was up to.

"I can't handle all of *this*," I cried, spreading my arms wide.

"What is *this*?" She mimicked my tone.

"Everything," I sighed. "My parents. My sister. The house. You. *Life*. It's all of it. It's catching up to me and this is the only way I know how to deal with it."

She made careful, measured steps towards me. "Caelan, getting high, *numbing* yourself to what's happening around you isn't going to solve anything."

"But it'll make me feel better," I snapped.

"I can't stop you," her lower lip trembled. "But when you walk away from me, and go to get whatever the fuck it is that you think you *need*," she glared, "I want you to think long and hard about what you're doing to yourself. To *me*. To any chance at happiness we might have." Tears streamed down her cheeks now. "Is this what our future is going to be? Every time something bad happens, or the memories get too much, you're always going to choose the drugs aren't you?"

I swallowed thickly, not wanting to answer her, but my silence was a confirmation and she knew it.

She bit the inside of her cheek and nodded. Crossing her arms over her chest, she slowly backed away. "I love you, Caelan, I do. God knows I love you more than I should. But *this*," she pointed to my sweaty and shaky body that was begging for the drugs, "I don't know if I can do it. I don't know," she repeated. "I want to be enough for you." She cried a bit harder. "But here you are, and you want the drugs *more*," her voice cracked painfully.

I wanted to make her see that I wasn't choosing the drugs over her. It was that I was too weak to fight the hold they had on me.

"I'm sorry," I whispered, bowing my head. She'd never know how much I meant those two words.

"Sorry isn't good enough, Cael. Not with this."

I closed my eyes, swallowing thickly. "It never bothered you before. You didn't seem to care."

Her sigh echoed through the hallway. "I didn't." Taking a shaky breath, she wiped tears from her eyes. "You started out as just another guy, a void filler for me. But then, I got to know you. The real you," she pointed in the vicinity of my heart, "and I saw what a beautiful person you are underneath the harsh exterior. You made me fall in love with you," her whole body trembled with her words. I wanted to step forward and wrap my arms around her. Hold her close and tell her it would be okay. But I couldn't move. My feet were stuck in quicksand and I was sinking down, forever being pulled away from her. An ocean was forming between us and I'd never be strong enough to swim the distance. "Because I love you," she continued, "I want better for you. I don't want you to depend on drugs or alcohol. I want you to be strong enough to deal with your feelings and memories instead of trying to repress them."

As her last word hung in the air, we were locked in a stare down. Our chests rose and fell in synchronized breaths.

I was the first to look away. I turned my back on her and descended even further down a path that might have no return.

Sutton

WATCHING HIM GO was the most difficult thing I'd ever had to do. I knew what he was going to do and I was helpless to stop it. I knew I could've kicked and screamed and put up a right good fight, but none of it would have fazed him. His desire for the drugs overwhelmed anything else.

I wiped the tears off my cheeks—angry at myself for even crying over him. I cared though. When you care, you *feel*. Feelings really fucking suck.

Picking up Brutus I went back inside. I stood by the window, watching for Cael. He came around the side of the building. His shoulders were hunched and his hands were stuffed into the pockets of his jeans. He bowed his head against the chilly wind as snow swirled around him.

I felt so helpless watching him go.

I wanted him to get better, to find help, but I knew I couldn't force him. He had to find the strength to make that decision on his own.

I only wondered if he ever would.

Or would this be our life? Me always watching him fight this? Having to turn a blind eye every time he snuck off to God knows where in the middle of the fucking night?

I leaned my head against the glass, my eyes followed the glow of his light hair, until I couldn't see him anymore.

I wasn't sure if I could do this.

I wanted to, but...

I sighed, pulling away from the glass. Seeing him struggle like this was taking a toll on me. He was trying so hard, but it was an impossible fight. Addiction was a fucking beast. It had sunk its claws into him and refused to let go. It was sucking the life from him.

What do you do when the person you love the most is spiraling out of control?

Do you fight for them?

Or do you let them go?

Little did I know that the decision was about to be made for me.

CHAPTER 24

Caelan

I CLUTCHED THE medium sized package in my hand. The movement wrinkled the shiny red surface. I'd already done a really shitty wrapping job and now I was only making it worse. I was nervous to give the gift to her. I wanted her to love it, but I wasn't sure she would. It was nothing fancy. I didn't even buy it at a store.

I raised my fist to knock on her door.

She opened it almost immediately. The smile on her face was contagious and I found myself mirroring her. Her dark hair hung in waves down her back and she was dressed in Christmas themed pajamas—the bottoms had dancing elves on them while her top was solid green.

"A gift?" Her eyes widened at the rectangular shape in my hands. "For me?"

I nodded, stepping inside. Scratching my jaw, I said, "You know, this is the first gift I've given anyone in a long time. It isn't much," I frowned, "but I hope you like it."

She closed the door behind me, shaking her head. "I'll love anything you give me, you don't need to worry."

I put the package down on the counter and reached for her hips. Once her body was flush with mine I made eye contact with her. "I know you're not very happy with me right now," I smoothed a finger down her cheek. Her eyes closed and her breath escaped lightly between her parted lips. "You have every reason to be angry. I know that. So, thank you for staying by my side."

Her fingers clasped my shirt and her whole body shook. "I want you to get help, Caelan." I opened my mouth to speak but she cut me off. "This isn't an ultimatum. If you decide to go to rehab, it has to be *your* decision. I'm smart enough to know that." She bit her lip and her gaze dipped down. "But I don't know if I'm strong enough to wait till then."

She leaned her forehead against my chest, inhaling deeply. She didn't cry. She wasn't upset. She was making a statement. If I didn't get my shit together, I'd lose her. I didn't want that to happen, but I understood. When we'd first messed around, it had been just that, but once real feelings got involved... it changed everything. For her and me. I wanted to be the right man for her, but in my gut I knew I wasn't. I wasn't ready to walk away yet. I still had hope that I could find the power within myself to get help.

"I don't want to talk about this anymore," she whispered, stepping out of my embrace. "Not today at least. It's Christmas. We should be celebrating."

I reached for the gift once more and handed it to her. "Open it."

"Not yet," she smiled, heading towards her coffee maker. "I need my coffee first."

"Of course," I chuckled, sitting down on the couch with the present on my lap, "you must have your coffee."

While Sutton tended to getting her daily dose of caffeine I watched Brutus bat at an ornament on the tree and then proceed to try to climb it.

"Brutus! No!" Sutton yelled as she ran over to remove the cat from the limbs.

She put the cat on the couch beside me and went to fetch her coffee. She sat down, took a few sips, and set the mug aside. "Gimme." She held out her hands for the present.

With a laugh I handed it over.

Like an excited child she ripped the paper off.

"Oh," she gasped, raising a hand to her mouth. "It's *beautiful*, Cael."

"You like it?" I asked nervously.

"Like it?" She looked at me like I had lost my mind. "I love it. This is... I'll cherish this forever," she hugged the canvas to her chest. "I do have one question, though."

"And what would that be?" I laughed. She looked so cute with her nose wrinkled in confusion.

"Why a hummingbird?" She tilted her head to the side, studying the painting.

"It's you."

"Me?"

"Yeah," I shrugged, squirming where I sat. I didn't want to sound like a pussy. "You're my hummingbird—my light in darkness. That's one of their symbols you know? I thought it was appropriate."

She looked down at the painting and then back at me. "That makes it mean even more to me... I... wow." She tucked a stray piece of hair behind her ear. "I'm blown away."

I couldn't help smiling. That's what I'd wanted to do. I wanted to give her something she could always have and look upon with fondness. Even if it all fell apart she'd still have a piece of me.

She stood and leaned the canvas against the wall. She studied it a moment longer before returning to the couch. She wrapped her arms around my neck and hugged me. I closed my eyes and did the same. I wished I could hold her forever, because when she was in my arms everything was okay. There were no bad memories. There were no cravings. There was only peace.

"Thank you," she whispered against my neck.

"It's just a painting," I chuckled, rubbing my hands up and

down her back. "I'm so pathetic I couldn't get you anything from a store."

She sat back, her hands on my biceps. She shook her head adamantly. "That painting means more to me than anything you could've bought at a store. Anything that comes from the heart," she placed her palm over the left side of my chest, "will always mean more."

She stood then and went over to the tree. She picked up the lone package lying there and turned around to hand it to me. "I hope you like it," she whispered and there was real fear in her eyes.

Before I opened it, I reached over to where she'd sat down beside me once more, and cupped her cheek. "Don't be worried."

"But—"

"Don't," I assured her.

I carefully peeled back the layers of the paper, unlike her chaotic tearing, revealing the gift underneath.

"Kyle helped me," she whispered.

I stared at the picture frame in front of me—one of those that had individual slots for multiple pictures.

Most were pictures of my family—family picnics, vacations, parties, that kind of thing. All happy moments. There was one of Kyle and me too, after a football game. We were both still in our gear, hair sweaty, but smiling for the camera and our arms outstretched to proudly point at the scoreboard in the distance. A few of the pictures were of Sutton and me. They were candid shots, taken on a phone. In one we kissed, in another we made silly faces, and in the last we looked at each other and the love there was palpable. I'd thought someone like me didn't deserve love, and that I'd never be able to return it, but Sutton taught me that I could.

"Are you crying?" She gasped.

"No."

I totally was.

I hadn't expected this gift at all, and I definitely couldn't have anticipated my reaction. The only picture I had of them was the lone one I'd taken the day at the house. Now I had many pictures—and not just of my parents and sister, but Kyle and Sutton too, because they were my family as well. *Family* wasn't defined by the blood running through your veins. It could also be the people that came into your life and left a profound mark on your soul. Kyle had done that by not abandoning me like everyone else and Sutton had done it by not judging me. She might want me to change now, but she still didn't judge me for my misgivings. She wanted better for me, and wasn't that what everyone wanted when they loved someone?

I reached over, cupping the nape of her neck, and drew her lips to mine. The kiss was slow and sweet, noticeably tender. Her body trembled. I loved the way she reacted to me—how her pulse raced, her long lashes fluttering against her sculpted cheekbones, and how when she wanted me to do more her tongue would slowly slip out from between her plump lips to wet their surface. She was doing all those things now. But I wasn't going there, not yet at least. I wanted to give her the Christmas she was missing out on with her family.

"There's something else I got you... well, us." I shrugged, watching as her eyes slowly opened, displaying dilated irises sparkling with lust.

"Really?" She hummed. "Can it wait?"

"No," I chuckled, pulling her hand from my shirt. "It can't, but this can."

"I don't want to wait," she pouted.

I stood and pulled the item from my back pocket. She took it and studied it for a second. I hadn't bothered to wrap it.

"*Miracle on 34th Street*? You want to watch a movie?" She regarded me as if I had lost my mind.

"It was a family tradition in my house," I explained. "I know you're feeling bad about not being with your family and I thought I'd share something from mine with you..." I trailed off, scratching the back of my head.

"Oh," she breathed. "This is..."

"It's dumb I know," I groaned, reaching for the movie to take it back.

"No." She wrapped her arms around it, refusing to let me take it. "We're going to watch it."

"It's okay, Sutton. I can tell you're not into it, it's fine." I grabbed her arms, trying to get her to relinquish it.

She catapulted over the back of the couch, belly flopping on the other side. "Ow," she groaned.

"Did you really jump over the side of the couch to get away from me?" I covered my mouth with my hand to suppress my laughter. With my knees on the couch, I peered down at her lying on the floor. She'd rolled onto her back, that damn movie still in one hand. Her hair fanned around her and she rubbed her forehead. She was definitely going to get a knot on her head from that.

"I did," she mumbled. "I'm not very graceful."

"That's obvious," I laughed.

She glared up at me. "If you were nice, you'd tell me that I was graceful. Like a swan."

"Ah, but I'm not nice," I smirked. Crossing my arms along the back of the couch, I leaned forward to peer at her on the floor. "In fact, I'm very, very bad."

Her laughter filled the air as she finally sat up. "You're lucky I'm a sucker for hot bad boys."

"Lucky, huh?"

"Yeah," she chimed, clambering to her feet. Pointing to her body, "You get to experience all this awesomeness on a daily basis. Most people would consider that lucky. I hear I'm a hot commodity. Exotic, even." She shimmied her hips, doing a little dance.

"You know," I grinned slowly, "I've seen your lap dance skills, but I've never experienced it on a personal level."

She rolled her eyes and muttered, "Down boy."

"Oh, so *now* you want to watch the movie?" I threw my hands in the air and flopped down on the couch as she popped the DVD into the player.

The movie started up and after she'd popped some popcorn, she settled against me on the couch. She stretched her body over top mine and placed the bowl on the floor within reach.

"Comfortable?" I asked.

"Very," she giggled, wiggling around.

I smoothed my fingers through her hair.

I didn't pay much attention to the movie, instead focusing on the way her body felt against mine, and the soft orchestra of her sighs and breaths. This was what happiness looked like—being with the person you loved. I wished I felt like this all the time. But eventually the self-doubt and anger and all the things I wanted to shut out became too much.

Addiction was a fucking poison, suffocating your mind and body. It took all control. I knew I didn't even have it as bad as others, but I still struggled.

Even now, as I lay with her, the overwhelming need was in the back of my mind. It urged me to go back to my apartment and let the drugs seep through my veins—to numb me from the world.

"Are you okay?" Sutton asked suddenly, raising to look at me. Her dark hair tumbled forward, tickling my face.

"I'm great," I forced a smile. "Just enjoying the movie."

She studied me for a moment and then returned to her previous position. "Okay," she sighed.

She didn't believe me, but she wasn't going to push me.

I wasn't sure if she let it go because she loved me, she had given up on me, or she was scared of me. She'd seen my outbursts and no doubt wanted to avoid that at all costs.

I glided my fingers down her back and she shivered. "That feels good," she murmured.

I did it again.

In turn, she started drawing something on my chest.

I closed my eyes, humming in contentment.

BEAUTY IN THE ASHES

In the back of my mind though, I kept thinking, *a love like this can't last forever.*

CHAPTER 25
Sutton

WE SPENT THE next two days in my apartment, wrapped in each other's arms.

It was easily the best two days of my life.

Until someone had the balls to knock on my door and pull me from bed.

"Don't go," Caelan grabbed my arm, trying to pull me back in to bed. "They'll go away eventually."

They knocked again.

"Not anytime soon it seems." I rolled further away and out of the bed, fumbling around for some clothes. I found Caelan's shirt first and pulled it on. It was long enough to cover my bottom half as well, so I ceased searching for bottoms.

When the person knocked again, I yelled, "Coming!"

"You could be coming in another way right now if you'd get your ass back in bed," Caelan commented.

I grinned and rolled my eyes as I backed away. "Later."

My feet tapped against the cold wood floors and I shivered as I unlocked the latch. I smiled over at Caelan lying in my bed before opening the door.

When I opened it I expected to see Daphne, or Frankie, maybe even Cyrus. What I didn't expect to see was tousled dark hair framing a pair of hazel eyes. His build was stocky, filling up the doorway, and the scent of his cologne was overwhelming.

"Marcus," I gasped.

"Marcus?" I heard Caelan mutter behind me, trying to figure out how he knew that name.

"What are you doing here?" I forced the words out of my throat and held on to the doorframe for support. I felt like I was as light as a leaf and it would take nothing to knock me over. My breaths were loud and my chest constricted painfully. Was this what a heart attack felt like?

His smile was slow—the smile of a predator about to devour its poor, helpless prey. "I've come to take you home. Mom and dad miss you. I miss you. Everyone misses you. You shouldn't have run away like that. We love you." Peering around me into the apartment, he chuckled with distaste. "Aren't you going to invite me inside, *sis*?" The word was said as a slur.

I couldn't breathe and all I heard was the blood rushing through my body.

This couldn't be happening.

How did he find me?

Oh God, I was going to throw up.

I couldn't do this.

I couldn't face this.

All the horrors of my past were rushing in rapid flashes through my mind. I'd worked so hard to block it all, but no matter how many walls I built it was still there only hidden.

"I think you should go."

The new voice came from behind me.

Belatedly I realized that the new voice wasn't indeed 'new' it was merely Caelan. His hand settled on my waist, offering silent comfort.

My world was crumbling around me, and even he couldn't hold me together.

I'd put thousands of miles of distance between this bastard and myself, yet he still find me. How? Was he a fucking FBI agent in his spare time and had special gadgets for tracking people down?

"Who the hell are you?" Marcus glared at Caelan, looking him up and down as he sized him up.

"Who I am is none of your fucking business and you know it. You need to leave. If I have to ask you again, I won't be nearly as nice." His tone was icy, the threat of danger imminent.

Marcus was undeterred. He slammed the palm of his hand against the half-open door and pushed his way inside.

Caelan grabbed ahold of my wrist and shoved me behind him. He was more forceful than he meant to be and I fell to the ground, banging my elbow in the process.

"I know what you did to her!" Caelan screamed, his anger visible in his stance. "You're not going anywhere near her!" He grabbed onto Marcus' shirt, but Marcus pushed him away easily. With a roar Caelan charged forward and tackled him to the ground. Apparently there was still a little bit of football player present in him.

I crawled backwards, out of the way, not wanting to be caught in the crossfire of the arguing men.

Silent tears streamed down my cheeks.

I wasn't scared of much.

Only one person.

And he was in this room.

I'd foolishly believed I'd never see him again, but here he was. I couldn't escape him. He was always there. If not *here*, he haunted my memories.

Caelan punched him in the face repeatedly, shouting at the top of his lungs. Marcus got in a few good hits too. As they rolled around a floor lamp fell to the ground. It didn't faze me.

Marcus looked towards me, his eyes connecting with mine, and it was like I was that scared little girl again and he had snuck into my room. His hands were on me, telling me to be quiet—that mom and dad would hate me if I told on him. I was so scared and I felt so alone. I wanted him off of me. I didn't like it. I didn't want it. Make him stop. Someone make him stop!

I screamed then as the memories assaulted me. I clapped my hands over my eyes, sobbing. I didn't want to see. I didn't want to relive it. I only wanted it to be over. I wanted to bury it six feet under and start fresh. That's what I'd tried to do until he showed up. As long as he lived there would never be a safe place for me. The only hope I had of escaping Marcus was death.

"What's going on?" Cyrus yelled over the noise of the two men fighting.

I slowly peeled my fingers away from my face. His mouth fell open when he got a look at me. "Make it stop," I begged. "Please, make it stop."

He sprung into action and tried to pry the men apart.

That hadn't been what I was asking him to stop, though.

I wanted someone to make the memories go away. I realized that would never happen. They were trapped inside, forever a part of me. There was no getting rid of them.

I had thought I was a strong person.

I saw now though, with Marcus' reappearance, it had only been a mask I was wearing.

I wasn't strong.

I was weak.

I was damaged.

I was broken.

I'd only been blocking what I really felt with false smiles. The fact of the matter was, I wasn't okay. I hadn't been for a while. I was struggling. The horrors of what he'd done to me would haunt me for the rest of my life—unless I did something stop it.

I saw now that I just wanted it to end.

I needed the silent suffering to go away.

Cyrus eventually got his arms around Marcus and pulled him away from Caelan. Frankie was there now too, standing in front of Caelan. Daphne stood in the doorway surveying the scene with confusion.

"What the hell is going on?" Frankie asked.

"Get him out of here!" Caelan pointed a finger at Marcus, his teeth clenched as he said every word. "Get him out of here before I kill him!" He lunged forward past Frankie, his arms outstretched like he was going to strangle Marcus. Calmly, Frankie wrapped his arms around Caelan's middle and pulled him back a few feet.

"Get it together, Gregory," he hissed.

"Come on," Cyrus started dragging Marcus away and out the door, "you need to leave."

Once they were out of eyesight Frankie released Caelan who came running to my side. I still sat on the floor with my back against the wall. He dropped to his knees, running his fingers along my cheek. "Sutton, sweetheart, are you okay? Please, talk to me."

When I said nothing he pulled me against his chest and let me sob into his shirt.

I wasn't okay and I didn't want to lie to him.

I felt more shattered than I ever had before.

The pieces of my life that I had so carefully reconstructed had been flawed. There were gaps and they didn't fit together right. It had all been a façade and now I was too broken to rebuild.

"Sutton, please say something," he begged, smoothing his fingers through my hair.

"He found me," I sobbed. My fingers tangled in my hair and I forced my head up to look at him. "Don't you see? No matter where I go or how much distance I put between us, he'll always find me. He's always going to haunt me."

"Who was he?" Daphne asked, tiptoeing closer to us.

"Go," Caelan snapped at her. "Can't you see she's not okay?"

I peeked over his shoulder to see Daphne pale. "Okay, fine. I'm going." When she saw me looking at her, she added, "If you need to talk to someone, I'm here."

I nodded, letting her know I heard and understood.

The other guys had left, so she closed the door behind her.

We were alone now, but Marcus' presence still lingered. He'd tainted this place for me and it would never be the same. It was no longer safe. It was like he got some kind of sick twisted joy out of seeing me suffer.

Caelan held me tightly in his arms, letting me cry.

I knew what I had to do and I only hoped he'd forgive me for destroying him.

"I'm so sorry he hurt you," Caelan whispered, his lips brushing lightly over my forehead. The tender gesture only served to make me cry harder. I wanted him to stop being so sweet, because I was about to hurt him in the worst way imaginable.

I untangled myself from his hold and came to my feet. I was still shaky and he immediately jumped up and grabbed ahold of my arm to steady me.

"I'm fine," I assured him.

"You're not. Don't lie to me."

I turned my head slightly away from him, instead looking out the window. That's when I saw Marcus standing on the street. His hands were shoved in his pockets and he was smirking at me through the window. I knew there was no way he really saw me, but it didn't stop him from getting under my skin.

I swallowed thickly, walking away.

No more.

I couldn't let him control me anymore.

And I couldn't keep running.

This ended now.

It had to, because I couldn't live in fear anymore.

I'd been doing fine up until this point. But I realized now that he'd never let me get away.

Rubbing my face, I mumbled, "I'm going to take a bath."

"Okay," Caelan whispered. Before I could go, he grabbed me by the neck and pulled my body against his once more. He rubbed his nose against the top of my head, inhaling the scent of my shampoo. "I love you, you know that, right? I live for you, Sutton. Only you. We'll get through this. Together. I'll make sure he never bothers you ever again."

I dammed back any more tears that might have fallen. I clung to his body, never wanting to let go. I wanted to believe him, but I couldn't.

The fact of the matter was, we were both too broken to ever be whole together. We couldn't save each other. We couldn't even help each other. I think we both needed each other at this point in our lives. We needed someone to *understand* us. Caelan Gregory was the best thing to ever happen to me, but his love wasn't enough to hold together the fragile pieces of my broken self.

"I love you too," I whispered. My eyes closed and tears that did not fall clung to the fine strands of my lashes.

With one last lingering kiss to my lips, he let me go.

Only he didn't know it would be the last time.

I closed the bathroom door behind me and leaned my back against it.

I was scared, but this had to be done. I couldn't live like this—it wasn't a life at all.

Damn Marcus for ruining everything! It's all he ever did! He ruined my childhood and then he took away this too! The lengths to which he'd go to torture me were endless. He found pleasure in my suffering.

Pushing away from the door I worked on autopilot. The water filled the tub and steam swirled around me.

Can you really do this? I asked myself

The answer was immediate and simple. *Yes.*

I had to escape the pain, the memories, the heartbreak.

But more than that, I had to escape Marcus and this was the only way.

I should've done it a long time ago.

Coming here was supposed to be a fresh start.

It wasn't anymore and I had nowhere left to go.

As I stripped my clothes and lowered into the steaming water I felt comfortable with my decision.

I'd thought about killing myself many times.

Daily, even.

Like I'd told Caelan, the only thing that always stopped me was that I'd be letting Marcus win.

I realized now, that even if I was alive he won.

He always won, because I lived in a constant state of suffering. I may have depressed it, but it was always there, threatening to choke me.

He ruined me.

Pretending to be okay wasn't going to work anymore. I'd always worry that he lurked in the background ready to destroy any life I created.

I sank below the surface of the water.

I opened my eyes, staring at the cloudy ceiling of the bathroom. It wasn't my first choice of what I'd like to look at as I died, but it was all I was going to get.

I opened my mouth and let the water enter my lungs.

I began to choke and sputter—my body fighting the need to get air. My hands dug into the sides of the tub as I forced myself to stay submerged. My feet kicked on their own—my body fighting against the demise my brain so clearly wanted.

Spots danced across my vision and my eyes grew heavy.

My last thought before everything disappeared was: *Drowning is a lot like falling asleep. Peaceful.*

Caelan

"SUTTON?" I STOOD outside the bathroom. The sounds of splashing had gotten my attention. What the hell was she doing in there? "Sutton?" I called her name again, jiggling the locked doorknob. "Are you okay?" No answer. More splashing. Something was seriously wrong. "Sutton!" I yelled her name, thumping my fist against the door. "Let me in!"

The splashing stopped and with it an icy dread trickled down my back.

"SUTTON!" My scream echoed through the whole building.

I hit my shoulder against the door, trying to force it open, but it didn't work.

I took a step away, cocked my leg back and kicked as hard as I could. I had to get to her. I had to stop this.

The door flew open, slamming against the opposite wall with the force.

I ran inside and dropped to my knees, which quickly became drenched with water.

"Oh God," I breathed, choking on the bile quickly rising in my throat. "Sutton!" I cried. My arms wrapped around her as I pulled her naked body from the bathtub. I smacked my hand against her cheek. "Wake up! Wake up! *Wake up!*" Her head lolled to the side. I frantically pressed my fingers against her neck, searching for a pulse. Nothing. I tried her wrist next. There was no flutter of life. She was fucking *gone* and there's was nothing I could do. Just like last time I was helpless. "You can't die, please. I need you," I sobbed. I didn't know I could cry so hard. "Please, I love you. Don't do this to me! I *live* for you, Sutton! Without you there's nothing else! You can't die. You just can't." I cried against her wet neck, drenching it further with my tears. I felt like what was left of my soul had been ripped from my body and was now being violently stepped on. I wasn't okay. *This* wasn't okay. I didn't know what to do. It was like my brain had suddenly stopped working and I was at a loss.

"Phone," I mumbled to myself. "Get your phone dumb ass."

My hands fumbled through my pockets but it wasn't there.

"Shit!" I screamed.

I didn't want to leave her on the cold tile floor by herself, it seemed wrong, but I had to. I gently laid her down, stuffing a towel under her neck to keep it elevated—that's what you were supposed to do right? Fuck. I didn't know. I was clueless.

I ran out of the bedroom and found my phone. I fumbled to dial 911.

"911 what's your emergency?" The lady spoke with a pleasant, calm tone.

"Help! You have to help her! She's dead! Oh God I think she's really dead!"

"Who's dead?"

"She's my... girlfriend," I said for lack of a better term. I knelt down beside her. "Please, she was in the bathtub and I think she tried to kill herself!"

"Do you know CPR?"

"Don't you think if I knew how to perform CPR I would've done it by now?" I screamed into the phone. "Please, send someone as fast as you can! I can't lose her! I can't!"

"Help is on the way," she said.

"Don't you need the address?" I asked. I didn't want them to get lost. They needed to get here now. She needed help. Seconds were precious commodities that could not be spared.

"Sir, you used a cell phone. I already have your location."

"Thank God," I muttered and hung up. I probably wasn't supposed to do that, but I didn't care.

As minutes ticked by and I searched weakly for a pulse, I saw her color begin to pale and her body fall slack.

There would be nothing they could do.

But there was something I could do.

I wasn't going to sit here and watch someone else I loved be ripped away from me. It was too painful. I couldn't keep living while everyone else I loved was dead. Even if they were all in Heaven and I was destined for Hell, that would be better than living this pathetic existence.

I left her once more, but not for long.

I went to my apartment in search of the one thing that would take it all away.

Once I had it grasped in my hand, I was ready.

In her bathroom once more, I curled my body around hers.

I reached for the syringe and inserted it into my vein. Every last bit of heroin I had in my possession entered my blood system. I knew it was more than enough to be deadly. Dropping the syringe to the side I wrapped my arms around her and kissed her cold neck.

"I'll see you all soon," I whispered.

Sirens sounded in the distance, but they meant nothing.

They were too late.

This was it.

I was Romeo and Sutton was my fucking Juliet.

CHAPTER 26
Sutton

PEOPLE WHO DIE and come back from the dead always seem to fail to mention how much it hurts.

I was surrounded by darkness and it felt like something was pulling on me.

Everything hurt and I couldn't fucking breathe—until I could.

A gasp tore out of my raw throat and my hands reached up, clawing at whatever was attached to my face.

Hands grabbed me by the wrist and restrained me. "You don't want to do that," someone spoke. I assumed the voice belonged to whoever held me down.

I blinked my eyes rapidly, searching for anything familiar.

Where was I?

"I'm Gail. I'm a paramedic, sweetie," she said. "You're going to be okay."

My eyes roamed around the confines of the ambulance.

I was alive.

"We're almost to the hospital. I'm going to give you something to make you sleepy. Okay?"

I don't know why she asked. I was helpless to speak or to stop her.

I felt the needle pierce my vein and cold liquid entered my

body. I fought against the sleepiness but there was nothing I could do. My lashes fluttered once, then twice, until they closed and I dreamed.

I WAS AWAKE.

I knew that much.

But I couldn't get my eyes to open and cooperate. I wiggled my fingers and sluggishly moved them up my body. All my muscles hurt and didn't want to move. It was like they'd been inactive for too long. Maybe they had.

When my fingers reached my eyes, I rubbed and slowly blinked them open. The lights were bright but I didn't want to close my eyes and submerge myself in the darkness any longer.

Looking around, it was obvious I was in a hospital room.

I remembered the time in the ambulance and then I realized what I had done.

"Oh God," I gasped—or tried to at least, since I had no voice and my throat was so raw it felt like it had been scrubbed with sandpaper. I heaved over the side of the bed, but nothing came up. I was sickened by what I'd done. I had tried to kill myself all because of that fucking psycho. What the hell was wrong with me? A single tear slid down my cheek. I couldn't believe I'd tried to do that to Caelan and myself. How selfish was I?

Where was Caelan?

Shouldn't he have been here with me?

He wasn't though. I was alone.

About the time I started to panic, the door to my room opened and a doctor strode inside.

"I'm happy to see you awake." He smiled kindly, looking at the chart in his hand. "You did quite a number on yourself. Luckily, everything here seems to look good. Your throat is going to hurt for a few weeks though. I recommend you stick to eating something soft, like baby food." He set the chart aside and grasped the bed rail in his hands. "You're a lucky young woman, Sutton. The paramedics almost didn't reach you in time."

"I know," I croaked.

"Now, the man they found with you wasn't so lucky." He frowned.

"W-what?" I forced the words out of my mouth even though it hurt more than I cared to admit.

"Don't worry, he'll be okay with time. He's stabilized, but it was touch and go there for a while."

I wanted to cry but no tears came.

Instead I felt hollow inside.

Because of what I'd done Caelan had tried to take his own life too. What had I been thinking? Clearly, I hadn't been. Anytime I was around Marcus he always seemed to make me do stupid things. It was like he screwed with my brain or something.

"I want you to go on an anti-depressant," the doctor continued, "and I'd be really happy if you'd go to therapy. I can't make you, of course, but I think it would be beneficial." I tried to speak, ready with a rebuttal, but he raised a hand and his look told me to be quiet. "You don't need to make a decision on the therapist now, but I want you to think on it." He sighed, looking at me sadly. I was sure he wondered what horrors could have possibly driven me to make such a choice. "I'll let the nurse know you're awake."

With that statement he was gone.

Nice fellow. Not.

A nurse entered a few minutes later, fussing over me. I begged her for water but she was reluctant to give it to me because of my throat, stating that the IV was providing more than enough nutrients.

Fuck that stupid IV. I wanted some damn water.

"Someone's here to see you," she said before she left. "Would you feel up to a visitor?"

I nodded, figuring it was Daphne, since it definitely wouldn't be Caelan.

I was wrong.

Marcus strode into my room with that damn proud smirk twisting his lips.

My heart rate spiked and the machine I was hooked up started screaming—at least that's what it sounded like to me.

"GET OUT!" I screamed, not caring that it felt like I shoved a knife down my throat when I yelled.

The nurse's eyes widened at my outburst and she looked from me to Marcus. Tears streamed down my cheeks and panic rose like a rollercoaster high in the sky.

"OUT!"

She grabbed his arm, trying to pull him away from me.

He didn't budge.

"Sir, I think you should leave. You're obviously making her distressed and that's the last thing she needs right now."

"But I'm her brother." He gave her the most charming smile he could muster and I saw her caving. He had that affect on people. He always fooled those around him into thinking he was a fucking angel.

"GET THE FUCK OUT!" I yelled again. It felt like spikes were being jabbed down my esophagus but there was no way I was going to be left alone in this room with him. There was no telling what he was capable of doing and I wasn't about to find out. He'd hurt me enough. He'd even driven me to the point of hurting myself. This ended now. "Go away," my voice cracked, "and leave me alone." I didn't say it out loud, frankly I didn't have the strength, but if he didn't back off and leave I'd get a restraining order filed. I probably needed to do that anyway. I couldn't live feeling like he was always lurking over my shoulder. Who could? Fear was crippling, especially when it was constant. I refused to be his victim anymore. I had rights and I would fight that motherfucker tooth and nail from now on to make sure he never hurt me or anyone else ever again. I'd been weak before, but resurrection from the dead gave me a much-needed clarity. I wasn't defined by him, and I'd been living far too long like I was. By coming here, to my *home*, he'd made an enemy out of me. I may have had a moment of weakness, of relapse so to speak, but it wouldn't happen again.

The look in his eyes changed and he must have seen that he'd pushed too far.

"I'll go," he told the nurse. The look he gave me said, *But I'll be back.*

I answered with a challenging smile. He wasn't going to beat me down anymore.

He didn't own me.

I owned myself.

With that thought I looked down at the tattoo adorning my wrist, partially obscured by hospital bands. *Freedom*.

I was truly free now.

They released me five days later. I wished it had been sooner but apparently I was under observation.

Lovely.

I was the resident basket case that might try to hang herself with the IV wires.

"Get lots of rest," the nurse warned as she helped me into a wheelchair. I didn't need it, but apparently it was protocol.

"I will," I promised her. I was too weak to do much of anything so rest wouldn't be a problem. As she started down the hallway I cleared my throat. "Can I see him?"

She knew the him I was referring to. I'd asked about him many times in the last few days. I needed to apologize to him.

"I'm not supposed to," she whispered.

"Please?" I begged. I couldn't go home without seeing him.

She sighed and turned down a hallway. "I could get in trouble for this," she grumbled.

"Thank you!"

"Shh!" She hushed me. "I can only give you ten minutes. That's it."

I'd take any time she'd give me with him.

I didn't reply. My throat was still raw and I needed to save my voice for when I saw Caelan.

"He just got moved from the ICU or else I couldn't do this," she said.

She wheeled me into a room and only a curtain separated me from him.

"Ten minutes," she warned again, holding up both hands and waggling her fingers.

The door closed behind her and I heard stirring on the other side of the curtain. I reached up, clasping the flimsy blue material in my hand and pulled it aside.

"Hi," I whispered.

Caelan stirred, turning his head towards the sound of my voice. He blinked rapidly like he couldn't believe his eyes. "Hey," he smiled weakly.

We both acted as if we were war battered. Maybe we were—it was just a different kind of war, one of the heart and mind.

"I'm so sorry," I choked out the words. I meant them and I hoped he saw that.

"It's okay." He reached out with a shaky hand to gently touch his fingers to my cheek.

"No, it's not," I shook my head adamantly. "I shouldn't have done that. It was a moment of weakness."

"I'm not mad," he whispered. Those same fingers touched my lips. It was like he was reminding himself that I was alive. I couldn't imagine how he must have felt seeing me like *that* after what he'd already gone through with his family.

"I was so selfish," I sobbed. "I didn't think about what it would do to you. What *did* you do?" No one had given me any details about how or why Caelan had ended up here, but I had a good guess.

He looked away from me and his Adam's apple bobbed. His head swiveled back to face me. "I wasn't going to let you go without me."

"Oh, Caelan." I buried my face in my hands. I was so ashamed of my actions and what had transpired because of them.

"I need to talk to you about something," he said, swallowing thickly. His eyes glimmered with tears and I knew something I didn't want to hear was about to come out of his mouth. "I know you're not going to like this, but it's for the best."

"W-what is?" I asked.

He took a deep breath, the air entering his lungs with a mighty whoosh.

"They're forcing me to enter rehab once I'm well enough. They said I'd probably leave in the next week or so. I had already decided to go to rehab on my own, once I woke up. I need help, Sutton. *Real* help." He stopped to cough. "I wanted to deny that I had any real addiction before, choosing to sweep it under the rug like it was nothing. I want to get clean for *myself*. I have to before I throw it all away for..."

"For something stupid... like me," I finished for him.

He nodded weakly. "I was ready to give up my *life* for you," he choked. "I'm as addicted to you as I am the drugs and alcohol. It's unhealthy. I need to stand on my own two feet. I can't do that with you." He looked away from me and up at the ceiling. I saw how hard this was for him but my heart hurt and I wanted to be angry. I bit down on my tongue so hard that I tasted blood, but I knew it was better that I didn't speak, because nothing nice would come out of my mouth. "Needing you is my fucking downfall. We're all wrong for each other, Sutton," he continued. "I think we did help each other. We helped each other heal, and we learned to love. But we're too fucked up to ever work. At least right now. Maybe one day, but I'm afraid one day won't be soon enough. I have to say goodbye to you. I'll be gone for a while and even once I'm out, I don't know if I'll be strong enough for this," he pointed to himself and then me. "Don't wait for me. Please, whatever you do," tears streamed down his face, "don't fucking wait for me. I'm not sure if I can come back here. It's okay to move on. I love you, I do. More than you'll ever know and that's why I have to end this. I think you know in your heart," he placed his palm over my chest, "that I'm right. I hope one day I'll be ready to see you. Maybe even to love you, but don't wait," he repeated.

I cried harder than I ever had in my entire life. I loved Caelan Gregory with every fiber of my being and his words ripped me apart, because deep down I knew he was right. We weren't meant to be. He wasn't *the one*. Maybe there never would be a perfect guy for me.

"I love you," I sobbed, "but I understand."

I scooted the wheelchair closer and he grasped the back of my neck, rubbing his thumb in slow circles. "I wish I was a strong enough man for you." His lips glided against my forehead.

My tears soaked his hospital gown. "I don't want to lose you."

Even if we weren't a couple I couldn't imagine not having him in my life. I would feel so empty without him. I needed him... but I guessed that was why we didn't work. *Need* was not a good quality in a relationship. It created a lethal bond that slowly self-destructed. In the very bottom of my heart and soul, I'd known this was coming—it was necessary.

We would both end up stronger people because of this.

That didn't mean I liked it or that it was easy.

Looking into his eyes I knew he was struggling with this as much as I was.

"You'll never lose me," he declared. "I'll always live here," he touched my chest, just over my heart once more, "and here," he tapped my forehead, "in your memories."

"Can I call you?" I asked.

He shook his head, looking at me pityingly. "I don't think that would be a good idea. Besides, I don't think rehab facilities let you talk to outsiders. It's all about the cleansing process. Please, don't make this harder than it needs to be."

I took a deep breath, gathering myself. "Okay." I felt gutted. The right thing can sometimes be very painful.

The nurse returned to wheel me away. He grasped my hand and held on tight. "I live for you."

I closed my eyes, savoring his words as I knew it would be the last time I ever heard him speak them.

With a whisper that carried behind me as I was taken away, I said, "I live for you."

I did. And I always would.

CHAPTER 27
Sutton

I'D THOUGHT I'D had my heart broken before.

I was wrong.

This was what having your heart broken really felt like.

Couldn't breathe, Couldn't think, couldn't feel.

It was like the moment our hands released each other I shut down. I knew he was doing what was best for him, and ultimately me, but that didn't make me feel any better.

I felt lost.

My buoy was gone and I was adrift at sea.

He'd etched a permanent scar on my heart.

The sliding glass doors opened onto the pickup line at the hospital.

"Do you see your friend?" She asked.

I searched the cars for Emery, but couldn't find him. He was supposed to be taking me home since Daphne couldn't.

"No," I said. I hoped he didn't take much longer to arrive. I was tired and I wanted to get in bed and sleep for the next ten years.

A few minutes past and Emery still hadn't shown. I was about to ask the nurse to go inside and call him—I didn't have a cell phone with me—when a car I didn't recognize stopped in front of us. The driver hopped out, heading towards us.

"Memphis," I gasped. "What are you doing here?" I asked as he stopped in front of me.

"Griff needed Emery's help," he shrugged. "So, he called me."

Of course he did. I could hear Emery's proud voice in my head saying 'fate.'

"I take it this is your ride?" The nurse asked. I looked up at her to find her checking out Memphis.

"Yep."

She wheeled me over to Memphis' car and with their help I was secured in the passenger seat.

"Thanks," Memphis said to the nurse.

I gave her a weak wave. She'd been nice, everyone had, but I wanted to get home.

Memphis turned the radio down.

Great. He wanted to talk. I really didn't feel like talking anymore.

"You know, I was really shocked when Emery told me what you did."

I rolled my eyes looking out the window at the scenery passing by. "Is that so?"

"Yeah," he said, scrubbing a hand over his face. "I never realized you were depressed. This has made me see that sometimes you just don't know people."

"No, you don't." I replied in a short, clipped tone.

"I wish you had said something to someone." He whispered and I could tell from his voice that he was hurt. "I would've helped you."

"It was a rash decision."

I wasn't looking at him, but I knew he was undoubtedly rolling his eyes. "Suicide is not a rash decision."

I whipped my head in his direction, letting my anger shine through. "You don't know me. You don't know what I've been through. Don't judge me for trying to make the hurting stop."

"Whoa," he said, braking for a stoplight. "Calm down. I'm

not."

"It feels like you are," I snapped. I was losing my voice at this point. If my doctor knew I was talking this much he'd bust a vein in his forehead. I rested my head against the window, letting my eyes drift closed. I was so, so tired.

"I care about you... more than I should, which has been pretty obvious. I thought I was your friend. I wish you could've trusted me with whatever hurt you so much that you thought you had to kill yourself to make it stop."

I swallowed thickly. There was only one person I trusted and I didn't have him anymore. He was gone. He was never really mine to begin with.

"My dad killed himself," Memphis whispered.

Jesus, Christ! Did everyone in this fucking town have a dead relative?!

I didn't say that out loud though. I let him talk.

"None of us knew he was depressed. I was fifteen and I couldn't understand why someone would do that." He let out a sigh. "But I'm older now and I *do* understand. The traumas of our past can seem like such a big deal. However, they're really not. There's always a tomorrow and with tomorrow comes the promise of a better day."

"Were you a philosopher in another life?" I questioned, fighting the desire to fall asleep.

He chuckled—the sound deep and husky, entirely masculine. "You never know."

After picking up my prescription Memphis took me home. He helped me inside and then didn't leave. Why wasn't I surprised?

"You can go now," I told him, searching through a drawer for pajamas.

"I'm not going anywhere." He plopped down on *my* couch, put his feet up on *my* coffee table, and proceeded to turn on *my* TV.

I was going to throat punch him if he didn't get the hell out of my place.

"Leave." I said the word through clenched teeth. I glared at him with every ounce of hatred and annoyance I had left in my body.

"No." He grinned and dimples popped out on both of his cheeks. How had I not noticed them before? "Get changed, sweetie," he waggled his brows, laughing under his breath. "It's going to be a long day and night and the next day and the one after that."

My mouth fell open. "What the hell?" I gasped, my voice sounding scratchy—kind of like what a demented cat would sound like if it tried to talk. Right on cue, Brutus jumped up on my bed, meowing that he wanted to sleep. Thank God Daphne had taken care of him while I was... indisposed. "You can't just," I floundered for what to say next, "move in here."

"I can," he changed the channel, "and I will."

"Ugh!" I groaned, the sound causing my throat to hurt even more.

I was too tired to argue, and seconds away from losing my voice. Memphis could stay if he wanted. Whatever. I didn't care. I totally did, but he didn't need to know that.

I changed into pajamas in the bathroom. I tried not to think about what had taken place in there, but it was impossible.

Without looking at Memphis, so he didn't see my tears, I climbed into bed. I was asleep before my head even hit the pillow.

When I woke up hours later, Memphis was gone.

I felt joyous and did a little fist pump. I really didn't feel like dealing with him. He was nice enough—too nice for me—but I wanted to be alone. Wallowing must be done alone and right now I had a date with the quart of ice cream hiding in my freezer.

I didn't bother with a bowl. I squirted chocolate syrup straight into the half-eaten container of ice cream, added sprinkles, whipped cream, and a cherry for good measure. Oh, yeah. It was perfect.

I sat down on the couch and took my first spoonful.

I moaned in pleasure, my tongue snaking out to wipe my upper lip free of whipped cream.

"You know I never knew someone could make eating ice cream sexy."

I screamed and fell off the couch—and there went my ice cream.

"Memphis!" I cried, my voice cracking. I picked up the container of ice cream and found that it was unharmed from the fall. "What are you doing here?"

"I told you I wasn't leaving," he replied, sitting down several bags on the counter. "I went to the grocery store and Chick-fil-a."

"Why'd you go there?"

"To get you food." He looked at me like I was dumb. "You need things that are soft to eat. And since canned soup *sucks* and I can't make any homemade, I picked you up some from Chick-fil-a, hence the stop there."

"Why are you being nice to me?" I gasped, overcome with an emotion I didn't recognize. Let's face it, I'd been pretty shitty to Memphis. Most guys would've moved on by now, deeming me a lost cause.

He ceased removing items from the bag and turned his head slightly to study me. His brows furrowed together and his lips formed a thin line. "That's what friends are for and I'm your friend."

I swallowed thickly. "I don't have a lot of friends."

"Well, then I count myself lucky to be such," he bowed slightly, smiling for my benefit.

"I don't deserve you," I breathed, my hands tightening around the container of ice cream.

He chuckled. "That's true."

Of course he'd agree.

Desperate to get away from the seriousness of the conversation, I mumbled, "You know, you better be really glad this didn't touch the floor." I pointed at my ice cream.

He shook his head as he went back to unloading the grocery

bags. "What would you have done to me if your precious ice cream was ruined?"

"Hmm," I tapped the end of the spoon against my lips. "I'm thinking a food fight would've been appropriate."

"You're something else, you know that, right?" He gathered up the plastic bags and tossed them in the trash. Without giving me time to answer, he leaned against the counter and said, "You should eat this soup before you devour that ice cream."

I clutched the container in my hand tighter. "Don't touch my ice cream."

He laughed. "I have two sisters, I know not to come between a woman and her sweet tooth."

As I ate my ice cream he put the groceries in their rightful place. He never, not once, stopped to ask me where anything went. He looked through the cabinets and figured it out himself.

Once every last bit of my delicious treat was gone I found myself chilled. I grabbed the blanket off the back of the couch and wrapped it around myself.

"Cold?" Memphis asked.

I nodded.

"Here," he shrugged out of the sweatshirt he wore and handed it to me. "Put this on. It'll keep you warm."

I was reluctant to take it at first, but finally did. The blanket pooled at my waist as I wiggled my body into the sweatshirt. Dang, there was a lot of extra material here. My head finally poked through the opening and I felt like a turtle.

"You know," he smiled, tapping a finger thoughtfully against his pouty lips, "you look really good in that sweatshirt. I think you should keep it."

I rolled my eyes and tucked stray pieces of dark hair behind my ears. I turned my back to him and faced the TV. "Not likely."

His chuckle reverberated behind me and I jumped at his close proximity.

"Jesus! What are you? A fucking ninja? First you manage to get into my apartment without me hearing you and now you're hovering behind me like an uber creeper."

"You have a very dirty mouth," he whispered huskily, his fingers brushing ever so slightly against my collarbone. My heart accelerated at the feather light touch and my throat constricted. It shouldn't have felt so good when he touched me, especially after what had happened with Caelan. I was heartbroken—but my damn heart still reached out for Memphis. I think it always had been and I'd denied it for far too long.

I wasn't going to rush into things though.

I needed time to heal and I wasn't going to be the woman I'd once been—jumping from man to man, because she knew nothing else. I had to gain my independence.

Memphis sat beside me. The couch squished down and I dipped closer to him, which I was sure was his goal. He held the bowl of soup in his hand and a spoon poised above it. He dipped it into the liquid and held it up to my mouth. A bit of broth dripped onto my bottoms and a noodle hung precariously on the edge. "Eat up, buttercup," he chirped.

Was he crazy? He had to be.

"You're not feeding me." I shook my head back and forth and tried to scoot away from him like a young child would from its mother when they didn't want to take medicine.

"Oh I am."

My mouth fell open in shock and he used it to his advantage by shoving the spoon into my mouth.

I sputtered and choked as the hot liquid hit my tongue and trickled down my throat.

Once I had swallowed I narrowed my eyes at him. It really hurt too much for me to continue to argue with him. Frankly, it wasn't worth it. If the smug jerk wanted to hand feed me soup, then so be it. If his fingers got too close I'd be more than happy to take a bite.

Once half of the soup was gone I could stomach no more. I shook my head adamantly that I was done. With a reluctant sigh he set the bowl on the coffee table.

"How are you feeling?" True concern showed in his eyes.

I pondered his question. "I don't know," I answered honestly.

"You've got to give me more than that." He stretched his arm across the back of the couch and his fingers hovered dangerously close to the back of my neck.

"I'm glad I'm alive," I whispered as I toyed with the sleeves of his sweatshirt. "I see now that I have so much to live for." I looked at him out of my peripheral vision.

A small gasp escaped my lips when he reached up and took a strand of my hair between his fingers. He rubbed it leisurely and he seemed to be waiting for me to tell him to stop.

I didn't.

"I'm glad you're okay." His voice was soft and hesitant, like he wasn't sure he should admit that out loud.

"Why?" I forced the word past my parched lips.

He shrugged and looked away from me. A muscle in his jaw jumped. When his gaze connected with mine once more I saw a vulnerability there that I hadn't been prepared for. "I care about you."

To most people they were four simple words. But I wasn't most people and they meant a hell of a lot to me.

I slid my body closer to Memphis'. He appeared skeptical as to what I was going to do. It shocked him completely when I burrowed my body against his. His arms wound around me as I laid my head against his chest.

I wanted to be held. There was nothing wrong with that, right?

No more than a minute had past until I croaked, "He ended things."

I felt every muscle in his body stiffen from my admission. "Are you okay with that?"

What a stupid question.

"No," I admitted. "I understand where he was coming from, but I... I love him."

Memphis smoothed the hair off my forehead and took my

chin between his thumb and forefinger so that I was forced to look at him. "You'll love again."

Was he right? Could I possibly ever love someone as much as I loved Caelan?

"I hope so," was my reply.

CHAPTER 28
Caelan

I WAS IN a fucking cell.

Okay, so it wasn't a jail cell, but it might as well have been.

Three large steps were all it took for me to walk from one side of the room to the other. Was this part of rehab? Did they put you in the smallest room imaginable in the hopes of driving you insane? If the answer was yes, then it was working.

I sat down on the bed and it was so hard that it didn't give an inch with my weight.

I really didn't want to be here, but I knew it was the best thing for me. I was far too dependent on the drugs and alcohol, ultimately becoming that way with Sutton. Apparently I was addicted to everything.

I placed my head in my hands and my clawed at my hair.

I wanted out of here.

I was desperate to escape the stark clinical whiteness.

This wasn't home.

There was *nothing* here that was me. The room was a blank slate. No pictures. No rugs. No TV.

It was empty.

Kind of like me.

I sighed heavily and let out a snarl. I'd only been there—I

looked around for a clock but found none—I'd guess thirty minutes, an hour at most.

And this was going to be where I lived until the doctors believed I was stable.

Fuck.

At this point I'd never be stable. This white box was going to drive me mad.

There was a window though, and it looked out onto a grassy picnic area where the inmates could hang out and eat. Yes, *inmates*, because that's essentially what we were. I didn't know who'd want to utilize it now though. It was winter. Who wanted to sit outside in freezing temperatures? Not me, that was for sure.

I lay back on the bed and stared up at the plain ceiling. I tried to conjure of shapes in the swirls of paint, but came up empty.

The door to my room opened and I sat up.

The prison guard—I was totally sticking with the whole prison comparisons—smiled and said, "Group therapy in five minutes. Someone will be by to get you."

Before I could answer she closed and locked the door—from the outside—once more.

I found it laughable that they locked us in our rooms. I guess they found that they had to, but still. Who was I a threat to? That question was probably better left unanswered.

While I waited for the person responsible for taking me to group therapy—and really, *therapy?* I didn't need therapy—I counted the seconds in my head.

Five minutes on the dot the door was unlocked. It was a man this time.

"Caelan Gregory?" He asked.

I huffed as I came to my feet. "The one and only. Who the fuck else would be locked in this room?"

"I hate firstdayers," the man grumbled.

Great, he had a fucking nickname for it.

"So," I said as he led me down the clean white hallway, "are you my guide dog or something?"

He sighed, shaking his head. "You're all the same when you get here."

I laughed at that. "Trust me, there's no one else like me."

"Well," he shrugged and opened a door, "you're about to find out that there are a lot of people just like you."

"I doubt that," I grumbled as I followed him inside.

"Sit," he ordered, pointing to one of the chairs set up in a round circle. They were blue and plastic—the only spot of color in the—of course—white room. I had never hated white as much as I did right now. Normally, I loved it. Especially when it was a canvas I looked at and there was the promise of endless ideas.

The man took the seat at the head of the group.

Was he a patient here too? If he was, why the fuck had he gotten me from my room? This was fucking weird.

"As you all know," he motioned to the other guys, and a few women too, in the chairs around me, "I'm Alex." Looking straight at me, because as luck would have it I was blessed with the seat directly in front of him. "I'm the therapist here." Staring me down, he continued, "You will have a group therapy session twice a week and three one on one sessions with me a week. Saturday and Sunday are your free days." Ha! Free days! Wasn't that a bunch of bullshit! I was locked in a fucking room! "You do not have to participate in the group today. Think of this as a warm up. You will, however, be expected to participate the next time. No excuses."

Fuck, this guy was a hard ass. He wasn't going to cut me, or anyone, any slack.

"Now," he clasped his hands together and tilted his chair on the back two legs, "I'll go first."

Now I was thoroughly confused. I didn't even understand why we were doing therapy in the first place? Was that normal? I didn't know. I should've researched this place before I allowed myself to be sent here. I wasn't one to talk about my feelings or any shit like that, so this was going to prove interesting.

"I'm thirty-eight. I've been clean for twelve years now. At seventeen years old I was a heroine addict. I got involved in the wrong crowd and wanted to lash out at my parents. They were very strict, you see," he steepled his hands together and leaned forward with his elbows on his knees. "So, like you," he pointed at me, "I've been through the same things. I sat right where you're sitting and questioned why the hell I was here. In my mind, I wasn't an addict. I didn't have a problem. I was fine. Guess, what? I was lying to myself, just like you've been doing to yourself," he pointed at me. "Addiction is a bad thing, but it doesn't make *you* bad." He sat back and crossed his arms over his chest. "The first step to healing is admitting you have a problem."

I wasn't sure if I was supposed to respond, but I did anyway. "Uh... haven't I admitted that I have a problem by being here?"

"In a way," Alex agreed, "but having sat right where you are now, I know you're probably already thinking of leaving and wondering why you agreed to this."

I swallowed thickly. He was exactly right. I kept my mouth shut after that.

"Alright," Alex clapped his hands together, "we'll start here," he pointed to the person on his left, "and go around."

"My name is Kasey," the woman spoke, "I'm an alcoholic."

"Would you like to say anything else?" Alex asked her.

She shook her head. Alex surprised me by not asking her to speak further.

The next person said, "I'm Ray. I'm a cocaine addict. I got addicted when I was only fifteen. Both my parent's were druggies, so I guess I was destined to become one too," he muttered, scratching his arm. "I've been here a month now. It's been the hardest thirty days of my life so far. But," he looked directly at me, "it's worth it."

And so it went.

Everyone spoke—some more than others. I could tell that the ones that didn't say much were new here. I guess we all had to work ourselves up to the deeper stuff.

When the session was over we were dismissed. Alex walked me back to my room once more. I felt like a child being shadowed by a parent so that they didn't run off. Alex seemed nice enough, but I didn't like him. I could tell he was going to push my buttons.

Before he left me alone in my room, he said, "I'm looking forward to seeing you tomorrow."

Boldly, I lifted my hand and showed him my middle finger, waving it through the air with emphasis. If he thought he was going to get me to talk about my feelings, he was mistaken.

Sutton

"WELL, WELL, WELL," Emery chimed the moment I walked into the coffee shop, "if it isn't the mermaid."

I shook my head and ignored him as I headed to the back. He wasted no time followed me.

"How have you been?" He asked.

I grunted and turned around to face him, my hands planted firmly on my hips. "You're best friends with Memphis, right?"

"Yeah," he nodded, clearly wondering where I was going with this.

"Then you should know everything, seeing as how the stubborn ass has lived at my place for the last week!" I cried, stomping my foot in irritation. No matter how hard I tried to get him to leave, Memphis refused to go. I don't know what he was afraid I'd do, he never voiced it out loud, but I was rarely alone anymore. He'd been nice—he was always nice—but it was weird having him around all the time. Especially since I got along with him better than I'd care to admit. He was easy to talk to, fun, and let's face it, nice to look at. But none of those things meant I was okay with him living with me for the time being. He had nothing to worry about. I wasn't going to hang myself from the ceiling rafters. I was okay. I was taking my medicine—even though I didn't think I needed it—and I felt okay. I missed Caelan and a part of me was still scared that Marcus would show up, but I was coping in a healthy way. I'd learned my lesson. Yet, I was still being punished for my moment of weakness. I knew Memphis, Emery, Daphne—all of them—deserved to know the truth about why I'd tried to take my own life. I was trying to get up the courage to tell them, but I hadn't had the guts yet. Telling my parents and boyfriend had gone horribly. While Caelan had been fine, I worried about what the others would think.

"Whoa," Emery lifted his hands in the air, "I was trying to be polite."

"Sorry," I frowned. *Stop acting like a bitch*, I scolded myself. But let's face it, I was one and I'd probably always be one.

When life hands you lemons, become a sarcastic snappy bitch—that was my motto.

I ran my fingers through my hair as I searched for the right words. "This has been a really tough time," I admitted and—oh God, was I going to cry? I better not.

"I'm sure it has," he nodded in agreement. "But you have friends, Sutton. You can talk to me. To Memphis. To Daphne. You're not alone. People care about you. Don't shut yourself off from us."

I grabbed the apron from my locker. "I know I can," I assured him.

"Have you seen a therapist?" He asked.

"I've only been out of the hospital for a week. What do you think?" I replied as I tied the piece of fabric around my waist.

"I think you should," he shrugged. "It would be good for you to get help."

"Ha!" I chortled. "Yeah, and let someone pick my brain, learn all my dirty secrets, and sit there thinking what a horrible person I am? I don't think so!"

"I think you're making a mistake," he said, blocking me from leaving the room.

"Emery," I said his name as calmly as possible, "*please*, I'm begging you, let it go. Don't worry about me. I'm fine. What I did was a dreadful mistake. I'm sorry if I hurt you with what I did, but it happened. It's in the past now and I'm ready to move on."

"Three weeks is in the past? You think that's enough time to move on from a suicide attempt? You're crazier than I thought," he shook his head, laughing humorlessly.

His words stung but I tried my best not to show that.

Upon noticing my frown, he mumbled, "Oh, crap. I shouldn't have said that. I'm sorry."

I raised my shoulders slightly, feigning that I was unaffected. "It's okay. You're right. I am crazy."

"Fuck," he groaned and scrubbed his hands over his face. "I'm the shittiest friend ever."

"I think we both are," I told him.

Shaking his head, he said, "Let's start this over... I'm really worried about you."

"Don't be. Honestly." I pulled my hair back into a ponytail and secured it with a hair tie.

"I can't *not* be," he insisted, still blocking my exit. He was persistent and I wasn't going to leave this room until he was done talking. I sighed, hoping he would stop talking soon. I wanted to get to work and return to normal—well, as normal as my life could be.

I forced a smile and prayed that if I played nice this conversation might end. "I'm sure between you and Memphis I won't be able to do anything stupid. Not that I'm planning to. I know I owe you all an explanation," I nibbled my bottom lip nervously, fuck I hated getting personal with people and showing vulnerability, "but I can't right now. Just know, I had my reasons for doing what I did. It wasn't a decision I took lightly. But *fate*," I tossed the word he so often used back in his face, "had other plans and here I am now." I spread my arms wide. "Looks like you're all stuck with my bitchy and sarcastic self for a while longer."

He chucked and reached out to wrap one arm around my shoulders.

"We're not stuck with you. In fact," he grinned as he ruffled my hair, messing up the ponytail, "we all kind of like you."

I WASN'T SURPRISED when Memphis showed up at the end of my shift to walk me home.

Emery grinned widely at seeing us leave together. Creeper.

"You really don't need to do this." I told Memphis once we were on the street outside. My breath fogged the chilly January air and I pulled my gloves from the pocket of my coat and put them on. The cold air felt good to my heated skin but I didn't want to get sick.

Memphis reached up and adjusted the beanie he wore. "I know, but I want to." Looking at me significantly, he added, "I never do anything unless I want to."

My breath left my body with a shaky rhythm. "I don't understand why you're still here," I shook my head and looked at the sidewalk below my feet. I watched him from the corner of my eyes, and added, "I'm not very nice to you."

He laughed at that. "No, you're not, but I've learned some things are worth fighting for." He stopped on the sidewalk and grabbed my hand so that I was forced to halt. With his other hand he reached up to tenderly cup my cheek. Despite the cold temperature his touch was warm. I found my eyes drifting closed as my body relaxed against his touch. While from the moment I met him my brain and heart had fought against what I felt for him I could never seem to control my body. I hadn't given Memphis a fair shot. I'd been to enamored by the mystery that lurked across the hallway in the form of a tortured artist.

"Don't push me," I gasped, "I'm not ready." My heart wasn't ready to love again—it was far too soon—but that didn't stop my body from curling into his. I'd argued with him non-stop for weeks, because I wanted him to leave. I never told him, but the real reason I wanted him to leave wasn't because his presence was unwelcome. It was because it felt *right*. More right than Caelan had, and that scared me something fierce. I didn't know how to handle these feelings. It seemed unfair to fall for someone else when I'd loved Caelan so fiercely, but I couldn't be alone forever. I did need time to heal, though. Maybe one day I'd be strong enough to be the woman Memphis saw, but I wasn't there yet.

"I know you're not," he forced my chin up so that I couldn't look away from his searing gaze. "I won't push you for more. I may hope, but if you never feel anything for me it's okay."

My heart wrenched painfully at the sincerity in his gaze and tone. Memphis was a *good* guy. I'd never been with a good guy before. Even my ex, Brandon, had been one of the bad ones—always taking his temper out on me with his fists. Back then, though, I'd craved that. I felt the need to be punished, because Marcus had managed to delude me into believing what he did to me was my fault. Guys like him were cunning and they knew how to get inside your head and mess with your thoughts. He'd fucked me up.

"Can I hug you?" I whispered. I was suddenly overwhelmed with the desire to be held—nothing more—and Memphis made me feel *safe*.

He didn't answer. He didn't have to. He held his arms out at his side and I dove in to his chest. His cologne, something woodsy and sweet, clung to his coat. My arms wrapped around his lean body. He was taller and more muscular than Caelan had been and it felt strange for a moment to hug him, but then I relaxed into it. His arms wound around my body and he brushed his lips against the top of my head. "It's going to be okay."

Caelan

I SAT ACROSS from Alex, not saying a word. If he thought he was going to get me to talk about my past and feelings and shit then he was out of his mind

"I don't understand the purpose of this," I said, my voice a growl. "I thought this was rehab—as in, get me sober—not a fucking psych evaluation?"

"You're a very angry young man," Alex remarked. "Why do you think that is?"

I shook my head roughly. "No, no, no, no, no," I chanted. "Do not answer a question with a question."

Alex sighed heavily and adjusted the glasses he wore. "I can see you're going to be one of the most difficult patients I've ever had. Lucky for you, or maybe not so lucky depending on your perspective, I love a challenge."

"Seriously," I muttered, "I don't understand why this is necessary. I'm here to get clean, not hold hands and talk about my feelings."

Alex sighed and fisted his dark hair between his fingers. He was clearly frustrated with me. Good.

"You and I both know why you need this," he remarked and my eyes widened. "Don't act so surprised. I do find out what I can about my patients. You see, an addict doesn't become one because they *want* to. Who wakes up and says, 'Today I want to throw my life away?' No one, that's who. Something has to trigger the need for such dangerous substances. True, some people grow up watching their parents do it and follow suit. Or they grow up where drugs are more prevalent than candy. But most people," he pointed at me, "have been through something traumatic and they see it as a way of escaping. Guess what?" He eyed me. "You're not. You're only adding to your problems."

I rolled my eyes and proceeded to slow clap. "Did they give you that diploma there for saying the most ridiculous things?" I pointed to the document in the fancy frame that hung on the wall behind his desk.

"No," he shook his head and I swore his lips twitched as if he fought a smile. "I *earned* that after I got clean and decided I'd spend my life helping the very people that I once was. But you know something, Caelan?"

"What?" I asked when he didn't continue.

"We'll always be addicts. There will always be a fight and a struggle not to go back down that road." He sat back and began rolling up one of the long sleeves of the button down he wore. He stretched his arm out in front of me. "See these?" He asked, pointing to the scars that adorned the veins of his arms. "They're a constant reminder of the life I used to lead. These scars won't go away, just like the ones inside you can't see. But guess what, with my help and the others here you can learn to move past those negative thoughts whenever you have them," he rolled his sleeve back down. "There will be good days and bad days—but if you work hard enough, one day those bad days won't seem so... well, *bad*. You have to find something you love to grasp onto to carry you through the darkness. It doesn't have to be a person, maybe a hobby," he said, and instantly I thought of my art. "I want you to decide on a goal for yourself. That will be what you work towards. Strive to be something."

I let his words sink in, mulling them over.

Alex looked at his watch and said, "Your session is almost over. But before you go, I want you to look at this." He grabbed a picture frame off his desk and handed it to me. He tapped the top of it and said, "Getting better is a struggle, but it's worth it. Don't you want this for yourself?" He asked.

I stared at the picture of him, his wife, and two kids who were obviously his children. They were all smiling and happy.

Alex held his youngest son in his arms and both wore beaming smiles.
Family.
"I do."

CHAPTER 29
Sutton

"Did Memphis move in here or something?" Were the first words out of Daphne's mouth when she entered my apartment.

"I'm happy to see you too," I laughed.

"Answer the question," she demanded as she looked around at all his stuff strewn everywhere.

"Well, if you're really wanting to know if I've asked him to stay, the answer is a big fat no. He kind of never left," I shrugged simply, picking up my evening cup of coffee. People that said coffee was bad for you were liars. I drank at least three cups a day and I was perfectly normal... well, almost. My nose crinkled at the smell of it. It seemed off. It hadn't smelled like that when I had some earlier. "Does this smell weird to you?" I asked Daphne and held the cup out towards her.

She sniffed it and looked at me like I'd lost my mind. "It smells like coffee."

I smelled it again and my stomach rolled. I put the cup down on the counter and stepped away from it. "I must be getting sick," I mumbled. Now that I thought about it, I had felt fatigued the past week and slightly dizzy several times.

"How are you holding up?" Daphne asked as she sat on the couch. Man, she always knew how to make herself at home.

I knew she wasn't asking me about my attempted suicide and instead about the break up. I sighed and sat down on the floor, crossing my legs. I picked up a candy wrapper—Memphis was always sucking on Jolly Ranchers—and crinkled it between my fingers.

I pondered her question. "Okay, I guess. It's been weeks and I haven't heard from him. I didn't think I would, but still... I'd like to know he's okay. I can't make myself stop loving him or caring about what happens to him."

"I'm so sorry, Sutton," she frowned.

"It is what is," I mumbled and that was the truth. "I tried to call him, even though he told me not to, but his cellphone has been cut off." I wasn't sure if I should admit what I did next, but thought what the heck, and told her. "I wrote him a letter. I haven't mailed it yet. I don't know if I should."

"How medieval of you," she joked. Sobering, she added, "I think you should. Even if you never get back together I think you deserve closure. Don't you? What's the harm in sending it?"

She was right. "I think I will."

"So, when are you kicking Memphis out?" She giggled and picked one of his socks off the couch, wrinkling her nose.

"Uh... don't you think I've tried that? He's more stubborn than me and that's saying something," I laughed. God, it felt good to laugh. "He won't leave."

Dropping the sock on the floor, she said, "He might be messy but at least he's hot."

That was true. Just because I wasn't ready for a relationship didn't mean I was blind.

"Did you just come over here to grill me on Memphis and the catastrophe that is my love life?"

Brutus settled in my lap and began to purr.

"Of course not. I ordered pizza and we're going to binge watch Supernatural," she clapped her hands together excitedly.

"My life is so exciting," I mumbled.

"Hey," she frowned, "The Winchester brothers are sexy, so this *is* exciting."

I snorted. "You need to get out more."

She narrowed her eyes and opened her mouth to say something but fell quiet when there was a knock on the door.

Just like every time I heard a knock, my heart leapt in the hopes that it was Caelan. But then I'd soon remember that he was gone and it would fall once more.

"Oooh! That's the pizza!" Daphne clambered off the couch and rushed towards the door. After signing the receipt she shut the door with her hip. "I'm so hungry and this smells *so* good."

It did smell good. My stomach rumbled at the smell of it. I hadn't realized how hungry I was before. I grabbed plates and we settled on the couch to eat and watch TV.

After hours of watching Supernatural I said goodbye to her.

I picked up the letter I'd written days ago and began to read it over.

Dear Caelan,

First off, it seems really weird to send you a letter. I tried to call you and your phone was cut off, so I thought I'd sit down and write this. Although, now that I'm doing it, I feel strange about it. I'm not sure if you even want to hear from me again. I need to do this for myself though. I'm happy you're getting help and I understand why you ended things. That doesn't stop it from hurting though. I want you to know that I'm not angry. Love is crazy and ours was one of the craziest—but that kind of love can be dangerous. I hope that when you're out and come home that I'll get to talk to you in person. I don't want us to become strangers.

I'm not sure if you're allowed to write back, and even if you are and you don't want to, that's okay. I needed to get this off my chest.

I live for you Caelan Gregory. Even if we're not together, that statement will always be true.

Thank you for giving me your love, even if I wish I could've held onto it for much longer.

**Love,
Sutton**

I folded the letter and slipped it into an envelope. I didn't have the address for the rehab he was at, so I sent Kyle a text and asked for it.

I didn't work tonight and Memphis would be home in about an hour. He'd been here so long now, that I wasn't sure what I'd do when he left. It was actually nice having the company and not being alone all the time.

Deciding to be nice, since I constantly gave him a hard time, I made a fancy pasta dish. The scent of garlic and parmesan cheese permeated the air. I wasn't hungry after eating pizza, but I knew Memphis would appreciate the gesture.

I was stirring everything together when he walked through the door.

"Mmm, something smells delicious," he rubbed his stomach.

My smile was small. "I thought I'd make you something. It's the least I could do."

"Well, thank you." His grin was wide, showcasing his adorable dimples. "I'm going to get a shower first."

I nodded and set about putting the pasta in a bowl. I even poured him a glass of wine. I truly felt bad for acting like a bitch to him most of the time. I knew he was only doing what he thought was right and I appreciated it.

I set everything down on the raised countertop, including a

napkin and utensils.

A few minutes later I heard the bathroom door creak open. I looked up from my spot on the couch where I'd sat down to read a little bit. My mouth fell open and a small gasp escaped me. I couldn't help it. Memphis stood there in nothing but a towel hanging low on his waist. Water droplets clung to his muscular chest and his copper colored hair was darker than normal as it shined with wetness. I licked my lips—my throat suddenly dry.

He smiled sheepishly and I swore there was a slight blush staining his cheeks.

"I—uh—forgot clean clothes," he mumbled, unable to make eye contact with me as he rifled through his bag.

I was a horrible person, because I sat there willing the towel to drop.

Snap out of it, Sutton! I scolded myself, but it did no good. I couldn't look away.

The bathroom door closed behind him and I was able to breathe again.

Jesus, he was gorgeous. I might not be looking for a relationship but I couldn't deny his hotness.

I think I needed another shower.

A very cold, very long shower.

Dressed, and clearly still embarrassed, he made his way over to the counter with his head bowed.

I felt like something had shifted in our relationship—there was no denying the mutual attraction now.

"There's only one bowl," he commented, turning to look at me over his shoulder.

I nodded, tucking a stray hair behind my ear. "I ate pizza with Daphne." With a playful smile I added, "Feel free to ask her if you don't believe me."

He chuckled but said nothing. He picked up the bowl and glass of wine. He sat down beside me on the couch and smiled crookedly. "It was lonely over there, so I thought I'd sit here where I'd have the company of the most beautiful woman in the world."

I laughed at that comment. "You're full of it." I turned the TV off and settled in for some conversation. "How was work?"

He chuckled, taking his first bite of pasta. "It's bartending, so it's always eventful."

"Did you always want to be a bartender?" I asked.

He watched me from the corner of his eye. "Why so many questions?"

I shrugged casually. "Just trying to get to know you."

"I went to culinary school," he muttered. My eyes widened in shock. "My dream is to own a restaurant one day. Until that day comes, I'll continue to bartend. I don't hate it, but it's not what I love."

"Your own restaurant," I gasped, mulling it over. Memphis was determined and a natural leader, so I could see him having success with it. "I think that would be so cool."

"Really?" He asked. "My dad always thought it was stupid. He thought I should do something more manly."

I laughed at that. "I think owning your own business is a big responsibility. Besides, what's so wrong with doing what you love?"

"What about you?" He questioned. "Surely you have bigger dreams than working at Griffin's?"

I swallowed thickly. "I have a business degree, but I honestly have no idea what I want to do. I know at my age I should have it figured out, but I don't."

"There's nothing wrong with that," he took another bite of food.

Frowning, I asked, "How bad is it? Now that I know you went to culinary school I'm never cooking ever again."

He laughed at that—the kind of laugh that shakes your whole body. "It's delicious."

I let out a sigh of relief. "Glad to hear that."

"Are you sure you don't want some?" He stretched his legs out, crossing them at the ankle.

"I'm sure. I ate..." I blushed and stopped myself.

"You ate?" He prompted.

"Well, I kind of ate half of the pizza. I was *really* hungry." I fiddled with the remote in my hand, wishing I hadn't turned the TV off.

He chuckled. "Why are you embarrassed about that?"

"I'm not," I said vehemently.

He said no more as he finished his dinner.

I went to grab the empty bowl from him so I could clean it, but he refused to relinquish it. Instead, he stood and trekked over to the sink.

I yawned, suddenly feeling absolutely exhausted. I gathered my pajamas and changed in the bathroom.

I grabbed my cellphone off the coffee table and saw I had a text from Kyle with the address. I smiled. I was scared to send the letter, but I knew I needed to.

Once the dishes were clean Memphis settled on the couch. He grabbed the blanket and draped it over his body. "Night, Sutton."

"Goodnight," I whispered, laying my head on the pillow and letting my eyes drift closed.

Caelan

IT TURNS OUT Saturday and Sunday were legit free days. The door to my room was left unlocked and we were all encouraged to explore the facility, get to know one another, and utilize the outdoor area. I noticed a lot of people chose to go outside. It had snowed the night before and I wasn't sure I wanted to brave the frigid temperatures. I understood why most were doing it though. We were cooped up in our small rooms all week and it was nice to inhale the fresh air.

"Aren't you coming?" One of the women from group therapy

asked as she headed towards the door.

"Uh..."

"Come on," she begged, "it may be cold but at least it's not, well," she looked around, "*here*."

After a moment of hesitation, I agreed.

I grabbed my sweatshirt from my room and shrugged it on. The woman had waited for me. I didn't even remember her name.

Outside the dusting of snow on the ground crunched beneath my feet. I sat down at one of the picnic tables where several people I recognized sat. I hadn't really bothered to get to know any of them. I hadn't cared. Looking at them now, I realized that was a mistake. Essentially, we were all in this together. We'd all been through similar things. If I couldn't talk to these people, then who could I? I'd been able to tell Sutton everything and yet I had trouble opening up to these people. Even now, I didn't open my mouth to speak to them. I sat there, a silent observer to their conversations.

I rubbed my hands together, trying to generate some heat.

"What about you, Caelan?" One of them asked.

"Huh?" I replied, feeling bad that I wasn't paying attention.

"What made you start using?" The guy across from me repeated.

"Oh," I looked down at the wooden table. "I..."

"It's okay if you don't want to tell us. We know how hard it can be to talk about," the woman beside me spoke. I thought her name was Bree.

"No, it's okay," I said, "it's just hard to talk about."

"Take your time. I'm Josh," he added, as if he knew I'd forgotten their names.

After a moment of gathering myself, I answered, "I found my family murdered. I started using so I could forget what they looked like when I found them. In the process, I started to forget other things about them—the good things. It was hard once I lost them. I went off the deep end and people told me I was a screw up instead of getting me the help I needed. By the time they realized how bad off I was it was too late for them to force me into rehab." I sighed, deciding to recant the whole story. "Then, this past summer, I met a woman and she changed everything. I wanted to be better for her. I didn't use as often and I didn't drink as much as I used to. She knew everything about me and she didn't care. She still loved me. But she had struggles too," I whispered. "When they caught up with her, she tried to end it. So, I followed suit. I tried to take my life so I could be with her. I realized how fucked up that was. She'd become another unhealthy addiction for me. So, I ended things and I agreed to come here," I spread my arms wide. "And that's my story."

Silence greeted me and then they went back to talking about random non-sense. Like favorite foods, where they lived, that sort of thing. My life didn't matter to them. Not in a bad way, but they didn't pity me. They'd been through hardships too. We were all the same—equals. And I'd be lying if I said it didn't feel nice to belong.

CHAPTER 30
Sutton

I SENT THE letter and I waited. For what, I don't know. An answer? A sign he still cared?

You know what I got?

The fucking letter was sent back to me, unopened.

I crinkled it in my fingers, but couldn't make myself throw it away. Instead, I shoved it in one of my dresser drawers. I was mad. Really mad. Could he seriously dismiss me so easily that he couldn't even read a letter I wrote him?

Apparently so.

"Hey, are you okay?" Memphis asked. He sat at the kitchen counter with his laptop. He ran his fingers through his shaggy hair and then pushed his glasses further up his nose. I hated to admit it, but he made those dorky thick-framed glasses look pretty damn hot.

"I'm fine," I forced a smile and twisted my hair into a bun. A few strands escaped the confines and framed my face.

"And I know you well enough to know that's a big fat lie." He closed the lid of his laptop and stared me down.

He knew about the letter so I figured there was no point in lying. "The letter got sent back."

He frowned, his eyes filling with compassion. His look made

me squirm. He was the last person on the planet that should be concerned about me. He was always so nice to me and while he made it clear that he hoped for more with me, he never pushed.

"Please, don't look at me like that," I whispered.

"Like what?" He chuckled, picking up a pen and chewing on the end.

"Like my pain hurts you." My voice was nothing more than a meek squeak. Since my suicide attempt and the break-up I'd felt more vulnerable. My tough girl façade had fallen away, revealing the damaged woman I was.

He frowned, a wrinkle marring his normally smooth forehead. "It does, though. That's how it works when you care about someone."

I bowed my head in embarrassment and didn't address his comment.

"As for the letter being sent back, maybe he's hurting and couldn't bear to read what you'd written."

I snorted at that. Caelan was not a romantic enough guy to have that sort of reaction.

"Or," Memphis continued, ignoring my reaction to his previous statement, "maybe they don't allow outside communication."

I frowned at that. When Caelan told me not to call—which I tried to anyway because I'm an idiot—I remembered him saying that he didn't think they'd let him talk to anyone on the outside. So, it was a possibility, but still... that didn't make it hurt any less. Especially since I didn't know if it was true or not.

I settled on the couch, trying to dismiss the returned letter from my mind. But it proved impossible.

Memphis got up and put a pack of popcorn in the microwave. As it popped my nose wrinkled and bile crawled up my throat. "What's wrong with the popcorn? It smells gross," I gagged.

Memphis' brows crinkled together in confusion. "It smells fine."

The microwave dinged and he took it out. As soon as the bag

opened I went running for the bathroom, emptying the contents of my stomach.

I heard Memphis' heavy steps against the floor as he hurried to me. His long fingers gathered my hair away from my face. "I threw it away. Are you okay?" He asked as I heaved against the toilet.

"Do I look okay?" I coughed.

He released my hair and wet a cloth, which he then handed to me.

I cleaned myself up and brushed my teeth. The whole time Memphis stood in the doorway with his arms crossed.

"Why are you looking at me like that?" I questioned before rinsing my mouth.

He appeared nervous, like he wasn't sure if he should say something, but eventually he said, "I know I don't have a vagina or anything, and I really don't know anything about this, but..." He ran his fingers nervously through his hair. "Could you be pregnant?"

I dropped the bottle of Listerine and since it was lidless blue liquid sprayed across the tile floor. We both hurried to grab the bottle and wipe up the mess.

My heart raced and sweat broke out across my forehead. Could he be right?

"Oh God." I slapped a hand across my mouth and thought I might be sick again, but there was nothing left in my stomach.

I crumbled to the floor and tears streamed down my face.

I hadn't even thought there was a possibility that I was pregnant. I'd chalked up all the weirdness I'd been experiencing lately to what I'd gone through.

I wrapped my arms around myself, trying to hold it together, but it wasn't working. Memphis sat down beside me and soon his arms joined mine. He coaxed my head to his chest and let me cry. He didn't say anything comforting. His hold on me was enough. He was a better friend than I deserved but I clung to him with all the strength I had left.

My tears soaked his shirt and the mascara coating my lashes stained the white material.

"It's going to be okay, Sutton. I'm here for you and I'm not going anywhere. We'll get through this together." He rubbed a soothing hand up and down my arm.

His kind words only made me cry harder. I didn't deserve him. Not at all.

His fingers tangled in my hair and he continued to whisper sweet words—each one an individual stab to my heart, because if I was honest with myself, I was falling for him and now I could be pregnant with another man's baby. True, I wasn't looking for a relationship yet, but that didn't mean I planned on being alone for the rest of my life. Memphis was good for me. I'd been fighting against him and my feelings for far too long and now there could possibly be a very large obstacle standing in our way. But I wasn't only crying because of Memphis and the possibility of a future with him. I wasn't *that* selfish. I was mostly crying because if he'd guessed right, and I was having a baby, I was going to be raising a child by myself and that was a scary thought.

"Please, stop crying," he begged, trying to soothe me with soft touches and kind words.

"You shouldn't be comforting me right now." I removed myself from his embrace and rubbed at my eyes.

"Sutton," he put a hand on my shoulder and forced me to look at him, "I want to be here for you. Why are you so afraid to let me in?"

I laughed at that. "Memphis, you're a good guy. A *really* good guy. And I'm fucked up. I don't deserve your kindness. You shouldn't waste your time on someone like me."

"Someone like you?" He repeated my words back to me. "Don't you realize, we don't choose who we fall in love with, it just happens."

"Are you saying that you love me?" I gasped, scooting away from him.

He shook his head. "Yes. No. I don't know," he mumbled. Meeting my eyes, he said, "I feel like I'm on my way to that point." Swallowing thickly, he added, "I know you don't feel that way about me, and I'd never pressure you, but..." He trailed off. "Maybe one day?" He framed it as a question.

"I-I—" I gaped, at a loss for words. "I don't know. Maybe." My voice was softer than a whisper, but he nodded like he heard me.

He stood and held his hands out to me to help me up. "There's no point in staying cooped up in the bathroom."

He settled me on the couch and draped the blanket around my shoulders.

"We'll schedule you an appointment to see a doctor in the next few days." He pressed his lips to my forehead in a soft, lingering kiss. He cleared his throat and stepped away from me. Something about that way he'd said *'we'* had made my body go cold. He acted as if we were in this together. I hadn't ever had anyone in my life before that treated me the way he did. I'd be lying if I said I didn't like it. I was fighting my feelings for Memphis tooth and nail, but they were there and they weren't going away. I couldn't help but echo his words in my head.

Maybe one day.

MY FINGERS TAPPED against the arm of the chair I sat in. I didn't think I had ever been this nervous in my entire life. Sweat dotted my skin and I couldn't get enough oxygen to reach my lungs.

Memphis sat beside me, his leg bouncing up and down restlessly.

"You don't have to be here," I reminded him for the tenth time that day.

"I know," he assured me, "but I want to be."

I didn't argue with him, because the fact of the matter was, I needed him. Without him, I wasn't sure I could do this. I didn't know what made me do it, but I reached over and entwined my fingers with his. He smiled and gave my hand a reassuring squeeze.

I knew I should be brave and face this alone, but I was tired of doing everything by myself. For once, I wanted someone else to be the strong one while I crumbled.

I held my breath as I waited for my name to be called.

I was beyond nervous and while a part of me hoped I was pregnant with Caelan's child, because then I'd have a piece of him forever, there was another part that hoped I wasn't. If I were having a baby, this would change my whole life. In the span of a few minutes I could be told I was going to be a single mom. I wasn't stupid and I knew raising a child was a huge responsibility.

My name was called and I stood slowly, wiping my sweaty palms on the fabric of my jeans. I thought I might pass out. Memphis stood too and put a reassuring hand on my waist.

"Do you want me to go back with you?" He asked. "I assumed you wanted me to stay out here, but I'll go if you want me to."

"I don't know," I admitted, biting my lip as I eyed the nurse waiting for me.

"How about this, I'll go back with you and if you change your mind at any time, I'll leave? Sound good?" He peered at me with clear gray eyes. He was far too kind to me. I didn't deserve him.

I nodded and still holding hands we walked to the nurse. She led us through the office and into a private room. She gave me a gown and instructed me to change in the connecting bathroom. I could hear the blood rushing through my body. There was still a very real possibility that I'd pass out.

When I exited the bathroom Memphis had his back turned so that he didn't see anything that he shouldn't.

I sat down and waited.

"It's going to be okay," Memphis murmured as he took my

hand once more.

"How can you say that?" I peered up at him. "This isn't your life. Or even your child if I'm pregnant. You can walk away at any time. We're not a couple," I laughed humorlessly.

He chuckled. "Why do you doubt me? You've never asked me to be here, so did it ever occur to you that maybe I'm here because I want to be?"

Moisture clung to my lashes. "You shouldn't *want* to. Not after everything I've put you through."

He clenched his teeth, grinding them together.

The doctor walked in and my throat became dry. She asked me the normal questions and I answered them as best I could. When it came down to time for the ultrasound, Memphis asked, "Do you want me to go?"

"No," I grabbed on to his hand and held on tight. "Please, stay. Don't leave me." My words encompassed more than this moment. I didn't want to lose him at all, but realistically I knew the chances of him sticking around were slim.

He nodded. "I'm not going anywhere."

Everything after that happened in a blur. It was like I was there in body, not in mind. I pretty much shut down after the doctor confirmed I was having a baby. There were so many things running through my mind. Memphis had to basically carry me out of the doctor's office. I couldn't seem to stop crying either—I was going to blame that on pregnancy hormones.

Memphis parked the car and I finally looked up. I expected to be parked outside the apartment, but instead there was a restaurant in front of us.

"You need to eat something," he whispered.

"I'm not hungry," I mumbled as I stared out the window.

"Sutton," he groaned. "You can't shut down."

He was right, but that still didn't make me feel like moving.

Eventually he got out of the car and came around to my side. He opened the door and pulled me out.

"Memphis," I whined, "I look like crap," I pointed to my face where there were bound to be streaks of mascara. "Don't make me go in there."

"Excuses, excuses," he muttered as he took my hand and dragged me inside.

Nobody paid us any attention as he led us to a booth in the back.

I wiped underneath my eyes and picked up a menu. I wasn't hungry, not at all, but I knew he was right and I needed to eat. When the waitress came by we both ordered a glass of water.

I perused the menu, hoping something would taste good to me. Even though it was well after lunchtime, the restaurant served breakfast all day, so I decided to order an omelet. I figured I couldn't go wrong with that.

Memphis clasped his hands together and eyed me. "How are you feeling?"

I traced my finger along one of the wood grains in the table and mumbled, "Scared."

"I believe that is perfectly normal," he assured me.

"Normal or not," I commented, taking a sip of water, "I don't enjoy the feeling."

He reached across the table and put his hand atop mine. "This isn't the end of the world, Sutton."

"You're not the one having a baby," I muttered.

"That's true," he agreed with a nod. "But I'll be there for you, I know Daphne and Emery will too. We may not be *family* but we're not going anywhere. You're not alone in this. He might be gone—"

"Caelan," I interrupted. "You can say his name. It doesn't bother me." Actually, it did, but it was better if I heard it. I needed to become desensitized.

He cleared his throat. "*Caelan*, might be gone, but you don't have to raise this baby by yourself."

"Are you proposing marriage?" I kept a straight face, even though I meant the question as a joke.

Memphis paled and then laughed. "As much as I'd like to

marry you someday, I have feeling if I asked you right this second, they'd end up carrying me out of here in a body bag."

"You've got that right," I smiled. Tugging my hair over my shoulder, I let out a sigh. "I know this isn't a bad thing unless I make it that way. But this is a human being we're talking about. I can keep myself alive, and my cat, but a baby? I'm not good with kids!" I cried. "The moment they start screaming I'm done and hand them back to their parents. I can't do that if it's my kid!" My hand went to my flat stomach and I rubbed it absentmindedly. "I want my baby, so please don't doubt me there, but I'm not sure I can do this."

"You can and you will," he assured me.

I wished I had as much faith in myself as he had in me.

MEMPHIS DROPPED ME off at the apartment and headed to work. Once inside, I grabbed a piece of paper, a pen, and began to compose my second letter.

Since the first had been sent back, it was probably a stupid idea to try to send another, but I didn't have any other options at this point. Also, I found writing to him to be therapeutic and cleansing. Even if he didn't read it, I'd feel better.

Dear Caelan,

The first letter I wrote to you was sent back to me. Unopened. I don't know whether you never got it, or if you simply didn't want to read it. I was mad at first, but since things are over between us I have no real reason to even talk to you. I know it would be best for me to move on and forget you. I'm trying, even though I don't want to. I'm beginning to realize, that when I move on (and I say when, because I won't pine for you forever Caelan Gregory) I'll always love you. You hold a special place in my heart. That kind of love doesn't go away.

But that's not why I'm writing you this letter.

I went to the doctor today. I'm not sick, but I am pregnant. I don't know how this happened, but I can't bring myself to be mad. I'm scared out of my mind, but I'm not mad.

Our love may have ended, but it lives on in our baby.

I hope you're getting better.
I miss you.

Love,
Sutton

I read through the letter three or four times before I slipped it inside an envelope. I addressed it and stuck a stamp in the corner so that it would be ready to mail in the morning.

Banging across the hall had me sitting up straight.

My heart went in to overdrive as my ears focused on the sounds. Someone was definitely in Caelan's apartment. Was he back? Had he not been able to cope with rehab? Was that why my letter was sent back?

I forced the questions from my mind and ran to the door. It swung open and I gazed across the hall. I hoped to see Caelan, but of course it wasn't him. I wasn't that lucky.

The sight that met me only served to shatter my broken heart further.

The door to Caelan's apartment was propped open with a box. Inside, I saw Kyle with more boxes, packing Cael's stuff away.

He wasn't coming back.

He needed to start fresh and that hurt. When he got out of rehab I wouldn't get to see him and I wouldn't know where he was going.

We're all wrong for each other. Caelan's words echoed through my skull. *I have to say goodbye to you. I'll be gone for a while and even once I'm out, I don't know if I'll be strong enough for this.* He wasn't sure if he was strong enough for *me* was what he really meant.

"Hi, Kyle," I whispered. He didn't hear me. "Kyle," I repeated his name louder.

He looked over his shoulder and saw me. "Hey, Sutton," he smiled, but it was forced. He stopped packing the boxes as I slowly made my way into the apartment.

"What are you doing?" My question was unnecessary, but I felt the need to ask it anyway.

He put his hands on his hips and tilted his head slightly to the side. The look he gave me said, *do you really want to know?* My answer was, of course, yes.

"Cael is going to move in with me once he gets out of rehab. He has a minimum of two months left, but I thought I'd go ahead and get his stuff cleared out." He shrugged, looking at the ground. This was awkward for the both of us. It was clear he knew that Caelan and I were no more. But had there ever really been an *us* to begin with? "How have you been?" He asked, trying to remain casual.

"Busy," I mumbled. No way was I telling him about the baby.

I looked around at the canvases, paintbrushes, and other random items littering the space. Soon they'd be gone and this place would be empty until someone else came along. It was really hitting me that I was never going to see him again. I wouldn't get to talk to him or see him smile. I would never argue with him again, or have the chance to piss him off by making too much noise. It was really and truly over. I had to accept that and move on with my life. Caelan was right when he told me not to wait for him. We were a dysfunctional, chaotic mess and I loved every second of every moment we shared. But chaos didn't last. Eventually it disappeared like dust in the wind and ceased to exist... just like us.

CHAPTER 31
Caelan

"You're making good progress," Alex commented, looking over his notes.

I didn't need him to tell me that. I knew I was. Things had changed for me once I opened up that day over a month ago at the picnic tables. It had been quite the eye-opener for me. For far too long I'd pitied myself, but these people didn't. They were all experiencing the same things. They didn't offer condolences or hugs. They listened and moved on.

"You know," he cleared his throat, "in two weeks you'll have been here for ninety days. You're not required to stay past that, unless you want to."

"I know," I nodded. "I think I'm ready to go home."

Although, I really didn't have a home anymore. When I'd last saw Kyle in the hospital we'd discussed it and both agreed it would be best if I terminated my rent agreement at my place and moved in with him. I needed someone to keep an eye on me. Basically, Kyle was going to be my glorified babysitter so that I didn't do something stupid.

"I'm happy to hear that," Alex smiled. Leaning forward, he asked, "You remember our first private session?"

I nodded.

"I asked you to focus on a goal for when you got out of here."

I nodded again.

"Would you mind sharing that goal with me?"

"Uh..." I didn't see why not, so I forged ahead. "I want to own my own art gallery. I want to be able to display my own art, as well as other locals, and maybe offer classes to children and adults that are interested."

Alex's smile widened further. "I'm proud of you, Caelan. You've done an exceptional job here. At first, I thought you were going to be one of my hardest patients but you've really been a breeze."

I rested my elbows on the arms of the chair I sat in. "I realized that I was constantly making everything about me. I was acting like my problems were worse than everyone else's and that's not true."

"I think you have a very good goal for yourself, but if it doesn't work out, you should consider being a therapist."

I snorted at that. Me? A therapist? He was definitely crazy.

"Yeah, so not happening doc."

"Well," he chuckled, "it was worth a shot."

We spent the rest of the time talking about what I wanted to do on the outside—see, prison talk—and he told me if I ever felt myself slipping to never hesitate to call him day or night. I took the business card he handed me but I didn't intend to use it. I felt great—not healed or anything, but like a normal human being. The hurt and aching was still there, I think it always would be, but I didn't feel the need to make it go away. *Feeling* was a part of being human. Trying to mask your emotions was a dangerous thing.

"I'll see you again soon," Alex said as my time was up. I left quickly, but I wasn't desperate to escape Alex's company. While, initially, he'd pissed me off I'd quickly learned that he really was on my side and having gone through this same stuff I could confide in him. Talking to people that could relate was a gift. I'd fought hard against going to rehab before, but I was glad I'd done it. I knew a part of me would probably always ache for the drugs and alcohol—probably the alcohol even more so, since it was much easier to acquire—but I could make the choice to stay away. Saying 'no' was a powerful thing, even when it was yourself you were denying.

Sutton

"ARE YOU TWO dating?"

My eyes threatened to bug out of my head at Daphne's question. Memphis chuckled beside me and Emery grinned from the other side of the table.

"I hate to inform you, Daphne, but she doesn't like me like that." Memphis stretched his arm across the back of the booth.

I laughed and shifted my head to look at him. "Who's saying I don't? And, in case you forgot, I'm kinda pregnant and last time I checked you weren't the father."

"Doesn't mean you can't date," he countered, smiling widely.

"That would be fucking weird," I mumbled.

"You've got the arguing like an old married couple down pat," Emery interrupted.

While things with Memphis had been friendly lately, and he made his attraction clear, it just felt strange. What could he possibly see in me? I'd pushed him away and now I was having a baby. What sane male wants that kind of baggage?

"I don't see what would be weird about it," Memphis addressed my previous comment. "It's not like I've recently developed feelings for you. I've known you for over six months now. It's not like I have some disturbing fetish you should worry about."

"Like wanting to bang a pregnant woman?" I asked.

He had been taking a sip of his soda and it sprayed out of his mouth across the table at my question. He coughed and tried to regain his breath. "You're something else," he told me once he'd regained his breath.

Smiling, I chirped, "I know."

Memphis wasn't staying with me anymore, but we did hang out a lot. I enjoyed his company and it was nice not being alone. He didn't pressure me for more, even though I knew he wanted it. He was waiting for me to make the first move. While the desire was there, I was scared. My feelings for Caelan hadn't disappeared—they never would—and I was pregnant. To have a relationship with Memphis seemed wrong. I felt like I'd hold him back from bigger and better things. Did he really want to handle a baby and me? And what if things between us ended a few years down the road and it hurt my child too? It was a lot to consider, but I also knew I couldn't let fear hold me back.

I hadn't said anything to Memphis about Marcus yet, but I knew I needed to. Now that I was having a baby, I definitely needed to get a restraining order filed against him. I didn't only have myself to worry about anymore. I wouldn't let that psycho fucker mess with my baby. Toying with my bottom lip I watched Memphis from the corner of my eye. I needed to tell him. Daphne and Emery too. They'd all been far too good to me and I was harboring secrets. It wasn't right. For my wellbeing I needed to get it out in the open. Caelan had helped me to see that I wasn't ruined because of it. Still, it was something that was hard to talk about.

As they all chatted away about randomness, I gave myself a silent pep talk.

When I was ready, I said, "Guys, there's something I need to tell you. I know I should've told you a long time ago, but this is hard for me to talk about." And there came the damn tears. *Go away, tears! I don't want to cry!* "I know you were all shocked about me... well... you know... trying to kill myself," I muttered. "But I had my reasons." They all grew quiet and sat with rapt attention as I recanted the story from the very beginning. It was hard to force the words out, but I did it. When I finished, Memphis punched the table and walked out of the restaurant. I was hurt by his reaction but I tried not to show it. When he didn't return a crying Daphne and worried Emery urged me to go after him.

I slid out of the booth and headed outside. I found him at the side of the building. His hands were braced against the stone surface of the restaurant wall and his head was bowed so he didn't see me approach.

"Memphis?" I said his name cautiously like he was a wild animal that might attack me.

Upon hearing his name he turned to face me. His eyes were red rimmed and he scrubbed a hand over his face in the hopes of hiding the depths of his emotions.

"Are you okay?" I took a hesitant step closer.

"Am I okay?" His look was incredulous. "Are you seriously asking me that right now?" I opened my mouth to respond, but he barreled on. "*I* should be asking *you* that. I knew something had to have happened to push you over the edge but I never guessed *that*. Then, for you to say that he showed up at your fucking door?!" I startled at his language and raised tone. Memphis was the guy that was always calm, cool, and collected so to see him lose it like that was a bit disconcerting. I mean, I guess I should have expected it, but I didn't. "I can't stand the thought of anyone laying their hands on you like that." His fists clenched at his sides and his jaw flexed. "It's not okay. He needs to be sent to prison for what he did to you."

I shook my head. "That may be true, but it's too late for that. The only thing I can do now is make sure he can't hurt me again or the baby."

"He's never getting near you ever again!" Memphis shoved a finger in my direction to drive home his point. "That's it," he paced back and forth, "I'm moving in with you."

I rolled my eyes at his dramatics and in a calm tone said, "Didn't you already try to do that? I finally got rid of you," I laughed so it took away any possible harshness my words may have had, "you don't need to worry about me. I'm fine."

"I worry about you because I care. I can't just stop my feelings for you. God," he shook his head, "you get under my skin like no one else can." He closed the distance between us in a few long strides. His breath left him in heavy gusts. He was clearly worked up and nothing I said seemed to calm him. His movements were quick and I didn't realize what he was about to do until it was too late.

His large hands covered my cheeks and he tipped my head back slightly as he covered my mouth with his. This kiss seared me straight down to my very toes. I'd kissed Memphis before, but it was nothing like this. *This* was a kiss. That day, so many months ago when I'd burst into the restaurant and kissed him... yeah, this is what I'd been trying to feel then. It was like the kiss brought all my feelings flooding to the surface and my God, I realized I'd been falling for Memphis for a long time—even when I'd been with Caelan. Emery's words from so long ago echoed in my head, *"I don't need to play matchmaker when fate will do the work for me."*

He was right.

I'd denied it at first, but fate was definitely at work here. I might've fallen in love with Caelan first, and needed him to heal the parts of me that were too dark for others to see, but Memphis was the one my heart belonged to. I'd never believed in soul mates or fate like Emery, but in this moment I believed there was definitely some cosmic force at work that made sure I stood here right now kissing *this* man.

My mouth opened beneath his and his tongue slipped inside. A soft, light moan escaped me and he growled low in his throat in response.

My body curled against his and he wrapped his arms around me in a protective embrace. His warmth surrounded me like the heat of a sunny day. Memphis was magnetic and I couldn't help but be drawn to him. He was the kind of guy all girls dreamed of finding—but circumstances, like my epic fuckedupness, had kept us from being together when we met.

We were getting a second chance, and I was ready to embrace it. No more running. No more hiding.

Memphis broke the kiss. He breathed deeply and couldn't hide the smile on his face. "Did you feel that?" He grinned as he asked the question.

I knew what he meant. Did I feel the *rightness* of us? "Yes."

His smile widened impossibly further, his dimples showing in both cheeks. He kissed me again, this time it was a simple quick brush of his lips, but it was enough to leave me shaking.

"I know you probably have a lot of concerns," he looked meaningfully down at my stomach, "but I want you to know, that wherever we end up I will love your baby like it's my own. It doesn't matter to me. This isn't a burden you need to worry about scaring me away. It'll take a lot more than that," he chuckled. He cradled my cheek in one hand and I let myself lean in to his touch. A huge part of me was screaming that this was too fast, but it wasn't like I was declaring love or jumping into bed with him. Memphis knew I needed slow and he wouldn't push me, I knew that. Holding back a laugh, he questioned, "Does this mean you'll stop pushing me away now?"

I laughed at that, bowing my head slightly to hide my smile, but he forced my chin up so that I couldn't conceal myself from him. "I guess so."

"That's better than no." His gray eyes met mine and there was so much happiness reflected in their depths that I couldn't help but smile.

"This doesn't mean we're dating, though," I warned him.

"Are we pre-dating then?" He quipped.

"Uh... I guess so," I laughed—the sound so light and genuine that it surprised me.

"I don't want to ruin the moment," his hands fell to my waist, "but I want you to know that I understand you're still struggling with what happened between you and Caelan, and of course the

Marcus thing as well. I think I've proved that I care about you and I'm here for you. If you need to talk or a shoulder to cry on, I'm your guy," he chuckled. "I know you've been keeping a lot of stuff in like the letters—"

I flinched. I'd tried to push that to the back of my mind. The second letter I'd mailed had been sent back just like the first—the same with the third and fourth and fifth. I still wrote them, but I'd stopped sending them. Caelan might never read them, but writing them gave me a much needed clarity and sense of relief. It bothered me that he didn't know about the baby, and he might never. I knew I could contact Kyle, but something about that didn't seem right. Caelan had made it clear by cutting off his phone, moving out of his apartment, and not reading one damn letter, that he didn't want anything to do with me. We'd said our goodbyes and he didn't need any more closure. I wasn't going to force him to be a part of the baby's or my life. I certainly wouldn't keep him from the baby either, but reaching out to him had become too painful. It was like I was continually taking a punch to the heart where Caelan was concerned. It'd been over three months since I'd last seen him. He wasn't coming back, that was obvious. While I was conflicted about moving on so soon, didn't I deserve to find love and happiness like everyone else? Or was I destined to be the heartless wench of my own tale?

"Sutton?" Memphis snapped his fingers in front of my face.

"What?" I shook my head free of my thoughts.

"Are you okay?" He peered at me. "You zoned out there for a minute."

"Yeah, I'm fine." I rubbed my face. "I'm just really tired after everything."

"Oh," he paled, "of course you are. I'm sure you're hungry too, since you came storming out here after me and we hadn't eaten yet."

At the mention of food my stomach rumbled. He chuckled, having heard it.

I turned to head inside, but he grabbed my hand to stop me.

He smoothed the strands of my hair away from my face. I expected him to say something swoony and romantic because it was Memphis, but that didn't happen. Instead, his face darkened and rage stormed in his eyes. "After we leave here, I'm taking you straight to the police department and you're filing a restraining order against Marcus. No excuses. You have to think about your safety and the baby's. I won't allow him to come within a hundred feet of you. I'm not typically a violent man, but if I *ever* see that man I will make sure to put him in a grave."

I put a hand on his shoulder in a reassuring gesture. "Don't worry, I know that needs to be done. I've been putting it off, because let's face it I'm not the most brilliant person on the planet. I won't let him hurt me again. I'm burying him—figuratively, of course," I laughed.

"You're not stupid," he brushed a gentle finger down my cheek, "you just think you're stronger than you really are. Everyone has breaking points, but you want to believe you don't."

"Geez," I shook my head, "it's like you know me better than I know myself."

He chuckled as his hands fell to his sides. "I pay more attention than most people. It's called being a bartender," he winked. "You pick up on human behavior real fast in that job."

We both laughed at that as we headed inside the restaurant. Daphne had stopped crying and Emery smiled as we approached. Those two weren't dating yet, but I still had my hopes. They both noted that something had shifted in my relationship with Memphis, but they managed to keep their mouths shut. I knew it wouldn't be long until they asked questions. For now, I didn't have an answer as to what we were and that was okay. It was nice to just... be.

CHAPTER 32
Caelan

I'D BEEN OUT of rehab for three weeks. I thought it would be easy to adjust back into the real world. I was wrong. It was the fucking hardest thing I'd ever done. Kyle was trying to understand, but he truly didn't get it. I was beginning to regret my decision to move in with him. I had no place to escape to be alone. I thought it would be good to have someone to keep me in line and to be honest, I hadn't wanted to see Sutton. My time away had given me a much-needed clarity. I was right to end things. We weren't good together, that was obvious to anyone with eyes, and I wasn't ready to face her. I knew one day, I'd find her and we'd have a discussion about things but it couldn't happen now. If I saw her... it would be a reminder of how fucked up I'd been and the lengths I'd gone to, to never lose her. Most women thought it was so romantic when a couple would go to extreme lengths to be together, but I had news for them, it wasn't romantic. It was fucked up. You shouldn't be willing to die just so you don't have to live without a person. That shows a startling dependency that is entirely unhealthy.

Oh, shit. I was starting to think like Alex now.

That couldn't be good.

"Want some breakfast, man?" Kyle poked his head through

the doorway of the bedroom that was temporarily mine.

"Sure," I replied.

"I'm heading to a diner down the road. Get dressed and meet me in the car."

With a groan, I pushed myself from the bed and got dressed. Some of my art supplies were scattered around the small room, but I hadn't bothered to paint very much. I hadn't felt like it. This wasn't my home and I didn't want to mess up Kyle's stuff. I would start looking for an apartment soon, but I wanted to live here for at least another month—I needed to know in my heart that I was ready to deal with everything on my own. The pull was still there, but I was fighting it. Kyle had gotten rid of all the alcohol in his house so that I couldn't get any from him. Smart man. I might've been tempted to sneak a few times. I knew staying sober was necessary for my wellbeing and any chance at a happy future I may have.

Kyle drove us a few blocks down the road and we walked into the diner.

Our conversation was easy as we ate. While Kyle had stuck around after I went off the deep-end, our relationship had changed and it wasn't an easy-going friendship anymore. We were getting that back though.

When we left, Kyle offered to drive me home before he went to work, but there was somewhere I needed to go. Kyle appeared reluctant to leave me alone, but I assured him I'd be fine. He couldn't keep me on a leash.

With my hands in my pockets, I walked around town for a while before heading to the cemetery. I knew there was a chance I could see Sutton and that scared me. Luckily, I didn't encounter her. I wasn't sure what I would've done if I had spotted her.

I entered the cemetery with my head bowed. I had the walk memorized and didn't need to look where I was going.

When I reached their graves, though, I was startled to find a woman there.

At first my mind played tricks on me and I thought it was

Sutton. But the woman kneeling on the ground had red hair, not raven-colored. I was relieved. After all, it couldn't have possibly been Sutton. I'd never told her where my family was buried. Although, with her handy-dandy Google search skills she could have probably found them if she really wanted to.

The woman stood, wiping beneath her eyes. When she finally turned and saw me she nearly jumped out of her skin.

"Oh my God!" She placed a hand against her chest, taking a few steps back. "You scared me."

My eyes scanned her familiar features and my brows furrowed together as I tried to place her. I knew her, but I couldn't quite remember how. The memory was there, in the back of my mind as a hazy image.

I studied her shiny red hair, emerald green eyes, and the dusting of freckles sprinkled across her nose. "Leah," I gasped as I finally recognized her. I hadn't seen her since the night of the murders. Okay, that was a lie, I probably had seen her after that but I ignored everything and everybody. I'd retreated into myself and everyone ceased to exist. All that I'd had was the hurt I felt.

"You remember me." Her smile was small and hesitant. She was slightly afraid of me.

"I do." I rocked back on my heels at a loss as to what I was supposed to do.

"It's been a long time," she commented, clutching her purse.

"Six years," I confirmed with a nod of my head. "You look good." Was that an appropriate thing to say?

"Thanks." A slight blush blossomed across her cheeks. "You look good too. Kyle said you were getting help for the…" She trailed off and swayed back and forth like she was unsure whether or not she should proceed with her statement.

"Substance abuse," I supplied. "You can say it. It doesn't hurt my feelings. I was a drug addict and an alcoholic. I own my sins instead of drowning in them." Yep, I was *definitely* turning in to Alex. The fucktard had messed with my mind.

"So, you're doing better?" She asked. Her gaze darted to the ground and I wasn't sure if it was because she suddenly felt shy or if she really was that afraid of me. I didn't want her to be scared. I wasn't the boogeyman.

I nodded, then realized she couldn't see me, so I said, "Yes. It'll always be a struggle, but I'm much better."

"I'm really happy to hear that, Cael." Her smile was genuine and something about hearing her say my name made sparks tingle through my body. Once upon a time I'd had a crush on this girl. Back then, I'd fucked her, but if things hadn't ended the way they had with my family I might have married this girl. She was beautiful and sweet. My mom had loved her. That would normally send most guys running from a girl, but everyone loved Leah. She had that kind of sweet and sassy personality that couldn't help but make you like her.

"Why are you here?" I asked the question that had been bugging me since I saw her.

"Huh?" She lifted a hand to her forehead to block the sun filtering in through the tree branches.

"Why are you here?" I repeated. "At my family's graves?"

"Oh," she shook her head, "yeah, that. Of course you're wondering why I'm here," she rambled. She was definitely nervous. "Like I said, I talked to Kyle—I ran in to him at the grocery store a few days ago. We got to talking about you and what happened. I... l hadn't been here since the funeral and I thought I should visit. They were good people and they shouldn't be forgotten. I brought flowers for them too," she moved out of the way so I could see. "I got lilies for your mom. They were her favorite, right? And daisies for Cayla. I figured your dad would come back from the dead and haunt my ass if I got him flowers, so I—uh—got a football instead."

The blush that had been highlighting her cheeks had now spread to her neck and the tops of her breasts.

I was touched by the gesture, but tried not to let it show. "That was nice of you."

She took careful steps around me and whispered, "I guess I'll see you around."

I watched her walk away, itching to call out. When it was almost too late, I yelled, "Leah!"

"Yeah?" She turned around, waiting for me to continue.

I looked at the graves and back at her. I'd walked around town for a while and it was getting late, so I asked, "Would you want to go to lunch... with me?" I don't know why I tacked on the *'with me'* part, as if that wasn't already obvious.

"Oh, um," she fiddled with the curly strands of her vibrant hair. Finally, she nodded, and said, "Sure."

I smiled so big that my cheeks hurt. "Great." I looked at the graves once more. "Would you mind waiting ten minutes?"

"Not at all," she smiled. God, she had a pretty smile. She was more beautiful now than she had been in high school. Those old feelings were resurfacing and I didn't know what to make of them. "I'll be in my car," she pointed over her shoulder towards the parking lot.

"Wait for me," I pleaded.

"Always."

Something about her reply made me think. I'd avoided her like I had everyone else after the murders. I'd assumed I'd never see her again—well, I'd honestly kind of forgotten about her. It was easier not to remember the people from that time of my life. It was a shock seeing her here today, but I was glad.

I turned to the graves and sat on the ground.

"Hey, guys," I started. "I'm sorry I haven't come to visit you in a while. I was getting help. I'm much better now. I've been working hard to get my life back on track. I'm hoping to open my own art gallery. I haven't thought of a name yet... maybe something to honor mom and Cayla since both of you were the true artists in the family. I'm trying my best to make you proud. I know you wouldn't approve of all the shitty things I've done in the last few years." I plucked some of the grass and twisted it between my fingers. "I sold your house. I hope you aren't angry, but I just couldn't hang on to it anymore. I couldn't go back there again and someone else deserves to make memories there. We had some good times in that house and I want that for another family, instead of it being tainted with what happened that night. I'm trying to move on, and while it's hard, I think I'm doing a pretty damn good job... now, at least. It only took me six years after you died to get my shit figured out," I chuckled humorlessly. "I want you guys to be proud of me." Tears pricked my eyes. No more words left my lips as I let the tears fall. I'd said all that I could say.

I didn't hear Cayla's voice, in fact I hadn't heard her since that day at the house. Maybe she had moved on. Or, possibly—okay, most likely—I'd merely hallucinated her voice.

I sat for a few more minutes before I gathered to my feet. Dusting the grass from my jeans, I murmured, "I guess this is goodbye for now. I'll visit again, but it'll probably be a while. I'm sorry for that, but I think I'll heal faster if I stay away. I love you guys."

I kissed my fingers and touched them gently to each gravestone.

I strode out of the cemetery as a feeling of peace settled around me.

I found Leah sitting in her car. She rolled the window down when I approached. "Lunch is on me, but do you mind giving me a ride? I don't have a car," I admitted.

I was a bit embarrassed by that fact but she smiled like it didn't matter. "That's fine," she replied.

I settled into the passenger seat and told her to pick the place. We ended up at a local Italian restaurant a few miles away. I held the door open for her as we walked inside. The hostess led us to a booth in the back and I was glad that we were relatively alone. I was looking forward to catching up with her. For once, I wasn't scared of being reminded of what happened. I was ready to embrace it as part of my life.

"So," I said as the waitress sat down glasses of soda, "what have you been doing since graduation?"

"Well," she smiled as she tucked a stray hair behind her ear, "I went to college and got a degree in social services."

"Really?" My brows rose in surprise.

"I know it's not very glamorous," she chuckled as she brought the glass to her mouth. I had to force myself to look away from the delectable sight of her lips wrapped around the straw. "But I wanted to help kids."

"I think that's pretty admirable," I noted. My fingers tapped nervously against the top of the table and I couldn't seem to make them stop. "So, you like it?"

"I love it." Her smile widened and there was a sparkle in her green eyes. "It's a hard job, I'm not going to lie about that, but it's also extremely rewarding. When a kid smiles at me for making things better for them..." She trailed off, a nostalgic smile playing on her lips. "It's nice," she finished.

"I'm sure it is," I agreed.

"What are you up to?" She asked. Bowing her head, she let out an nervous laugh. "Besides the obvious of course."

"And by obvious you mean... rehab?" I knew that's what she meant, but I liked watching her squirm. While there had been some fear when she first saw me, that was all gone now. She wasn't as sassy as I remembered from high school, but I figured that had to do with nerves. It had to have been a shock to see me.

"Yes," she squeaked.

I took a sip of soda, making her sweat it a bit longer. "I'm not really doing anything right now. I moved in with Kyle and I haven't gotten a job yet. I'm hoping to move out of his place in a month or so, but I really want to open my own art gallery." I launched into everything I wanted to do with it and her eyes widened. Her mouth parted in shock too. Was it really so surprising that the addict might have dreams and aspirations too?

"Wow," she gasped when I was finished, "I think that's a great idea, Cael. It would give you something to focus on, but you love it so it wouldn't feel like work."

"Thanks," I smiled.

Our food came and conversation lulled for a bit. When the waitress returned to take away our empty dishes, she asked if we'd like some dessert. I looked to Leah for an answer.

"Yes, please," she smiled, and I noticed how she lit up the room when she did, "tiramisu."

"Great choice," the waitress chimed. "It's made fresh daily. Would you like any coffee to go with it?"

"No, thank you," Leah replied. Turning to me, she admitted with a wry smile, "I know it's a bit early for dessert, but I can't resist. I have quite the sweet tooth."

"Dessert is a very important food group," I quipped.

The waitress set the plate of tiramisu on the table with two spoons. I didn't want any, so I pushed the plate over to Leah's side of the table.

"Please, you have to eat some," she begged. "Don't make me feel like a pig."

I chuckled and lifted a finger. "One bite, but that's it. I don't really like coffee flavored things."

"How is that possible?" She gasped. "Coffee is delicious."

I couldn't help but think of Sutton with her words, but I pushed those thoughts out of my mind. I was sitting here with Leah and she deserved my undivided attention.

I took a bite of the mousse-like dessert and swallowed it down. "There," I put the spoon down, "now you can say that you didn't eat the whole thing."

"Thanks," she smiled beautifully before digging in.

The waitress dropped off the check and I put down my credit card.

I was either going to have to get a real job soon or start selling my paintings again. I couldn't live off my saving's forever and I was planning to use the money I'd made of the sale of my childhood home to open my gallery.

We walked out of the restaurant and I found myself yearning

for more time to spend with her. I knew I couldn't take up any more of her day though.

"Do you need a ride home?" She asked.

"I'm fine. I enjoy the walk," I shrugged.

"It's no trouble, really," she opened her car door. "Don't be stubborn."

I chuckled. "Fine." I accepted her offer. I gave her directions to Kyle's place and she pulled up to the curb. "I hope I get to see you again."

"Me too," she smiled. "What's your phone number?"

"Oh, uh, I don't have one," I scratched the back of my head. When I'd made the decision to go to rehab, I'd thought it would be best to start clean, and that meant forgetting about everyone that had become a part of my life once I started using.

She frowned. "Can I reach you through Kyle?"

I nodded. "Yeah. He'll let me know you called."

"Great," she smiled. I started to get out of the car, but her hand landed on my arm to halt my progress. I looked over my shoulder at her and raised a brow in question. "I'm really glad I ran into you today. I've missed you." Her lashes fluttered against her cheeks.

"I've missed you too," I admitted and the words were true. I hadn't realized how much until now.

"Bye," she whispered.

I gave her a small wave as I jogged up the steps into Kyle's townhouse. I closed the door and peeked out the window, watching as she left.

The strangest emotion was filling my body.

I was... *happy*.

CHAPTER 33
Sutton

"MEMPHIS!" I CRIED, my voice full of urgency. "Come here! Hurry!"

He came running out of the bathroom, half of his face was shaved and the other half still boasted white foam. "What is it? Are you okay? Is the baby coming?" He fired questions at me in a rapid fashion. One hand held the towel around his waist, which was dangerously close to slipping off.

"No," I giggled. "The baby kicked."

"You nearly gave me a heart attack because the baby *kicked?*" His look was incredulous.

Men.

I grabbed his hand and placed it on my rounded stomach. His mouth gradually fell open in awe and his eyes widened. "Wow," he gasped, moving his hands over my stomach to better feel the baby. "That's the most amazing thing I've ever felt." He reached up to cup the nape of my neck. "Thank you for sharing that with me." He pressed his lips to mine in a soft, but lingering kiss.

To an outsider we were a couple sharing a special moment over our growing child. Although, while we were now officially a couple, the child was not his.

Enough time had passed that I knew Caelan was out of rehab.

He hadn't called or come to see me. He'd ceased all contact and made it pretty clear he wanted nothing to do with me. That stung, but I was okay. In fact, Memphis made things more than okay.

"Are you ready to find out if the baby's a boy or girl?" He asked.

"Yes," I grinned, barely containing the squeal in my voice. "I can't wait!"

I wrapped my arms around him and held him close. Once I stopped fighting my feelings I saw that what I had with Memphis was a beautiful thing. Our relationship was as easy as breathing.

His hand continued to rub absentmindedly against my stomach. Peering into my eyes, he said, "You know, this apartment isn't quite big enough for a baby."

"I know," I agreed, nervously biting on a fingernail. I knew I needed a better place to bring the baby home to, but this was all I could afford.

"I have an extra bedroom at my place." His tone was very persuasive. "It could be yours and the baby's, or," his voice grew husky, "it could be the baby's and you could sleep in my bed." He ran a finger along my jaw in a light caress. My neck arched and I moaned. I hadn't told Memphis I loved him yet, but I knew in my heart I did. I wasn't ready to say the words yet, soon though. We hadn't had sex either. I knew we both wanted to, but I was making myself wait to progress things to that point. In the past, that's what all my relationships had been based around—even with Caelan—and I wanted things to be different with Memphis. However, my patience was wearing thin. I wanted him.

"I-I—" I stuttered as his fingertips skated over my exposed collarbone. I didn't know how he could fill my body with *want* by one simple touch or glance. He was a freakin' magician—the panty magician, because I was about to throw mine across the room and beg him to take me right here. But then I gathered my senses and told myself to calm down. It wasn't time. I wanted it to be different with him, romantic. I didn't want it to be a clash of lips and limbs. I think that this was the first time I'd ever craved slow, sweet love.

Memphis was a miracle worker.

"I need to think about it." I gasped, finally finding my voice.

"Don't take too long," he murmured as his lips ghosted down my neck. "The baby will be here before you know it."

"I know," I whispered.

He released me and pointed to his face. "I better finish shaving."

"Too bad you're lopsided now." I smiled wryly and reached up to caress his smooth cheek. "I like you with some stubble."

"Is that so?" He chuckled. "I'll stop shaving then."

I laughed under my breath as he retreated to the bathroom. I was ready to go, so I sat down to wait. Normally, Memphis waited for me, but I was so excited to find out the gender of my baby that I'd been ready for hours.

Memphis walked out of the bathroom dressed in a pair of dark khaki cargo pants and a white v-neck shirt. "You look nice," I grinned, looking him up and down.

He chuckled huskily and grabbed his wallet off the dresser and put it in his back pocket. "I thought maybe we could have a picnic in the park after your appointment."

"That sounds great." I meant it too. Normally, that would have been something I would've frowned at—anything overly romantic gave me hives—but not anymore.

He looked at his watch. "We better head out."

He was right. This was one appointment I didn't want to be late to.

I twitched with excitement the whole drive to the hospital. Memphis eventually grasped my hand to cease my movements.

I was a buzzing bundle of nerves by the time I was called back to the room to wait.

My doctor believed that Memphis was the father of my baby. Neither of us had bothered to correct her. It was easier not to.

Besides, Memphis had proven himself to me and I believed him when he said he wanted to raise my child as his own.

I held my breath as I waited for my doctor. I had no preference over whether my baby was a boy or girl, but I was desperate to know.

"Breathe." Memphis rubbed his hand soothingly up and down my back. "You're going to pass out if you keep holding your breath like that."

I let my breath out with a gust. "Sorry," I smiled sheepishly. "I hate waiting."

"Me too," he chuckled, pulling up a chair and holding my hand as he sat down beside me.

We both fidgeted nervously, our eyes on the clock as we waited for my doctor. It always took awhile for her to come back to my room, but this time it seemed to take even longer.

When she finally came in, I asked, "Can we speed up this process?"

She laughed. "Someone's excited."

"We both are," Memphis added.

She asked me several questions and looked things over. "So, you want to know the sex?" She moved the wand over my rounded stomach.

"Yes!" Memphis and I exclaimed simultaneously.

She laughed. "Are you really sure?"

"Don't play with me," I pouted.

She clicked around the screen and moved the wand until she saw what she needed to. "It looks like you're having a..." She paused for dramatic effect. "Girl!"

"A girl?" I gasped in awe. "I'm having a daughter?"

"You are," she smiled, wiping the goo from my stomach and putting everything away.

"Wow," I breathed in shock. Somehow, knowing I was having a girl made it even more real. In a few months I'd have a daughter to hold. I looked over at Memphis and saw that he had tears shimmering in his eyes.

"We're going to have a daughter," he breathed, leaning over to kiss me. His words affected me more than he knew—it was a turning point for me. We were in this together. He wasn't running from me. Memphis and I were going to be a family—him, little bean, and me.

"Here you go," the doctor handed the ultrasound sound photos to me.

I clutched them tightly, not wanting to let go. I stared down at them, tracing the soft curves of little bean's nose and mouth. She was perfect and I couldn't wait to hold her.

After a few moments to overcome my emotions I got dressed and we headed home to pack for our picnic.

I felt so light and happy. Things were falling into place for me. All the bad shit I'd gone through had been a really crappy stepping stone in this thing called life. Now I was where I wanted to be, and because of all the bad I could appreciate the good even more.

"Why are you smiling?" Memphis asked me as he made sandwiches.

I sat down at one of the stools and propped my head on my hand. "I didn't know I was."

"You were," he chuckled, carefully watching what he was doing. His copper hair fell in his eyes and he flicked his head so that the strands were out of his way.

"I guess I have a lot to be happy about."

"I like seeing you like this." His gray eyes flicked up to meet mine.

"You're a big part of the reason I'm so happy," I confessed.

His grin was infectious. The dimples in his cheeks winked at me and I resisted the urge to lean across the counter and kiss them. "Really?" Surprise colored his tone.

I nodded. The words *I love you* were on the tip of my tongue, but I did not proclaim them. Instead I decided to wait until we were at the park. That seemed like a better, more romantic, spot to confess my feelings.

Memphis packed everything in a cooler and we were on our way once more. It was a nice spring day—the birds chirped and the sun shone like a halo over the world.

He parked the car and took my hand, the cooler clasped in the other. We didn't walk very far until we found a shady spot under the trees.

"Shit!" Memphis cursed. "I forgot a blanket for us to sit on."

"It's okay," I assured him. "It's only grass. We'll be fine."

He seemed unsure. "We can sit at a table if you'd prefer," he pointed to one of the many tables scattered through the park.

Rolling my eyes at him, I sat on the ground and patted the spot beside me. "It's a nice *grassy* blanket. Same difference."

He sat down, chuckling under his breath. "You are so different than other girls."

"I take it that's a good thing, since you're sitting here with me and not one of those 'other girls' you speak of," I laughed, grabbing a sandwich from the cooler.

"It is," he smiled, the motion crinkling the corners of his eyes.

I pulled the sandwich from the baggie and took a bite. "Mmm," I moaned, "this is delicious."

"It's a sandwich," he stated.

I looked at him out of the corner of my eye, and said, "I'm pregnant, therefore always hungry. So I'm sorry that I'm thoroughly enjoying this sandwich."

"Don't be sorry," he grinned and grabbed the sunglasses dangling from his shirt, slipping them on to block the sun.

We chatted as we ate and once the food was gone, we decided to stay a bit longer. We moved to a sunny spot and lay down beside each other. Memphis crossed his arms behind his head and stared up at the clouds. Taking the opening, I scooted my body against his, curling around him, and rested my head on his chest. A hum sounded in his chest. His fingers lazily trailed up and down my arm. I felt content and entirely at peace in his arms.

My eyes grew heavy, but I forced myself to stay awake.

Memphis' breaths were heavy, like he had a lot on his mind. He leisurely rolled to his side and propped his head on his hand. He trailed a finger down my nose, his eyes far away.

"What are you thinking about?" I said the words softly, like I was afraid of his answer.

"I love you." The words tumbled out of his mouth and shock slithered through my body. I hadn't been expecting that. "I love you," he repeated. "I don't expect you to say it back or anything, but I thought you ought to know. I couldn't keep it to myself any longer. I love you," he brushed a piece of hair off my forehead, his fingertips gliding in a feather-light touch over my face. "I love you." Grinning, he said, "It feels so good to say that."

Pushing him onto his back, I hovered above. My hair fell forward, creating an intimate shield around us. I lowered my head, like I was going to kiss him. When my lips were only millimeters from his, I breathed, "I love you too."

His gasp was my undoing and I couldn't hold myself back from closing the small distance between us. I kissed him with every ounce of passion I had in me. I wanted him to know that I wasn't just saying the words. I really meant them.

Memphis had burrowed a space into my heart the moment I met him, and while I fought my feelings for him and immersed myself in Caelan, those desires never went away. In the past months, my love for him had grown every day—even when I'd done everything to push him away, that love was building inside me. I fell in love with him slowly—the way you're supposed to. I got to know him and he got to know me. There was nothing *instant-love*—about us. We worked hard to get to this point and went through a lot. Sadly, it took me falling for someone else, and subsequently ending up broken hearted, to see that this man right here was the one for me. He wasn't my second choice. He was *the* choice.

Memphis broke the kiss and turned his head to the side as he panted. He sat up with me cradled in his lap. He took my face between his hands. "Are you sure?"

"Abso-fucking-lutely."

"You and your potty mouth," he chuckled.

"Face it," I pressed my forehead to his, "you love all the things I say."

With a serious look, he said, "It's you I love."

"You really love me?" I burrowed my head in the crook of his neck, absorbing the heat of his body and familiar scent.

"I really do," he breathed. "I love the way you're so passionate about things you believe in. I love the way you smile in the morning when you're still half-asleep. I love the way you sing in the shower when you think I'm not listening. I love the way that you're this crazy self-confident woman, but sometimes you show this soft shyness and I can see a glimpse of what you were like as a child." Grasping a strand of my dark hair in his fingers he tugged gently. "I love everything about you."

I grinned at that. "I'm glad, 'cause you're kinda stuck with me."

"Oh, am I now?" He laughed, his hands grasping my waist where I straddled him—probably not the best position we could have been in, in a public park.

"Yeah," I smiled—the kind of smile that makes your face hurt, "now that I have you, I'm never letting you get away."

His laughter made his whole body shake. "I think I should be saying that. You didn't have to chase me. You had me from the beginning." His face grew sad. "It was hard watching you fall for someone else."

My heart clenched painfully at the hurt etched into the handsome lines of his face. "I'm sorry."

He shook his head and took my hand, pressing his lips against my fingers in a tender kiss. "Don't be. All that hurt I felt makes this moment that much sweeter."

"Are you sure you're a bartender and not a poet?" I asked him, wrapping my arms around his neck.

"I'm sure," he winked.

"I wish I was better with words," I whispered and lowered my arms as I laid my head on his shoulder. "I wish I could express to you how strong my feelings for you are."

"Don't worry," he kissed the top of my head and then my forehead, "we have the rest of our lives for you to show me."

WE CRASHED INTO the apartment, tearing at each other's clothes. With both of our declarations at the park, neither of us could wait. I needed him to feel my love.

My legs wrapped around his waist and he carried me to the bed.

In the back of my mind, a silly insecurity reared its ugly head—would he be disgusted by me? I was pregnant and my body didn't look like it used to, and as a guy would he be grossed out?

My fears overcame me and I pushed at his shoulders. "Stop. Stop. Please, stop."

He pulled away, looking at me with a raised brow. "What's wrong? Tell me."

I swallowed thickly, fiddling with my hands. "I... I'm pregnant."

He laughed. "Yes, Sutton, I'm well aware. I've been to every appointment and I've watched your belly grow."

I frowned. "No, you don't get it. I'm *pregnant*. I don't look like I used to and this baby," I wrapped my arms around my stomach, "it's not even yours. How can you even want to do this with me?" Tears coated my lashes.

Memphis cupped my cheeks, forcing me to look at him. "Get those silly uncertainties out of your head. None of those things matter to me, you *know* that. Don't let fear hold you back. I love you and I love this baby," he placed his hand on my stomach, overtop mine. "If I didn't want you or this, I wouldn't be here. I would never lead you on, Sutton. I love you," he declared, "and when you love someone unconditionally, nothing else matters." He stared at me for a moment, studying my facial features. "I won't push you for more. If you're not ready to progress our relationship to this point, I'll wait. Do I want you right here and right now? Hell yes. But I won't push. I've waited this long, and I can wait some more." Brushing his lips against my ear, he whispered, "I can be a very patient man when I know the reward will be well worth it."

I processed his words and tried to push my insecurities away. A shiver rocked my body. I wanted this. I wanted it now. But I was *scared*.

I grabbed the collar of his soft shirt in my hands and drew him closer to me. "Slow," I breathed the words, "be gentle with me. I can't handle another heartbreak."

He kissed me deeply and pulled away, running his thumb over my bottom lip. "Your heart is a precious gift and I will never look at it as anything else."

I scooted back on the bed and his body followed mine. He pulled his shirt off and tossed it somewhere behind him. I ran my hands along the smooth planes of his abs and chest. God, he was perfect.

He took things slow, just like I asked, making sure I was comfortable and truly ready. I was. I wanted all of him and I wanted him to have all of me.

He stared into my eyes as our bodies joined and he saw when I gave him that last piece of my broken heart—it might not have been whole, but every part now belonged to him.

He kissed me tenderly and our breaths were in sync. Everything about us was *right*.

Afterwards, wrapped in his arms, I couldn't stop smiling. I was so incredibly happy. There was no longer a black cloud hanging over my head. For the first time in my life, things were good.

But good things never last, and soon it would all come

crashing down.

CHAPTER 34
Caelan

I'D SPENT A lot of time with Leah since the day at the cemetery. We went to dinner and just hung out. It was nice reconnecting with her. I'd even spent some time with a few of the guys I'd been friends with from the football team. It was weird seeing these people again, but I needed this. I'd been avoiding anything that might be too painful for too long. It was time to stop running and hiding. I needed to live.

"What are we watching?" Leah asked, sitting down on the couch with a bowl of popcorn and drinks.

"I don't care," I shrugged and reached for a handful of popcorn.

"Hmm," she perused the row of DVD's, "aha! Found it!" She chimed and slid the disc into the player.

We'd decided to have a relaxing night at her place and watch a movie.

My feelings for her grew every day. I found myself going out of my way to make her smile or laugh. I thrived off of seeing her happy.

The movie started to play and she put the popcorn bowl between us, creating a barrier.

I wasn't sure if she didn't have feelings for me, or she was scared that she did, but she was always careful to make sure we never crossed a line. I was growing impatient. I wanted more than this. Although, I knew that this was better than nothing and I shouldn't rush things. I was a recovering addict after all. Slow was good for me. I didn't want to do anything stupid that could hurt me and ultimately send me back to that dark place.

The movie started, but I didn't pay much attention to it.

Instead, I watched Leah from the corner of my eyes. I noted the way she flicked her hair over her shoulder or twitched her lips when there was a part in the movie she didn't like. I liked how her eyes sparkled when she laughed at a funny part or filled with tears when it was sad. She was the kind of person that felt things deeply. When the movie was over, she turned the TV off and cleaned up the popcorn bowl.

I hovered in the doorway to her kitchen, my hands in my pockets. I felt so out of place and awkward. I'd always been a 'charmer', or so I'd been told, but I now found that I never knew the right thing to say. I felt so out of place.

"Are you okay?" She asked me, pulling her long red hair back into a ponytail.

"I have a lot on my mind," I replied.

"Do you want to talk about it?" She asked, grabbing her car keys off the counter to take me home.

I shook my head and decided to change the subject. "I'm going to look at spaces for my gallery on Saturday... would you want to come with me?"

"Saturday?" She looked to the side and I knew she was internally going through her schedule to see if she was free. "Yeah, I can go." Smiling, she asked, "So, you're really going to do it?"

I nodded. "I am. I'm going to use the money I got from the sale of my parent's house to buy it."

"I think that's great, Cael," she clapped her hands together. "I'm so happy for you. You deserve this."

"Thanks."

As she drove me home she asked me questions about what I thought I wanted to do with the gallery. I answered them the best I could.

To be honest, I was scared to take this leap. I'd be taking a risk opening a gallery, but it was what I wanted to do and for once I was going to follow my dreams.

I said goodbye to Leah and just like every time we parted, I longed to close the distance between us and kiss her. I never did. I didn't want to push her away and I valued our friendship too much to jeopardize it.

"Wow," Leah gasped, looking around the space. Her voice echoed through the expansive area. "I love this one. It feels like we're in New York City."

I had to agree with her. The ceilings were high with large windows, exposed ductwork, and brick walls.

"This one also has an apartment attached," the relator spoke.

"It does?" That fact definitely piqued my interest. Not only would I have my own gallery, but I'd have an apartment too. I'd been looking for a place for a couple of weeks and kept coming up empty. Everything was either too expensive or a complete dump.

"Yes," Bob, the relator, nodded, "it's just around here."

I followed him to a staircase that led to a door. The apartment was set up much the way my last one had been—everything open except for the bathroom.

"What do you think?" Bob asked.

"I think I'll take it."

Leah squealed with excitement and jumped into my arms. She shocked me by kissing my cheek, dangerously close to my mouth.

"Oh," her cheeks reddened as she realized what she'd done. "I'm sorry."

Bob cleared his throat and quietly left us alone.

Leah started to leave, but I grabbed her arm and pulled her against me. "Don't be sorry."

She mumbled something and her gaze dropped to the ground. I grabbed her chin and forced her to look at me.

"There's something I want to try," I whispered, leaning in. I'd wanted to kiss her for so long and with what she had done, she'd let me know she was ready.

She swallowed thickly and her pulse fluttered in her throat.

I lowered my head and sealed my lips over hers.

The kiss started out slow, but quickly built. Her arms wound around my neck and her fingers into my hair. She tugged lightly as she moaned into my mouth. Her body fit perfectly against mine as I held her, almost as if she'd been made for me. Her mouth parted beneath mine, drawing me in. The tip of my tongue touched hers and it was like a thousand fireworks went off in my body. I'd never believed you could experience that feeling until it happened to me. She moaned softly as I grasped her waist, pressing her hips into mine. My old tendencies started to rear up and I had to squash my desire to take here right here, right now, pinned against a wall. I couldn't do things like that anymore.

When the kiss ended we both were out of breath and clung to each other. Her body shook and I held on tight so she didn't float away.

With a shaky hand she reached up to touch her slightly swollen lips.

"I hope you're not mad," I spoke, "but I've been wanting to do that for a while."

"Not at all," she smiled beautifully. "Can we do that again?"

I didn't answer her with words. I didn't need to. I kissed her again, taking my time. I wanted her to know how much I craved her, but at the same time I didn't want the intensity of my feelings to scare her. There was a reason I'd been so drawn to her when we were in high school. She was special.

"THAT'S IT," KYLE said as he dropped the last box down on the floor.

I felt an overwhelming sense of satisfaction as I looked around the space that would soon be my gallery. But then once I saw just how little boxes I had a frown formed on my face. It was pretty sad that my entire life fit inside ten boxes. That was it. I didn't even have any furniture. I'd made Kyle get rid of everything from my old place. I'd only kept the necessities. I wanted a fresh start, but now as I looked around I felt pathetic that I was twenty-four years old and this was all I had.

"Looks like someone needs to go shopping." Kyle clapped me on the shoulder. He must have been thinking the same thing I was.

"Yeah," Leah piped in. "You need a bed, and a couch, and—"

Kyle made a loud snoring noise, his head lolled to the side as he pretended to be asleep.

Leah rolled her eyes.

Jolting, as if he'd just come awake, Kyle said, "Once people start talking about shopping, that's my cue to leave. I don't shop. Have fun you two." Waving to us over his shoulder, he left.

"We should probably see if we can get you a few things." Leah stood, brushing her shorts free of invisible dust. I couldn't help but appreciate how nice her legs looked in those little white shorts. "Caelan?"

I shook my head free of my thoughts. "You're right. Let's go."

I'd finally bought a car, so I drove. I had no idea what to look for in furniture so I went with what Leah liked.

"Come on, Cael," she groaned. "This is your place, not mine. It should reflect your style."

"Do I even have a style?" I grumbled, sipping on a Coke the sales lady had offered.

"Everybody does." Leah rolled her eyes like I was stupid.

"I really don't care," I shrugged. "Pick out what you think looks nice and I'll be happy."

I could tell Leah was getting frustrated with my obvious lack of interest, but honestly, what the hell did I know about furniture?

Leah told the sales lady what items we wanted and then I paid. They couldn't deliver it for a few days, so it looked like I was stuck sleeping on an air mattress. Wonderful.

We walked out of the store and got dinner before going back to my place. Leah helped me unpack the boxes before she headed home. As soon as she walked out the door I missed her company. To distract myself I grabbed one of the canvases I'd bought and decided to paint.

Almost instantly my mood changed with each stroke of color. It was undeniably therapeutic to bring something to life on a canvas. It was created from my mind and didn't exist until I picked up a brush. Within art magic existed.

When I painted, it was like something else took over. My hand made the necessary movements to bring alive her image. I chose pink for her hair and it dripped down the canvas in tiny rivulets. Her eyes came alive and her lips pouted at me. Only someone that knew her would know the woman on the canvas was Leah.

For hours I painted. I didn't want to sleep. I wanted to create. So, I did.

I TOOK LEAH with me to the storage unit I'd had Kyle place my belongings in. I hadn't wanted to keep my furniture, but I had told him to make sure nothing happened to my paintings. I noticed other boxes stacked in the corner of the unit, stuff he hadn't bothered to bring to his house.

I started going through the paintings, looking for any I could hang up in the gallery and wanted to sell. There were plenty I knew I would leave here. I didn't want to get rid of them but I couldn't have them hanging in my apartment either.

I stopped when I got to one of my paintings of Sutton.

It was like the air had been kicked out of my lungs. I'd known these were here, but I hadn't thought about what I'd feel when I saw them.

In one word, sadness.

I was sad because when I looked at her I saw our good times and our bad. I saw two broken people who were so desperate to feel alive they clung to anything that made them feel safe. But there was nothing safe about the two of us together. We'd been a fire burning uncontrollably, leaving behind a path of destruction across our hearts. I'd loved her in the only way I knew how at that time, but it had been a poisoned love. I'd never been able to give her everything. I knew we'd both tried and we thought we were better, but we'd only masked the pain like a Band-Aid over a fresh wound.

"Who is she?" Leah asked, stepping up behind me. Her hand lingered on my back as she peered over my shoulder at the painting.

No one would have been the easier answer, but I couldn't reduce Sutton to that. She was special to me, even if I had said goodbye to her. She'd always have a place in my heart. She helped me get through so much and I'd always be appreciative of that. I hoped one day I'd have the strength to thank her in person, but I needed to get my life on track first.

"She was someone I loved," I whispered, hoping my words didn't upset Leah.

"She's beautiful," she commented.

"She is. She's got quite the fiery personality too," I smiled fondly as I thought of Sutton.

"Do you mind me asking... do you still love her?"

I turned around to find Leah nibbling on her bottom lip and wringing her hands together. She was upset. I didn't want that, but I had to be honest.

"Yes," I answered. "I still love her. I'll always love her. But I'm not *in* love with her." I took Leah's cheek in my hand and rubbed my thumb over her soft skin. "There's a difference," I smiled lightly.

"So..." She paused, her eyes darting to the ground. "It's over between you two?"

I chuckled at that. "I think we were over before we even started. We weren't good for each other, but it took me being with her to finally accept that I needed help. She gave me the clarity I needed, but we had too many issues to ever make it."

"Do you miss her?" Leah's voice cracked with the question.

I thought about that for a moment, not sure of an answer. "I miss what we could have been had circumstances been different. But it's over now and I'm sure she's moved on," I shrugged. "I'm moving on too... I hope," I looked at Leah meaningfully. I curled my hand around the nape of her neck and pressed a soft kiss to her lips. I felt her relax and all I wanted to do was put her mind at ease. "You're the one that I want."

She smiled at my words. "That makes me happy."

"It does?" I questioned, continuing to stroke her cheek. A huge part of me still worried that even though I was clean I would never be good enough for her.

Leaning close to me she stood on her tiptoes to reach my ear. "You want to know a secret?"

I nodded.

I felt her smile as her lips touched my ear. "I want you too."

We clashed together, our lips fighting to reach one another's. She tasted sweet—like sunshine and popsicles on a summer day. I couldn't get enough. She fisted my shirt in her hands and my fingers tangled in her long hair. We hadn't gone past kissing, but I felt the desire for more build between us. In the back of my mind I remembered the night at The Cove with her. I'd been so carefree and content then. Everything had come crumbling down around me that night and I had pushed her away, because I was stupid and didn't know how to cope with grief. I'd been a boy, but now I was a man and I knew exactly what I wanted, and it was Leah.

We bumped into the boxes and canvases went tumbling to the ground as we bumbled through the storage unit. Neither of us seemed to care though.

She wrapped her legs around my waist and I pinned her against one of the walls. My hands were braced beside her head and her hips rolled against mine. I growled low in my throat. She was testing my restraint.

My lips made a path down her neck and her soft pants filled my ears. "Caelan," she breathed my name before I claimed her mouth once more. My fingers dug into her hips. I was desperate to take her clothes off and sink myself inside her, but I knew I couldn't.

I forced myself to pull away from her and laid my head in the crook of her neck. I panted heavily as I tried to catch my breath.

"Why'd you stop?" She asked, sounding out of breath too.

"We're in a storage unit," I answered, "not exactly the best place to have sex."

"Oh," she replied, as if she was only now realizing where we were. "Right." She lowered her legs from my waist and I stepped back so she was no longer caged between my arms. The moment was gone, for now, but it wouldn't be long until I made her mine.

CHAPTER 35
Sutton

AS I WAS packing boxes to move, I came across all the letters I'd written Caelan. I didn't know what made me continue writing them after they were returned, but it made me feel better, even if he never read them. It had been three months since I wrote the last one—the day I found out I was going to have a daughter and Memphis and I declared our love for one another. I picked that one up now and started to read it.

Dear Caelan,

I have a lot to tell you since last time.
I guess I should start with the good news (it's all good news, but this is the best news). We're having a girl! Can you believe it? I sure can't. Sometimes it still doesn't feel real that I'm having a baby. Unlike most girls, I never imagined myself having kids or a family. You gave me this gift though, and it's the best thing that's ever happened to me. I love her so much. Feeling her move inside me fills me with immense joy and pride. I often find myself

wondering what she'll look and be like. I hope she's an artist like you. Wouldn't that be nice? Regardless, I know she's going to do great things.

The other thing I wanted to tell you is I've fallen in love. You told me not to wait for you and a part of me wanted to ignore your request, but my heart had other plans. I've fallen in love with an amazing man that's loved me through it all. He knows everything, but doesn't look at me differently for it. I have to thank you for that—for giving me the courage to open up to people and tell the truth. You were right. I have nothing to be ashamed of. I didn't do anything wrong. I haven't done it yet, but I'm thinking of starting a group for women and girls who have been raped to come and share their stories and talk to people who've been through it. I think I would've benefited from something like that, and knowing that I'm going to have a little girl... I don't ever want her to be scared like I was. I want her to have the strength to talk about things and not bottle it up inside like I did. I'm trying to be a good role model for her. I hope you get to meet her someday.

Best,
Sutton

I folded the letter back up and put it away in the box with the others. Memphis kept telling me to contact Kyle and send them, but I wanted Caelan to live his life first. I didn't want him to feel obligated to do anything for our daughter. He'd already thrown so much of his life away and I didn't want her to become another burden to him. I knew in my gut I'd see him again one day, and when that day came, we'd have a lot to discuss and I hoped he wouldn't be angry with me. It hadn't been an easy decision not to tell him and I did it from a place a love.

I closed the flaps on the cardboard box and taped it shut.

Memphis had managed to convince me to move in with him. He could be highly persuasive when he wanted something. The baby wasn't due for another month, but we'd already cleared out his guest room and were getting it ready. He'd painted the walls a soft pink—a color I'd been against, but he'd insisted the room be pink. The crib was put together, but in need of sheets. I'd gone a bit crazy buying clothes and she had enough to last her until middle school—well, you know, if she stayed baby-sized. The only thing I didn't have figured out was a name. Memphis hadn't asked me about it. I think he believed that was one thing he shouldn't be a part of. I had a couple of ideas, but nothing felt right. I'd resolved to pick a name once she was here and I had a chance to see her and hold her.

I was startled from my thoughts when I heard a knock on the door.

I grumbled under my breath as I came to my feet. Memphis had gone to get more boxes and no doubt, his hands were so full that he couldn't get to his keys. Why couldn't men figure out how to put the stuff down, open the door, and pick it back up? It wasn't rocket science.

I waddled my way to the door and swung it open, while speaking, "Why can't you just put the stuff down and open the damn door?"

"It's nice to see you too, Sutton."

That voice did not belong to Memphis. Ice slithered down my spine and my hands shook. My throat closed up as I tried to close the door. He thrust his foot through the gap, effectively jamming it. "Tsk, tsk," he snapped his tongue against the roof of his mouth, "that's not very nice. Aren't you going to invite me inside? It's been far too long." Peering past me, he smiled evilly.

"And look at that, your keeper seems to have disappeared, and oh," his eyes dropped to my stomach, "he left you a present."

"Go away, Marcus!" I screamed through gritted teeth. "Leave me alone!" I looked around blindly for anything to throw at him. Unfortunately, almost everything was packed away.

He smiled and there was nothing nice about it. "Did you really think a measly restraining order would keep me away?" Shaking his head, he chuckled, "I got quite the laugh out of that when it arrived in the mail." He pulled an envelope out of his back pocket and dropped it on the floor in front of my feet. "I would've come sooner, but I've been busy." He looked around at all the boxes, and added, "Looks like I came just in time. It doesn't matter though. You can't hide from me, Sutton." My back ran into a wall and he stopped in front of me. I swallowed thickly as my eyes darted from side to side, looking for a means of escape. There were none. He had me trapped against the wall. I was completely vulnerable and I had to think about my baby. I couldn't do anything stupid. His hand closed around my throat, squeezing. "I will always find you." His lips brushed against my cheek and he dipped his head towards my ear, taking the lobe between his teeth. "I own you."

Tears leaked out of the corners of my eyes. I'd never been more afraid of him than I was right now, but I was more concerned for the well being of my daughter than I was for myself.

Black dots floated across my vision from lack of oxygen. He smiled as the light faded from my eyes. I fought against unconsciousness.

Fight back, Sutton! Fight! You're stronger than this!

Somehow I found the strength within myself to head-butt him. He grunted and released his hold on me. I fell to the ground, gasping for air. I didn't have the strength to stand so I started crawling.

"Help!" I tried to scream, hoping Cyrus, Frankie, or Daphne would hear me, except my voice was nothing but a weak croak. I pushed at boxes, sending them tumbling to the ground in a crash. It was the best I could do and I had to hope someone would come to investigate the cause of the disruption.

"You bitch!" Marcus yelled and I felt his hand close around my ankle. He pulled and I slid across the floor towards him. He flipped me onto my back and straddled me. His hands held my wrists in a vice-like grip as he pinned me down.

I struggled against him. I wasn't going to make this easy for him. I tried to find the oxygen in my lungs to scream, but couldn't. I lifted my head and opened my mouth, trying bite his arm. When my teeth hit flesh I bit as hard as I could.

He howled in pain. Releasing one of my wrists he slapped me across the face. He hit me so hard I tasted blood in my mouth and heard a ringing in my ears.

"You never knew how to listen to anybody." He shook me, his fingers digging painfully into my arm. "I had to teach you a lesson. And it looks like," he skimmed a finger lightly down my jaw, "you still haven't learned."

"Why are you here?" I gasped around my raw throat. "Why won't you leave me *alone?*" I sobbed. Didn't I deserve a happy life? Why did Marcus have to continually ruin everything for me?

He lowered his head to my neck and inhaled my scent. "Because no one has ever felt as good as you."

The guy had serious psychiatric problems. If I made it out of this alive, because something told me I might not, I would make sure he was put away—be it in jail or an institution, this fucker was going down.

"Get off of me," I rasped, struggling to get loose, but he was so much stronger than me. I felt the baby move restlessly inside me. She sensed my distress and was responding.

Oh, God, please don't let anything happen to my baby.

"You're a sick son of a bitch," I spat on him when he reached for my panties—easy for him to grab since I wore a dress today.

"Face it, Sutton," he growled my name, "you like it."

"Help!" I tried to scream again. My voice was a little louder this time, but still not enough that anyone heard me. "Help!"

He released my hands as he undid his belt buckle and started on the button and zipper of his jeans. I used his distraction to my advantage and reached around blindly for anything that might be lying on the floor. I wasn't going down without a fight. I wasn't the meek, scared Sutton that Marcus remembered from those endless nights where he snuck into my room. With my love for Caelan and Memphis I'd found the strength to overcome the tragedies of my past. I wasn't crippled by fear.

Finally my fingers latched on to something. Whatever it was, was heavy enough to be used as a weapon. I swung the object at his head and it connected with a resounding thump. He fell to the side and a smidgen of blood leaked out of a cut on his forehead. He wasn't dead, but he was knocked out.

I struggled to get to my feet and run to the door, before I made it though, it swung open. "What the hell?" Memphis dropped the empty boxes he'd been holding. He got a look at the mess and the man slumped on the ground. He took me into his arms. "Holy shit! Are you okay? Please tell me you're okay. Who is that? We need to call 911. I can't believe this." The words tumbled out of his mouth, one right after the other.

He was in shock and so was I. I couldn't speak and I could barely think straight. My body hurt all over and I breathed like I'd run a marathon. Pain radiated in my abdomen and I clutched my stomach.

Memphis called 911 and spoke with the operator, reporting a break-in.

Finding my voice, I said around tears, "Tell them to send an ambulance."

"An ambulance? Why? I mean, the guy's knocked out but he isn't hurt that bad."

Flinching in pain, I gasped, "I think the baby's coming."

He dropped the phone and then scurried to pick it up. He rattled off information to the operator and then stayed on the phone with them as we waited. He helped me to the couch and I sat down. The pain I felt was unlike anything I had ever experienced.

Marcus began to stir and I whimpered.

"Do you know who that is?" Memphis questioned. It was then that I realized he thought he'd walked in to a burglary.

I nodded, since I couldn't find the words to form a response.

Memphis' mouth fell open and realization lit his eyes. "Oh."

It wasn't long until the police and paramedics showed up.

"It hurts so bad," I told Memphis, tears wetting my cheeks, "and it's too soon. What if something happens to her?"

"It's going to be okay," he took my cheek in his hand. "We're going to get through this. Don't worry."

I was scared out of my mind that something was wrong with my daughter. If something happened to her... I feared what I might do to Marcus.

As the paramedics helped me onto a gurney the police told me they'd need a statement once I was up for it. They handcuffed Marcus and hauled him away. He was still half-unconscious. Apparently I'd hit him harder than I thought. Was it bad that I didn't care if he bled internally and died? I wanted the fucker to suffer like I had. Yeah, that was definitely wrong of me, especially considering I was going to be a mom, but I didn't care.

Memphis held my hand all the way to the hospital and spoke soothing words to calm me. It did no good. I wouldn't feel better until I knew if my daughter was okay.

A doctor looked at me immediately and discerned that the baby was in distress and needed to get out *now*. I'd thought if I was in labor they might be able to stop it, but that wasn't the case.

"No!" I screamed. "It's too soon! She's not ready!" I started to sob and scream hysterically. Memphis grabbed my arms to restrain me as I lashed around.

"The baby will be fine," the doctor assured me in a calm tone. "It is early, but not too early. Breathe."

I didn't believe him. He wasn't my regular doctor. What did he know? Nothing, that's what.

From there things moved even faster as they prepared me for a cesarean section. This wasn't how I planned to give birth to my little girl, but life rarely went according to plan. Especially mine.

I was wheeled back to the operating area and eventually Memphis joined me. He grasped my hand tightly and with his other he massaged my forehead. "It's going to be okay. She's going to be fine. Don't worry. Relax." His words did nothing to soothe me. I wouldn't be okay until I heard my daughter cry and got to hold her.

Within minutes she was pulled from my body. She didn't cry at first and my heart momentarily ceased to beat as fear overcame me. Once her cries filled the air I was able to breathe again and my heart picked up with its regular pattern.

They gave me a brief glance at her, but it wasn't enough. She was carried away from me to be checked out. Tears slid down my cheeks and Memphis wiped them away hastily. He kissed my forehead and murmured, "Please, don't cry."

"I want my baby," I told him. "Tell them to give me my baby."

"Oh, Sutton," his voice cracked and I knew this affected him as much as it did me. "I know you want to see her. Soon, I promise."

His words didn't comfort me. As a mother I needed to hold and feel my child. I needed to breathe in her baby smell and count her fingers and toes. Watching a stranger carry her away from me was difficult.

"I'm so sorry," Memphis apologized as he continued to rub my forehead. I didn't know what he was sorry for. He hadn't done anything wrong.

I let my eyes drift closed at the feel of tugging on my abdomen as the doctor stitched me closed.

I shut down after that.

I DIDN'T REALIZE where I was when I woke up. But once I recognized that I was in a hospital, I began to panic. My hand immediately went to my stomach and found my womb empty. I looked around, a scream about to leave me when I spotted Memphis asleep on the couch in the corner.

"Memphis," I croaked his name, my voice hoarse from lack of water. "Memphis?" I repeated a little louder when he didn't hear me.

He startled awake, looking around for any threat. "What's going on?" He rubbed at his tired eyes and sat up fully.

"I want to see her," I pleaded with him.

His face softened and he stood, taking my hand in his. For a moment, I thought he was going to tell me something had happened and she didn't make it, but he didn't. "I'll talk to a nurse and see what's going on."

"Thank you." I squeezed his hand. I was thankful that I had him. He truly was the most amazing man. I didn't know what I'd do without him. He was always there to pick up the pieces when I crumbled. "I love you," I whispered.

"I love you too." He lowered his head and pressed a tender kiss to my lips.

He wasn't gone long until he came back with a nurse. She handed me a Styrofoam cup full of water and raised the bed so I was in a sitting position. "Everything's fine with your little girl," she assured me with a smile. "She's been checked out thoroughly and despite the early delivery she's perfect, just on the small side. I can bring her to you if you want me to?"

Did she even need to ask? "Please," I begged. "I want to hold her."

"Give me a few minutes." She smiled kindly as she looked over my vitals. "I'll be right back," she said as she exited the room.

Memphis grabbed the chair and slid it over so that he was beside my bed. I held my hand out for him and he gladly took it. "I'm so sorry you've had to go through this."

"Don't be," I whispered. "I'm fine and the baby's fine. That's what matters."

"I can't believe he came after you again," he shook his head in dismay. "It's like he's obsessed with you or something."

"Yeah," I agreed. "He's got issues, but he's not getting away with it this time."

He smoothed the tangled knots of my hair off my forehead. I knew after everything I'd been through in the last however many hours, I had to look like crap, but he still gazed at me like I was the most beautiful woman he had ever laid eyes on. "This is only a small bump in the road. It's all up hill from here," he assured me.

I smiled at him and he leaned over to kiss my forehead. The overwhelming sense of trust and completeness I felt with him was nothing I'd ever experienced. I'd thought I'd known true love—and maybe I had—but this was a forever kind of love and it was a totally different thing. Where Caelan had shot into my life like a falling star—brightening it for a moment, before disappearing—Memphis was the blanket that kept me warm at night. He was always there for me. Things with us were easy. He was a breath of fresh air. He was the man I didn't know to hope for and when I found him, I ran like hell into another man's arms. I couldn't regret our lost time, though, and without Caelan I probably would've never realized my true feelings for Memphis. Love was messy and never perfect. Real life sucked and the person you thought was 'the one' turned out to be 'just for now'. But if you stayed strong Mr. Right came along and all the heartbreak was worth it, just so you could tell him you loved him every night as he fell asleep. I knew my love for Caelan would always be there, but it was a different kind of love now—one of fondness and the bond we shared of our child. I knew that without him I wouldn't have found peace. We might not have been meant to be a couple, but we were meant to change each other's lives—I was sure of that.

The nurse breezed into the room, pushing one of those clear bed thingies they kept the babies in. Oh my God! Did it make me a horrible mother that I didn't know the name for them? Had I already failed at this whole parenting thing before I even had a chance?

She picked the baby up and placed her in my arms. "Here you go, mommy."

Mommy.

I was a mom.

I was responsible for this tiny human being.

She was mine for the rest of my life.

I really hoped I didn't fuck this up.

My daughter stared up at me, her pink lips pouted. She wiggled her arms out of the pink blanket she was wrapped in, like she was trying to reach out to me. I held my finger out and she wrapped her tiny hand around it.

"Wow," Memphis gasped from beside me. "She's perfect."

He was right. She was. I'd never seen a more perfect baby.

I kissed her wrinkly forehead and felt tears spring to my eyes. I was so relieved that she was healthy and we had nothing to worry about. I'd been so afraid I might lose her.

I pushed the hat she wore off her head and was shocked to discover a dusting of blonde hair. I'd expected it to be dark like mine, but she was all Caelan except for her lips. Even her eyes were his shade of blue.

"I love her so much." My words were thick with tears. "How is that possible?" I asked Memphis.

He reached over, running his finger over her plump cheek. "Because she's amazing."

Even though she wasn't his daughter I could see the love in his eyes.

Kissing my temple, he murmured, "We're a family."

I closed my eyes, absorbing his words. I was so happy and I knew I was exactly where I was always meant to be.

Tweaking her nose, he asked, "What are you going to name her?"

As soon as I looked at her, I knew exactly what her name was supposed to be. "Cayla," I breathed. "Her name is Cayla."

CHAPTER 36
Caelan

"Do you know what today is?" Leah asked, her excitement palpable as she jumped on the bed.

I rubbed my eyes, racking my brain for what she could be talking about. "Uh... I have no idea. Enlighten me."

"It's your one year anniversary!" She clapped.

"We haven't been dating for a year," I stated, looking at her like she'd lost her mind.

She rolled her eyes and sat down on the bed beside me. "I meant you've been clean for one year."

"Oh."

Was it crazy that I wasn't even aware a year had past?

"We need to celebrate!"

"We really don't," I replied. "Unless," I grinned, "celebrating involves getting you naked?"

"No," she rolled her eyes. "Nice try."

I crooked an elbow over my eyes. "Then let me sleep."

"No," she pulled my arm away. "You're not going back to sleep. We're meeting Kyle for lunch."

"I seriously don't want to make a big deal out of this," I told her.

"But, Cael—"

"It seems weird to celebrate the fact that I've managed to stay sober for a year," I grumbled.

"It's an accomplishment you should be proud of." She leaned towards me, her red hair tickling my bare chest.

"I am proud of myself," I defended, "but it seems like a stupid thing to make a fuss over."

"Don't be a fun sucker," she pouted.

I chuckled and sat up, rolling on top of her. "Fine, I'll go to lunch," I kissed her, "but first I think I deserve a present, you know, since today is a celebration."

She wrapped her arms around my neck and her lips ghosted along my ear. "Your wish is my command."

"Hey!" Kyle greeted us at the restaurant. Balloons were tied to the chairs and confetti sprinkled the tabletop.

"It's not my birthday," I stated. "So, what's with all the birthday shit?"

Leah clasped my hand. "We wanted to make it fun."

"I had plenty of fun *all* morning," I chuckled.

"Rub it in," Kyle groaned and sat down.

"What happened to Stephanie?" I asked him. "I thought things were good between you guys?"

"She was too clingy," he grumbled as he perused a menu.

"And it sounds like *you're* too picky," Leah piped in. Looking across the table at Kyle, she said, "No one's perfect, you have to give them the chance to prove that their flaws aren't everything."

He set the menu down. "How insightful of you. I'm sure you have to overlook a lot of flaws with this one," he pointed at me.

I chuckled, running my fingers through my hair. The blond strands had grown too long and I knew it was time for a trim. "Flaws? I have no flaws?"

Kyle and Leah both laughed at that.

Conversation moved to my gallery. It was doing better than I ever thought it would. I'd named it Marayla's a combination of my mom and sister's names. I knew most people didn't understand the name, but it wasn't for them.

I'd held my first workshop last week and the turn out had been more than I anticipated. It made me happy to do what I loved. Everything had worked out for me.

Well, almost everything.

I knew in my gut that it was time to see Sutton. I needed a proper goodbye with her. I'd moved on and I was sure she had too, but I knew I would never truly feel at peace until I apologized.

As we left the restaurant, I said to Leah, "There's somewhere I need to go."

"Oh." Her face fell. "Do you want me to go with you?"

"No," I shook my head, squinting against the sunlight. "I need to do this on my own."

She nodded in understanding. I dropped her off at the gallery and headed to Sutton's place.

I kept going over in my mind what I wanted to say, but none of it felt right. To be honest, I was scared to face her. I'd hurt us both when I ended things, but it was what needed to be done.

I parked my car and sat there for a few minutes, trying to muster up the nerve to get out and face this.

Finally I jogged up the steps of the building and stopped outside her door.

I knocked and no one came. I knocked again. Maybe she was at work. I could wait. If I left, I might never come back. I sat down on the ground beside her door, settling in for however long I had to stay.

Twenty minutes later the door to Cyrus' apartment opened. He startled at seeing me.

"Gregory?" He rubbed his eyes. "Do my eyes deceive me? I wondered what happened to you."

I didn't have time for Cyrus' bullshit.

"When will Sutton be back?" I asked, rising to my feet.

Pity filled Cyrus' eyes and I didn't understand why. "She doesn't live here anymore."

"Sh-she doesn't?" I stuttered. Had she moved back to Texas? I couldn't imagine her doing that, but maybe I didn't know her as well as I thought.

Cyrus nodded. "She's been gone for *months*." His mouth parted slightly in shock. "You don't know, do you?"

"Know what?" I asked, brows furrowing together in puzzlement.

"Never mind," Cyrus waved a hand dismissively.

He started to pass me but I grabbed his arm in a tight hold and he was forced to stop. He glared at my hand until I dropped it. "Do you know where she's living now?"

"Yeah," he replied. "I don't know if it's really a good idea for you to see her though."

"I have to," I pleaded. "I need to see her. If you're trying to protect me from being hurt by seeing her with a guy, it's fine. I've moved on and I told her not to wait for me. I don't expect anything from her. I just... I need to see her," I pulled at the strands of my hair, yanking to the point that it was almost painful.

"That's not what I'm protecting you from," Cyrus huffed. "I can see you're not going to leave this alone." He pulled his phone out and began to type. Seconds later my phone beeped. "There. Now go. And don't say I didn't warn you," he muttered before storming off.

I read off the address and headed for my car. It only took me fifteen minutes to get to her new place. It was another apartment, but these were bigger and nicer.

I didn't give myself any time to think as I got out of the car. I checked my phone again for the apartment number.

When I stood in front of the door, I closed my eyes and took a deep breath to prepare myself for what lay behind.

I raised my fist and knocked.

"Just a minute!" A male voice called out.

A moment later the door swung open and I was face to face with Lap Dance Guy or at least that's what I called him in my head. I shouldn't have been surprised, but I was. Even though Sutton had always denied that there was anything between them, I'd known better.

Lap Dance Guy held a baby in his arms. As soon as my eyes landed on the baby an overwhelming sense of ownership flooded me. She was mine. I knew it. I felt like some physical force pulled me towards her, but I forced myself to step back.

My body shook all over with shock. *This* was what Cyrus didn't want me to see. Sutton had my baby and she never told me. I was hurt, sure, but I understood. I'd never contacted her once I was out of rehab, and I'd done everything I could to make sure I never saw her. I gave her no reason to trust me with our child. As my eyes scanned my daughter, I happened to get a glance at the man's hand where it was wrapped around the wiggling bundle.

They were married.

I had expected her to move on, but to be married? And with a baby? *My* baby? Nothing could have prepared me for that.

I swallowed thickly and muttered. "Sorry. I've got the wrong address."

I walked away.

I walked away from the woman I'd once loved.

I walked away from the baby I knew in my soul was my daughter.

It was the right thing to do.

I didn't deserve to have them in my life. I may have gotten myself cleaned up and wasn't doing too shabby, but I still didn't feel good enough.

I wasn't a strong enough man for them. I hoped her husband was loving and kind, and took good care of my girls. If he didn't, I'd always be waiting in the shadows, ready to swoop in and save them.

I wasn't angry with Sutton.

Instead, I felt peaceful. I understood now, that even when everything crumbled and your world turned to ash, there was still beauty—just like a phoenix rising from the ashes.

Shoving my hands into the pockets of my worn jeans, I stepped onto the sidewalk, bracing my shoulders against the cold wind as I took the first real steps into my new life.

A life without Sutton.

A life without pain.

A life worth living for.

Sutton

"WHO WAS THAT?" I asked, coming out of the kitchen. I reached for Cayla and Memphis slipped her into my arms. He wrapped an arm around me, like he was trying to protect me. "What's wrong?" I asked. I lovingly rubbed his cheek with the hand that wasn't holding Cayla. My wedding ring sparkled in the light, and like every time since it'd been place on my finger a month ago I found myself smiling at it.

A year ago, I never would've thought I'd be Memphis Allen's wife, but I was and I couldn't be happier.

All he said was, "I think it's time for you to mail those letters."

CHAPTER 37

Caelan

I HADN'T KNOWN what to think when all the letters arrived from Sutton. She'd labeled each one with a number so I knew to read them in order.

They came only a few days after I'd left her place without seeing her. I guessed Lap Dance Guy had told her I showed up—and I really needed to stop calling him that.

After I'd returned I told Leah where I'd gone and what I'd seen. She'd been upset at first, but once I told her about the baby she grew angry with Sutton. I explained to her that Sutton had every right not to tell me. I'd been nothing but a fuck up the last time she saw me and I'd made no effort to contact her since.

As I read the letters I discovered she had tried to tell me, and when the letters returned to her unopened, she assumed I didn't care. It broke my heart reading those letters. I'd never even seen them. The first handful was addressed to the rehab I'd been at, but they had a strict policy of zero outside contact. They'd been the ones to send the letters back. I wondered if I had gotten these if it would've changed things. I didn't think so though. We were both exactly where we were always meant to be.

I got to the last letter and it was dated only two days ago.

Dear Caelan,

    I really don't know what to say in this letter other than I'm sorry. I'm sorry I didn't try harder to tell you about the baby. I'm sorry I wasn't strong enough for you. I'm sorry that I hurt you. I'm just... sorry. I know I've said that word so many times already in this letter that it's bound to have lost all meaning.
    I was shocked when Memphis told me it was time to mail the letters.
    I'd given up on you and assumed I'd never see you again. I thought, and I hate to say it, that maybe rehab hadn't worked out for you and you were in an even darker place than before. There were times I wondered if you'd died. I hoped you had moved away, or even that you hated me so much that you couldn't bear to see me. Either of those things was better than the thought of you suffering. Why? Because, while my heart might now belong to Memphis, there is a part that will always be reserved for you. I care what happens to you. I want you to be happy and healthy and get your life figured out. I know I could've tried harder to contact you, but the fact of the matter was, I was terrified of what I might find out if I dug too deep.
    Memphis said you looked good. That makes me happy. I only want the best for you.
    I'm sure you figured out that Memphis is my husband. I hope you don't hate me for moving on. You told me not wait for you, and at first I did anyway. I held myself back from any connection, but what I felt for him quickly

overcame the pain of losing you.

Despite that, I miss you every day. You had an overwhelming impact on my life and without you I wouldn't be where I am. I wouldn't have found my own self-worth and saw that I was worthy of sweet, pure love.

Thank you for giving me our daughter. Within her I've found something worth fighting for. She's given me the strength to seek help for my past. I want to be a better, stronger woman for her. So, I've been seeing a therapist. My doctor wanted me to see one a year ago, but I refused. Better late than never, right?

Marcus came back a few months ago. I'd filed a restraining order against him a little while before and it didn't sit well with him. He's not in jail, but he's being forced to get help. I'm keeping tabs on him. I'm not going to let him hurt me, our baby, or any other woman ever again.

I don't have your phone number, hence the letters, but you can call me anytime. I'd really like for you to meet our daughter. It was never my intention to keep her from you. We might not be together anymore, but that doesn't mean we can't be a family—an unconventional one, but a family nonetheless. I want the best for our daughter and she deserves to have her amazing daddy in her life. I know you'll be great with her. She's so wonderful and I love her so much. I want you to experience that.

All the best,
Sutton

I read over the last letter three or four times. I reached up to feel moisture clinging to my cheeks.

"Cael?" Leah asked from the doorway of my bedroom.

I wondered what she thought as she saw me sitting there with all of those letters scattered over the bed.

"Here, read them." I told her. I had nothing to hide. She needed to read these as much as I did. I knew the past couple of days she had feared I regretted not being with Sutton. The thing was, I didn't regret anything anymore. Regrets were really just puzzle pieces, they were all different shapes and sizes, but they fit together to make one large picture—the image of your life—and it wasn't all that bad.

Tears streamed down Leah's face as she read the last one with a hand clasped over her mouth to stifle the sounds she made.

"Cael," she croaked, "you have to meet your daughter. You can't stay away."

"I know," I whispered. Taking her hand in mine, I added, "I can't believe that I have a daughter. Isn't that crazy? Me? A dad?"

"It's not crazy at all," she replied, stroking my cheek with one hand. "You're going to be an incredible dad."

My heart felt exceedingly full of love at the thought of my daughter. I wanted to hold her and sing to her and protect her from monsters—those that were real and merely fictional.

"When are you going to meet her?" Leah asked, wiping away her tears and proceeding to pick up the letters.

I shrugged. "I don't know. I'll have to call Sutton."

"Whatever you do," she reached over and put a hand over mine where it rested on the bed, "don't wait too long."

She was right. If I waited I'd talk myself out of it. I'd come up with some excuse as to why I wasn't good enough for my daughter, how she deserved a better father. But I was her dad, and I was going to be in her life no matter what. I wasn't going to fuck this up like I had everything else.

I picked up my phone and called Sutton.

Sutton

THE MOMENT I saw the unknown number flash across the screen of my cellphone I knew it was Caelan.

I took a deep breath and closed my eyes, taking a moment to calm myself.

My hand shook as I brought the phone up to my ear.

"Hello?" My voice quaked with nerves.

"Hi, Sutton."

It had been over a year since I last heard his voice and the moment he spoke it was like I could finally breathe. It was still the same low, throaty growl and instantly memories of the two of us flooded my mind.

"How are you?" I asked. They were the only words I could force between my lips.

"I'm good," he replied. "I got your letters."

"I figured." I paced the length of the living room as I talked to him, nervously fiddling with the hem of my shirt.

"I want you to know that I didn't send them back to you. I never got them."

"Oh," I breathed.

"Don't feel bad," he hastened to add, "but I didn't want you to think I had ignored you."

"It would've been okay if you had," I said, taking a seat at the dining room table. I was glad Memphis was at work and didn't have to see me freaking out like this. He already worried far too much about me.

"No, it wouldn't have." I heard him sigh and then he continued, "I'm sorry for the way I handled things with you."

"Sorry?" I was taken aback. "What do you possibly have to be sorry about? I think we might have had the most peaceful break-up in the history of break-ups."

He chuckled at that. "You're not angry?"

"Nope," I assured him as I drew random designs on the table. "I understand why you did it. Let's face it, if we hadn't broken-up then, it would've happened eventually. We weren't right together. Two people as messed up as we were... that only spelled disaster."

We both grew quiet.

Eventually, when I knew he wasn't going to speak, I said, "D-do," I had to clear my throat, "do you want to meet her?"

"Yes," his voice cracked. It almost sounded like he was crying, but I didn't think that was possible.

I suggested we meet at Griffin's on Saturday of the upcoming weekend. It would be neutral grounds and he wouldn't have to feel uncomfortable by coming here.

"Sounds good," he replied.

"I'll see you then," I smiled, even though he couldn't see me. "And Caelan?" I added before he could hang up.

"Yeah?"

"Thank you." He didn't need to ask what I was thanking him for. He knew.

"STOP IT," MEMPHIS commanded, grabbing my hand to cease the destruction my teeth were doing to my fingernails.

"I'm nervous," I mumbled, using my foot to rock Cayla's carrier and keep her asleep. The last thing I wanted was for her to be fussy when Caelan got here.

"It's okay to be nervous," Memphis assured me and he rubbed my shoulders. His words and gesture did nothing to ease my nerves. I couldn't believe I was about to see Caelan after more than a year. For the last few days as I thought of him, I kept remembering the broken Caelan I'd seen in the hospital bed. He'd been so thin, and unhealthy looking.

Cayla started to stir and I reached down to pick her up. Her sweet baby smell instantly put me at ease. Her blue eyes widened as she stared up at me, cooing softly. I rubbed gently at the downy soft blonde hair covering her head. From what Memphis said, Caelan had gotten a good look at her the day he showed up. I wondered what he thought—if he was as wowed by this little miracle as I was.

Emery came by the table and set down cups of water. "I didn't think you'd want coffee, Sunshine. You're already jittery enough." He winked. "And are you even allowed to drink coffee when you're breast-feeding?"

"Emery!" I laughed. Leave it to him to make this situation not seem so dreary. As he grinned at me, I thought back to how insistent he was that Memphis and I were perfect for each other. He had been right, but I wasn't going to tell him that.

Emery walked away, laughing at my exclamation.

I didn't get to see him as much anymore. I'd quit my job to stay home with Cayla and I used my spare time to help Memphis look for a spot to open his own restaurant.

The door opened and I looked up. I knew in my gut it would be him and I wasn't disappointed.

He looked different from all my memories of him. He'd filled out more and his skin had a rosy, healthy shine to it. His blond hair had gotten longer and his eyes weren't cloudy with what whatever drug he'd been using. When he saw me, he smiled. I hadn't been expecting that. More so, I hadn't been expecting it to be the smile of the boy I saw in the online article when I'd first tried to find out about him. When I saw it, I'd been determined to make him smile like that again. Only back then, I wanted him to be smiling at *me*. He wasn't though. He was smiling at the squirming baby in my arms. Seeing him light up like that brought tears to my eyes. I was so relieved to know he was happy and healthy.

I startled when I saw a beautiful woman with vibrant red hair come in behind him and clutch his hand.

I was shocked and I was sure it showed, but I quickly smiled once more.

I stood and Memphis joined me in walking over to Caelan.

"You look good," I smiled fondly.

"Thanks." His smile was crooked and almost boyish. He looked his age now, except for his eyes that held the pain no one should have to experience.

"Hi." I turned towards the woman beside him. While I didn't feel any jealousy towards her, I did hope she was good to him. Caelan deserved to love and be loved, but I didn't want him to be taken advantage of. "I'm Sutton."

"I know," she replied, forcing a smile. I could tell she was nervous around me. "I'm Leah."

"It's nice to meet you. This is my husband, Memphis," I nodded my head towards the man playing bodyguard. He shook hands with both and said a few words. "Should we sit down?" I suggested.

They both nodded and we all sat down at the table Memphis and I had previously occupied.

I had no idea where to start, but seeing as Caelan and I were going to be connected for the rest of our lives, the rest could come later.

Right now was about introducing him to our daughter.

Memphis cleared his throat and pointed at Leah. "I'm going to get some coffee, would you mind coming with me?"

I smiled. That was my Memphis, always trying to do the right thing. He saw that this moment needed to be between Caelan and I only.

"Sure," Leah agreed, knowledge shimmering in her pretty green eyes.

As soon as they were gone, I moved to sit beside Caelan. "She's beautiful," he whispered, reaching out to touch Cayla's smooth cheek.

"She's perfect," I added. "Here, you hold her," I tried to hand her to him but he flailed. "Caelan," I laughed. "What's wrong?"

"I don't know how to hold a baby," he admitted. "I don't want to break her."

I bit down on my lip to contain my giggles. He was dead serious and I didn't want to embarrass him. "Just hold your arms like this," I nodded down at the way I had her cradled in my hold, "and make sure you support her neck."

He mimicked my pose and I eased our daughter into his arms. "Wow," he gasped as she stared up at him. "I can't believe we made her."

"Me either," I laughed.

"I love her so much already."

"Babies are pretty amazing like that," I agreed.

He kissed her head and then his eyes flicked up to meet mine. "What's her name?"

I let out a breath and answered. "Cayla. Cayla Hale Gregory."

He gasped. "You named her after my sister?"

"Of course," I replied as he looked down at her with even more awe than before. "No other name was right."

I saw Memphis and Leah take a seat at another table. I was thankful that they were giving us more time.

I grew quiet, watching Caelan gaze at Cayla. I laid my head on his shoulder and he stiffened at first, but then relaxed.

"I live for *you*," he breathed as he cradled our daughter in his arms. His finger tenderly stroked her pouted lips.

Tears pooled in my eyes at the words he spoke to her—words he'd once told me.

We both lived for Cayla now and it was the best thing either of us had ever done.

The End

COMING SOON

saving TATUM

Trace + Olivia Series Book 4
(September 2014)

AND

WHEN WE FALL

A companion novel to *Beauty in the Ashes*
(Late 2014)

Saving TATUM

Sneak Peek

Even tough girls need saving.

JUDE BROOKS IS bad news. He's the kind of guy that leaves behind a string of broken hearts and Tatum O'Connor is not about to be one of those girls, despite all of Jude's advances. They have a past, and Tatum's determined to make sure they don't have a future.

Unfortunately for her, "no" isn't a word in Jude's vocabulary.

The more she backs away, the more he pushes.

But what if he pushes too far?

Tatum's hiding a pain that no one sees and holding on to a hurt that may never heal. Letting Jude into her heart could shatter her completely—and what if she opens up to Jude and he can't handle her baggage?

Love is never easy—especially when the person you're falling for is the person you blame for the worst event in your life.

Love, heartache, and despair.

That's the name of the game when you're Saving Tatum.

PROLOGUE

Unedited and subject to change

I JOLTED AWAKE at the sound of someone trying to beat our front door down. I sat straight up, the blankets pooling at my waist. My head twisted to look at the blinking orange numbers flashing on the clock beside my bed. Three in the morning.

Fear slithered down my spine like a serpent.

Nothing good came from someone at your door that early in the morning.

I heaved my tired body out of bed. My muscles were stiff and overworked from a rigorous cheerleading practice the night before.

I opened my bedroom door and poked my head out. I saw my mom and dad coming out of their bedroom. A baseball bat was clutched in my dad's hand. What did he think he was going to do to an intruder with that? Knock them out? Besides, if someone was trying to break in, why would they be knocking on the door?

"Stay up here, Tate," my dad warned, quietly tiptoeing down the steps. My mom followed him even though he warned her to stay put as well.

I kept watch on the door.

My dad looked through the peephole and muttered, "What the hell?"

Swinging it open, I saw red and blue flashing lights and an

officer stood at our door.

I rolled my eyes. The neighbor's kids were probably vandalizing again.

I was about to close my door and get back in bed, when I heard the officer speak.

"Mr. and Mrs. O'Connor?" He asked. He was young and nervous, obviously new to the police force.

"That's us," my dad answered, "is there a problem?"

"It's about your son, there's been an accident. I'm so sorry to tell you this, but he didn't make it." His face was somber, eyes downcast.

My mom let out a piercing, soul-crushing wail, and started to fall. My dad's arm held her upright.

But there was no one there to hold me up.

I crumbled to the floor, clutching at my chest.

I couldn't breathe.

I was suffocating under the pressure.

He didn't make it.

He was dead. My big brother—my best friend—was gone.

"I'm sorry," I heard the officer say one more time before my dad closed the door. His cries soon joined the sound of my mother's.

Tears streamed down my face, but my sobs were silent.

Graham was gone. In a matter of hours he'd been ripped from my life forever. I'd just seen him at dinner! We'd been talking about school and how I'd be cheering at the football game on Friday! He was telling me how proud he was of me!

Everything had been perfect! The way it was supposed to be! Something like this wasn't supposed to happen!

Graham was a senior! This was his last year! He was supposed to leave for college and study to be a lawyer like our dad!

He. Wasn't. Supposed. To. Die.

None of this was supposed to happen.

My perfect life wasn't supposed to explode like this.

But it did.

Over night, I went from having it all, to having nothing.

I watched my mom close herself off from everybody.

I watched my dad spend his every waking hour slaving over his job so he didn't have to think about Graham, or mom, or even me.

I watched myself slowly spiral from a carefree happy girl, into a complete and utter cynic.

And I knew exactly who was to blame for everything.

Jude Brooks.

ACKNOWLEDGEMENTS

Wow, I don't even know where to begin. I have so many people to thank for helping me with this book and keeping me sane. This has been my hardest book to write, but I'm definitely the most proud of it. *Beauty in the Ashes* pushed me as an author. It challenged me and forced me to think differently. I've been trying to write this story for five or six years, and now finally felt like the right time. So, I went back to Caelan and Sutton's story and finished it once and for all.

Becca, Haley, Kendall, Stefanie, and Heather, I can't thank you all enough for beta reading and keeping me sane through this whole process. I was beyond stressed while writing this book and your words of encouragement kept me going. Thank you for shaping *Beauty in the Ashes* into the book it is today. In other words, thanks for making it better.

Harper James and Regina Bartley... ladies, I don't know what to say. Thank you, doesn't begin to cover it. You guys are always there for me when I'm freaking out. You tell me when something sucks and when it's awesome. You keep me motivated when I feel like falling apart. Through the good and the bad you're both there. I'm so incredibly thankful to have friends like you.

Thank you to all the bloggers who took time to read *Beauty in the Ashes* and for those that participated in the Blog Tour. I appreciate everything you do for me and other authors. Without you most of us would fall into obscurity.

Thank YOU for reading *Beauty in the Ashes*. Whether you

loved it or hated it, THANK YOU for taking a chance on this book. If you've read my other stuff then you know this is quite the departure for me. Thank you (are you sick of me saying that yet?) to every single person who has ever read one of my books, because of you I get to do what I love, and for that I will always be grateful. I wish I could meet all of you and express in person just how thankful I am. Since I can't, I hope this rambling paragraph has done the job.

Of course I have to thank Jenessa and Jeff for being the cover models. Thank you for being a part of my book and bringing my characters to life. You both did an amazing job and I couldn't be happier.

Regina Wamba (Photographer and Cover Designer Extraordinaire) I have three words for you... You. Were. Right. I was so against having a "paint picture" on the cover, but you wouldn't let it go and in the end it was exactly what the cover needed. Thank you for always being amazing and giving my books the most beautiful covers.

Angela, thank you for the amazing formatting and for being such an awesome, nice, beautiful person.

Lastly, Grammy deserves the biggest thanks of all since she's stuck living with me and I was a complete psycho while writing this book... well, more than usual. Anyway, thanks Grammy for always believing in me even when I don't. When you look at me with concern when I'm having a rare meltdown, you'll still say, "You can do it." Those four words might not seem like a lot, but they mean everything to me. When I doubt myself, I hear your voice in my head encouraging me to keep going. You've always been there for me and I don't know what I'd do without you. I might not always say it, but thank you. For everything.

ABOUT THE AUTHOR

Micalea Smeltzer is a bestselling Young and New Adult author from Winchester, Virginia. She's always working on her next book, and when she has spare time she loves to read and spend time with her family.

Follow Micalea:

Facebook:
https://www.facebook.com/MicaleaSmeltzerfanpage?ref=hl

Twitter:
@msmeltzer9793

Instagram:
micaleasmeltzer

Pinterest:
http://www.pinterest.com/micaleasmeltzer/boards/

Made in the USA
Monee, IL
25 March 2025